D1058731

Shelf Life

Shelf Life

A NOVEL

MARTIN SNEIDER

JEWISH
LEADERS BOOKS

Published by Jewish Leaders Books, an imprint of Forefront Books.
Distributed by Simon & Schuster.

Library of Congress Control Number: 2022924060

Print ISBN: 978-1-63763-168-3
E-book ISBN: 978-1-63763-169-0

Cover Design by George B. Stevens
Interior Design by Bill Kersey, KerseyGraphics

To Jill, my soulmate for fifty-five years. I dedicate this book to you who believed in me more than I believed in myself and who inspired me to write Shelf Life.

Acknowledgments

I AM GRATEFUL TO MARYANN KARINCH, WHO AGREED TO READ THE very rough first draft of *Shelf Life*, saw promise in it, and advised me to transform it into a family saga.

And my eternal gratitude to my coach, Michael Levin, who painstakingly helped me bring the fictional Feldman family to life.

"Going through life with a conscience is like driving your car with the brakes on."

Sammy Glick, in *What Makes Sammy Run?*
by Budd Schulberg

Prologue

MAX FELDMAN'S FIERCE EXPRESSION AND LASER-LIKE GLARE LEFT NO doubt that he expected me to do right by him. After spending so many years watching my father, studying him, learning from him, and being verbally abused by him, I stared back in a sense of wonder. How odd, my father waiting for my decision, after all the years of me waiting for him.

Finally breaking eye contact, I turned my attention to my mother, who had assiduously avoided meeting my eyes or those of my brother.

I shifted my attention to the iconic St. Louis Arch, the Gateway to the West. We were in the fifteenth-floor law office conference room, and the view was spectacular, with the afternoon sun giving a jewel-like luster to the stainless steel structure. The Arch had been much ridiculed at the time of its construction. The *St. Louis Post-Dispatch* had published a cartoon depicting it as a giant croquet hoop with the mallet and ball on the Illinois side of the Mississippi. But to the surprise of many, the city's signature monument had succeeded beyond anybody's expectation.

I took a moment of comfort in this visual diversion. Few had foreseen the impact of the Arch. And no one gathered around me at the table in this conference room could foresee the consequences of our ballots on the crucial and divisive issue facing us. The only certainty was that the verdict would have profound repercussions for the family business and for the Feldman family itself.

In the days leading up to this meeting, tensions had run high. There was no mystery about my father's and mother's wishes. The two were diametrically opposed and totally irreconcilable. The ultimate verdict would rest, it would seem, on how my brother and I voted. All the shares of Fratelli Massimo Inc. were divided among us four family members.

Joining us at the table were a high-priced local attorney and my mother's father, my grandfather Gunther Harris Berg. He was a high-powered New York attorney who had cleverly and, in my father's view, with malice aforethought drawn up the incorporation documents and other legal formalities when my father opened his first Fratelli Massimo high-fashion women's shoe store. Now several hundred units existed nationwide.

The fact that my mom and dad were on opposite sides, and were barely speaking to each other, put me, Joshua Feldman, in a mind-numbing bind. I loved my mother from the bottom of my heart and wanted her to be happy, but I worked for the family company, and my professional future was in my father's hands. He was founder and CEO, and he was grooming me to one day succeed him.

Disappointing either parent was unthinkable. But the unthinkable was also inevitable.

Chapter 1

I'VE SPENT MY ENTIRE LIFE IN RETAIL, AS DID MY FATHER, MAX, before me, and his father before him.

My daughter, Allison, will not carry on the tradition, though it's not because she doesn't care or lacks the talent for it. A look in her closet would confirm her fashion passion and intimate relationship with Anthro to Zara. No, it's not a lack of interest or aptitude. It's that she understands how the turmoil in modern retailing crushed our family's business—and threatened to crush our family as well.

"Too much blood in the streets," is what she concluded. "If your mom or my mom hadn't been so strong, God knows what would have happened to the family, or to you, Dad."

She's right about my mother and my wife. Without them, who knows what might have happened?

My father was a retailing superstar. With the financial assistance of my mother, Maddy, he founded and developed the Fratelli Massimo brand chain of stores—at one time, seven hundred of them, from coast to coast. When I was a kid, I worshipped him. It didn't happen often, but when he had the time, he would sit me down and go on about the business. Stories of triumph poured out of him: spotting a hot shoe before the competition, negotiating a below-market rent, outsmarting an annoying supplier, and so on. His punchline to each story was predictable: "Not bad for a sodbuster from Omaha!"

I would listen with rapt attention, and at the end, he would pick me up with his giant hands around my tiny chest and tickle me until I squealed, "I'm going to wet my pants!" Finally, he'd release me into a bounce on the sofa and plop down next to me.

"One day, Josh, you will have an office next to mine and we will be business partners and run Fratelli Massimo together."

This became my dream.

When I was around ten years old, Dad would sometimes take me to his office on Saturday if he was not doing any store visits. My little brother, Rand, was two years younger than me and usually declined the invitation so he could stay at home to read, play, or go shopping with Mom. But I was eager to be with Dad.

He would show me the top-selling shoes and samples of what was coming in the next season. I began to pick up the lingo: high heel, mid-heel, needle toe, mule, stripling sandals, and sport shoes, to name a few. He would sometimes test me to see if I remembered what was hot and what was not. Afterwards, Dad would head to his office to catch up on paperwork and sales reports.

I always enjoyed the minor tasks he would have me do. I made copies, collated, and stapled. The office had a brand-new copier, and I remember hearing him say, "I don't want to see a picture of your hand or your behind, Buster!" It was as if Dad could read my mind. When he was finished with his work, he'd take me to Steak 'n Shake for a hamburger and shake. We'd talk about the business, the Cardinals baseball team, and what I was doing in school. On those Saturdays, he was like a pal or maybe like an older brother. I couldn't help but feel secretly glad that Rand wasn't along. Just me and Dad.

Occasionally, when I had finished my clerical tasks at the office, he would show me the boxes of newspaper clippings that his assistant, Carly, maintained. Many of the periodical stories featured Fratelli Massimo and how successful the company was. The headlines talked of store-opening records, high sales, and soaring profits. Others focused on my father. I remember seeing "Feldman's Forecast for Fall Footwear" or "Feldman: Sky's the Limit for Fratelli Massimo." I especially liked the article titled, "When Max Speaks, Seventh Avenue Listens."

The earliest stories were in a scrapbook that Mom had kept. The more recent ones were neatly filed by Dad's assistant. "Your wife found it boring," Carly told my dad.

Digging through the files one time, I came across a story where a reporter from the *St. Louis Post-Dispatch* had interviewed Dad. After a few details on Fratelli Massimo's latest success, he asked my dad how he had gotten into the business.

"I hated school. Honestly. It was boring. As soon as the bell rang, I would dash to my parents' small grocery store on North Twenty-Fourth Street in Omaha. That was my classroom!

"There were dozens of little lessons and bits of information that I soaked up, walking up and down the four aisles of the store. It was like retail radar. I'd spot something, like we were running low on Campbell's tomato soup but had too much cream of mushroom.

"Well, it didn't take a genius to figure out what to do. Mark down the cream of mushroom, order more tomato soup, and raise the price by a few cents."

Reporter: "What other lessons did you learn?"

"Too many to tell. Take a $2.00 item and mark it down a penny to $1.99, and sales improve. Put high-profit items at eye level, smack in the customer's face. That same customer will search for the low-margin necessities like milk and eggs, but it's the impulse-item buys that pay the bills. Raise prices on paydays. Talk to customers. Ask them why they bought this and not that.

"But the route men were the best—these were the guys who refilled snacks and beverages for all the local stores. They had great info on what was happening. And they loved to talk. They'd let you in on what was selling and what wasn't. They'd tell you about new items, discuss competitor price points and displays—stuff like that. Of course, I had to bribe them with a free Coke or sandwich from the deli counter, but it was always well worth it."

Reporter: "Your dad must have been proud."

"Yeah, when Sy wasn't yakking with the ladies."

When I came to that last sentence, I went into Dad's office.

"Dad, Gramps was proud of you, wasn't he?"

"Long story for another time, Champ. Let's grab a burger."

Dad never did tell me the story, but Gramps did—years later. Even then, I was too young and naïve to understand what it meant. Nor could I understand what it foreshadowed.

When the school calendar permitted, we would spend Passover with Sy and my Grammy Rose in Hallendale, Florida. The most memorable of those trips occurred around the time I read the article with the reporter asking Dad about his father. Carly was supposed to reserve a four-door sedan, but all they had left by the time we got there was a Chevy coupe. We managed to shoehorn the luggage into the tiny trunk of the car, then all squeezed in. Off we went for the half-hour drive.

I loved Gramps Sy. He was loving and gentle. He would take Rand and me outside and show us how to weave palm fronds into whips. Then he would toss us around, play catch with an old tennis ball, and share stories about the old country and Omaha days. He seldom mentioned Dad.

That particular year, I remember that the sun was setting when Rose summoned the three of us inside after playing. We girded ourselves for a three-hour seder, which was a far cry from the slap-dash version we had at home when we couldn't make it down to Florida. In our St. Louis version, Mom would rustle up a seder plate with the customary horseradish, lamb bone, egg, saltwater, matzah, bitter herbs, and charoset. Dad would lumber in with four dog-eared, anglicized Haggadahs and shout, "Play ball!" We would tear through the highly edited Haggadah in about twenty minutes and tuck into a celebratory meal, prepared by a local gourmet grocery store, which was heated up and served by our housekeeper, Nora. Total time at table: sixty minutes, maximum.

No such luck in Florida. No, it was a seder with major-league Haggadahs. If the seder was to commemorate our people's exit from Egypt, the end of the seder was our exit from this torture of boredom. Hallelujah!

That year, with Sy and Rose, we took turns reading from the Haggadah—even the weird stuff in italics! Dad was clowning around, making faces and rolling his eyes, trying to make us laugh. When we got to the part about the plagues, Dad started shaking his head and in a stage whisper declared that he, for one, thought Moses was a loser.

Everybody sat in stunned silence. Except Sy.

"Our most heroic figure and you, the biblical scholar, think he's a loser?"

"Yeah, imagine going on bended knee and pleading with Pharaoh time after time to let our people go, and getting your ass kicked every time."

"Until the last time, Max, when Pharaoh himself lost his first-born son and we left for Israel."

"Yeah, yeah, that's the story, but that journey took forty goddamn years and 'our most heroic figure' didn't even get there."

Silence reigned at the table. Dad, relishing his role as provocateur, added, "At least Pharaoh died like a man, in battle, not wobbling on his staff and peeking at the Promised Land. Some hero!"

All hell broke loose, Sy yelling that Max had to leave the table. Then came Mom, begging Max to apologize. This led to Rose sobbing. Rand and I sat before our plates, mouths agape.

Why did Dad have to ruin the seder? Calling Moses a loser was like saying Albert Einstein was a dope, or Jonas Salk a faith healer. He couldn't be serious. It was Dad just being Dad.

"If you want me to leave, I'll leave." And with that, Dad went to the living room and turned on the TV.

Mom went after him, but Sy asked her to return to the table.

Rose pleaded for peace, and Sy muttered, "He's lost to us." He apologized for the disruption and then moaned, "I used to go to shul to thank God that he spared the firstborn sons of the Jews. I was thinking of Max, of course. What a curse!"

I said, "You can't be serious, Gramps!"

"You'll understand, Josh—when you get a little older."

In the years following that Passover's unpleasantness, my father's icy relationship with his dad manifested itself in subtler ways. One of them would leave the room when the other entered. At the dinner table, they hardly conversed, and if they did, there were only terse, cryptic, or sly responses. On the three-minute long-distance phone calls between our two households, Dad and Gramps were never on the line at the same time. It was as if there were an agreement, tacit or explicit, that we boys would never again witness their mutual antipathy. Mom certainly never addressed the issue with me, and I was afraid to bring it up with Dad.

But I never forgot that seder and didn't understand what had prompted Dad to utter such heresy. He had to have known it would disrupt the family seder and cause utter acrimony. The exchange that stuck with me was Sy's reminder that Pharaoh had lost his son, and Dad's response, "Yeah, yeah." Like it was nothing! Whatever had happened between Gramps and Dad back in Omaha must have been catastrophic.

Chapter 2

AFTER GRADUATING FROM HIGH SCHOOL, I WORKED FOR DAD. I HAD moved from the distribution center to the office and was tasked with auditing some stores, which was a euphemism for checking up on them and reporting back to Dad. One day, he decided to dispatch me to Miami to audit the store at 163rd Street. This was located on the north side of town in what was then a largely Jewish neighborhood. The center was anchored by the two big department stores in the area, Burdines and Jordan Marsh. Dad suspected that the manager of our store, Sam Goodman, was up to no good. He claimed that Goodman was "dipping his pen in company ink by either creating phony refunds and/or screwing the cashier." What was I, a house detective?

The fact that it was July and 110 degrees in Miami made the prospect of the visit grim, but it demonstrated to the home office personnel that the boss's son was not "on a boondoggle."

It also provided me with an opportunity to visit with Gramps Sy, who was living in what they used to call a rest home, operated by one of the Jewish agencies in Miami. Grammy Rose had died a few years before that and Sy, while mentally sharp and physically OK, was, according to Dad, "better off in that facility rather than trying to live by himself in Hallendale." Somehow Gramps had agreed to the wisdom of the move.

During the southbound two-hour flight, I gave some thought to what life would be like in the fall as a freshman at Washington U. But most of the time, I fantasized about climbing the corporate ladder and ultimately partnering with my dad.

After arriving at the Miami airport around four in the afternoon, I rented a car and drove to suburban Kendall to the Ida and Milton Silverstein Home for the Aged in order to visit with Sy. The store audit would take place the next day.

Palm trees, particularly to a northerner, signal rest and relaxation. You're at a resort—enjoy yourself! But the ones that dotted the lawn in front of the home elicited a different reaction. There were depressing brown fronds with metal sheaths near the tops to discourage rats from nesting; several of them were listing dangerously to the windward side. The gray asphalt road leading up to the entrance was rutted and in some spots even bubbling in the sweltering heat. A giant dumpster occupied two of the ten parking spaces reserved for guests.

The home itself had originally been a private residence, built in the plantation style against the sun and the weather. A large front porch with some (unoccupied and in need of repair) Adirondack chairs gave the place a welcoming appearance, though its colonnaded façade was in serious need of a whitewash, and the broken brick stairway begged for a lawsuit.

I entered the foyer and asked the receptionist where I could find Sy. She directed me toward a large public space where Sy and several *alter cockers* were seated watching the television news hour. Sy greeted me warmly, rising from his chair and giving me a squeeze. Then he backed up a couple of steps, put his hands on my shoulders, and gave me the once-over.

"You're big and handsome, Josh, just like your dad was at your age."

"Thanks, Gramps, you look pretty good yourself."

"I want to believe you, Josh, but the doc doesn't agree. But we'll pretend you're right. Let's get out of here before dinner."

"Sure, where would you like to go?"

"Wolfie's in Miami Beach." Predictable. He loved that place. After a bathroom visit, we made our way to the car and headed for the Arthur Godfrey causeway and Miami Beach. Perched near Collins Avenue, the very popular deli founded by a Catskills busboy was close to the grand resorts, such as the Fontainebleau, Roney Plaza, and Castaways—but none of them had the over-stuffed sandwiches like you got at Wolfie's. It was off-season, so we didn't have to wait for a table, and we were shown to a booth in a quiet corner of the restaurant.

As was his ritual, Sy schmoozed with the waiter in Yiddish. Evidently, he told him a joke, because both broke out laughing. We each ordered a sandwich, and Sy begged me not to tell my mother or his doctor that he had committed the horror of having a tongue sandwich and a bottle of Pabst Blue Ribbon beer—a favorite from his Omaha days.

I didn't want to darken this time together, but I did want to ask about his feud with Dad. I knew I would never find out about it from my parents.

Sy was the one to crack the ice. "So what do you think of the Ida and Milton Silverstein Home for the Aged?"

"It seems OK. Maybe a bit worn out, and it could use some work..."

"Unlikely to happen. It's partially funded by the state, and getting those goyim in Tallahassee to ante up some bucks for a bunch of old Jews in Miami is a long shot."

"But, Gramps, certainly there must be better places."

"There are. And your father offered to pick up the tab, though I suspect it was Maddy's idea."

"That's not fair. Maybe it was Dad's idea. Fratelli Massimo is gushing cash."

"You might be right, Josh, maybe it was your father's idea—but I doubt it."

"Gramps, what is it with you and Dad?" There, I had asked the question.

Silence ensued as each of us weighed the merits of a revealing and candid conversation. The waiter interrupted the silence when he arrived with our order and asked if everything looked OK. Sy nodded and we continued staring at one another.

Finally, he said, "Josh, it's a long story, and it happened a long time ago."

"You mean what happened at Passover back in Hallendale?"

"No, it's not that—though I've always felt bad about that day. You boys witnessed something you should have been sheltered from. No, what happened between your father and me took place decades ago in Omaha and changed forever the way we feel about one another. Sure you want to hear about it? I'm not very comfortable with this."

The ball had been returned to my court. If I said no and changed the topic, the rest of the dinner would simply be a memorable interlude of a time when Gramps and I palled around in Miami Beach. But it might be my last chance to discover what blew up the relationship. Was that selfish? There was my dear Gramps, getting a brief leave of absence from the home, and there I was on the cusp of ruining the moment.

"I know what you're thinking, Josh. We're on the edge of something really unpleasant. I promised dear Rose I would never tell you what happened in Omaha. But I don't know that I will have another chance. This tongue sandwich may finish me off! Still, I think I owe you the story, even though you might end up hating me or, even worse, hating your father. I think you're old enough to understand what happened and mature enough to deal with it and learn from it. OK?"

"Yes." I focused on his every word.

"We lived on North Twenty-Fourth Street in Omaha," he began. "In those days, it was a largely Jewish neighborhood. Most of us had come from Poland or Russia or somewhere in Eastern Europe in the 1920s. We were the lucky ones. We got out before Hitler and Stalin took over. We worked hard, cobbled together a living, bought little houses, and raised our families. But the war changed everything.

"During the war years we were united in our misery and fear. The shul was our meeting place; the rabbi was our leader. Most of us kept kosher and walked to shul for Friday and Saturday services. The neighborhood was a shtetl. Everybody knew everybody else and everybody's business. I was a peddler before I bought the grocery store. Grammy did needlework for some of the richer folks.

"The grocery store was on a good corner, but it was on the small side. I bought it from a German man in 1938. I think he knew that his days were numbered in that Jewish neighborhood when stories about the Nazis made it to the *Omaha World-Herald* and local radio stations. I felt sorry for him because he was a good guy, and he offered it to me at a bargain price. And, yes, it may have been a bargain price, but I wasn't exactly a Rockefeller. I had to borrow and pledge everything to raise the money. My brother Saul owned a service station that was doing well, and he loaned me some money and cosigned a note from the bank to help me.

"I knew I would have to depend on Rose and your dad to help me in the store. Rose ran the register, kept the store tidy, and paid the bills. I bought the merchandise, worked with our suppliers, took deliveries, and plucked the chickens." He paused and shook his head with a little laugh, perhaps seeing visions of those poor de-feathered chickens.

"And your dad stocked the shelves, stamped the canned goods with a blue marker, did odd jobs around the store on Saturdays and after school, and made some deliveries. He was in high school during the war, and—thank God—too young to be drafted. He could have joined up near the end as many of his friends did, but we felt blessed and maybe a little guilty that he stayed at home.

"He was a good worker, I'll give him that. He was tireless when it came to displays and thinking of promotions." Gramps paused again, but there was no laugh this time. His eyes narrowed.

Was this it? I wondered. What was he holding back?

"Max wasn't above putting his thumb on the scale when Rose was elsewhere. He knew how to add a penny here and a penny there to the cash register tape. No, it wasn't grand larceny, and I yelled at him for doing it, but I couldn't be there to keep an eye on him all the time."

That I could imagine. My dad liked to play fast and loose with the rules. What Mom told me when I was a kid about how Dad leached off vendors was sort of the same thing.

"But he always had his eye out for ways to do more business. When sales were slow, he would ride his bike ten blocks south toward Dodge Street to see what our competitor, Nathan Marcus, was up to. Nathan had a bigger store and a different clientele. His shoppers were Jews, Irish, Italians, and even some Blacks. It was also well known that he did a credit business with some folks, mostly Blacks, and squeezed a pretty penny from them. I, like a dumb schmuck, carried my customers' debts for nothing and even tore up the paper now and then if the customer was in a bind.

"It was in Nathan's store that your dad got the idea to stock liquor. But your dad would also check their prices and brands and compare them to ours. Nathan belonged to our shul, where he and his family had their own pew up front near the pulpit, while we Feldmans sat in the bleachers. We nodded to one another and chatted from time to time about business. We weren't what you would call friends, but we certainly were not enemies—until much later.

"I was content to run the store and gossip with my customers. They were like family to me. We joined them on their simchas, comforted them when their sons went off to war, and sat shiva with them.

"The war in Europe was going well until President Roosevelt died. We all felt we'd lost our favorite uncle. Finally, the war in Europe came to an end, and that *shtarker* Hitler was dead. What a day! But then the news about the camps came trickling in. Josh, we were all in pain. To see the newsreels at the movie theatre was a shock. And then we started finding out about family members who had died in the camps. The poor refugees who had survived, some of them settled right near us in Omaha. It was a sad time for us on North Twenty-Fourth.

But we all rejoiced when the Japanese surrendered, and nobody second-guessed President Truman's decision to use the A-bombs. We wanted that war to end! When it was officially over, we closed our stores and gathered in the shul, and the rabbi led us in prayers of thanksgiving. You could hardly look at our neighbors who had lost sons in the war. For them, the war would never be over.

"When the boys came home, we all made a big fuss over them. They had all changed so much. They hadn't just grown older in years, but in emotions—they had witnessed horrible things. All of them wanted to begin a new life. Your dad understood what that desire meant, and would mean, for our store and our way of life.

"He came to me one evening after dinner. We were living above the store, so we had a normal family life together. We closed the store at six, cleaned, and went upstairs. It wasn't unusual for Max to want to talk business; in fact, he talked business nonstop. And what he said that night made perfect sense.

"'Pops, these guys who are coming home aren't going to stay on North Twenty-Fourth. Maybe for a few weeks or months, but they're going to either move out of town, go to college on the GI Bill, or move west in Omaha.'

"He was friends with some of these returning servicemen, and it was no secret that they were anxious to get a good job, buy a car, start a family, and purchase a home. But they all longed for a home that wasn't in our neighborhood."

"'When that happens, Pops, our store is kaput. The only reason it's survived this long is because all the Jews have stayed in the neighborhood and been loyal. That won't last.'

"Of course, he was right—as he often was about those kinds of things. But I was stubborn just like him, and I continued to believe we could survive as we had for so many years.

"Little by little sales started to dip. One by one the families in the shtetl moved west, and their homes were purchased by Blacks who were moving north after the war. We sold more pork and more beer. Liquor sales helped keep us afloat, but the handwriting was on the wall. Only I was too stubborn or too stupid, or both, to realize the obvious.

"It was a day in early 1947 when Max showed up in front of the store in a car he had borrowed from Uncle Saul. He opened the door and called out to me. 'Pops, please come with me. One hour is all it will take. Take a break from gossiping with the ladies.'

"Such disrespect, and in front of my customers. But I was curious as to what was on his mind. So I took off my apron and asked Rose to mind the store. The car sputtered south and then headed west on Dodge Street. When he got to Fortieth Street and Dodge, he turned right and parked the car in front of a vacant hardware store. We both got out of the car and your dad pointed to the vacant store.

"'That, Pops, is the future! I've been scouting real estate, and I think we can rent this store at a bargain. It wouldn't take much to convert it to a grocery store.' I was growing irritated that he had wasted his time—and mine. I told him we didn't need a second store. We could barely keep the first one alive. And then he told me his big idea: 'Agreed! We don't need a second store. We need just one store and it needs to be here, not on North Twenty-Fourth.'

"I told him that Rose and I were not throwing away our lives and leaving our friends due to a few months of soft sales. He said our grocery store was doomed to go under in a year. I should sell right away, or I'd get bupkis for it. I asked him when God had made him the newest prophet."

"'I'm not talking about prophecy,' he said. 'You just have to open your eyes and stop being a stubborn schmuck.'"

I gasped. Calling your dad a schmuck? Unthinkable. If I did that to my dad, holy shit...

"Josh, I smacked him across the face. Never, ever had he spoken to me like that. And never before had I struck him. We stood staring at each other, neither of us willing to give an inch.

"Finally, he continued in that somber tone your dad has when he isn't getting his way: 'Are you telling me you're willing to throw away the equity you have in your grocery store because you put a higher value on your friends and neighbors, being walking distance from the shul?' His voice had gotten louder in a nasty combination of anger and self-righteousness. I told him yes, I put a higher value on people and my faith than I did on ringing the cash register.

"We got back in the car and, without saying another word, made our way back to the store.

"Your dad, as I said, was living upstairs with us. The most we could manage was a silent truce after that, but he moved out when he was nineteen. I wasn't surprised, but I was depressed. I was sad that we had fought, unhappy with the way I had handled myself, but still hopeful we could mend fences.

"That hope withered when I opened the store a few weeks later. In the mail slot was a letter from your dad. He started out with 'Sy.' He had never called me that before. I saved a copy of the letter but never read it again. If I ever want to have a heart attack, I'll pull it out and read it.

"The basic message was that he told my competitor Nathan Marcus about the location. Nathan signed the lease the very next day and hired your father as assistant manager in charge of the old store. So now Max and I would be direct competitors. His choice.

"My business went downhill fast; your dad was undercutting me on prices and extending credit at high interest rates to anyone that had a tuchus. Eventually, we were forced to sell the store at a distressed price to one of the Blacks who had moved into the neighborhood. It's funny. I had bought the store at a bargain price from a German who was nervous about the Jews in the area, and I sold it to a Black man who was part of the next wave of immigrants, so to speak.

"Nathan did well and opened up a chain of grocery stores in Omaha and Council Bluffs across the river. Your father got promoted and eventually managed one of the new stores, until he was drafted during the war in Korea."

By the time he had finished his story, the restaurant was nearly empty, our waiter gabbing with his coworkers and looking over at our table every two minutes. We got up. I paid the check, and we drove back to the home.

Grandpa was all talked out, and I didn't feel like talking either. We hugged tightly when I dropped him off. He ran his hand through my hair and muttered something about "being fifty years younger."

I had a lot to think about now that I knew what had happened, at least from Gramps' perspective. I didn't doubt him. I had witnessed Dad bully his employees, the gardener, the newspaper boy, and even Rand. He also pulled stuff with vendors, which violated FM's policy. He talked his way into Super Bowl tickets, a week's stay at a supplier's condo in Miami, and large cash gifts to me and Rand when we had our bar mitzvahs. "When you're boss, the rules don't always apply to you, Josh. Results are the only things that count." I couldn't wait to be boss!

I also knew that Sy was a softy and not much of a businessman. I loved Gramps a lot and sympathized with what he'd had to endure from his son, but I still, God help me, believed in Dad. He grew up poor, never went to college, and succeeded because of his grit and talent. He wasn't perfect, but I admired him. Dad had his eye on the prize and never wavered in his quest for that prize. To hell with those who got in his way!

I returned to St. Louis a couple of days later and went straight to the Fratelli Massimo office on Washington Avenue. Immediately, I saw a message on my desk indicating that Dad wanted to see me. My desk was one of twenty located in the basement of the building in what was called the bullpen. Most of the clerical staff worked there grinding out their comptometers with sales information or transcribing tapes recorded by the executives. It was a constant clatter that sapped your energy and drained your brain. Why was I given that desk? Dad wanted me to start at the bottom. Literally.

I took the elevator to the executive floor, where Carly, his secretary, greeted me, checked with Dad, and ushered me into his office. There, behind a desk the size of a pool table, sat Dad, rocking back and forth.

"So, boychik," he inquired, "how was Miami?"

"Like an oven."

"And Sam Goodman. What about him? Screwing the cashier?"

"Couldn't figure out a way to find that out. They were fully clothed during my entire visit."

"Very funny. Did you ask the hosiery girls? They know all the dirt."

"No, didn't want to get them involved."

Dad sighed. "And the refunds, were they legit?"

"Well, they appeared to be. I checked the refund book and all the numbers looked good, though there were about $540 in refunds during the last two weeks. Seems high."

"Right, Sherlock! Did you call any of the recipients of Sam's largesse?"

"Most of them were out-of-state addresses. Sam said lots of tourists visit the store."

"He did, did he? And you bought the story? Lots of tourists in the fucking middle of July visited the store, found the shoes they purchased not to their liking, and took time from their holiday to go back to the store and ask for a cash refund? Am I on the right track here?"

I stammered, "That's what he said. Seems strange, I admit."

"You realize that Sam just stole $540 from our family, Josh? How does that make you feel?"

"Resentful."

"Resentful? Hmmm...how about angry and seeking revenge? That's how you are going to feel tonight when you fly down there and fire him with no severance!"

"Wait a minute, Dad. First of all, I am a summer employee."

"You're a Feldman, kiddo!"

"OK, but Sam Goodman has trained and promoted almost every store manager and assistant manager in Dade County."

"And trained them to be thieves, you think? Big lesson here, Josh. Stealing from the company is a death-penalty offense. I don't care how many managers he's trained."

"How about probation?"

"How about you grow some balls? If you ever expect to run this place..."

Somehow the rules were strictly applied to Sam Goodman, but not with Dad. His anger seemed justified; after all, Sam was stealing from us. But the revenge part? What was he getting into? Maybe it was like what Dad had done to Gramps. He hadn't been content to leave the family business. Hadn't been content to go to work for a competitor. No, Dad had to drive Sy out of business by cutting prices and extending credit. It was a dirty game to play. What could possibly induce a son to do that to his father? It took me twenty years to answer that question.

Dad fingered through a stack of papers and looked downward.

"Don't let the door hit your butt on your way out.... Oh, and by the way, did you happen to see your grandfather while you were down there? The way you handled Sam reminds me of how Sy handled the customers who welched on him in the old days."

"Yes, I picked him up and we went to Wolfie's. Boy, that's some crappy place he's living in."

"Did he tell you I tried to get him to move to a nicer place? That I offered to pay the difference?"

"Yes, he told me."

"Stubborn son of a gun! Did you talk about anything else?"

"Nothing important." My eyes lowered to the floor.

"Now you're lying, Josh. I know the old man wouldn't miss an opportunity to dump on me."

"No, we talked about the Cards and other stuff," I told him.

"I'm glad you're lying. Means we don't have to dredge that stuff up and talk about the 'Honorary Mayor of North Twenty-Fourth Street.' He thought everybody in that ghetto was his friend, and he forgot to mind the business. Chatted up the ladies. A couple stories about Sentimental Sy and Mrs. Marcus. But they both kept their clothes on when I was around."

"Dad, can we drop it?"

"Josh, fly down to Miami. And this time, take care of business."

So I returned to Miami to take care of business.

Chapter 3

PICTURE AN AMERICA WITHOUT SHOPPING MALLS, LIFESTYLE MALLS, strip malls, outlet centers, category killers, discount stores, big box stores, or the internet. Close your eyes, and travel back to the early 1950s, when there was no interstate highway system, Americans owned .87 cars per family, and only 21 percent of households included a woman who worked full time outside the home. Department stores dominated general merchandise retailing, and the downtown store was where most of the action took place. Customers paid full price for goods except during sale times: post-Christmas and in the month of July. Men regularly wore coats and ties, and women wore dresses and heels to baseball games. That was America in the early 1950s—a country proud and confident in the years following World War II. The postwar retail boom gave way to five decades of nonstop growth. The latter part of America's retail expansion produced the rapid spread of malls, the explosive growth of superstores, and finally, the emergence of flashy websites.

When my dad took off his army uniform for the last time, after the Korean War in 1952, he set his sights on starting his own business, and the timing couldn't have been more favorable. That's not to diminish his hard work. Many other retailers managed to fail during this halcyon period of retailing. But businesses encounter headwinds and tailwinds alike, and Dad benefitted from gale-force tailwinds for almost forty years.

He caught another break as well. The army hadn't sent him to Korea when he was drafted from the plains of Nebraska. Because

he was a shopkeeper, the government assigned him to the
Quartermaster's Corps, the supply chain operated by the military,
which saw that troops were clothed and equipped. Yes, it resembled retailing, but the best part for him and his future was that
he served in Germany, near Frankfurt am Main. That allowed
him to travel throughout Western Europe during its post–World
War II rebuilding period instead of slogging through God knows
what in Asia.

In his travels, Dad discovered two master shoe stylists and
artisans when he befriended Sergio and Enrique Fratelli in Milan.

The story has become a legend at the company, and it famously
varies with each telling. It goes like this: Dad is traveling on a
crowded train with a ten-day pass from Germany to Florence,
Italy. He's seated facing a woman who is reading an Italian newspaper. Dad can't help but notice her shoes (and shapely legs). The
shoes are a lustrous shade of burgundy in supple calfskin, with a
low vamp and hourglass, three-inch heels.

He waits until she lowers the paper and then asks her where
she purchased the shoes. She speaks no English and is somewhat
taken aback by his approach. One of the other passengers offers
to translate, having learned some English from the GIs who
occupied his town.

One thing leads to another, and Dad scores not only the
address of the Fratelli brothers' atelier and store in Milan, but
also the woman's address and phone number in the same city.
Dad disembarks in Milan instead of continuing to Florence.
He's conflicted, of course, by the two opportunities, but quickly
figures out how to have his cake and eat it too. He makes a dinner
date with the woman, then hops into a taxi to visit the brothers'
atelier.

Instead of proceeding to the main shopping area surrounding the Rinascente department store, the driver weaves through the narrow, blighted streets of the industrial section of the city still pockmarked by war-inflicted damage.

This can't be right, Dad thinks. Is he in danger? A hostage? The cabbie is silent and unresponsive to Dad's nervous questions. Dad is in uniform but unarmed.

Suddenly, the taxi driver stops. Dad peers through the cab's window and sees a handmade sign on a dilapidated two-story brick building: "Scarpe di Fratelli." Relieved, he opens the car door, stuffs some lire into the driver's hand, and surveys the front of the building. It is not what he was expecting.

The door is flanked by large windows. Behind the left window are animal skins, bolts of fabrics, heels, insoles, and other shoe-making material tightly stacked on shelves. The right side is the display window for a sliver of a store. Featured in the center of the window is the exact style the woman was wearing on the train. In addition to burgundy, the shoe is shown in aubergine, moss, and silver blue. All terrific fashion colors.

He opens the door and is greeted by Sergio Fratelli, who holds a shoemaker's hammer in his left hand. Sergio is wearing a leather apron over his street clothes. Dad introduces himself and they shake hands. He is then presented to Sergio's brother Enrique, who is wearing a pin-striped suit, stiff white shirt, and narrow striped tie. Both speak a sort of pidgin English and exude the warmth and charm that Italians are known for.

Dad explains that he's temporarily in the army, but in civilian life he's a retailer—a merchant with plans to open numerous shoe stores when he returns to the States.

"How did you hear of us, signor?"

Dad fumbles in his pockets. "Signorina Mastrioni."

"Ahhh, Signorina Mastrioni. No, Signor Feldman, I'm afraid it's Signora Mastrioni."

"Ahhh," says Dad. The three of them glance at each other, sadly.

A tour of the store, workshop, and storeroom ensues. Dad asks to see the styles that Sergio is working on. The brothers glance at each other and shrug. "OK. But is secret." Dad signals his promise to not share the information, and Sergio opens a curtain in front of some shelving. This is the treasure Dad was searching for. He handles and inspects each model with the loving touch of a true merchant. He can't believe his luck—these are beautiful styles that would fetch very high prices in the States. He inquires about prices and can hardly believe the answers he is given. Such bargains!

"They are not Gucci, Signor Feldman. They only look like Gucci!"

During *la pausa* they bond over lunch and a couple bottles of Valtellina Rosso at a neighborhood trattoria.

They return to the store slightly drunk, but happy.

The brothers call a taxi for him, and then each embraces Dad in turn. Sergio, with his face a mask of sadness, tells Dad, "Ah Max, poor Signora Mastrioni still mourns for her husband who was killed in the war."

The three nod knowingly.

Dad promises to stay in touch.

He honors that promise through the mail and by visiting them annually. He goes even further by honoring them with the store's name, Fratelli Massimo. He figured Massimo was the Italian version of his name, Max.

The brothers will receive his very first order when he opens his first store..

Chapter 4

DAD HARBORED UNBOUNDED AMBITION AND POSSESSED ENORMOUS merchandising talent as he began putting together plans for a new shoe store concept. The only thing he lacked was capital. After his "apprenticeship" at a local department store, he again struck it lucky. He married my mom, Madeline (Maddy) Berg, who happened to be an only child from a wealthy family. His father-in-law was the smartest person I ever knew.

If my grandfather Sy was a sweetheart, Gunther Harris Berg was the opposite. Raised in Boston, he attended MIT where he studied engineering, but math was his passion. No doubt he recognized that wealth and power did not often accrue to mathematicians. In any event, he attended Harvard Law School, was editor of its *Law Review*, and proceeded to Wall Street where he made his fortune and reputation as a corporate lawyer with an extensive list of blue-chip clients. Mom told me that her dad advised corporate CEOs from IBM, General Motors, and U.S. Steel, as well as the heads of New York's biggest banks. He counseled power brokers like Robert Moses, who redecorated New York City; New York attorney general Louis Lefkowitz; and governor and presidential aspirant Nelson Rockefeller. They valued his realistic assessment of the situations they faced, his oft-quoted line that they must play "the long game," and his unvarnished, blunt opinions. But most of all they sought his unfailingly accurate analysis of the state of play, no matter how complex. Gunther Berg could see around corners.

Mom would laugh knowingly when she described her father. "To the unwary, my father seemed affable and engaging. Approachable and charming, ready with the perfect anecdote for any situation, he had mastered the art of being deceptively congenial. He also had the skill of feigning humility.

"For example, he would routinely buy a morning newspaper at the small kiosk in the lobby of his office building. He always took a couple of minutes to banter with the owner, Franco, about the Yankees, Dodgers, Giants, local politics, or some bubbling scandal. He would make small bets with Franco on ball games or election results. These were bets that Dad would frequently lose.

"Whenever Franco saw me, he would tell me how friendly my dad was, like a member of the family. 'You might want to give him some friendly advice, Miss Berg. Stick to lawyering, and forget about gambling.'

"When I told my dad what Franco said, he chuckled."

"'As for being "like a member of the family,"' he said, 'you realize that Franco's family is a big cog in the City's Democratic machine.'

"'Why bother, Dad?' I asked. 'Just buy a paper and be gone.'

"'Because I'm playing the long game. I have lots of clients who may one day need a favor in City Hall. You never know.'

"'And is that why you lose your little bets with Franco? You're a master poker player and a shrewd gambler.'

"'Maddy, those five-dollar losses might just turn into big-dollar payoffs for my clients!'"

Mom tapped her cigarette on the ashtray and continued.

"To Franco and many others, he *was* friendly, a man of the people. But Josh, lurking behind that bonhomie was an icy and calculating genius who mentally strip-searched the lesser beings he engaged with, examining, and silently condemning, their weaknesses, false facades, and self-delusions.

"In the early days your father was completely taken in by my dad's shtick. 'Your father and I are simpatico, dear,' he would proclaim to me.

"*In a pig's eye*, I would think to myself."

I had observed some of their interplay myself.

When we would visit Grandpa Gunther in New York, he and Dad would chatter away about the business, sports, and politics, and Grandpa would play the role of hail-fellow-well-met. Gunther would compare Joe DiMaggio, Ted Williams, and the Cardinals' Stan Musial, rattling off the stats. He would gently tease Dad about the Cardinals' lackluster performance during the fifties and boast about the Yankees but concede that rooting for the Yankees was like rooting for U.S. Steel. His patter inflated Dad's confidence and egged him on to making increasingly grandiose pronouncements, which Gunther would unfailingly honor with just the right utterance or facial expression. "Max, you've hit the nail on the head."

As we'd head to the airport, Dad would gather himself and magnanimously declare that "Gunther wasn't a bad old bird...for a New York lawyer!"

While I couldn't see Mom's face from where I was sitting, I could sense her shaking her head. She was well aware of how contemptuous Gunther was of Dad.

Maddy had always been her father's daughter but, mercifully, with some important variances. First, she loved my dad for many years. Second, she lacked Gunther's silent but merciless cynicism. It's not that she was unaware of her dad's modus operandi—she just knew what he was up to.

Her mother, Alice, died of breast cancer when Mom was a young teen, and this bonded her and her father. He saw and valued her potential, intellectual heft, incisiveness, and acerbic wit. He gladly coached her in the ways of his cosmopolitan world. Gunther hired tutors to teach her how to play bridge, and she often became his partner at the table; eventually she became a Life Master.

In their time together, he naturally shared his almost universally negative and skeptical judgments of the people he knew. While not outright rejecting his mordancy, she leavened it with a humanity that permitted her to like people—and to love my dad, at least in the early years.

Maybe it was his optimism and self-confidence. Perhaps it was his boldness, or his bluntness. ("He's as subtle as a sledge-hammer," my mom would say.) It might have been his candor. Or maybe, just maybe, it was because he was a good-looking Jewish boy—tall, barrel-chested, with slicked-back dark hair and nearly black eyes. He would free her from the closed-up genius of a father she lived with. Or perhaps it was the fact that she could read Dad like a book. Even though she had a close relationship with her own father, there might always have been a sliver of doubt as to what he really thought of her. Having been allowed to hear her father's harsh assessment of others, might she not have inferred that she, too, was one of his silent targets?

She could be herself with Dad.

• • •

I remember one Sunday, when I was a freshman in high school, Mom and I were in the den flipping through scrapbooks. Dad was away on a business trip. Rand was practicing hoops out back. Mom and I were seated comfortably on the sofa, with the photo albums open on the cocktail table. Adjacent was Mom's glass of Chardonnay, a pack of cigarettes, and her ashtray.

We were looking at an old black-and-white photo of a broadly smiling Max sporting an open-collared shirt, an Eisenhower jacket, pleated slacks, and sandals. His left arm is draped around Maddy, who's smiling with her lips pursed, her head swaddled in a polka-dot scarf against the wind. She has on a shirtwaist, a cardigan sweater, a necklace of seashells, and what look like Capezio ballet slippers.

"Max and I were aboard the Fire Islander ferry boat from Bayshore to Fair Harbor, to visit friends."

The photo made me curious about how they met. Maybe it was the influence of Mom's second glass of wine, or that she thought I was now old enough to hear the story.

Before opening the first Fratelli Massimo store, Dad worked for the Famous-Barr department store. It seems that Dad was in New York every six weeks, calling on vendor after vendor, examining their merchandise and negotiating prices. While he was hard-core in his business dealings, his soft skills enabled him to do what few in the industry could: cultivate genuine friendships, as he had with Enrique and Sergio back in Milan. Many of the guys he bested in deals attended his wedding, and some even made their way to St. Louis for my bar mitzvah.

In defiance of Famous-Barr's rules, Mom confided, Dad took full advantage of their largesse when he was a buyer. He welcomed dinner invitations at fancy New York restaurants, did not decline tickets to Broadway shows or Knicks games, and was not one to reject holiday gifts conveniently delivered to our home, never to his office.

On one of his New York trips, he was invited to join a vendor at the 21 Club restaurant on West Fifty-Second. He arrived early after his trek from the Hotel Abbey, the dump where he stayed at the north end of a then-squalid Times Square. He sat at the bar and found himself seated next to a fairly tall and attractive—but not quite beautiful—brunette, who was to be my mother.

"I was waiting for my roommate with whom I shared an apartment in Murray Hill. We'd both graduated Smith and Horace Mann. I was working as an editorial assistant for a literary magazine and thinking of enrolling at Columbia in their graduate program of Arts and Sciences. I loved the written word and was a voracious reader," she told me.

Mom would spend many of her later years studying nineteenth- and early twentieth-century American and English literature. Not at Columbia, of course, but at Washington University, in our hometown of St. Louis.

"I was sitting at the bar at the 21 Club when this big, handsome hunk of a guy with a completely garish suit plopped down next to me and started chatting me up. He was waiting for a vendor to join him, but in the twelve minutes we had together he managed to get my phone number. I didn't quite know what to make of him. He was good-looking, as I said, but it was his confidence and optimism that I found so captivating. Honestly, I sort of liked his Midwest twang and his naïvety. I was definitely interested, and so was he."

Getting together with Maddy became a regular part of his New York visits—and he knew how to show her a good time.

Dad didn't hesitate to ask his vendor buddies for two tickets for Broadway shows and even two tickets to Knicks games, which my mother-to-be "endured with grace." They went Dutch treat for dinners, as Dad couldn't bring himself to scrounge dinner-for-two favors from the boys.

Their relationship blossomed and the inevitable moment arrived when she had to introduce Max to the celebrated Gunther Berg. Plans were made for the three of them to have a quiet lunch at the Harvard Club. (What other kind of lunch is there at the Harvard Club?)

It's impossible to know what my dad had on his mind as he made his way from 1407 Broadway, where his buying office was located, to the club on Forty-Fourth Street. Was he anxious to meet Maddy's exalted father? Did he resent having to go to the Harvard Club and be surrounded by all those smug Ivy Leaguers? Was he self-conscious about his appearance or his lack of a college education? Or was he the intrepid and confident winner of Maddy's heart? My bet is on the last of those.

"Your dad elbowed his way through the swells at the club who were clothed by Brooks Brothers and Rogers Peet, the more daring by Paul Stuart, and the more traditional by J. Press. Dad was clothed by Ripley's of Times Square! Josh, your father wore a padded-shouldered tan gabardine double-breasted suit. He had on a dark blue spread-collared dress shirt and a wide—well, very wide—floral tie that could have served as a tablecloth in a pinch."

Gunther, who had traveled to midtown from his offices at 26 Broadway near Wall Street, was well-known at the club. The manager, maître d', and waiters all greeted him. His friends and associates nodded politely.

"The three of us were seated with me between the two of them," my mom recalled, taking the final sip of her Chardonnay. "After introductions and an exchange of pleasantries, Gunther served up a couple of gossipy anecdotes on the late-night escapades of Yankee stars Mickey Mantle and Billy Martin. Your father was spellbound. Any nerves he might have had about Gunther evaporated. A man after his own heart. A huge baseball fan, Max couldn't wait to share these salacious stories with his buddies on Seventh Avenue. Thus emboldened, he opened with the retailer's ritual question."

"'So how's business, Gunther?'

"Josh, dear, never in his fifty years on earth had Gunther been asked that question. How's business, indeed? He was a lawyer, a renowned lawyer. The law is a profession, not a business. But your father asked this question of everybody he greeted. He'd ask the same of a rabbi.

"But it's not for nothing that Gunther was revered as a genius. He read the *Wall Street Journal* daily and knew the lingo: 'Well, Max, in your vernacular we're up about 10 percent versus last year.'

"Your father was speechless, his smile wide, his eyes glowing.

"Gunther went on, with a speech I had heard ad nauseum. 'Yes, business is good. It's always good. When the economy is booming, stock and bond offerings soar. When the property market collapses, our bankruptcy and distressed loan departments prosper. When the tax law changes, our phones ring off the hook. The trust and estate planning department works well into the night. And the best news is that companies are always filing lawsuits against other companies. Yes, Max, business is good—it's always good.'

"Max responded, 'It's not like that in retail. When chenille sweaters die, they're as dead as Kelsey's nuts. And who knows what will replace them? That's why I'm here pounding the pavement. Looking for something new. Won't get much inspiration in this place, if you don't mind me saying.'"

Mom smiled. "My dad came back with the perfect reply."

"'True enough, you'll find many fine things at the Harvard Club, but the latest in fashion is not among them.'

"The waiter served drinks and hot popovers," Mom continued. "We chatted about this and that. And then after lunch when coffee was served, the interrogation portion of the event ensued."

"My dad led off: 'Madeline tells me that you two are seeing a lot of each other.'"

Mom recalled, with another smile, that she and Max had rehearsed likely questions and responses the night before. "So then your father said, 'Yes, Gunther, we are seeing a lot of each other, and we plan to get married in the spring.'"

Mom exhaled. "My dad was taken completely by surprise. Max's declaration of our intention to marry had been my suggestion at our rehearsal session. I knew Dad would be wrong-footed for a minute or so. I was apprehensive, but knew I held the trump card. Gunther's many years of courtroom experience had prepared him to deal with surprises. I could see his mind running through scenarios and narratives. He reached the inevitable conclusion.

"I was going to marry this guy, regardless of what Gunther said or did. Forbidding, objecting, protesting, or threatening would not change the outcome. On the contrary, it would only stiffen my resolve and complicate his task going forward. His fatherly goal would be safeguarding my interests in this marriage and maintaining the loving relationship he had with me. Gunther always played the long game."

She halted for a moment and looked me in the eyes. "You see, Josh, since my mom's death, at least, your grandfather had sheltered and protected me. And I could always count on that. When he returned to the office that afternoon, Gunther, of course, would do his due diligence on Max. I doubted he would find anything serious enough to convince me to abandon my plans.

"Of course, he still would not bless the marriage. I knew him too well for that. I would expect some expressions of fatherly concern, which we would parry. But all my dad had to do for our father-daughter bond to continue was to follow the implicit, invisible script which I, well-schooled in the ways of Gunther, had composed.

"A long silence ensued, but finally Gunther spoke. He said that he had hoped I would wait awhile to get married. 'Madeline has been on her own for only a few years since Smith. She's working her way up in publishing and might even return to school. This talk of marriage seems rather hasty to me.'

"Then he turned to Max and said, 'I'm not sure what your current or future position pays, but I imagine it won't permit you two to live as she is accustomed to living.'"

"Apologizing for his vulgar Yiddish, Max made it clear he was 'not the kind of schmuck who's going to wait around to be promoted.' He told Gunther he would open his own store. 'I have the location picked out,' he said."

Mom told me that Gunther offered him an alternative. He would talk to his good friend, Sidney Solomon, a senior executive at Abraham & Straus—at that time, the keenest competitor of Macy's. Perhaps a phone call could pave the way for Max.

"But your father would have none of it," Mom said. "He stood his ground. Said, 'I want to be my own boss. I'm set to go.'"

"Gunther countered that this plan would require significant capital. He continued, 'Madeline has led me to believe that you're not a man of means. Not that I mind. In fact, I rather admire the way you've made your way in the world. You worked at your parents' grocery store during your school years, you served in the military, and you've climbed the ladder rather quickly at Famous-Barr. All are admirable accomplishments. But surely you haven't nearly enough capital to open a store, and I doubt many banks would back you!'"

Mom leaned in and continued. "Your father actually cocked his head and informed Gunther of my decision to commit a bit of my trust fund money to finance his start-up store."

"Gunther, putting on his squinty-eyed, reproachful look, said, 'Madeline and I agreed that she'd leave those funds in blue-chip investments until she was much further along in her career and had met a suitable young man.'"

"I asserted that I, in fact, had met a suitable young man, saying, 'I love Max and want to marry him. And I want him to have his own store. Besides, the store will need only a small percentage of the fund's assets. Not much risk, really, Father.'

"Gunther, looking every bit like a schoolteacher addressing a rather slow-witted student, berated me for 'knowing nothing about commerce, nothing about risk.'"

"For dramatic effect, I slammed my hand on the table. 'I love you, Dad! But I am twenty-five years old, and I know my own mind and heart. And I want to do this. I would really like your approval.'"

Mom sighed. "Poor Dad was trapped. He knew his role and his lines. He couldn't bring himself to break what he had with me—a bond that had sustained him after my mom died. Besides, he held a losing hand. He was shrewd enough to know that the marriage was inevitable. It would be best to fold, and fold graciously.

"With his eyes half-hooded he conceded, 'Well, I was quite stunned by your announcement, but I certainly won't stand in the way. Hell, you'd probably run me over if I tried.' He laughed. 'No, I wish you both the best.' And with that he stood, shook hands with Max, and embraced me.

"I whispered, 'Clever, Dad,' in his ear. Then he excused himself and departed.

"As he waited for a taxi, I said, 'My dad was already plotting his next steps, I'm sure. He lost this first round, and retreated, but he will not lose sight of his long-term goal of protecting me.'

"Max and I rose from our seats and made our way into the Harvard Club's foyer. We embraced, and your dad kissed, I mean really kissed, me. Poor Gunther probably got a letter of reprimand from the club manager, who witnessed our indiscretion."

Saying these words, Mom's eyes glazed over.

Six months later, Maddy and Max got married in a small private ceremony at Gunther's apartment overlooking the Metropolitan Museum. The rabbi from Temple Emanu-El officiated. Maddy's close friends and some of Max's from Seventh Avenue attended. His parents took the train up from Miami and gathered at the wedding with their New York family from

Brooklyn and the Bronx. Gunther invited no one, but he did give the bride away.

Mom slept in her childhood bedroom the night before the wedding. It was planned that she would have breakfast with her father in the morning. "I think we were both eager to reclaim the warm relationship that had been wounded at the Harvard Club lunch. I was a bit teary-eyed as I made coffee, toasted bagels, and retrieved my personal jar of peanut butter from the butler's pantry, the one with my name on the lid. I moved around quietly.

"For his part, Dad put down his copy of the *Times* and gazed at me while I was repeating for perhaps the last time my morning rituals in the family kitchen. Dad embraced me, which evoked from me a full-on sob. My beloved father's eyes watered as well. Finally, he managed to say that he loved me and would miss me.

"I snuggled closer. 'Oh, Dad, I will miss you too. You've been my hero since I was a little girl. Promise me you'll give Max a chance. I know he'll be trying hard to please you because he knows how much you mean to me.'

"'I will, my dear,' he said. 'Nothing would please me more than to get to know him. I will try my best.'

"'I know you will, Dad.'

"With that, Gunther excused himself for a moment and returned with a beautifully wrapped jewelry box."

Mom sighed. "I opened it. It was the pearl necklace that my father had given my mother on their tenth wedding anniversary. He asked me to wear it that afternoon for my wedding, as an eternal symbol of our mutual devotion.

"I asked him to help me put it on. He fumbled with the clasp, and then stepped back to see how it looked.

"He beamed. 'It's gorgeous, Maddy. Your mother would be so proud and delighted.'

"'Even with these ratty flannel pj's I'm wearing?'

"'Yes, even with those ratty pj's!'"

Chapter 5

THE FELDMAN FAMILY SPOKE RETAIL.

To be more precise, my dad and I spoke retail.

"So, Dad, how was business?" I would ask when we were seated at the dinner table. That would prompt him to give the family a blow-by-blow analysis of Fratelli Massimo's performance that day. It might have been up, down, or sideways. Moreover, he would tell us why. After all, my father was not just the founder and CEO of the company, he was also the merchant. A merchant will anticipate what his customers want before they know it. Dad taught me that the merchant was the single most important person in a fashion business; without his instincts and foresight, the business would fail.

"In Hollywood," he would continue, "I would be called 'Bankable Box Office,' just like Gregory Peck or John Wayne."

If Dad had just returned from a buying trip to New York, he would share his triumphs, such as identifying a fashion winner, negotiating a favorable price or delivery date, outfoxing a competitor, or nabbing an exclusive for a certain style.

I was spellbound, pleased to hear of his wins, as each of these episodes cemented my role as Dad's future business partner and heir. How glorious it must be to be my father.

My brother was not similarly impressed. While my mom would nod and utter a wifely word or two of praise, no matter how dizzyingly triumphant Dad's achievement, Rand stayed mute.

After a particularly brilliant coup on my dad's part, recounted in sparkling detail, he turned to my brother. "Rand, what does it take to impress you? Your brother understands what it takes to win at retail and how important it is to the family's welfare."

Rand raised his eyes from his plate and said, "Nice going." Then he returned to playing with his food.

"Nice going? That's it?"

Rand said, "OK, Dad, you did a good job last week in New York."

Dad boiled over, his face crimson, eyes flashing. He turned toward Mom. "Maddy, please inform the little prince that I'm the one who puts bread on the table."

"Max, I think Rand has other interests and he's trying to be polite. I think all this business talk bores the hell out of him."

"Bores him, does it? How does he think we can afford to live this way? It's because I make it happen." Dad's engine was really going.

"We're all terribly grateful to Dad for making all this possible, aren't we, boys?"

Mom's question was met with two very fast answers of yes.

"Now, let's finish dinner in peace."

Rand asked to be excused and Mom quickly followed.

On more than one such occasion, Dad and I would be the last ones at the table. "That little ingrate," he would start. "When I was his age, we had nothing. We lived above our little grocery store in Omaha. I worked in that store from the time I was seven years old. I learned to be a merchant there. I worked my rear end off learning how the store operated and then improving things even when your grandfather objected. Everything from price points to placements to bribing the goddamn route men to feed me info—that was me. You name it, I did it.

"I did not sit at the table like a little prince. I did not have my mommy rushing to comfort me. No, I was my own man, not a momma's boy."

"Dad, Rand is a great guy and my best friend. He's the best backyard athlete in the neighborhood. He isn't interested in the business, just like I'm not interested in those dusty novels Mom reads. Give the guy a break."

"Mom's dusty novels don't pay the bills, sonny. Fratelli Massimo does, and I am Fratelli Massimo—and don't you forget it."

When it came time for his bar mitzvah, Mom took my brother to New York to get outfitted. This was in sharp contrast to the wardrobe I wore at my own. I was relegated to the local Brooks Brothers store where Dad picked out a blue blazer, gray flannel slacks, a button-down shirt, and striped tie. But for some reason, my mom thought Rand would be happier with the fashion selection in New York.

Rand was slender and handsome—everyone agreed on that. He looked a lot like Mom. He even had her graceful way of moving. He had thick, straight, dark hair, with a razor's-edge part. Add to that his piercing blue eyes, a Roman nose, and rather thin lips.

I took after my father. My face was round, I had curly brown hair, a fleshy nose, gray-blue eyes, and thicker lips. I was five foot nine and, to be truthful, a bit stocky.

I wasn't jealous. Why go all the way to New York for clothes?

Mom smiled when I asked her. "Your brother will be happier with the selection there."

Whatever.

My mom was right as usual. Rand couldn't wait to tell me about his weekend adventure.

"We stayed at the Stanhope, right next to Grandpa's apartment. Every meal was a treat. Gunther even took me to the Automat for lunch on Saturday and to Katz's deli on Sunday. The big surprise was going to Barney's on Seventh Avenue, where Mom introduced me to Barney Pressman, who is *the* Barney. He gave Mom a big hug and then escorted us through the store. Wow—what a store! Like nothing in St. Louis."

When his purchases arrived, he modeled them for Mom and me. Dad took a pass. Rand looked great. Instead of the boxy blazer I got at Brooks Brothers, his was made in Italy; it was snug in the waist and the lapels were a bit wide. His slacks had no cuffs, and his shirt was bright white with a spread collar. The only thing like my outfit was the tie, striped, but tied in a four-in-hand knot, not a dowdy old Windsor, like Dad and I wore.

Rand hung the outfit with care in his closet, and I would catch him sneaking a peek from time to time. Could he ever be a merchant like Dad? I doubted it—it was only his personal appearance that he cared about, then and now. Always the *dernier cri*, as my French teacher might have said.

Dad took great pride in being a self-made man. I think this may have been one of the reasons he was disappointed with Rand.

"He was born with a silver spoon in his mouth. You were too, Josh, but you're learning from the master and will someday be in charge. But Rand—who knows?"

Dad had told his rags-to-riches story a million times, but he never tired of repeating it.

When Dad got out of the Army in 1952, he decided to settle in St. Louis. "It's a big-league city!" he proclaimed. He landed a job with Famous-Barr, St. Louis's dominant department store, and worked his way up to a buyer's job in women's ready-to-wear.

In those days, when most department stores operated only a downtown location, such stores were far more popular than they are now. Price points ranged from modest in the bargain basement to premium on the couture floors. They were staffed for the most part by full-time veteran salespeople who worked weekdays and Saturday from 10:00 a.m. to 6:00 p.m., except for Mondays when they closed at 9:00 p.m. In those days, all department stores were closed on Sunday.

Those retailers offered the convenience of options such as charge accounts and easy returns to their customers. Most had elegant dining rooms, like the Oak Room at Marshall Field's in Chicago, or the Pompeian Room at Brandeis in Omaha. Famous-Barr in St. Louis had a restaurant and cafe serving the best French onion soup available outside of Paris. They wanted to keep shoppers in the store as long as possible. The longer they stayed, the more they purchased.

But these were more than just retail outlets. In a way, they were like my grandparents' grocery store—a place to gather and be seen as much as a place to shop. Philadelphians, for example, said, "Meet you under the clock" at Strawbridge & Clothier. Large rooms were made available to civic groups for their meetings. The department store owners, who were mostly founding families, were local bigwigs and celebrities; they were leading figures in local commercial and charitable causes.

A buyer's job, like the one my dad had in the 1950s, was a critical one. Each buyer had sales and profit/loss responsibility for his or her category. Many of Dad's buying colleagues were women. Retailers were smart, and they knew that women did most of the shopping. The department and specialty stores took advantage of their knowledge and skills and gave them decision-making roles. Women thrived in retail long before they could set foot in many other professions.

Buyers needed to plan early for each season: how many sweaters would be needed for Christmas? And they were responsible for pricing the merchandise, markdowns, selling costs, and advertising expenses. In a sense, each operated his or her own business.

And that job, along with his confidence and impetus and Mom's cash, gave Dad the experience he needed to start Fratelli Massimo.

• • •

At the opening ceremony of the very first Fratelli Massimo store, Mom cut the ribbon draped in front of the building. The store was located directly across the street from Famous-Barr.

A photograph shows my mother in a demure, longish skirt and a white blouse with a Peter Pan collar. Mom's also wearing a stylish pair of needle-toe, two-inch-heel pumps sourced from the new store's inventory. My dad, with a cat-that-swallowed-the-canary grin, stands to the side. His wardrobe has improved considerably since his lunch with Gunther. He's wearing a three-button sack suit, which was very popular back then, with a button-down collared shirt and narrow tie. On his feet are a pair of cordovan-colored Weejun penny loafers, a long-held St. Louis tradition.

I'm there, too, in utero. I was born six months later.

Peeking past my mother in the photo, you can see the facade of the store. It had double-glass doors adjacent to show windows. The window on the left was devoted to dress shoes, which carried the store's French Room Originals private label. They were priced from eighteen to thirty dollars. The right-side window contained casual shoes with the store's Country Club Casuals private label. Casual shoes were priced from twelve to twenty dollars, except for the nationally branded Keds tennis shoes.

The yellowed photograph appeared in the business section of the *St. Louis Post-Dispatch* under the headline, "European Footwear at American Prices." Three paragraphs captured the store opening.

> *A new concept in shoe merchandising opened today at the corner of Seventh Street and Olive Street downtown. Fratelli Massimo offers ladies the latest in European footwear styles at what the founder, Max Feldman, says are American prices.*
>
> *According to Feldman, "A customer can spend a lot of money trying to find the latest in fashion footwear at department and specialty stores, but Fratelli Massimo offers her stylish shoes at affordable prices. These aren't cheap knockoffs, but original designs by the best of Italian stylists."*
>
> *Feldman and his wife, New York–born Madeline (née Berg), live in Clayton. He was a clothing buyer at Famous-Barr until recently, and has been planning the opening of Fratelli Massimo for the past year. He confidently predicted that this store would be the first of hundreds, as malls are opening up*

across the country, and there "was nothing resembling Fratelli Massimo...developers are already calling."

Getting the store ready to open was a circus. As my dad recounted:

"I hired an architect with a giant broomstick up his rear end. Wouldn't listen to anybody. The building contractor was a thief who took kickbacks from every sub and supplier and missed every deadline. The city building code morons had their hands out and approval stamps locked up. The only stand-up guys were Enrique and Sergio, who honored every commitment and shipped the marvelous shoes, just as ordered—a full month ahead of the store opening. Even sent me and your mother a grand opening gift."

He saved the harshest remarks for his landlord.

"That son of a bitch who owns the building has no principles whatsoever. Changed his mind with the day of the week and whichever way the wind was blowing. He knew he had a prime location, and he made me jump through hoops to get a lease written. He even called the house at ten one night to say he had another tenant lined up. I had to get dressed, drive downtown, and kiss his ass as well as up the rent to seal the deal. And as I was leaving his office around midnight, he declared, 'I will need your articles of incorporation, ASAP.'"

Dad went on, raising his eyebrows.

"'Articles of what the fuck?' I asked myself. I got home around 12:30 a.m. and woke Maddy. She rolled over, yawned, and said she would call Gunther at 8:00 a.m. New York time and get the thing done. I was never so glad to have the old man around.

"Gunther was more than eager to help. He himself drafted the documents, which included articles of incorporation, officer designation, capital structure, and so on, and had them couriered to St. Louis. Didn't charge me a nickel. The guy's a real mensch."

Max and Maddy reviewed and signed the documents quickly and rushed to get them notarized. Copies were hand-delivered to the landlord, who inspected and OK'd them. Max was pleased with his titles: chairman, chief executive officer, and president. The legal documents gave him "the authority to conduct business on a day-to-day basis, sign checks and other legal documents, and make operating decisions necessary to the operation of the business." Maddy's title was less grandiose: secretary/treasurer. When Maddy asked her husband about her duties, he smiled and told her to "look pretty." When she asked Gunther, he promised to explain things to her when she visited New York.

Had Dad taken a bit more time to carefully read Gunther's documents, he just might have discovered that there was a hidden bombshell in the legal framework. It was something that neither Dad, nor any of us, would realize until an explosive family decision point, years later.

Gunther knew my dad was a man in a hurry who valued titles and public acclaim more than anything. What possible difference would all the legal gibberish make? After all, he was in charge—he was chairman, CEO, and president of his own company.

This original Fratelli Massimo concept bore scant resemblance to what would become the format that numbered hundreds of units throughout the United States. Developing a winning retail format is an iterative process. It starts with a vision and is reimagined, tweaked, and retooled as customers react positively or negatively to its offerings.

And, of course, competition doesn't stand still. Shops open their doors every day, so customers and competitors are free to examine each element of the store, including merchandise, pricing, décor, sales staff, and displays. There are no secrets, no patents, and no copyrights. Retailers are naked.

Dad was enthusiastic about his original formula. Famous-Barr, his prime competitor, offered more-expensive branded merchandise, such as Ferragamo, Herbert Levine, and Roger Vivier. By selling private label merchandise sourced from Italy instead of premium-priced brand names, he could undercut department store prices and still make good money.

But too much time had elapsed since Dad's European travels in his army days. Europe was in recovery mode and inflation was rampant, so there were few bargains to be had. This meant that the original markup on these purchases was insufficient to cover the inevitable markdowns and expenses generated by the store, including Dad's salary and travel expenses.

By the time I was born, the message was clear: the original formula would no longer work. Customers liked the merchandise well enough, but the margin on merchandise was not going to pay the bills. Fratelli Massimo was due for a reset, which would ultimately become several resets.

Unlike the founders of most undercapitalized start-ups, Dad had the comfort of knowing that his wife had lots of dough. He could have futzed around for years and not exhausted her resources, but that wasn't Dad. He was always driven to succeed, but this time he had some additional incentives. He was crazy about Maddy and had convinced her that he was the right guy for her, despite her father's reservations. Running through her money was antithetical to his pitch, and he now had a family to support. He had to make it. Also, Gunther's skepticism was posted on Dad's mental bulletin board. Dad would not fail and give the old man that satisfaction!

He set about finding a different formula, one that appealed to customers but would pay its own way. His ability to divine what customers wanted, as well as his depth of personal conviction and willingness to take risks, separated Fratelli Massimo's fortunes from those of a thousand retail failures.

Dad sifted through the selling results. The success of his Italian imports was unquestioned. Customers loved the shoes, but he had priced them too low to make the necessary profit margin. He experimented with his holiday line and increased the retail price on incoming merchandise, which were mostly dressy evening shoes. Results were positive, yet Dad was hesitant to reprice his incoming spring merchandise, which was much more casual.

Back in 1957, Black Friday bargains were the future, not the present. Holiday-happy customers typically paid full fare for apparel and footwear. So were the encouraging results generated by the higher-priced shoes at Fratelli Massimo a one-off, or were they a clue to future strategy? As Dad explained to me later, "There's a definite holiday shopping frenzy in retail. Customers throw caution to the wind. They're in an upbeat mood—they're buying gifts and expect to receive gifts. They're going to parties and family gatherings, so I viewed the Christmas selling results with skepticism."

Dad selectively raised prices on some of his spring merchandise—mostly the dressy pumps women bought for their Easter outfits. This worked, too, which gave him the confidence to gradually raise prices on most of his private label French Room Originals and Country Club Casuals.

While outcomes were improving, the store was still not reaching its potential. What was missing? Dad was determined to find the answer. He spent most of spring 1958 traveling the country, shopping and inspecting shoe stores from Los Angeles to Boston. He walked the newly opened regional malls and the shopping streets using his "retail radar."

His conclusion: Fratelli Massimo lacked an important ingredient found in most successful retailers—authenticity. As he explained to me years later, "People don't just shop at Saks Fifth Avenue and Lord & Taylor because they like the location, the merchandise, the pricing, or the sales staff. They shop there because the store has a point of view and conveys authenticity. And nothing conveys authenticity better than brand names."

Dad set about trying to convince branded shoe manufacturers to sell to Fratelli Massimo. You might imagine that most would leap at the opportunity, but that wasn't the case. The store was virtually unknown outside of St. Louis. Was its credit OK? Did it have the image those brands required? But the most challenging obstacle was Famous-Barr. Like many others of its kind, it carried only brand-name shoes. Why would a brand want to compromise its relationship with Famous-Barr to sell to a nobody across the street?

Seeking brand names, Dad pounded the pavement once again in New York. His failure rate was 100 percent when it came to premium-priced names like the kind carried by Famous-Barr. But he started to make headway with sub-premium brands like VANELi, DeLiso Debs, Daniel Green, and Capezio. These labels were more interested in volume than image and in some cases weren't terribly worried about Famous-Barr's reaction, since these brands could be found in a wide variety of specialty stores, in addition to department stores.

Dad invited the representatives of many of these brands to visit his store. He wined and dined them with Maddy at his side. One by one they agreed to ship him small quantities of their goods—with four huge conditions. Fratelli Massimo had to pay them the full list price for the footwear, not the discounted price Famous-Barr was entitled to. Dad had to promise that he would sell the merchandise at the same price Famous-Barr charged. The merchandise could not be marked down until the brand gave permission. And finally, Fratelli Massimo had to pay for merchandise upon receipt, so no thirty-day terms, which were customary in the industry.

Dad agreed. It was the "authenticity factor."

"Customers will see these brands as adding legitimacy to the store." And, he added with a chuckle, "They'll begin to appreciate even more the bargain prices on our French Room Originals and Country Club Casuals."

That was step three in the reset of Fratelli Massimo.

Step four would take a bit longer. Dad believed that he could attract even more customers if he offered a lower-priced private label product manufactured in New England, which was still a robust shoe-producing hub with huge manufacturing plants— unlike the tiny atelier Enrique and Sergio Massimo operated.

But Fratelli Massimo had to generate more volume to warrant purchases of hundreds and then thousands of pairs, rather than the dozens he was purchasing from the Massimo brothers. He would need half a dozen stores to command the buying power he was seeking.

Resets one and two enabled the store to break even in 1959, so Max Feldman set his sights on launching his first suburban St. Louis mall store in 1962. At that point, he felt comfortable tapping Mom's trust fund. Fratelli Massimo was on a firmer footing, and retailers and Wall Street analysts were convinced that regional malls were where Americans were going to shop. What had been an experiment in Natick, Massachusetts, or Northland, Detroit—opening a mall consisting of two major stores with specialty operators in between—became America's preferred shopping venue. The number of regional malls would peak at over one thousand by the end of the century.

My dad had his faults, but he was a genius merchant and visionary. Those gifts, combined with fortunate timing—a post–World War II hunger for things to buy—and the right venues, malls, propelled the company for decades.

Chapter 6

IN THOSE EARLY YEARS IN THE 1960S AND 1970S, FRATELLI MASSIMO consumed my father's energies and passion. He usually made it home for dinner when he was in town, but he worked nights and weekends and traveled frequently. He insisted on attending every new store opening; there were dozens and dozens, and then hundreds and hundreds, as malls were multiplying like rabbits.

With Dad traveling so often, it was up to Mom, with the help of our housekeeper, Nora, to manage our home and my brother and me.

While I was old enough to understand the reasons for Dad's hectic schedule, I never quite forgave him for missing most of my birthday celebrations—and those of my brother. Yes, I knew that Saturdays were a big day for retailers, and Dad wanted to be in the store, especially a newly opened one. It gave him a chance to "stress test" the crew and to see which shoes were selling. But this didn't sit well with me, particularly when I was a little guy. All of my friends' dads came to their parties.

Perhaps because of Dad's frequent absences or because she is a rank sentimentalist, Mom made our birthdays very special. In fact, she went through a special ritual each year on the day before our birthday celebrations. We would be treated to a screening of all of our previous years' birthday parties, filmed by Maddy on her ancient Kodak 8mm camera.

Mom scurried around arranging things in our smallish den. A wobbly screen was placed in front of our television set, and the Bell & Howell projector sat on a TV table behind the sofa. We were each given a bowl of popcorn, popped by Nora, and we plopped ourselves down on either side of Mom. On the side table, Mom placed her own bowl of popcorn, a pack of Viceroy cigarettes, her lighter, the ashtray, and a large box of Kleenex.

Rand and I loved this tradition. Dad would excuse himself groaning, "How many times do I have to watch these?"

"Strictly optional, Max," my mom would reply. "The boys and I will have a private tear-jerking screening."

Mom would turn on the clackety-clack projector and narrate, identifying kids and parents, and offering play-by-play commentary. Naturally, we were embarrassed by our infantile antics—playing with the gift wrapping instead of the presents, enduring hugs and kisses from Sy and Rose, and smashing slices of birthday cakes into our maws. Mom would laugh and cry at her boys on the screen. "Seems like just yesterday!"

The scenes from my fourth birthday party would bring tears to my eyes. There I was in my cowboy suit, surrounded by my preschool classmates. There was a sizeable pile of gifts awaiting me. My mom panned the assembled friends and relatives. I picked out my grandparents from Florida, the mothers of my classmates, and a high chair with my squalling two-year-old brother.

It seems that I was disappointed that the entertainment was provided by Ickle Pickle and not Kedzo. Mom stopped the film. "I tried everything to get Kedzo, but he was much in demand, so poor you had to settle for Ickle Pickle. Time for you to come to grips with it, kiddo."

I faked a smile, but what really upset me was Dad's absence. Once I asked Mom where he was.

"Oh, Josh, he was so sorry he couldn't be there. Nothing's more important to him than you boys. But your father was getting his first suburban store ready to open before Thanksgiving. The electricians, who make an ungodly amount of money per hour, were uncertain how to proceed with something. They called the house. He rushed over to Northwest Plaza to straighten things out and didn't get back until very late that night."

I couldn't really blame him. The future of Fratelli Massimo was on the line. This Northwest Plaza store was his second unit and his first regional mall store. The rents were high, but the location was great—right between Famous-Barr and Stix, Baer & Fuller, the other big department store chain in St. Louis. He knew there would be heavy traffic between them and gambled that the expensive location would produce terrific sales and profits even with the astronomical rent.

I was just four years old at the time, but I could sense his excitement the morning after the store's grand opening.

"You can't believe the traffic, Maddy. They were lined up outside the store waiting for the doors to open. We did more business in one day than we do all week downtown. I rented a truck and drove to our downtown store and loaded it with inventory and spent last night refilling stock at Northwest Plaza. At this rate we're going to run out of inventory in three or four weeks."

With that, he left the breakfast table, got on the phone, and begged his vendors to ship more merchandise.

This was the break that Fratelli Massimo needed. It didn't take a prophet to see that a second, third, and fourth mall would soon open in the St. Louis area. This phenomenon would be repeated in city after city across the country.

Suburban customers loved the convenience of the mall. They appreciated the proximity, not having to drive to the city, and they were simply drawn to it. The shopping center became the town center of the communities it served, offering acres of free parking, shopping, dining, movie theatres, holiday excitement including Santa and the Easter Bunny, meeting rooms, and special events in a climate-controlled (mostly crime-free) venue. In those early days it had special appeal to the moms who had yet to join the workforce, providing a pleasant environment in which to spend the day, meet friends, have lunch, and do a bit of shopping.

And it generated millions in tax revenues for those local communities, benefitting schools and local treasuries.

The losers, of course, were the downtown shopping districts, which saw traffic decline, crime increase, and retailers shutter. At first, it was the local mom-and-pop stores that faded, but eventually the major department stores and specialty stores (like Lerner's and Woolworth's) fell victim to the decline. One by one, the department stores shrank the size of their one-time downtown flagship units, and then they closed them altogether or converted them to closeout stores. Soon, most once-vibrant downtown shopping districts turned into ghost towns.

By 1962 the mall promised to be the launching pad for the largest retail expansion ever, and Fratelli Massimo was ready to blast off.

Perhaps because Dad was gone so much, Rand and I started hanging out together at a young age. At first it was building things with Tinker Toys, Legos, or Lincoln Logs. Rand took great delight in knocking over what we had painstakingly built. His laughter and beaming smile salved my distress over the rubble he wrought. My brother possessed a certain mischievous charm that enabled him to get away with murder, unscathed. The only exception was with Dad, who was not seduced by his charms and who also punished him mercilessly. Rand was grounded when he scuffed Dad's Cadillac Eldorado playing basketball in the driveway and endured a tongue-lashing when he tore the box scores from the paper before Dad had a chance to read them. Everybody else was, as the expression goes, putty in his hands— especially Mom, who would more often than not smile indul- gently at his hijinks and faux apologies.

We played sports together. It was clear, even in grade school, that Rand was a superior athlete. I was two years older, so I prevailed for a while, but he passed me like a Porsche overtaking a VW Beetle. And he took on the affectation of referring to himself in the third person on the playing field, as if he were the announcer. "Rand Feldman, all-star, comes to the plate!" or, "The wily Rand Feldman pops a left-handed layup around his clueless brother." By age twelve he was calling himself "Rand the Man," a moniker that would stick with him through high school. When he entered a basketball game, a student would announce over the loudspeaker: "Now entering the game, Rand the Man Feldman!" The crowd went crazy at home games. Even the opposing team's players laughed.

When weather permitted, he and I would play basketball in our driveway. Horse was our game, which required your oppo- nent to match the shot you made. Four misses and you lost. At first, I would win—I was six inches taller. But by middle school, he would clobber me. And to make matters worse, he would do a play-by-play inspired by the NBA commentator Marv Albert. "Rand the Man circles the free throw line and throws up a miracle hook shot. HEEEEEEEEE SCORES and the crowd is on its feet!" And on and on. As humiliating as it was to lose to a younger brother, I could only marvel at his wizardry and charm. After many of his victories, he would embrace me and say, "Josh, perhaps Rand the Man can help. Maybe a little work on your jump shot . . ." And we would fake wrestle on the lawn until we broke up laughing.

I don't remember Dad watching us play Horse, until one particular day. I was fourteen and Rand was twelve; Dad had just returned home after closing the offices at noon on a Good Friday.

He parked his car at the base of the driveway and appeared.

Rand began his play-by-play commentary: "Sellout crowd at Feldman stadium today to watch these two rivals battle it out for supremacy in the Horse league. Rand the Man gets the ball first. Will he try his famous hook shot from top of the key? Yes! He's dribbling to his spot, stops, turns sideways to the basket, and lets it go! It's good!"

Naturally, I missed my attempt at his "fucking famous hook shot."

"And now Rand, a righty, is dribbling toward the basket, cross dribbles, and sinks a layup with his left hand."

As a natural lefty, it meant I had to do it with my right hand—with predictable results.

"Oh no, fans, we were really hoping for a close match, but Rand the Man has taken an almost insurmountable two-shot lead."

Dad had seen enough and stormed into the house.

When we had finished playing Horse and smack talking, we burst into the house. There we found Dad and Mom squaring off in the kitchen.

"How can he let that little twerp beat him at a game of Horse? Answer me that, Maddy."

"Max, he did *not* let him win. Rand is better at basketball. That's all it is."

"Yeah, yeah. But it just isn't right. Josh is taller, has more experience, and is a better athlete."

"No, he's not a better athlete. If you were around more you would see that, day in and day out. It's clear who the better athlete is, and it's Rand."

My father noticed us, and turned to Rand, asking, "Is that right?"

Tilting his head and looking toward heaven, Rand replied, "Rand the Man, Clayton's best backyard athlete, pushes through the crowd to receive the NBA's player of the year..."

Before he could finish the monologue, Dad lunged for him but instead ran into Mom, who stood with arms folded, guarding him.

"Don't you ever even think of striking him, or Josh!"

I didn't really know what to think. Rand was better at basketball than I was. I knew Dad had great hopes for me, but why was basketball so important to him? And what did he have against Rand other than his lack of interest in the business?

Dinner took on a predictably somber cast that evening. Dad went on and on about how successful the Easter season had been. I, of course, played straight man and asked him some softball questions. Mom updated us about her day at school. She had been taking classes in American and English literature at Washington U. Rand asked to be excused and raced upstairs. Everybody was anxious for the day to end.

But it didn't conclude at dinner.

While pretending to do our homework, Rand and I were listening to the Cards game with Harry Caray and Jack Buck doing the play-by-play. Suddenly, we heard shouting coming from our parents' bedroom down the hall. We sneaked down to their closed bedroom door.

"Goddammit, Maddy, why do you always side with Rand and protect him? You're making a mommy's boy out of him."

Mom said, "I don't always side with Rand, but he needed my support tonight when you were being a bully. And I won't tolerate that, Max. You're bigger and stronger than the boys, and at least one of them still looks up to you. Stop being a boor."

"I suppose you're referring to Josh. Yes, he does look up to me, and he does have an amazing aptitude for the business."

"You mean you think he has an aptitude for the business. Because he can do all those computations you've taught him and he sucks up to you with his business questions." Her voice sounded very high.

"Not just because of that. He cares about the business, and he seems to be the only one in the family who does. You never ask or care. And when he's not hiding behind your skirts, Rand is too busy with his fucking Rand the Man bullshit to give the slightest thought to the family business."

Mom let him have it. "Are you feeling sorry for yourself, dear? Toiling away in obscurity without so much as a thank-you from the peasants you're handing bread to? You sound like you did when you were working for your dad. Poor, underappreciated Max."

"Maddy, I'm going to lose it, and you won't like it."

"Should I fear for my safety?"

"No. I would never hurt you, but you hurt me plenty. Not with your fists, but with your words. You're clever with words like your father, and you twist them around and make me look like the bad guy."

"Sometimes it doesn't take much twisting."

"Well, if I'm such a bad guy, how can you possibly stand to have me around? Is it the lifestyle I provide?"

"Oh, come now, Max, have you looked at my trust fund lately? And my save-the-day investment I made so many years ago in Fratelli Massimo? Why, my dear, I could be perfectly comfortable on my own. But I love my three boys, warts and all, and I want this family to thrive, just like you want Fratelli Massimo to thrive."

"Then why are we fighting?"

Their voices lowered and we couldn't hear much, so we silently scurried back to our bedroom, older, wiser, and sadder.

We were older, wiser, sadder, and worried. We were worried because we realized, for the first time, that our family was somehow fragile and vulnerable.

To hear Dad suggest that Mom might be happier without him around, and to then hear Mom remind him of her wealth, shocked both of us. To add to our anxiety, Rand and I felt personally threatened: me, by Mom's expression of skepticism of my abilities, and Rand, by Dad's caustic comments about him. We weren't completely mollified by Mom's declaration about "loving her boys, warts and all." And Dad's failure to reaffirm that love left us both at a loss.

With a pathetic but understandable childish grandiosity, we concluded that our actions alone would determine the family's fate. We could stave off a breakup only if we behaved ourselves.

Chapter 7

MUCH TO OUR RELIEF, THINGS AROUND THE HOUSE SEEMED TO return to normal in the days after the fight.

My brother and I resumed school after that Easter weekend. My dad dropped me off at Clayton High School, while my brother walked to Wydown Middle School, which was only a few blocks from our house in Clayton's Claverach subdivision.

Both of us were thankful there hadn't been a reprise of our parents' Easter weekend brawl following our basketball duel. But we remained vigilant and were cautious in our behavior so as not to set them off. We also confided in one other. And Rand became my banker. I was always short of cash. I liked to play poker with the boys and wasn't very good at it, unlike my grandfather Gunther, who turned out to be a stud at the tables, as I would witness in Las Vegas years later.

In my high school and college days, I smoked Lucky Strike cigarettes, which were a financial drain. For some reason Rand always had ten or twenty dollars to bail me out. In exchange, I advised him on how to play Dad. I didn't need help with Mom, who was always generous with her love. I also played big brother Joshua and tutored him on how to have his way with girls.

Our home occupied three-quarters of an acre atop a small knoll. The steep driveway posed a problem during winter when the rear-wheel drive cars of that era couldn't make it up the grade and were often left on the street. When Dad's big Cadillac Eldorado got stuck, he would fling open the front door and scream for Rand and me to help him dig out.

"Miserable St. Louis weather!" he'd yell.

We'd shovel, push, and rock the car until it was unmoored. Then we'd hop in, sweaty and exhausted, and he'd drop us off at school.

Mom's car was more modest. It was a Ford Country Squire station wagon that had seen a few fender benders. In fact, the front grillwork was so crumpled, she joked about taking it to the orthodontist for braces. Mom had not driven a car until she arrived in St. Louis and was still getting the hang of it twenty years later. Mom dared not drive it on snowy days. She was happy to walk the mile to Washington University. Smiling, she would tell us, "Reminds me that I'm a New Yorker at heart."

Our house was built in the 1930s and was Georgian in design, like most of the houses in our neighborhood. It had four bedrooms upstairs. My brother and I shared a large bedroom over the garage. Mom and Dad shared a master suite, while Mom used the third bedroom as an office. In addition to her desk and typewriter stand, it contained a file cabinet and floor-to-ceiling bookcases we had added after moving in. Mom filled every single shelf of those bookcases. She interspersed "trash" like mysteries and spy thrillers with what she deemed serious fiction. Most of the space was devoted to what was commonly called literature. No books published after 1935 need apply. The second floor also had a spare bedroom, which was originally a maid's room. It was used by Nora when she stayed overnight, by guests, or for out-of-season storage of Mom's clothes. The staircase to the second floor was flanked on one side by a large living room with a fireplace, a bow window, and a cozy little rear den, which had been added by the previous owner. We hung out there as a family in the evenings when we had no homework. That's also where Mom presented our birthday film shows. Dad was usually stationed in his Eames chair thumbing through the newspaper or his sales report, his feet crossed on the ottoman. Mom and the two of us (when we weren't sprawled out on the floor) sat on the big couch facing the TV-stereo console.

A large dining room and kitchen area occupied the other side of the first floor. The dining room was decorated in the style of the day. It was filled with Chippendale furniture, damask curtains, and a sideboard and hutch that housed fine china and sterling. Crown moldings and a chair rail were the architectural features.

The kitchen was rather large and accommodated a sizeable breakfast nook where we took our meals. The kitchen itself was rather modern, having been updated by the prior owner, who had chosen a suite of Kenmore appliances in avocado, which was the chic color of the day.

Rand loathed those appliances. "The color is like vomit! It's puke green."

Mom was indifferent to his whining. "I can't be bothered going to Sears to replace perfectly functional appliances."

But when it came to her wardrobe, she was far less practical and insisted on being *a la mode*, as the French put it. She didn't rely on St. Louis retailers for the latest in fashion, even after Plaza Frontenac opened and offered a Saks Fifth Avenue store and a Neiman-Marcus store designed by Stanley Marcus himself.

"He may have designed the store," Mom grumbled, "but he sure didn't design the clothes." She gave the assortments a grade of C–. No, Mom engaged in what she called "wardrobe refreshment" on her frequent trips to New York. Her return was followed by a tidal wave of parcels from Bonwit Teller, Lord & Taylor, Saks Fifth Avenue, and of course, that mecca of haute couture for the Upper East Side Ladies Who Lunch, Bergdorf Goodman.

Dad actually encouraged these shopping expeditions, as he delighted in Mom's appearance. She was leggy, slender, and athletic. Her visage, like Rand's, was perfectly patrician. Mom was known for her azure blue and rather mysterious eyes, silky smooth complexion, slightly rouged, rather thin lips, and ruler-straight nose. No wonder Sy and Rose thought when meeting Mom for the first time she was a shiksa! Her brunette hair in a pageboy cut was flecked, even at that time, with gray. When she sported her New York finery, she was, as Dad put it, "a fine-looking woman."

"Yes, Max, I am the finest looking woman in the English department at Washington U."

"Not much competition there, sweetie pie," he joked.

But Dad loved showing her off. When the company held galas to commemorate special events, she was a major attraction. When invited to dressy dinner dates or parties, she sparkled. An evening at Tony's, St. Louis's five-star restaurant, demanded Maddy's best. And she always delivered.

When they left the house on those occasions, Nora—our housekeeper, cook, and part-time sitter—would shake her head and mutter, "What a stunner!"

So, no, Dad didn't begrudge Mom those trips to New York.

Sometimes they went together when he had business reasons for being there. They stayed in posh hotels and ate in top-level restaurants.

When Mom went solo to New York, she palled around with her city friends. She filled her days with museums, shopping, lunch, tea, and cocktails. She said she frequented the Elizabeth Arden spa, where they worked magic for her "body and soul restoration."

She often stayed with her father. "Poor Gunther's all alone, so we go out to dinner and maybe theatre, or sometimes we play bridge with his buddies. Sometimes we talk about our memories of Alice, but we never stray into politics. Dad's a rock-ribbed Republican and I'm the opposite. We agreed years ago to not talk politics. But from time to time we talk about business."

"What kind of business do you discuss with him? Dad says you're not interested in Fratelli Massimo," I asked her once.

"Well, Josh, that's not true. I am interested in Fratelli Massimo, just not the day-to-day stuff your dad goes on about at the dinner table. Rather, Gunther and I talk about the future of the company and the role the family will play."

"Huh?"

"Well, in a nutshell, your dad has made a huge success of Fratelli Massimo, and with that success come certain complicated issues regarding its future. It's just legal stuff; you'd be bored stiff with it. OK?"

"I guess." I was a high school kid. What did I know?

Her St. Louis life was slow-paced by comparison, but I think she loved it all the same. Suburban life in Clayton was fine with her. She did most of the "mom" things women did in that era: shop for groceries, oversee the household, pay the bills, and supervise lawn-and-garden work. She also volunteered at our school library, attended PTA meetings, took us clothes shopping, and drove carpools when necessary. Mom even helped us with our homework. What she did not do was cook, except on weekends, but even then, it was catch as catch can. She'd manage with the barbecue or bring something home from a pizza joint.

"You see, boys, I was never allowed to do much in the kitchen. I may scramble some eggs or toast a bagel. My mom, Alice, died when I was young, so we always had a cook. And they were like Nazis, ferocious and territorial. I dared not enter their sanctum sanctorum. I couldn't even get a glass of milk or a scoop of peanut butter without setting off a nuclear explosion. And we do have lovely Nora, don't we?"

That, too, was fine with Dad. If dinner was served on time and frequently included his favorites, he never questioned the arrangement. Nor did we, since we never had setup or cleanup duties, except for the odd weekend.

In addition to volunteering at our school library, Mom played bridge—at the Life Master level. So, when my parents moved to St. Louis, she was determined to find bridge games that were her equal. Through trial and error, she aggregated a group of six highly accomplished and competitive bridge players. Some of these like-minded ladies became her best friends. They had regular games on Tuesday and Friday afternoons. They rotated houses and adhered to unbreakable rules. No food was to be served; it would be a distraction, and who needed the calories? Drinks were limited to water, tea, coffee, and, in later years, Diet Coke. Bridge rules were strictly adhered to with conventions declared, meaning there was no talking during play, no do-overs, and no temper outbursts. The most they could get away with was an anguished facial expression.

Mother's other great passion was reading, literature in particular. It's hard to remember Maddy without a book in her lap and a cigarette in her left hand.

In the early 1960s, right after Rand was born, Mom ventured over to Washington University in hopes of taking some English courses to, as she said, "revive the part of my brain which has atrophied since I left Smith and the New York publishing world."

She described it years later. "When I thumbed through their catalog, it was a thrill. I saw all the authors and books I wanted to study and hadn't had time for at Smith. And the school was just a mile down the road." Thus began Mom's exploration of all things literary, which she eventually narrowed down to nineteenth- and early twentieth-century British and American fiction. Jane Austen, Charles Dickens, George Eliot, Thomas Hardy, Henry James, and his friend and rival Edith Wharton were her favorites. She derived special satisfaction from what is called a close reading of their novels.

As I understand it, a close reading calls for a sentence-by-sentence parsing of the author's work. This involves meticulous interpretation of the author's intentions in language, structure, plot, character development, and so on. Of course, the reader's interpretation is subjective, so the student must read what respected critics have said as well.

Mom was relentless in her pursuit of her own defensible interpretation of dozens of these novels. Like a detective, she sought clues, references in other novels the author had written, analysis of what was taking place historically at the time the book was written, how the author's personal life influenced his or her writing, and on and on.

Sometimes Rand and I would tease her by chanting, "Sometimes a rose is just a rose." And if we wanted to be naughtier, "Sometimes a cigar is just a cigar."

Mom's inevitable reply was, "If you grew up with Gunther as your father, you knew that a rose was not just a rose and a cigar was not just a cigar. He would dissect every sentence you spoke, hunting for hidden meanings and motives. I was well trained."

Mom tried to educate me in the ways of fiction, but she failed. It began my freshman year at Clayton High, when I had to write a paper on *The Return of the Native* by Thomas Hardy. I mentioned something about it at dinner, and Maddy was all over it.

"Excellent. I had to read that book years ago at Horace Mann. Why don't I take a look at your first draft?"

"Uh, OK." What else could I say?

Three drafts later, Mom was still furiously scribbling on my offering with a red pencil.

I begged for mercy. "Mom, this isn't university, it's just a high school assignment." And then I showed her my trump card: "And we're supposed to do our own work." When that failed, I turned to Dad. "Pleeeease get Mom to stop."

Dad was getting a big kick out of our mini drama. "C'mon sweetheart, give the kid a break. He'll never need this stuff when he grows up."

"Max, we don't know what Josh's career will be. Yes, yes, I know you're hoping he goes to work at Fratelli Massimo, and maybe he will, but what if he wants to do something else? These skills are necessary, particularly in college, and if he goes to graduate school. It's critical thinking."

"Look, he's not going to any graduate school, and the kid's smart enough to get through college without spending three hours writing a three-page paper."

"Max Feldman, you never attended college, and you admitted you were a poor student. You're even proud of it. But you've been very successful without those skills, because you're a natural leader and a creative merchant and you've been smart enough to surround yourself with people who have the skills you lack. Why don't we do our best to educate Josh as best we can, so he has all the tools to choose any career path he wants?"

"It's a waste of time and energy, Madeline Feldman, trust me."

I was delighted and grateful that Dad had rescued me. But there was Mom again, doubting my potential career with Fratelli Massimo. She had done it the Easter weekend when she quarreled with Dad, and here she was, doing it again.

Freed from Mom's well-meaning but overwrought oversight, I proceeded to do the bare minimum to get through English class and many of the other courses I took. Getting B's and C's with the occasional A was good enough for me. Mom would look at my grades and shake her head. "Josh, you can do so much better." But she'd leave it at that, thank God. Dad glanced at my report cards, nodded, and went back to reading the paper.

I spent my high school years concentrating on sports, my buddies, and eventually, girls.

Not so my brother Rand. He sought all the tutoring Mom offered, and Dad didn't object. I think it was because he knew Rand wasn't destined for the business, and he wanted him to, at least, "have a trade." Whatever the reason, Rand and my mom were soulmates, just as Dad and I were.

Rand continued to do his backyard sports wizardry during his freshman year of high school. He then played a key role on the JV and varsity basketball teams. He eventually got involved with extracurriculars, like the yearbook, where he demonstrated his graphic design talent.

The whole family showed up for a ceremony at the student center in March of his junior year where he was named Pepper's King—Clayton High's version of "most popular guy." At graduation, he ranked among the top five students academically and went off to Stanford. I, as was preordained, had gone to Washington U.

Mom even accompanied Rand to visit Stanford. She was hoping he would go to an I-95 Ivy League school, but Rand wanted to go west. Maybe to escape from Dad and the frosty relationship he had with him. Rand liked the Stanford campus, but he fell in love with the City by the Bay.

"Josh, San Francisco is the coolest! We took a tour of the city—it was wild. The Tenderloin District is X-rated, the Castro District is home to lots of uninhibited homosexuals. The city is like the West Coast version of New York. It is the opposite of St. Louis."

Mom was cool with the decision. Dad was indifferent.

Chapter 8

As Fratelli Massimo continued to grow, Dad, while proud of his achievements, began complaining that he was working in obscurity.

"Josh, nobody but your mother and I and our accountant know how successful the company is."

"But Dad, everybody knows it's a great success with more than a hundred stores, and you're constantly quoted in the newspaper."

"True, but people think we're just a small family business; the reality is we make a ton of money, and if you stack us up against some of the public companies out there, we outperform them."

"So, it's our secret."

"You sound like your mother."

"Isn't it sort of like bragging to reveal all those numbers?"

"Well, podnah, like Dizzy Dean once said, 'It ain't braggin' if you done it.'"

I didn't care what the Cardinals great had to say. It was bragging, pure and simple, and to me, it was kind of obnoxious. Just like the kids at school who flashed their A papers around for all to see.

When I shared that conversation with Mom, she sighed and said, "Life is just fine the way it is. We do what we want, when we want, and nobody looks over our shoulder. End of story."

With the organization in place and a winning merchandising formula that basically broke down to 50 percent popular branded footwear complemented by 50 percent private label shoes, along with handbags and accessories, Fratelli Massimo powered on. Mom's trust had provided the seed money as well as the continued funding. But by the time the twentieth store opened, the company was starting to generate excess cash—even with an aggressive expansion strategy in place. Dad had culti-vated relationships with two of the big downtown banks and was able to obtain the necessary preholiday seasonal financing that the company required.

Regional malls were opening at a rate of four or five per month nationwide. Not all of them were winners, but suburban America seemed to have an insatiable appetite for these venues, and customers flocked to them. Tax-hungry suburban munici-palities eagerly paved the way for malls by making infrastructure improvements and offering a variety of tax incentives. Big finan-cial institutions, like insurance companies, parked their cash with real estate developers, who promised them healthy returns.

These malls needed department stores to pull in traffic and specialty store tenants, who paid the rent.

Everybody won. Certainly, Fratelli Massimo was no excep-tion. Its first few mall stores were in St. Louis, but Dad had his eye on the Chicago market, three hundred miles to the north. Would the St. Louis merchandising formula work in unfamiliar territory? Store openings in 1963 in the Old Orchard Shopping Center in Skokie and the Oak Brook Center in a western suburb of Chicago were successful. Shortly after that, a very desirable and expensive location became available on North Michigan Avenue. The family traveled to Chicago for the opening, with Maddy doing the ribbon-cutting honors. It was another Fratelli Massimo winner. Seizing the initiative, Dad opened stores in Detroit, Minneapolis, Cincinnati, and Kansas City. He then leased locations in the Southeast—Atlanta, Miami, Tampa, and New Orleans.

Not all of these stores were victories, of course. Some were outright duds and left Dad scratching his head. Was it the location within the mall? The co-tenants, the department store anchors, the competition, or the customer mix? Was it a weak manager or off-target merchandising or perhaps both? The answer was critical because mall rents were increasing rapidly and Fratelli Massimo had to sign ten-year leases. These contracts committed the company to operate the store and pay rent for the entire length of the lease, regardless of the store's results. Too many real estate mistakes could cripple Fratelli Massimo. Banks would get nervous and expansion might have to be halted.

Fast-forward to just after my second trip to Miami, when I had to clean up the mess at 163rd Street by firing the manager. Dad called me into his office. He had identified six dud stores and speculated with me about what might be causing the problem.

"Josh, you're great with numbers...always have been. I need you to get me the answer or answers to that question, and you've got the time and talent to get to the root of the problem. We're headed to the ICSC, the big shopping center dog and pony show in Las Vegas next month, and before we leave—and more importantly, before we sign another lease—I need the answer to that question."

I was staggered. This was new territory for me. But I did know how to crank the numbers, and I was analytical. Most of all, I wanted to please Dad and increase his confidence in me, particularly after the Miami trip fiasco. I also knew he was desperate for an answer, so I might be able to negotiate a few concessions.

"I'd love to do it, Dad, but I'll need some stuff."

"Yeah?" he squinted at me.

"First, you gotta get me out of the basement. With the clatter of comptometers and typewriters, I can't hear myself think down there."

"OK. For as long as this project lasts, and it better not last too long. Then it's back to the basement you go. And where does Mr. Big Shot want to plant himself?"

"Glad you asked. There's an empty cubicle out by Carly's desk. I'll also need her to do some typing and make some airplane and hotel reservations for me. Get me cash advances from treasury. You know, the usual."

Dad peered at me over the top of his glasses and grimaced. I knew he liked how I was handling this, but he dared not show it.

"Why don't you just take my office, wise guy."

"All in good time." I smiled.

Dad smiled back at me, and the deal was done.

And then he predictably got in the last word. "Better be on my desk by the time we leave for Vegas."

It took me a few hours to move and get settled.

I then had the accounting department get me the numbers for the problem stores. Real estate supplied the leasing plans and maps of the malls with the tenants identified. I interviewed the store ops executives about each of the units.

Next, I had Carly make travel arrangements. I asked for a thousand-dollar cash advance, which resulted in a cross-examination by our controller. I apologized for asking, but I didn't have a credit card to my name back then.

Two weeks later, after all the meetings, store visits, and number crunching, I found myself distilling and analyzing the information, preparing the final one-page report, late on a Sunday evening. Before leaving the office, I placed the following memo face-up on Dad's desk awaiting his Monday morning arrival.

Dear Dad,

Here's the down and dirty.

Westland Mall, Hialeah, Florida: Clientele is 90 percent Cubano. Merchandise is 100 percent white-bread. Transfer the inventory to malls like 163rd Street and Dadeland, and replace with Latino styles, vibrant colors, higher heels, and more open-toe shoes.

Evergreen Park, Chicago: Clientele is 101 percent Black. Merchandise is a mishmash of suburban Chicago Anglo. Need State Street, high-fashion merchandise, and a few Black salespeople—and perhaps a Black assistant manager wouldn't hurt!

Sharpstown, Houston, Texas: A great mall if we were in it. Whoever OK'd an entrance mall location should be canned. We're located between a guitar store and a travel agency. Need to be between Sears and Foley's, preferably on the first level. Attempt to relocate. If you meet resistance, threaten to convert our store to a wig store. (Fortunately, our use clause is very, very liberal.)

Castleton Square, Indianapolis: Fire the manager if you can find him. He's worse than Sam at 163rd Street. Guy is never there. Windows haven't been dressed or cleaned in weeks. I checked with accounting and the theft of merchandise at the store is at record levels. Comp decreases two years running.

Kenwood Towne Centre, Cincinnati: Dillard's and Nordstrom's shoe departments are spectacular. Virtually every brand we carry, they carry in breadth and depth—all colors, all sizes. Service in both is extraordinary. We could emphasize our private label assortments, but Baker's and Chandler's have us beat there. It's fourth down and thirty yards to go. We have five years to go on our lease. Losses as far as the eye can see. Punt! Maybe the landlord will take the store back.

Southdale Center, Minneapolis: A trip down memory lane. One of the first malls, but certainly not one of the best. We're paying rent for its past, not its future. Either try to close or trade for a location in one of the other Dales: Ridge or Rose.

Your trusted assistant and successor-in-training,

Josh

Naturally, I had all kinds of backup data, as well as photographs developed at Walgreens and conversation notes, but I knew with absolute certainty that Dad would want only the bare facts and recommendations. He never had the patience to wade through pages of work papers and narratives. He wanted decisive, and I gave him decisive.

We drove to the office together in silence on Monday morning. Dad was his usual nervous self because on a Monday morning, sales results would be pouring in.

I offered to let Dad out and parked the car myself. I wanted to give him a head start with the report.

I didn't have to wait long for his reaction.

I could hear Dad scream at Carly, "Get Josh in here!"

I appeared instantly.

Dad was beaming.

"Well, fucking finally. This is brilliant. You had me worried after you screwed up that Miami assignment—thought I sniffed a bit of Sy in you. But no need to worry. This report gives me just what I need. While we've been sitting here fat and happy with total sales going up, some rot has set in."

I fluttered my eyelashes modestly.

Dad continued. "And to be perfectly honest with you, I was afraid you'd deliver a dissertation. Something your mother might appreciate, but which would be completely counterproductive around here."

With that Dad shouted at Carly again. "Book airplane tickets and a hotel room in Vegas. Josh will be joining us."

I couldn't believe my ears. Las Vegas—the big retailing convention. All the mall developers and the big chain retailers . . . and if you believed the gossip, all the partying!

This was good—it was great.

And Dad never honored his threat to send me back to the basement! I was an upstairs guy from then on. I was on my way!

Nothing could have prepared me for the extravaganza in Las Vegas.

It was all there—hundreds of vendors, thousands of styles, a galaxy of garments, leggy models by the dozen, buttoned-up mall developers, and a gaggle of reporters and fashion insiders.

The stars of the event were the merchant princes: Milton Petrie of Lerner Shops, Sam Demoff of Edison Brothers, Ralph Lauren of Polo, Vince Camuto and Jackie Fisher of Nine West, Marvin Traub of Bloomingdale's, and, of course, Max Feldman of Fratelli Massimo. Each was besieged by the press. Each was followed by his retinue of retainers. Each handed out little morsels of insight while parading through the convention hall.

"Max, are pointy shoes on their way out?"

"Not if your foot is shaped like that!" Titter, titter. "But if you have a normal foot, you won't be caught dead in them."

"What about stacked heels?"

"My lips are sealed." Wink, wink.

"And ballet slippers?"

"Only if you're Margot Fonteyn." And so on and so on.

Cameras flashed, ballpoint pens scribbled, and there was a constant long line for the phone booths flanking the wall. So this is what Dad lived for. He was a rock star, not some mere Midwest family business boss. Here he was floating on air. He pointed to his favorite reporters, mimed one of his chief competitors, favored the women in the entourage with a slightly longer than necessary hug or a sly compliment about how they looked or what they wore. My dad was a red-carpet whiz.

This was the guy who worked in "obscurity"? Well, I guess he did in his St. Louis life, but not here, in Sin City.

The real entertainment began in the evening. First, there were drinks with vendors and mall developers, who provided top-shelf spirits and drop-dead-gorgeous cocktail waitresses. "Where have you been all my life?"

When the crowd around Dad started to break up, he winked at me and confided that he had pressing engagements elsewhere, with an emphasis on the word *pressing*.

Leveraging my filial connection to the rock star, Max, and being the youngest stud in the room, I made my own late-night arrangements.

Chapter 9

FOLLOWING MY LAS VEGAS ESCAPADES, MY FIRST SEMESTER AT Washington U was a total downer. I managed to flunk zoology, which was a class crammed with doctor wannabes. This failure turned out to be a blessing in disguise. I also bombed out in French; Madame Maddy had insisted I enroll, rejecting my preference, Spanish. As a result of those two dings, I found myself in the dreaded academic purgatory known as probation. Even worse—those on academic pro couldn't be initiated into the fraternity, so I became what was known as a neophyte. Only with a strong rebound in the spring, thanks to clever course selection, some coaching from the brothers, and access to the frat exam files, was I able to become an active member in good standing of Pi Lambda Phi. I returned the brothers' help by nabbing the intramural ping-pong trophy.

As for the blessing in disguise, flunking zoology—all the flunkees from zoology were automatically enrolled in a "rocks for jocks" course in the spring called Field Botany. The condemned dutifully filed into Mrs. Eisendrath's classroom. She went on and on about the wonders of vegetation, some guy named Linnaeus, ground rules for the course, and finally, the assignment of lab partners.

"In the past I relied on students to choose a partner for lab work. That has not worked so well. Friends chose friends, which left a number of students with no match. So, this semester I've paired you alphabetically."

"Oh, God," I silently prayed, "please pair me with somebody smart, someone smarter than me—smart enough to get me a C in this course."

Mrs. Eisendrath read off the pairings and asked the newly assigned partner teams to stand at one of the stations in the laboratory. "Abbott and Anderson; Arbuckle and Benjamin," she continued on. Finally, she arrived at "Epstein and Feldman."

I arrived at lab station five first and saw *wildly gesticulating Epstein* talking to Mrs. Eisendrath, who repeatedly shook her head no.

Defeated but undeterred, she trudged over to station five.

"Hi, I'm Josh Feldman."

"I'm Amy Epstein, and I'm sorry but Nancy Shapiro and I agreed to be lab partners. She's an all-A sorority sister of mine who was smart enough not to take Zo her first semester. I'm a complete dope in science. You must be too. I saw you in zoology with your head on your desk most of the time. Nancy and I are going to appeal to Mrs. Eisendrath during office hours."

"Gosh, Amy, you make a guy feel like a million bucks."

"It's nothing personal, Josh, sorry. I want to go to law school one day, and I can't afford to flunk this course. Zoology was bad enough. Besides, you're on academic pro aren't you? A ZBT told me."

The Zeebs, as members of Zeta Beta Tau are called, were notorious. They were rich (their fraternity is known to its legion of critics as Zillions, Billions, and Trillions, or Zion Bank and Trust). They were very well-dressed, in khakis, button-down shirts, and Baracuta jackets. And they were constantly trawling for impressionable freshman girls at the library.

Miss Amy Epstein was a 9+ and worth pursuing. Medium height, lush auburn hair in a ponytail, a body like those cocktail waitresses in Vegas, doe-like brown eyes, cute little turned-up nose, and very kissable lips. *Drama aside, I couldn't help but think of how pleasant it would be to be her lab partner. And who knows? One thing might lead to another.*

As instructed, we both studied the lab manual outlining procedures and protocols and played with the microscope that we would share; my fantasies ran wild. "Come hither, Amy, see this interesting bit of protoplasm. Can't see it? Let me help," as our bodies touched, and I guided her search on the microscope.

As class ended, she rushed over to her friend, Nancy Shapiro, and they scurried out of the classroom.

I decided to act.

"Professor Eisendrath . . ." She was gathering her papers as I approached.

"I'm not actually a professor, merely a lecturer, and you are?"

"I'm Josh Feldman and I wanted to tell you how happy I am to be paired with Amy Epstein. We'll make a great team. I don't know any of the students in class and didn't know who to be partners with, but your system worked perfectly for me. She'll be a super partner."

"Well, glad to hear that, Josh."

She smiled politely and exited the classroom.

Having sealed the deal, I spent the afternoon at the frat house sharpening my table tennis skills.

Evidently, Mrs. Eisendrath didn't mention our little tête-à-tête to Amy and Nancy when they met, but happily, she was implacable. Amy and I were a couple! At least in Field Botany . . .

Pursuing Amy would prove difficult. My time with her was limited to two ninety-minute class periods a week, and though she eventually reconciled herself to the partnership, she was still in a relationship with Mr. Zeeb. He invariably greeted her as she left the lab session, so I couldn't walk her to her next class. Even inviting her for coffee was impossible. I had to content myself with offering brilliant, jocular repartee as we sliced and diced specimens to study and classify.

By March I could get her to laugh out loud with my imitation of the Julia Child–like Mrs. Eisendrath, who swooned over this calyx and that corolla. Amy even deigned to wave at me when we passed each other on campus. I knew her schedule to a T. We occasionally stopped and chatted when she was unaccompanied by Mr. Zeeb. But my serious pursuit would have to wait until the next year, when I hoped she would dump the bastard.

• • •

By the end of my freshman year, my GPA had climbed to the required 2.0. Probation was lifted, and I became a full-fledged member of Pi Lam and qualified for transfer to the business school in the fall. "Voila!" as my French professor might have said.

I abandoned my room at the frat house and returned to the comforts of home during the summer. Of course, I worked at Fratelli Massimo doing a rotational program, learning all the staff functions, like human resources, accounting, logistics, real estate, and management information systems.

When I drove home with Dad at the end of the day, we talked about the fun stuff: what's selling, what's not, comp store sales, competitors who were doing well, and competitors who weren't. He assured me that once I graduated, I'd be assigned to the merchandise department, where he spent most of his time; this was clearly where the most important work was being done. I would learn from the master himself.

After transferring to B-school, my grades were OK. Finance, accounting, and marketing were naturals for me; HR not so much. But academic probation was just a bad memory and graduation was once again on the horizon.

Sophomore year, I carefully cultivated friendly relationships with a few of Amy's Sigma Delta Tau sorority sisters. I had two motives: I wanted to build up street cred with Amy, and I needed intel, since she was in Arts and Science and I was over at the B-School—so we had no classes together.

According to her sisters, Mr. Zeeb was out of the picture and she was playing the field.

So I took my chance. Summoning every bit of courage I could muster, I caught up with her as she left Olin Library, headed for class.

"Amy," I said breathlessly, "how about we grab something to eat Friday night and maybe go to the Esquire?"

"Josh, you're a laugh a minute, but I'm dating some other guys now."

My big break came when I visited a fraternity brother in Chicago over Christmas break. I took a chance and called Amy at her home in Highland Park. When she answered the phone, I blurted out, "Hi, your old lab partner from Field Botany is in town. How about joining me for a hot dog at Michael's—and if you have some time, I could use your help."

Tick, tick, tick.

"What kind of help?"

"Well, my family owns a store in Old Orchard Shopping Center I have to visit. Maybe you've heard of it. Fratelli Massimo?"

"You own Fratelli Massimo?"

"Well, not just me, but my family. I'd love to get your opinion about the merchandise."

"Let me get this straight. Your family owns that store?"

"We own all of them. My dad runs it … with my help." (This was a slight, but understandable, exaggeration.)

"Huh. Well, I'm not free today, but tomorrow might work."

Amy and I had a great day. Michael's is a Highland Park institution, as are its Chicago-style hot dogs, so we started there and then drove to Old Orchard. I had taken the precaution of alerting the manager that I would be visiting, so we were given the royal treatment upon arrival.

"Oh, Mr. Feldman, welcome!"

"Please, Frank, just Josh is OK. Mr. Feldman is my dad."

Amy and I shared some opinions about the merchandise; then she suggested we visit O'Connor & Goldberg, our strongest competitor. We made a day of it fighting holiday traffic. When we finished, I drove her home, and her mom, Adrienne, greeted us. Introductions were made. After a few pleasantries, she asked, "So, your family owns Fratelli Massimo? My husband is a partner at Price Waterhouse, the accounting firm—he'd be interested in meeting you."

I made the time to honor her request by having drinks with her and her husband before I took Amy out for dinner. Amy's dad, Ralph, was very friendly.

"That's quite a business your family owns," he began. "Still privately held? Not public, eh? Don't happen to know what accounting firm you use in St. Louis, where we have an office?"

"No, Mr. Epstein."

"First name, please, Josh."

"OK, Ralph, it's a local firm."

"I see. Let me give this some thought. You two have a good time tonight."

Amy and I dined at Don Roth's Blackhawk restaurant. It was a great meal, and we had a great time. No après-dinner fooling around—just a sisterly peck on the cheek, but the door had been opened.

My mom enjoyed hearing about the Amy adventure.

Dad said, "Whatever works, Josh, that's my motto." But when I mentioned Ralph's query, Dad lit up like a Christmas tree.

"Price fucking Waterhouse? Interested in us? See what I mean, Maddy? We're not just some local family-owned business."

"Yes, Max, they're interested in your business. Not exactly stop-the-presses kind of news. That's what they do."

"I know, but as I was telling Josh, Fratelli Massimo is like this undiscovered gem!"

"You're not exactly undiscovered, dear. You never miss an opportunity to talk to the press."

"Dad, are you forgetting your red-carpet treatment in Las Vegas? Mom, you wouldn't believe—he's a rock star. The garmentos and press couldn't get enough of Max Feldman."

"Max, sweetheart, tell me all the details. So, you're a rock star! Does that mean what I think it does?" She asked with a leer.

Dad shook his head. "No, Maddy, it's just the usual industry stuff. And yes, if you're in the retail business, you know about Fratelli Massimo. But that's a small fraternity."

I excused myself from the table. I really didn't want to hear them argue. Dad never missed an opportunity to complain about the company's low profile. Mom never missed an opportunity to shut him down.

• • •

Amy and I started dating sporadically that spring, but by junior year, we were more or less exclusive. We were still "undeclared," but neither of us was seeing anyone else. I took her to movies, dinner, parties, and the big event, the Pi Lambda Phi formal on Valentine's Day at the Hilton (after which we checked into a room and spent our first full night together). Before that, we had fooled around a lot and managed to have sex in the Porsche, which required circus performer-like contortions around the sadistically placed hand brake and the narrow sports seats.

Mom was naturally curious about our relationship and had all kinds of questions about Amy. Of course, she wanted to meet her. I stalled, not so sure how the two would get along. Mom can be intimidating. People—specifically, other women—could be put off by the way she dressed, spoke, and carried herself. She was Very Upper East Side Manhattan. I wanted nothing to complicate my quest.

Ultimately, Mom took matters into her own hands (as she always does).

On a spring day, I was having coffee in the campus snack bar with Amy when who should stroll in, but Mom. We never

ever saw each other on campus. The business school was in a converted dormitory, Prince Hall, located at the western end of the campus. Mom spent her days in Duncker Hall, on the eastern end, with all the longhairs and bookish literature types.

She spotted us sitting at a table for four and click-clicked her way toward us in medium-height Chanel heels. As usual, she was dressed to kill—a sober St. John suit with a contrasting shell and an Hermès clutch (which was completely wasted on her litera-ture buddies—but not on the lovely Amy).

I quickly reminded Amy that Mom was an English major and on campus a lot.

I then rose from my chair. "Amy, this is my mom, Mrs. Feldman, or rather Maddy. Maddy, this is Amy."

"I've heard so much about you, Amy. Do you mind if I join you?"

"Not at all, Mrs. Feldman."

"Maddy, please."

Mom sat down with us. I offered to get her coffee, but Amy glared at me with a look that said, "You're not going to leave me alone with your mother, are you, Josh?"

Mom sensed the situation and declined the coffee. She broke the ice with the old reliable Jewish geography gambit. "Amy, Josh tells me you're from Highland Park. We have friends there who live by the high school on Maple Avenue. The Nathansons. Do you know them?"

"No, I'm afraid not. Maybe my parents do, but I know where Maple Avenue is, of course. We live on Green Bay Road, farther south near County Line."

"Josh says that you're a good student." This was a perfectly natural and predictable "mother" question.

"Well, I do pretty well except for zoology, which Josh and I both flunked."

"Is that what brought you together—flunking zoology?"

"In a way, since we both ended up in Field Botany. That's where we met."

"And so, what do you intend to do when you graduate? Teach?"

"Not really. I plan to go to law school."

"Well, that is ambitious."

This totally awkward, stilted conversation had exceeded its sell-by date.

"Mom, Amy and I have to get to class."

"Of course, glad to have finally met you, Amy."

"Me, too, Maddy."

As she stood to leave, Mom turned to Amy, and in the most casual manner, asked, "Amy, I know it's last minute, but would you like to join us for Passover Seder next Wednesday? Unless you have other plans, of course."

Amy hesitated for a moment, then replied, "I'd love to."

"Well, Amy, I must warn you we have an extremely abbreviated seder. Sixty minutes, max. Does that work for you?"

"Perfectly. My family is quite Reform Jewish. We actually go to Sabbath services on Sunday. And we celebrate Christmas as well."

"Excellent. Seven o'clock?"

"Fine. Would you like me to bring something? A bottle of wine, or a tin of those vile macaroons? I can't really make anything at my place."

"No, nothing. And Amy, I quite agree with you about the macaroons. Ladurée, they're not. Just bring yourself. And it's casual."

We watched Mom stride out of the coffee shop, her heels hammering the tile floor.

"Wow, Josh, your mom is something else. She's not at all like my mother. Do you think she liked me?"

"What's not to like? You were brilliant." I smiled.

It turned out that Mom had carefully contrived to "run into us." She had checked our schedules at the registrar's office, knew we each had an open hour at that time, put two and two together, and swooped in.

I spent the next five days doing everything I could to insure a smooth and frictionless seder.

I worked with Nora to make sure we would have a Passover-ish menu. In addition to a proper seder plate and matzo, I asked her to get some chicken soup and matzo balls at Straub's. I also requested some of that red horseradish that Sy and Rose used to serve, not the white stuff. The big ask was brisket. Again, Straub's came to the rescue.

Mom watched from the doorway in her customary pose—a cigarette in her left hand and her left elbow cupped in her right hand. She signaled her assent with a nod and a smile, which was returned by Nora.

Next, it was Dad's turn.

Naturally, he was on to me and gave me some grief, but in the end he agreed to be a "perfect gentleman" when conversing with Amy. He promised to use sanitized language, minimal Yiddish, no double entendres, and to ask no embarrassing questions.

Last on the to-do list was a call to Rand, who was flying in from Stanford for spring break and would be at the seder.

"Rand, I need a favor," I opened.

"Is this about the much-discussed seder with Amy?"

"Yes. This is important to me, and I'm worried about Dad being a complete jerk."

"So, what else is new? What can I do for you, Josh?"

"Just be yourself and don't turn on the Pepper's King charm. I don't need the competition."

"No worries on that front."

"You haven't met her."

"Trust me."

"OK, I can count on you to play this straight?"

A few moments passed, and I heard him chuckle. "Yes, Josh, Rand the Man will play this straight."

Finally, Wednesday evening arrived. The table was set, and we were assembled in the living room.

"Don't all stand there like a firing squad!"

With that, the doorbell rang. I went to open the door.

Amy was standing on our front porch, waving goodbye to her roommate, who had given her a lift.

I helped her with her coat. She was wearing a lightweight black cashmere crewneck sweater, a string of pearls, and a short— but not too short—charcoal-colored wool pleated skirt. Her shoes were black leather mid-heel pumps with a little grosgrain bow. Wait a minute! Those shoes were from Fratelli Massimo! They came from last fall's French Room collection, SKU 97384, twenty-four dollars.

Dad would spot them from one hundred yards.

Mom came over and kissed her lightly on the cheek. She returned the peck. Dad and Rand followed with warm handshakes.

"Our best seller!" Dad exclaimed. I sensed he was winding up to offer Amy a Fratelli Massimo discount card. Yikes! It felt as if a grizzly bear had grabbed my throat. Mom sensed what he was about to do and came to the rescue.

"Max, I left the Haggadahs upstairs. Please be a dear and get them; they're on the hall table."

"I was about to ..."

"I know Max, but the Haggadahs, please."

Dad staggered upstairs to fetch them.

Stick save and a beauty by Mom.

The table was resplendent with fine china and the good silver. Some spring flowers sat in a vase as the centerpiece, and all the Passover props were perfectly placed: wine goblets, matzo platter, and the seder plate, each segment filled with the appropriate ingredients. There was even the just-polished Sabbath candelabra, a mysteriously retrieved wedding present from Sy and Rose.

Mom did the honors with the blessing over the candles.

Mom and Dad sat at either end of the table. Amy and I were together on one side facing Rand. We started in.

In honor of Amy, I think, Dad slowed it down a bit from his usual breakneck pace. We didn't set any records, but we cruised at seventy miles an hour, skipping the longer passages. Dad also resisted the temptation to bash Moses. We did lots of responsive readings in English. And it was off to the plagues and blessings over the wine, matzo, parsley, and (red) horseradish. I opened the door for Elijah, and we finished the pre-dinner portion in twenty-seven minutes. It was the Feldman family's version of seder's greatest hits.

Nora and Straub's came through with a great dinner, which we ate at a much slower pace than usual. During the meal, the rest of the family learned about Amy:

- She was majoring in Political Science and hoped to become a lawyer.
- Her two younger brothers were still in high school.
- No, Washington U wasn't her first choice (Dad's evil question)—Penn was.
- No, Washington U wasn't her safety school (the Stanford man's rude question)—University of Illinois was.
- Yes, she liked St. Louis, but preferred Chicago (uh-oh).
- She planned to go to Washington U's law school when she graduated (thank God).
- She had a stay-at-home mother, and her father was a partner at one of the big accounting firms, Price Waterhouse.

Dad said he'd like to meet him. Mom rolled her eyes. Dad wound things up by crooning "Dayenu," and we filed into the living room.

After profusely thanking Mom and Nora for the lovely seder, Amy politely announced that she needed to return to her apartment to study for a test tomorrow. I offered to drive her back. Before she put on her coat, Mom hugged and kissed her and said, "Amy, you are a lovely young woman. Maybe we can have coffee on campus one of these days if you have time?"

"That'd be great. Tuesday and Thursday afternoons work best for me." They traded phone numbers.

I, of course, was over the moon. Take that, you Zeeb SOBs!

Chapter 10

AFTER GRADUATION, I JOINED THE COMPANY AS A MERCHANDISE planner in the fall of 1979, right as Amy was beginning law school at Washington U. As a planner, I helped the buyers schedule their purchases and distribute the merchandise they had ordered as it came into our distribution center in downtown St. Louis. The job entailed a lot of insight into what individual stores needed, hours of number crunching, creation of spreadsheets, and contact with our suppliers. I was a long way from actually picking styles, but the planner's role is essential in the merchandising process, so I was eager to master it and impress the buyers.

Unless she had tons of homework, Amy and I got together for dinner or a movie on the weekends—which more often than not happily ended at the apartment I had rented in the Moorlands in Clayton. A couple of years before, I had bought a used Guards Red 1972 Porsche 911. Mom loaned me five thousand dollars, and I took out a thirty-six-month bank loan. I've owned many Porsches through the years, but none as cherished as that original. A photograph of the car with Amy and me, arm in arm, hangs prominently on the wall of my office.

It felt great to be working full time, being independent and out of school—finally.

Fratelli Massimo was thriving even during the 1970s, when interest rates soared and people had to line up at the gas pump during the Arab oil embargo. The company operated three hundred stores in thirty-eight states, though we had yet to open in Manhattan. Dad didn't think we were ready for that, and rents were sky-high. Sales for the company amounted to more than $250 million, with profits of about fifteen million. As mentioned earlier, Dad had depended on bank loans for seasonal needs, but since the company was generating lots of cash, we had no long-term debt on the balance sheet. And though we were a private company and didn't have to publicly report our financial status, it was no secret that Fratelli Massimo was thriving and had lots of room to grow. Our landlords received our monthly sales numbers as required by the leases, so I'm sure they shared the positive news with the financial firms they themselves depended on. The Fratelli Massimo story was catnip for the boys on Wall Street, who began trying to sell us on going public.

It wasn't as if the idea of an initial public offering or IPO was new to Dad. He had been itching to do it for some time. Though Maddy steadfastly opposed the idea, going public had been suggested by his stockbroker, Bobby Weil, his accountant, Justin Brooks, and his lawyer, Ray Weinberg, all golfing buddies of Dad's. They were also members of Highland Hills Country Club, which Dad aspired to join.

I was at home with my parents one Sunday when Amy was studying for finals, and the going-public subject came up.

"Max, what can the investment banks do for us that we can't do for ourselves? The company has loads of cash. Why share it with anybody? Why open our books to the public? Local gossip is enough—why would you want your salary and our personal wealth to be headline news in the *Post-Dispatch* and *Business Journal*? And what happens when business dips? Will local stockholders, your buddies in particular, give you a pass? No! There'll be awkward situations and whispered criticisms. It makes no sense. This is our family's business; let's keep it that way."

"Well," Dad said, "Bobby and the others suggested that being a public corporation would benefit us enormously. The proceeds from the offering would mean that we wouldn't have to borrow seasonally from the banks anymore. And with interest rates in the teens, that's a big bite out of earnings. All we're doing is making the banks rich with our risk-free loans. We could also offer stock options to our key employees. And they intimated that it would help with estate planning. Evidently, passing on a private company to your heirs is a mess."

"I'm sure Bobby knows what he's talking about," Mom said. "I'm also sure he stands to make a tidy sum if we go public. Did he mention that? Max, dear, I like privacy. That's one of the reasons I wanted to leave New York, where my dad was a public figure. We Feldmans live well, travel, and do what we want without worrying about what the public might think. And I like my anonymity at the university, where I am just another mature student slaving away. I don't want them knowing how much we have."

"You don't think people know we're wealthy? I don't mean the hippies at school, I mean our friends, the girls you play bridge with, my foursome, my buddies. C'mon."

"Max, they know we have money—but not how much. They can speculate, and probably do, but it's our business, not theirs."

"OK, I get it, but let's just say it's an open question. No final decisions have been made."

The pressure from Dad's friends, and the phone calls and letters from New York bankers, kept coming, and it gnawed at him. He took me to lunch one day and explained.

"It's all well and good for your mother—who's always had money—to want to be discreet about it, but she's being hypocritical."

"Dad, you're talking about Mom, who's the greatest. You can't mean what you're saying."

Dad smirked. "You think she's so perfect, don't you, Josh? Maybe not like blind-as-a-bat Rand, who worships her. But, news flash, she's human. She's plenty smart. Clever. She and Gunther are like twins. Don't you think she's a bit insincere about being a 'mere mature student' at WU? Wake up! She flashes those Gucci and Louis bags around old Duncker Hall. Even those pointy-headed profs must know that she didn't buy them at Target. Don't tell her I told you, but she just donated one hundred thousand dollars to the school's capital campaign. They sure know she didn't get that much money taking in laundry."

"But Dad, Mom is a private person; she's discreet, despite her wardrobe. Look at the car she drives, that broken-down Ford station wagon. She's still living in the same house I was a baby in, for God's sake. Maybe the better word is *private*. Mom likes being private, particularly about family matters. Fratelli Massimo is a family matter, and she wants to keep it that way."

"You still don't get it, Josh, and you better smarten up if you know what's good for you. Keeping the business private deprives me of the recognition I deserve for creating and growing the company. Your mother wants me out of the spotlight. That's fine with her. Born with a silver spoon in her mouth, she never had to prove herself to anybody, anywhere, except at the bridge table. So la-di-da, she can pretend to be just another hard-working student and hausfrau, while her wealth grows thanks to M-A-X F-E-L-D-M-A-N, the man behind the scenes. Well, I've had it with playing second fiddle!"

"Dad, everybody knows you're the maestro at Fratelli Massimo. And every business person knows that the company's a huge success. You get full credit for all that! I don't get it, and I don't understand what you mean by 'playing second fiddle.' Mom is happy to stand in the wings and let you take all the bows and applause."

And then he resorted to his tedious routine. "I grew up poor, Josh. I started with nothing and I'm proud of what I've accomplished. I'm not ashamed or embarrassed about it. I'm proud of it, goddamn it, and I want the world to know it."

"But Dad, it's not all roses. Business is not always great. You yourself tell me tales of companies that failed—Woolworth's, A.S. Beck, Kresge. And what about having stockholders to answer to and those Wall Street wise guys second-guessing you? What about your independence and ability to do what you think is best for your company?"

"Do you think for one minute that I would let those empty suits tell me how to run my business? I'd sooner quit and let them try to manage it. They'll figure out that Fratelli Massimo is nothing without Max Feldman now—or Joshua Feldman in the future." He winked.

He had that power over me, dangling my glorious future in front of me. I always succumbed and rationalized his personal shortcomings. I ignored the way he treated Rand and what he had done to Sy. Never for a minute did I stop to think it could happen to me.

It was clear that Dad was counting on my support in the upcoming battle to take the company public. Rand was another story. He would probably back Mom, since they were so tight. Dad had a lot of work to do to convince her that going public was in everybody's best interest. I think Dad believed that, but his real motive was making sure *everybody* knew in black and white how damn successful and loaded he was. That group included the Highland Hills members, his suppliers, and, of course, a skeptical Gunther who would have to concede that Max had triumphed.

Things quieted down until 1979's numbers were in. The results revealed that Fratelli Massimo had turned in another record performance. We achieved those numbers with virtually the same formula Dad had refined in the late 1950s, with half our shoes sourced from respected brands and half private label items created by our team. A smaller and smaller percentage came from the Massimo brothers in Italy. Most were sourced in New England, and a growing proportion came in from Asia, priced at 30 percent less than our branded merchandise. Handbags, accessories, and hosiery added to sales and were very profitable. Our shopping center locations were high quality, if expensive. The stars were aligned, and the pressure mounted for a public transaction.

On a Sunday in early March, I stopped for deli and drove the few blocks up to Claverach.

When Mom opened the door, I knew something was wrong. She had on a terry cloth robe and floppy bunny bedroom slippers, and wore no makeup. Mom wouldn't usually come downstairs unless she was prepped and dressed.

"Are you feeling OK?"

"Yes, Josh, it's just been a bad day." We went into the kitchen to stow the deli stuff.

"How come?"

"Your father and I have been going back and forth about Fratelli Massimo ever since Bobby Weil left late this morning. He had some information Dad asked him for about going public."

"What kind of information?"

"Maybe it's better if Dad explains it to you. I'm flattened."

I noticed that Mom had a Kleenex in her hand and a bunch in the sleeve of her robe.

"You've been crying."

"So I have," she said.

"Over Fratelli Massimo and the stuff Bobby dropped off?"

"Yes, it started off with Fratelli Massimo. Bobby didn't merely drop off the material, he wanted us both to review it with him. It was underhanded and sneaky—a betrayal."

Dad opened the kitchen door. I backed up and leaned on the door to the back porch to hear about it.

"It wasn't sneaky, underhanded, or a betrayal, Maddy. You're being too emotional. I told you he was coming over."

"That's right, Max, 'coming over,' as you put it, is not what I was referring to. Being subjected to a sales pitch booklet that you both obviously had worked on was underhanded and disloyal to me. And now your good friend Bobby Weil—who is married to Evie Weil, the biggest gossip and tramp in town—knows that we sharply disagree about this going-public thing. That's just a taste of what awaits this family if we go forward. Everyone knowing our business…"

"Maddy, Bobby's very discreet. He must be in his business. And I don't know where you're getting your information about Evie. I know she's not your type. She's not book smart like you, but she is street smart. She didn't come from money. But yes, she's flamboyant and very popular."

"I'll bet she is! She's a notorious flirt. And the girls at bridge bet it goes beyond flirting. Wake up, Max! He and his firm stand to make a pile of money if you follow his advice. And he's not so discreet. Didn't he disclose that others in the firm were enthusiastic about going public? Is that being discreet?"

"He wanted their opinions."

"Did he also want his foursome's opinion? And Evie's? Will 'flamboyant and popular Evie' be calling me to meet for coffee as part of the 'sell Madeline' campaign? Or will she take the direct approach and go after you herself?"

"That's unfair. You're really nuts, my dear."

"Nuts, am I? It's you who won't face reality. There are many people who will benefit financially if we take the company public. You cannot trust any of them to give you an objective opinion."

"And what makes you so smart about these guys on Wall Street?"

"Gunther Harris Berg—that's who made me so smart! I spent many years listening to his tales of the rich and famous and how they got that way, and it wasn't because they discovered a cure for cancer. It was because they were clever financiers and lawyers who divvied up the spoils from companies just like Fratelli Massimo." Mom gave him a knowing look.

"Jesus, you have gone off the deep end! And you accuse me of being disloyal? You'd rather listen to your father than to your husband who has worked hard to provide you with everything you could possibly want. The same husband who allowed you to prance off to Washington U to analyze and dissect every line of some dusty novel and have an orgasm over some insight that won't mean anything to anybody except those bearded geniuses you hang out with."

"*You* allowed me to go to WU? Master Max? You'd still be drawing a paycheck at Famous-Barr if I hadn't invested that money you needed to get Fratelli Massimo off the ground. Who defied her father in doing so? Who got Gunther to prepare all those incorporation papers in forty-eight hours? And who has played the nice wifey while you ... do what you do?"

"Don't go there, Maddy! I don't know that you're such an angel, either. I don't know what you get up to on those frequent New York adventures. And I've never asked."

"Right. How considerate of you. Do I really just shop, see my friends, visit museums, dine with Gunther, and seek my physical pleasures at the Elizabeth Arden spa? Or do I have a pretty boy stashed in my secret pied-à-terre, breathlessly awaiting me? Go ahead and ask if you dare, Mr. Big Shot."

"I don't want to, not in front of Josh," he shot back.

Maddy's head swiveled. Her eyes widened. She'd forgotten I was standing there. And then she started to cry and wiped her face with the tissue stuffed in the sleeve of her robe. She rushed over to me, hugged me, buried her face in my chest, and cried her heart out.

"God, God, Josh, forgive me," she said. "You were never ever meant to witness a scene like that. Tell me you forgive us. Please."

I was choked up myself, but I managed to say that I forgave them.

This was a moment that each of us three would remember forever.

Dad went upstairs, but I stayed with Mom as she calmed down. I got her a generous pour of Chardonnay, and we went to sit on the couch in the den. Mom put her head on my shoulder. I reminded her that we used to watch our birthday films from this very sofa. We thought back to those happy times and Mom's happy tears.

"Josh, I wish I could erase what just happened," she whispered.

"I'll get over it. I love you, Mom. You're the best. I believe in you."

"I know, and we both let you down. There's something devastating about disappointing you and Rand. You do forgive me, don't you?"

"Always and forever," I replied. What else could I say?

When I finally left the house, I stopped at Steak 'n Shake for a hamburger. I needed to give myself some time to think about what I had just witnessed. I reached two conclusions. First, I would not tell Amy about what happened. For some reason I wanted to preserve the family's *Leave It to Beaver* image I had tried so earnestly to portray. And I certainly didn't want to spread any dirt about Evie Weil. Amy was a good friend of Evie's daughter, Jenn. Second, I knew that I needed to call Rand as soon as I got back to my apartment.

Luckily, Rand was in his dorm suite, and his roommates were away on a skiing trip, so we could speak freely.

After I told him about what happened at home, there were some uncomfortable moments of silence. Finally, he responded.

"You OK, Josh?"

"Well, I'm shaken up, but I'll be OK."

"You sure?"

"What do you mean? Yeah, I'll figure this out."

"That might mean facing some nasty stuff."

"You don't think I faced some pretty nasty stuff this evening?"

"Yes. Sorry you had to endure it. But you also need to wake up and face some facts."

"Like what facts?"

"Sure you want to listen to this? I'm coming home in a couple weeks for spring break and we can do this face-to-face."

"Let's cut the drama and suspense. What great insights does Rand the Man have?"

"Look, I don't have a lot of time, but here goes. For Dad, going public is the popular affirmation of his prowess. All that bullshit about stock options, bank interest rates, and estate planning is just a smoke screen. He wants the world to know how smart and successful he is. For Mom, taking Fratelli Massimo public is akin to taking the family public. And she abhors that. Every time the annual report comes out, every time the *Business Journal* publishes the company's details, every time there's an article on executive pay and benefits, she'll be miserable. She's happy in her world: family, school, books, bridge, and the occasional buying spree in New York. Life is good. But not for Dad—he's hungry for adulation."

There was no way we could all come out winners. If Mom got her way, Dad would be monstrous. He would unleash his anger and seek revenge.

"We need to talk," I blurted out.

"Fine, but not now. I've got to run. Let's talk when I come home. In fact, I'll book the TWA red-eye from San Francisco and you can pick me up that Saturday morning. We can have breakfast in a booth at Toddle House. I need to tell you something personal about me, but it can wait till then. OK?"

"Rand, is everything alright?"

"Absolutely, but one last thing: don't side with either of them until we talk."

"Got it." I hung up the phone.

Chapter 11

Heeding my brother's advice, I did my best to avoid both of my parents. I dreamed up a reason for a business trip to Chicago, where we operated fifteen stores. Fortunately, Dad traveled a lot, so we hardly saw each other during the two weeks before Rand came home. I left a message with Nora that I couldn't do Sunday night dinners for a couple of weeks.

I continued to see Amy, but I never mentioned the family fight (or the going-public issue). I needed to keep it all private. If Amy suspected anything, she never let on. First-year law students are buried with work, so she had other things on her mind.

A week before Rand was scheduled to come in, I got a message from Mom. She notified me that I needed to reserve some time on the Wednesday and Friday afternoons of the week Rand was in town. It was something to do with the business at some law firm. It also turned out that Gunther would be visiting, so I figured it had something to do with the going-public issue.

Customarily, Gunther would see us in St. Louis a few times a year on his way to Las Vegas, but he usually stayed for only one night.

When I was younger, I asked Mom why my staid and proper grandfather would go to "Sin City" several times a year. She laughed and said, "My father loves to gamble. His math skills come into play at the blackjack table, or when he plays craps. I can assure you that he never makes the incorrect bet. That does not mean he wins. You never win in Las Vegas if you stay long enough, but he does minimize his losses."

"But Gunther doesn't seem the gambler type."

"And what is a gambler type, Josh?" she asked.

"Oh, I don't know…kind of sleazy."

"Does Sean Connery seem sleazy when he's in a casino?"

Then it was my turn to laugh. "No, but Grandpa is no James Bond."

Mom chuckled again. "That's for sure, Josh. But lots of respectable people gamble, and not just in casinos. Stockbrokers bet money every day on the stock market. Life insurance executives bet you'll live a long life. Why, even your dad gambles when he buys shoes for the next season."

"That's not what I meant, and you know it."

"Well, my son, many people think that life is made up of hundreds or thousands of gambles."

"Like what?" I asked.

"Picking somebody to marry, for example. When I chose to marry your father, I was betting that he would make me happy for the rest of my life. If you and Amy get married, you'll each be making the same bet. But it does not always work out." Mom paused for a moment. "Sometimes you win and sometimes you lose. The marriage bet is a bigger bet than you can ever make in Las Vegas."

Just the year before, I had been in Las Vegas for one of the shoe shows. By coincidence, Gunther was staying at the Desert Inn—his usual Las Vegas haunt. He asked me to join him if I had some spare time. We met up in the lobby of the hotel at 8:00 p.m. and instead of heading to dinner, I asked if I could watch him gamble. He was curious. "Why, Josh?"

"It seems out of character. You're...well, you're a buttoned-up gentleman. And I just can't picture you in one of those casinos." His only concession to the casual, tawdry, unkempt attire most gamblers sported in Las Vegas was the absence of his Harvard tie. He still wore gray flannel pants, a boxy Brooks Brothers blazer, a button-down pima cotton shirt, and cordovan brogues.

"Let's go to a blackjack table, so you can watch and learn," he said.

Gunther led me through the noisy, raucous casino (not at all like the ones in the 007 movies), and he took a seat at a blackjack table. The other gamblers were just what I had pictured when I called them "sleazy" back when I was talking to Mom. Three women seated at the table had blinking brides-maid tiaras on and were in town from Milwaukee for a bach-elorette party. All three were totally wasted. One guy with a cowboy hat, jeans, and Western shirt had a cigarillo hanging from his lips. The gambler in the last chair looked like he slept on the streets. There he was, filthy and disheveled, but with a huge pile of chips in front of him.

I thought the play was rather boring, hand after hand. People won. People lost. The dealer was taciturn, but for some reason was given tips when somebody won a lot. The pit boss did take note of Gunther and nodded in welcome. I saw that Gunther was never indecisive. He split, doubled down, and took a card, or not, quickly and unemotionally. After maybe fifteen hands, the other players, especially the girls, starting turning to Gunther to get advice. The dealer even motioned to Gunther when one of them was debating a play. It was just as if he were in a corporate board-room, and he had all the answers.

After about an hour, he made to leave. The bachelorette girl next to him shrieked, "You can't go! You're the man!" And with that, she rose to embrace Gunther and give him a kiss on the lips. Gunther blushed, bowed, and smiled. "Sorry, I must leave. I have a grandson to feed. The dealer will help you. Good luck, girls!"

When we sat down in the hotel's coffee shop, he asked if I had learned anything.

"Well, first, you're a near robot."

"I'm sure I appear that way. Anything else?" he asked.

"Well, the sleazeball at the end of the table was a gambling robot, too, but he looked like he didn't know where his next meal was coming from."

"Well, Josh, that particular 'sleazeball' owns three hundred feet of frontage on Las Vegas Boulevard, The Strip. He's worth millions. He's a regular. I've known him for years."

"Unbelievable."

"Appearances can be deceiving here in Vegas, but that's true everywhere. And the cowboy is a car dealer from New Jersey who wants to be a different person in Las Vegas. Tell me, Josh, what did you think of the girl who kissed me?"

"Well, I'm sure not used to thinking of my grandfather like that."

He grinned and said, "Just because I'm an older man, doesn't mean I've lost my . . . I'll call it magic mojo, Josh."

That made me squirm a bit. I couldn't picture that. I didn't want to picture that.

"Let me ask you a question, Josh. I hear from your mother that your father may be interested in taking Fratelli Massimo public. What do you think?"

I really had to be careful. Gunther was so wily. I wasn't in his league, so I just repeated what Dad had said without revealing how I felt about it.

"Well, Dad thinks there are a lot of good reasons to take that route: There's the big payday, of course, stock options for the employees, and what he calls estate planning. Also, he said he wants the world to know how successful the company is."

My grandfather had a few things to say. "All true, Josh. And in the process, the world will learn how incredibly successful your father is. But I believe he may be underestimating some of the drawbacks. When you run a public company, your life is an open book and you become responsible to thousands of stockholders. When results are good, they are rather pleasant and supportive, but when business is not good, they can descend on you like a pack of hyenas; that goes for the Wall Street analysts, as well."

"Dad said he wasn't worried about that."

"I imagine he did. Up to now, he's been fortunate that Fratelli Massimo is entirely held by the family. He must answer to only Maddy, you, and Rand. A luxury he may one day miss if the company is public. But enough of this. I want to get back to the tables."

I wondered what involvement Gunther had in all of this going-public business. That became all too clear at the showdown in St. Louis.

"And, Gramps, I want to get back to betting which shoes will sell next season!"

We parted in the lobby, and silver-haired Gunther soon disappeared from view, lost in the fugue of smoke, throngs of gamblers, and the chaotic cacophony of bells, whistles, chimes, shrieks, and moans.

The morning Rand was to arrive, I called TWA to check on his flight. His plane was on time and would arrive at 7:00 a.m.

As arranged, I picked him up and we drove down to the Toddle House diner on Lindell Boulevard. We both ordered breakfast steaks, eggs, toast, and coffee.

"Love the 911, Josh." Rand was fascinated with my car.

"Yeah, Mom loaned me some dough and just shook her head."

"Well, Josh, that's just a little indulgence. You can afford it. If you ever visited California, you'd see tons of Porsches, Ferraris, and other sports cars. It's car heaven."

He went on, "And as for San Francisco, it's like the Wild West. Take it from me, someone who frequently visits San Francisco. It's a wide-open town. I'll never forget the time Mom and I went on a tour. What an eye-opener! Completely uninhibited stuff. Sex, clothes, language ... anything and everything is OK. Not at all like St. Louis, which is so buttoned-up. Can you imagine live sex shows in St. Louis? And not just boy-girl stuff."

"And what do you think, Rand?"

"I am kind of mixed. I could do without the rank profanity, panhandling, and raunchy sex shows, but I like the freedom. I can't quite describe it. I feel I can be myself, with all my flaws, vices, and desires. In St. Louis, I feel all tied up and living my life the way others want me to. Don't get me wrong. I love our family, minus Max, and wouldn't trade it for anything, but I'll never live my life here."

"Mom and Dad will be disappointed. And I'll be sad without Rand the Man around." I took a sip of my coffee.

"And I'll miss you too. But I'm pretty sure Dad won't be disappointed, and I'm almost positive that Mom won't be surprised."

"Yeah, I guess you and Dad have never hit it off. But why do you think Mom won't be surprised if you don't come home?"

"She sees things, and she's from New York."

"What's that got to do with anything?"

"Josh, you know I love you. I want you to always remember that. OK?"

"Yeah, but what are you trying to tell me?"

"Do you remember when you called me before that seder and warned me not to turn on the charm for Amy because you didn't need the competition? And I told you not to worry?" he asked.

"Yeah, so?"

"You didn't have to worry because it's not girls I'm interested in, it's guys."

I was dumbfounded, speechless, and stupefied, so I uttered an absolute inanity.

"But you were Pepper's King at Clayton High!"

And then we both started laughing and laughing, until it hurt.

We embraced and I hugged my brother tightly. If he was happy, I was happy. It would take me a while to digest the news, but my brother was my best friend. I loved him dearly.

"I'll relinquish the Pepper's King title, if that would make you happy. It will certainly make Mr. Congeniality, the runner-up, happy as he will now assume the title and duties of King. Or I can be retitled Pepper's Queen!"

We laughed again.

Then the reality sank in. Rand wasn't coming home. He was homosexual and would never have children, and it might be impossible for him to adopt a child.

"Are you going to tell the folks?"

"Well, I'm pretty sure Mom has figured it out. She's from the big city. She was with me when we visited Stanford and then San Francisco. When we were on our college trip we toured NYU in the Village, and she was watching me closely. She won't be surprised. It's Dad who will read me the riot act. But yes, I'll tell them when the time is right. I don't want to live a lie. I know I can count on you, Josh."

"Always and forever," I told him.

And I meant it. I never loved Rand as much as I did at that moment. My little brother, with his secret. And his love for me, as well as his willingness to confide in me. I almost wept at the intimacy. I could admire his bravery and only hoped that he could lead a good life and deal with the intolerance he was sure to experience. But knowing Rand as I did, I knew he would be strong.

We headed back to my apartment, where we both got some shut-eye until early afternoon. We spent a few minutes discussing the Fratelli Massimo dilemma and agreed that we would both try to appear neutral and let the two of them decide what was best. Rand also intuited that there might be deeper issues between them that we didn't want to know about—and didn't want to get involved in.

"Let's just get through this week in one piece. God knows what Gunther wants with us. Guess we'll find out Wednesday afternoon."

"Agreed," I said.

I dropped him off at Claverach midafternoon and picked up Amy.

Mom invited all of us to dinner on Tuesday night. It would be a rare family reunion with Gunther and Rand in town. And since Amy and Gunther had never met, Mom thought it would be a good opportunity for a family gathering. The fact that we were meeting at the lawyer's the next day cast a cloud over the affair, but all things considered, it went well.

At cocktails, I introduced Gunther to Amy, who had just been named to Washington University's *Law Review*. It was never easy to impress Gunther, but I think Amy won him over—at least, I hoped so. I hung with them for a few minutes to make sure things went smoothly. Gunther started off doing his man-of-the-people shtick, but then I detected a change. They actually started discussing substantive legal topics, and Amy was holding her own. It went over my head and I was barely listening when I heard Gunther mention that he might be able to help Amy get a summer position at a Wall Street law firm: Weil, Gotshal. Before I had a chance to intercede, Amy thanked him and told him that she had already accepted an internship at Hotchkiss and Hamilton—a big-deal St. Louis firm.

The conversations at dinner were pleasant. Dad and I caught up on business. Rand and Mom kibitzed with one another when they weren't chatting with Amy. Gunther held forth on the rumors of a possible strike by the major-league baseball players, a subject Dad and I cared about a lot. We both were avid Cardinals fans, and their prospects for the upcoming season looked good. We hoped there would be no strike. The Yankees were in decline, which made the two of us quite happy.

Things heated up a bit when the conversation turned to the fall's election. President Jimmy Carter and Ted Kennedy were vying for the Democratic presidential nomination, and Ronald Reagan looked like he would be the Republican nominee. Thankfully, everyone, including Dad, kept the chatter light even though I knew Dad was a big Reagan fan and Mom loathed him.

Things broke up around eight thirty, as we engaged in the usual departure chitchat. Before driving Amy back to her apartment, I checked with Rand to see if he was OK. "Yup, my news can wait," he replied.

Chapter 12

AT PRECISELY ONE THIRTY IN THE AFTERNOON ON WEDNESDAY, THE four Feldmans presented themselves at the law offices of Dewey & Martin in downtown St. Louis. We were conducted into a small conference room with an eastern exposure that gave us a dramatic view of the Gateway Arch. Gunther was already seated at the round table. Next to him was a conservatively dressed man in his fifties who was introduced to us. Harrison Balding, a senior partner at Dewey & Martin, had worked with Gunther before moving to St. Louis.

After introductions and pleasantries were exchanged, we were all seated. Gunther began to speak.

"Madeline asked me to arrange today's meeting, and I welcome you all. Harrison is present because he has helped to advise Madeline and me about some legal matters that affect all of you. He is also familiar with Missouri law, which differs in some important respects from the laws of New York State. That knowledge has proved very worthwhile in the drafting of the documents that are contained in the envelopes in front of each of you. I, of course, have been involved in this work in an advisory capacity only. Should you have any questions, Harrison will do his best to answer them. But should any or all of you wish to retain the services of your own attorney, you are encouraged to do so.

"Please refrain from reading the documents contained in your envelopes until you've had a chance to hear what I, Harrison, and Madeline have to say. First, I will give you a bit of history.

More than twenty years ago, Madeline decided, quite against my wishes, to fully fund Fratelli Massimo. She did so from her trust fund by buying the entire capital stock of the then nascent Fratelli Massimo Corporation for five hundred thousand dollars.

"Maddy, you and Max will recall the packet of corporate material I prepared and couriered to you many years ago. You were both anxious to receive the articles of incorporation in order to finalize the lease for your first store location. The envelope I gave to you contains copies of the original signed and notarized documents. One specific item is relevant to today's meeting. The seed money Maddy provided was used to fund the company's early preopening start-up expenses, such as salaries, travel, rent, utilities, working capital, and fixed assets requirements of the company."

Dad's eyes widened and his jaw dropped. He, Rand, and I were beginning to put two and two together.

"Wait a fucking minute!" he said. "I barely read those papers. Maddy and I were equal partners. Husband and wife. Both investing in the business. Maddy with money, and me with sweat equity. You're not suggesting otherwise?"

Gunther raised his eyebrows. "Max, copies of those very papers are in your envelope for your perusal. You were, as the documents indicated, named chairman, chief executive officer, and president of Fratelli Massimo. Madeline was the sole investor. You had no equity in the business. Now, if you will permit me..."

Dad was apoplectic. He rose to his feet and shouted, "You fucked with me, Gunther! You and my loving wife!"

Mom said, "At the time, Max, I barely read the documents myself. I remember vividly: we were in a big hurry to get them notarized, and we sent them off to the landlord and the bank. In fact, when I asked you what my title as secretary/treasurer meant, because I didn't honestly understand, you smiled and said, and I quote, to 'look pretty.' Remember?"

Dad collapsed in his chair. "I've been hosed, and Max Feldman doesn't get hosed. I'm going to get my own attorney involved in this farce."

I sat up in my chair; Mom used to warn me to be careful when Dad referred to himself in the third person.

Gunther continued, "As you wish, Max. You are welcome to seek the advice of an attorney.

"As the company grew under Max's stewardship, Madeline's original investment was drawn down and was supplemented by another five hundred thousand dollar infusion from her trust fund. Eventually, the excess cash the company was generating—in addition to seasonal bank borrowings—sustained the company. But no other equity capital was raised, which means, in simple terms, that Madeline Berg Feldman *was* the sole stockholder of the Fratelli Massimo Corporation."

That was a stunner! Dad stood and started to blurt something out, but Gunther ignored him and continued.

"Max, you need to hear what follows. I purposely emphasized the word *was*, because all that has changed. In 1965 Madeline became uncomfortable with her ownership situation. She confided to me that she felt it was the family's business, and that the boys—meaning the three of you, Max, Joshua, and Rand—should be equity partners in the business. We discussed this over a number of years. I, for one, saw the wisdom of her desire, and sought Harrison's counsel as to how to go about achieving this objective under Missouri law."

Dad sat back down, giving Gunther a venomous look.

"The three of us met in New York on numerous occasions." Gunther chuckled. "I believe Maddy told you she was spending time at Elizabeth Arden. It was a great cover. In any event, we discussed a number of ways to approach the issue. At first, I was determined that Madeline retain voting control—at least 51 percent of the voting shares. She was strongly opposed to this suggestion. She believed it was a family business, and she didn't want to be the boss. After much back and forth, I convinced Maddy to retain 40 percent of the shares, with Max, Josh, and Rand each receiving 20 percent of the outstanding shares. She reluctantly agreed to that, rather than a distribution of 25 percent of the shares to each member of the family. Madeline, will you please explain why you settled on the 40-20-20-20 distribution?"

Still fuming, Max turned his attention to Mom, his eyes blazing.

"Thanks, Dad. Here was my reasoning. I thought that if Fratelli Massimo confronted a potentially contentious matter— say a hostile takeover bid or an ambitious acquisition proposal—a majority vote would be required. If Max and I agreed on a critical decision, which was customary in the early days, the two of us would have voted our combined 60 percent of the shares identically, and we would have gone forward. If, on the other hand, I alone was opposed, and all three of you guys were in favor, your 60 percent of the share would carry the day, and we would proceed. In any event, it would take at least two of us—and in some cases, three of us—to carry the day. As Gunther pointed out, I didn't want to be the boss, but I didn't want the shares split evenly, as that would mean three members would always be required to make a difficult decision, which is some-times a high hurdle. Fifty-fifty votes could lead to dissension within the family. I didn't want that possibility. And if I am being a pigheaded so-and-so about a decision, and if you, Max, as CEO, and Josh and Rand are of the opposite mind, you will prevail." She remained calm in her explanation.

By this time Dad was glaring at Mom, no doubt doing the math. Sixty percent of the shares would be needed to go public or stay private. The combinations were few. Mom plus one of her boys would get to 60 percent. All three of the boys would have to be in favor of going public if Mom voted no. Mom was adamant about staying private. That meant Rand was the key, because if only Dad and I voted to go public, we could muster only 40 percent of the votes between us.

Gunther continued, "Once we agreed on the formula, Harrison and I worked on affecting the transfer of shares in the most tax-efficient and efficacious way possible. Each of you was receiving shares during the past dozen or so years, and you are now fully vested and possess the rights and responsibilities of being 20 percent partners in the Feldman Family Partnership, which owns 100 percent of the Fratelli Massimo Corporation. Harrison, if you will..."

His partner jumped in. "Thanks, Gunther. I'd like to add a couple more things. The trusts, which you can read at your leisure, require you to vote all your shares either for or against any proposal that comes before you four. That, too, was Madeline's idea, as she did not want the family members splitting votes and engaging in internecine squabbling over a share here and a share there. Additionally, ballots on proposals are confidential. While the results will be announced, how each of you voted on a proposal will not be disclosed. In fact, the ballots will be destroyed after they are tabulated and the results announced.

Again, Maddy was insistent that she hoped that while there would be instances where the members of the family disagreed, it was important to respect the final results and move on with no recriminations. These arrangements are quite unusual, but Gunther and I feel they honor what Madeline wanted."

Gunther said, "I might add that this arrangement, along with the stellar results Max has achieved, make each of you quite wealthy. Joshua, you and Rand are very lucky guys. But along with the wealth come weighty responsibilities. None more so than your deliberations and decision regarding the company's going public. I say that because no investment bank will want to go forward with an offering unless the family has reached at least a 60 percent majority favoring that action. Questions?" Gunther folded his hands on the table.

My brother and I were blown away.

Dad was not so moved. Keeping himself under control—but obviously seething—he started speaking. "So, if I understand this scheme, which was concocted in the dark of night without a moment's consultation with the founder, chairman, CEO, and president of Fratelli Massimo, Rand and Josh and I have equal equity stakes in Fratelli Massimo?!"

"Yes, Max, that's right," Gunther serenely responded. "But Maddy's generosity means that you are many millions of dollars richer than you thought you were when you had breakfast this morning. And you have a significant percentage of Fratelli Massimo stock, which will give you a strong voice in the governance of the company. The original incorporation documents that you have in your envelope—and which you were very happy and anxious to agree to and sign—indicate that you are, indeed, chairman, CEO, and president, and have complete control of the company's day-to-day operations. So your opinion carries great weight here. And, as Maddy just pointed out, if you, Josh, and Rand agree on something, or if you and Maddy agree, you will move forward."

"But I *am* the company," Dad countered. "I barely looked at those documents. I was in a tight spot, time was precious. You knew that and took advantage! I signed them to get the goddamn first store open. Without me, there's nothing. Without my sense of urgency and my merchant skills, the company would fail. You sucker punched me!"

"I'm sorry you feel that way, Max," Gunther said. He was as calm as a man ordering his favorite drink at his usual watering hole. "But if Maddy were so inclined, she could have retained sole ownership of the entire company for as long as she wished. And should you be as uncomfortable with your current situation as you described, you are free to try to sell your shares by giving each of your three family members the right to buy them at a price equal to that offered to you by a qualified outside bidder."

"And," added Harrison, "I remind you that you are encouraged to consult with any attorney you choose, to examine and understand the documents and to enter into litigation if you feel it is warranted. But if you want my opinion, I would avoid that path for a couple of reasons. First, the documents have been drafted with extreme care and vetted by experts in the field, and second, litigation can be protracted and expensive. With the going-public decision at hand, you may not want to elect to follow that course."

Dad was frustrated and devastated, to put it mildly. Clearly, bombast would not work with these two legal heavyweights. With Maddy clearly opposed to going public, he would have to persuade Rand to vote his shares with him. I saw him eyeing Rand.

Rand was poker-faced. He showed no indication at all of which way he was leaning. But if I were a betting man...

As for me, who was buttering my bread these days?

Gunther concluded the meeting. "I urge you each to examine the documents in your envelope. Feel free to address any questions to either Harrison or me. Also, given the urgency Max has placed on proceeding with the 'go-public' option, I suggest we reconvene on Friday at 1:30 p.m. to discuss that alternative, vote on it, and discuss any other matters pertinent to the Feldman Family Partnership. That is, unless you, Max, wish to defer that decision for another time."

"Fuck you, Gunther. You know this can't wait!" Dad snatched up his envelope, his hand trembling, and quickly exited the room without saying another word.

I had left my car at the office and come to the meeting with Dad, so Mom drove me back. On the way, Mom, Rand, and I avoided discussing what had just transpired and talked about inconsequential drivel. Each of us was pondering a weighty decision.

Chapter 13

I steered clear of Dad when I got back to the office. Instead, I dug into some paperwork and, toward the end of the day, called Amy and told her I had something very important to talk to her about. She was curious, but I told her I needed to speak to her in person, and to meet me at my place. I then took my phone off the hook, as I wanted to avoid a call from Dad. He could find me, of course, but I hoped to have some quiet time to figure out what to say to Amy.

I knew she was technically not a lawyer, not yet anyway, but she had a stake in this, and I valued her advice.

I picked up a pizza on the way to my apartment. She was waiting for me in the living room. We embraced and went to sit at the small corner table in the kitchen.

"Josh, you scared me. Should I be worried about something? Are you all right?"

"Yeah, sorry. This is all about Fratelli Massimo, and it's strictly business. I need you to help me figure something out."

I summarized, as best I could, what had transpired at the afternoon meeting.

"Wow, Josh, that's great news, isn't it?" She looked hopeful.

"Yes and no," I said. "It's awesome that I'm a partner in the family business. I can't quite wrap my head around the money part, but I'm nervous, and I'm frightened about Friday's meeting and the going-public vote I will have to cast."

"Give me some time to read through the documents, just to make sure I understand them."

About an hour later, Amy was smiling and shaking her head. "Your grandfather deserves the reputation he has. He is incisive and clever. Those original incorporation documents are a masterpiece. And they're all perfectly legal. He puffed up your father with titles and made sure your mother owned the company—lock, stock, and barrel. He knows how to play the long game. I would never play poker with the man. Gunther lost the first round at the Harvard Club lunch; he won the next one with the ownership arrangement.

"The family partnership idea is good and works from a tax and estate point of view," Amy continued. "He failed to convince your mom to keep a controlling 51 percent stake, but Gunther must have become aware early on that Rand was never going to be a fan of your dad's. So this arrangement gives the appearance of your parents' sharing the control of the business, but the reality is somewhat different."

"Explain, please."

"OK. Let's use the example of the going-public proposal. It requires 60 percent of the shares to succeed. You tell me your mother is bitterly opposed, so Max must convince you and Rand, both, to vote his way. He'll assume that you're a done deal, so he'll probably want to work on Rand. Knowing Rand and his relationship with your dad, or rather the lack of it, convincing him to vote to go public won't be easy.

"One more thing, sweetie. Your mother ain't so dumb, either. She's giving you cover. You can vote with your dad, which takes the pressure off you and keeps you in good odor with your dad. But if Rand votes no, the business stays private—which will mean that Maddy gets her way, and she and your brother take the heat. Your brother is almost out of the house, and your mom will soldier through. She will still have an ace up her sleeve in the family partnership, which means your dad must stay in line if he wants to share in the wealth that the business generates. Maddy and Gunther are two very smart individuals."

"Amy, you're not so far behind in the smarts department either. So, you think I should just vote for going public?"

"I didn't say that. I said your mom is enabling you to do that, if you think it's best."

"Well, Dad will go crazy if I don't vote his way—and I'm supposed to follow in his footsteps." I looked straight into her eyes.

"Maybe you don't wear the same size shoes."

"What are you driving at?"

"Josh, I love you and I want to share my life with you, but it's important for you to understand that just because your dad sees you as his successor, and just because you want that role, there's no guarantee that it will happen. You are twenty-three years old, and lots of things may change. You often say retailing is a Darwinian business, that concepts come and go. You may find another opportunity that suits you better. And forgive me for saying this, but I don't trust your father. Remember what he did to Sy? That was a horrible betrayal. He's fully capable of betraying you too."

This was hard to hear. "Amy, he was a goddamn teenager at the time."

"Do not defend him. Look how he's ostracized Rand and openly criticized Maddy. That man is capable of brutality."

"I've done some crazy stuff too."

"Look, Josh, you're precious, sweet, loyal, funny, sexy, and smart. But do you have your father's sixth sense about what merchandise will sell six months from now? And do you have his dark side? His ruthlessness? Sometimes business leaders need that quality as well. And are you willing to subordinate family life to the laser-like focus Max devotes to his work? I'm not a businessperson, dear, but you need to think about what the long term might look like."

"I don't know if I have that sixth sense, or that mumbo jumbo about ruthlessness. I am sure that Fratelli Massimo, like all businesses, will have its ups and downs. But let's assume it all works out. You're basically a member of the family, so how do you think I should vote?"

"A 'basically' member of the family is one wedding ring short of being an 'actual' member of the family. Friday's vote is completely up to you. I am in your corner, either way. And now I need to get back to my own challenges at school. Let's get together Friday evening after the meeting. I can't wait to find out how it goes."

With that, Amy departed, leaving me with my own thoughts.

A merchant is like a world-class artist or a great athlete. All the practice in the world can't make you into one. You have to have talent. I wasn't sure I was a merchant, but I knew I was a great retailer, a good numbers guy, and I had a flair for the business. But if a "dark side" or ruthlessness was a prerequisite, calling your dad a schmuck or bullying your son, I wasn't so sure I had that in me.

• • •

When I got to the office Thursday morning, Carly had left a note taped to my cubicle asking me to see Dad ASAP.

"Well, Josh, I spent eight hours yesterday and last evening with my lawyer, Ray Weinberg. It was a complete waste of time and money. Gunther and Balding did a real number on me. The documents are airtight. We could fight it out in court, but Ray says we have a less than 1 percent chance of winning. And that would mean more money and more time." The look on his face was sour. "Your mom has completely fucked me over."

I sprang out of my chair. "Don't ever say that about Mom. First of all, she's not like that. She had no idea that the going-public option would be front and center when those documents were written, or that you two would see things so differently. And neither of you even looked at what you were signing. Second, Mom voluntarily gave each of us 20 percent of the business. Because of her money and family loyalty and your skills, we are rich! If you think that's being fucked over, you're nuts."

Dad shook his head. "Maybe she didn't know back then, but your bastard grandfather knew what was around the corner. It's odd, but in some ways—not many—we're alike, the old man and me. We think about the long term. For me, it's next season. For him, it's decades into the future. I'll tell you one thing, if I had to pick a lawyer in a critical situation, I'd call Gunther, even though I hate the motherfucker. Nobody's smarter or more devious than that son of a bitch. That being said, we're screwed.

"I know I can count on you, Josh, but convincing Rand is another story. He's a mama's boy and always has been, even with his athletic skills and good looks. And I'm odd man out. I don't think the kid has asked me a question about the business in years."

"Dad, Rand isn't interested in the business. Nor does he ever want anything to do with it, or you. He's a creative guy and plans to stay on the West Coast when he graduates."

"Any advice on how to bring him around on the vote?"

"Yes. Do not try. Just take your chances. No offense, Dad, but you and he are like oil and water, and you'll only make things worse. Think of this from Rand's point of view. He doesn't get along with you and has no interest in the business. He might just decide to vote to take the business public, sell his shares, take the money, and run. That way, he severs his relationship with you and the business."

Dad lightened a little. "Maybe you're right. That does make sense.

"You know, it's a pretty sad situation when the guy who made Fratelli Massimo what it is can't take it public. It's all the more galling because it's your mom and brother who will probably stop me. I don't know if I can ever forgive them."

"You can't mean what you're saying. Even if it stays private, you can run the business, make tons of money, and come home to Mom. That's a pretty soft downside to this whole mess."

"You've got some growing up to do, Josh. You're not in my shoes. Coming home to Maddy isn't quite the treat you think it is. She never asks about the business. Her head's stuck in a book, or her mind is elsewhere. She's paranoid about the Weils, Evie in particular, since that Sunday dustup you witnessed. She could care less about Highland Hills.

"I had to sit and watch Sy bollocks up his business because he couldn't see the future. I goddamn guarantee you I won't sit by and watch Fratelli Massimo fail to reach its potential. Don't take me for granted. And don't go wobbly on me, Josh."

I muttered some words of reassurance and left his office, but honestly, I was torn. Staying private with Mom holding 40 percent of the voting power, me 20 percent, and Rand 20 percent gave me a terrific chance of taking over for Dad one day. On the other hand, going public would make me rich. But once we were public, the family's power would be diluted. Anything could happen. The board of directors might want a different successor. We could merge or be acquired. And either way, the business needed a happy and motivated Max to succeed. What a mess.

• • •

On Friday, I drove down to Dewey & Martin because I had agreed to take Rand to the airport after the meeting.

When we entered, we saw that it was the same conference room and the same arrangement around the table. And the same Arch.

Gunther led off.

"Welcome. I trust you've all had a chance to read the documents you received Wednesday. Does anybody have any questions for Harrison or me?" He paused. "Seeing none, let's get to the business at hand. Maddy has asked me to chair today's meeting in accordance with the bylaws of the Feldman Family Partnership. Any objections? Thank you. Three items on the agenda, a copy of which is in front of you.

"First up, old business. Second, the vote for or against the exploration of taking Fratelli Massimo public. A ballot and envelope are also in front of you. Third, new business."

Everyone murmured their agreement with the agenda.

"Any old business? No? Then let's proceed to the vote. Before you mark your ballot, is there any discussion about the proposal?"

Dad shrugged his shoulders and exhaled. Rand and I avoided eye contact with everybody but Gunther. Mom was cool. She has lots of leverage.

"Well, then, let's proceed," Gunther said. "Your ballot summarizes the proposal. And you need only draw an X in one of the two boxes on your ballot. I remind you that your name should not appear on your ballot, except for Madeline's, as she represents 40 percent of the outstanding shares. As soon as you have voted, please place the ballot in the business envelope, seal it, and hand it to Harrison. The two of us will retire to a separate room, tabulate the results, destroy the ballots, and then inform you of the final tally."

We marked our ballots, put them in the envelopes, and delivered them to Harrison, who then left the room with Gunther.

It shouldn't have taken long, but the clock in the room seemed to stop, as if the electrical power had been interrupted. Mom and Rand were composed. Maybe the ballot counting was just a formality for them because they already knew the outcome. That seemed likely to me. Rand and Mom had probably voted no. I was fidgety and tried to avoid eye contact with my father. He, on the other hand, stared at each of us in turn—Mom, Rand, and me. There was a strong current of tension zapping between each of us and Dad. He was desperately trying to divine the tally by reading our facial expressions and body language.

He almost jumped out of his chair when he heard a door open down the hall. Max had staked so much on going public. He had to figure that Rand's vote would be decisive. I wondered whether he regretted how he had treated Rand through the years. Probably not. Dad never looked back unless it involved a triumph of his.

The door to our meeting room finally opened, and the two lawyers entered.

Harrison Balding looked down at his legal pad and announced, "By a vote of sixty to forty," Dad shut his eyes, "the Feldman family has approved the proposal to explore going public."

Dad was exultant, but to his everlasting credit, he resisted the urge to gloat. He simply said, "I think your boys got it right, Maddy, and I'll do everything I can to make this work."

Maddy, ever gracious, though I detected a tear in her eye, thanked Dad and replied, "I trust you will, darling, and I can only say that I am happy this miserable episode is over."

Gunther asked if there was any new business. There was none. As the directors were gathering their papers to leave, Dad turned to Gunther and asked, "Will you stick around for a few minutes after the meeting? I have a number of questions regarding the whole going-public process."

Gunther nodded, told us that the meeting was concluded, and reminded us once again that Mom didn't want us to disclose how we voted. As Gunther put it, "Once a decision has been reached, it's final and not to be discussed." I'm not sure how realistic that was, but I, for one, was relieved.

Rand, Mom, and I left the room and headed to the garage. Not a word was spoken until we got to the cars, where Mom hugged and kissed each of us and wished Rand safe travels. She then asked me if I could meet her for lunch the next day at Parkmoor. "We need to talk—just the two of us."

Chapter 14

WHEN I MET UP WITH AMY AND TOLD HER WHAT HAPPENED, SHE just shook her head.

"Well, how did you vote, Tiger?"

"It's supposed to be confidential."

"You make me laugh, Josh, that's one of the reasons I love you. Well, I am going to make a guess and you can keep your little secret. Sixty percent of the votes were for going public. Since we know how your dad voted, there's only two ways that could happen. You three 'boys' voted for it. Or, your mother and father voted for it. I would bet that your mom caved. She values the family's happiness over her own. I know Rand, and he would never, ever give your father what he wanted; he hates the guy—and with good reason. So, I think you two voted no."

"It's confidential, Amy. How many times do I have to tell you?"

She went on, "Oh, I keep forgetting, but just supposing I'm right, you'd better never let your father know how you voted. Of course, you won't, because it's confidential, but you'd better hope Rand keeps his mouth shut! Just sayin', because you're a dead man at Fratelli Massimo if he squeals."

I remained silent.

"Your mom's a marvel, loving and lovely and clever like her father. I adore her, as you worship her. But she's going to take some grief from your father, because he'll assume she voted no. I want you to know that I'm no Maddy. Her energy, her entire being, is spent ensuring that 'her boys' are taken care of. Please forgive me for this—I think she's spoiled you and Rand. She runs interference for you. And she gives your father too wide a berth. I would never tolerate being treated and bullied like that, and I know you wouldn't behave like him. She's of the generation when moms made family their sole priority. But it's 1980, and times are different.

"I will be a loving wife and mother hopefully, and I also want to be a successful attorney. In fact, I will want to become a partner. That is my ambition, as yours is succeeding your dad. And Josh, sweetheart, you can always look for my support, but I will be far more independent than Maddy, and far less able to cushion every blow that befalls you. I have my own ambitions and battles to fight."

"I understand, Amy. Maddy is a tough act to follow—and an unrealistic act, at that. I want you to be successful at home and at the office. My mother never had to worry about the latter. And, you're right, she's been my protector. I get what you're saying."

After a few moments, I continued. "I guess Gunther lost this round. Dad got his way."

"It may seem that way, Josh, but never bet against the Sage of Wall Street. He plays the long game. There will come a day when Maddy will win the next round, and Gunther is sure to play a role."

· · ·

When Mom and I met at Parkmoor the next day, we embraced and then slid into our booth. I ordered a Kingburger, fries, and a Coke. Mom had a salad. We agreed to split a hot fudge cake sundae for dessert.

"Josh, I have two favors to ask of you. I guess that you figured out how I voted yesterday. Please don't ask me why I did what I did. It's best left unsaid. OK?"

I shrugged. "Sure, if you want it that way."

"Good. Secondly, I don't want you to ever tell your father how you voted. Never, ever...even if he asks you point-blank. He'll never forgive you if he knows you voted to stay private. I know it's wrong to lie, even by omission, but I want you to lie, if it comes to that. For the sake of the family. Will you promise me that?"

"Yes, I promise."

The waitress brought our order.

"And now, let me tell you how touched I was by your vote. I won't ask you why you did it, but it overwhelmed me. I was prepared to have you vote with your dad, which would have been fine with me. But when the tally was announced, I could barely speak. You were willing to endure your father's wrath and put your career in jeopardy by voting no. You're a brave boy, but that vote showed me you love me almost as much as I love you. It's a mother's dream."

"I do love you, Mom. You're the best." I meant it. Her keen desire to keep the business private was one of the factors that led to my vote, but that wasn't the compelling reason, though I didn't mind the fact that Mom thought it was. I knew in my heart that I had voted for what was in my own best interest. I was thinking of my own future in a privately held Fratelli Massimo where Mom, Rand, and I would control Dad's succession. To be honest, I was growing uneasy with my father's reassurances. I couldn't completely trust him—not after what I'd heard from Sy. Not with the way he treated and spoke of

Mom when the subject of going public arose. If we had stayed private, I would have the votes.

• • •

It was chaos when I got to Dad's office on Monday.

Carly was rearranging the conference room and loading banker boxes on the table while her phone kept ringing. Dad yelled at me to pick it up, as he was on his private line. I picked up Carly's phone, and it was some guy from Lehman Brothers named Peter Kahn who insisted that Dad pick up. I put him on hold and signaled to Dad that it was important. Dad raised his index finger, meaning he would be off in a minute. It turned out to be only ten seconds before he switched to the Lehman call and waved me into his office.

"Yeah, hi, Peter. Gunther told me you would be calling. Let me put you on the speaker. My son Josh should hear what you have to say." Dad pushed some buttons on the phone.

"We need to get going if we hope to get the IPO done by September/October," Peter began. "The election in November will spook the market, and the outcome either way will unduly impact the offering. Traders come back after Labor Day, and your auditors will have OK'd your first-half earnings report by then. By the way, who are your auditors? I forgot to ask Gunther."

"A local firm: Justin Brooks, CPA."

"You're joking. Got to dump them, like yesterday, Max. You need a top-seven accounting firm to baptize this baby."

I was going to mention Price Waterhouse where Amy's dad was a partner, but Dad cut me off.

"But Justin's been with me since day one."

"Admire your loyalty, Max. I really do. But kiss them goodbye. Trust me. Or, if you must retain them out of some sense of loyalty, give them some bullshit stuff to do like internal audits or the tax returns for the Feldman Family Partnership. Something, but not your books. Got it? I'll call somebody from Ernst & Ernst. They do a ton of retailer audits. They must have an office in St. Louis. Somebody will call. OK?"

"Yeah, but I'm not happy."

"You're not paying us to make you happy, sport. You're paying us to make you M-O-N-E-Y. Capisce?"

"Uh-huh." Dad nodded.

"Great. We're on the same page. And your local counsel?"

Dad knew where this was heading. "A great guy, smart, knows all the ins and outs. A real professional. Discreet. Ray Weinberg."

"Never heard of him. Will look him up in Martindale-Hubbell." Kahn screamed at someone to look him up in that directory of attorneys. A moment or two passed.

"A nonstarter, this guy's a nobody. Max, look, I understand. I've done dozens of these IPOs of family businesses. These guys you've been using are loyal and competent. No question. But they're overmatched here. They have no credibility on the Street. Make up your mind to something right from the get-go: You're going to play in the majors, my man. You need to bring your A game. Ask your father-in-law—who, by the way, should handle the New York end of things, legal-wise. He and his firm are the best in the business. Your banks?"

"Boatmen's and Mercantile," Dad mumbled.

"No New York banks?"

"No, Peter. Believe it or not, banks with billions in assets do exist outside of New York."

"I guess we can live with that at least until we get you public, but then its Manny Hanny, Chase, or, God forbid, Chemical Bank."

"Whoa!" Dad was boiling mad at this point. Nobody had talked to him like this since a drill sergeant in his basic training days. "Wait a fucking minute, Peter. This is my business. I started with zip, nada, zilch, and built this into a terrific business that you guys want to get a slice of. I don't mind that. But I want you to know that I know my way around the block. I also know that there are plenty of I-banks that want to take us public. There's a pile of letters from them on my desk. So, show a little respect. Get it?" Dad nodded at me, showing Peter who the boss was.

"Got it. Call Gunther, cry on his shoulder, and then splash your face with cold water. Then call me back when you're ready to get serious. Two o'clock, New York time. I have a board meeting at three, bye." Click.

Dad shook his head and gave me a look.

"I don't know who this Peter guy thinks he is. But he's messing with the wrong CEO, sonny. Gonna teach him a little Show-Me State lesson. First order of business with your grandfather is finding another I-bank. Maybe Goldman Sachs. That'll bust Peter's chops. Let him explain to his boss how he lost this 'baby,' as he called it.

"Carly! Carly! Get Gunther on the phone, pronto. And Josh, I need you to scram. Carly will give you a list of things to get. Gunther gave it to me Friday before he left town. Ciao." Dad waved me out of his office.

I wasn't invited to listen to the Gunther call. But Carly whispered to me later that a somber Max had phoned Peter Kahn at precisely 2:00 p.m. New York time, and that he was placed on hold for fifteen minutes before Peter got on the line. And yes,

Mr. Kahn and his team would be at Fratelli Massimo at 11:00 a.m. sharp tomorrow morning. She said that I should be there with a blank legal pad in hand.

That was the first time I had ever known Dad to back down. I wish I had a transcript of his talk with Gunther.

Luckily the conference room could accommodate fifteen people, because that's how many filed into the room on Tuesday morning at eleven. I sat with Dad and Carly. In walked our new best friend, Harrison Balding, from Dewey & Martin. I saw the head of the local office of the Ernst & Ernst accounting firm, Henry Morrison. Two of Dad's direct reports were there, as well as his head of leasing and finance. Next came Walter Benning and his store op guy, Andy Frain. And then there was the SWAT team from Lehman Brothers: Peter Kahn, two of his lieutenants, and three analysts—graduates of Ivy League schools, all. They would do the number crunching and the grunt work.

Other than Dad's brief welcoming remarks, he, Carly, and our execs were mostly silent for the next four hours. At most, they muttered, "Yes," "I understand," and "by then, really?"

The bankers, accountant, and lawyer, on the other hand, rattled off the timeline, the priorities, the dos and don'ts, who you could talk to and what you could say, who you couldn't talk to, what needed to be disclosed, what needed to be private, and so on. The immediate goals were a Securities and Exchange Commission filing and preparation for what's known in the trade as the "road show."

This last item elicited a broad smile from Dad. He knew that a road show would spotlight him; he would tell the story of Fratelli Massimo and his role in its success. He would travel to cities across the country with Peter, or a stand-in, accompanied by a couple of analysts and a gal Friday. The team's mission would be to convince institutional investors like Fidelity and Vanguard of the wisdom of buying shares in Fratelli Massimo. The entourage would travel in a corporate jet, be driven from place to place in stretch limos, stay in elite hotels, and eat in the finest restaurants—all paid for by Lehman Brothers. Their payday, of course, would come on the day we went public, and this payout would be in the millions of dollars. Naturally, I would try to hitch a ride on the jet and accompany them for a couple of days . . . as a learning experience.

But my main function would be much more mundane. I was told to deliver tons of information—leases, loan documents, financial reports, and assorted files and data—to the three analysts who would examine them, massage them when necessary, create spreadsheets and slides, and "sanitize" them for the protection of all concerned. After all, nobody wanted to get sued. This process, known as due diligence, would take many days and nights. The conference room became the epicenter of the going-public process.

• • •

Most of my office time that summer was spent gathering and delivering the goods and tracking down the answers to dozens and dozens of questions. I relied on Fratelli Massimo's department heads and staff for many of those answers, but I had to head to our former CPA and law firm and grovel for our documents and data. It was awkward. Those people had helped our company become a success. No one blamed me for their dismissal, but feelings were hurt. The changeover bothered Dad, but not enough to distract him from reveling in his upcoming celebrity status.

He did take time out to feel a bit sorry for himself about Justin and Ray's fate. "I've got to live in this town when Lehman clears out, and both those guys are voting members of Highland Hills." He dared not say this in front of Maddy, who might have given him an "I told you so" look and lecture. But he felt comfortable whining to me.

For her part, Maddy was her usual pleasant self. She continued taking classes at the university and even earned, almost by accident, enough credits to get her MA degree in literature that spring. This meant that she had to take some big exam. No problem for Mom. She claimed the MA was no big deal, and she wouldn't hear of our going to commencement. She played bridge that Friday. She bid and made slam to her delight.

When Maddy heard about the road show, she marched Dad to his closet and assessed his wardrobe for the big trip. Predictably Mom found it wanting, and they agreed to go to New York for some suitable replacements at Paul Stuart, rather than relying on our local men's stores, Brooks Brothers or Famous-Barr.

For their part, Lehman Brothers provided a coach to help with the drafting and delivery of the pitch. He also prepared index cards with likely questions that potential investors might ask. Dad and the coach practiced until he had the answers down pat.

• • •

The pieces were coming together in late June and early July, so a preliminary schedule was prepared with stops in half a dozen major cities and, of course, New York. It was important to go there in July because "everybody who was anybody decamped for the shore or the mountains in August." A tentative date of September 15 was established for the initial public offering. This would be inevitably delayed because we needed approvals from government agencies, the lawyers, and the accountants. October 1 would probably be the Big Day.

Chapter 15

THAT SUMMER WASN'T ALL GRUNT WORK FOR ME. ONCE I FINISHED at the office, I would usually pick up Amy, who was just down the street at Hotchkiss and Hamilton. We'd go out with friends, go to a club or two, or grab something to eat and usually spend the evening at my place. No weeknight overnight stays for Amy, as she had to professionalize herself for work each morning. She needed to wear a sober blazer and ladylike skirt, a white or off-white shell, a mod scarf, hosiery, and two-inch heels; she had to be fresh as a daisy to impress the powers that be. And impress them she did, as she secured a full-time offer when she graduated.

We were both anxious to be engaged, and so I promised to go up to Highland Park over Labor Day to make our intentions known and ask her father for his blessing, which Amy assured me was a mere formality.

The Epsteins and the Feldmans had met a couple of years earlier, when Amy's family came to St. Louis for her undergraduate graduation. We had them over for cocktails and dinner. Given how different our parents were—cool and precise Ralph Epstein and bombastic Max, the rather full-figured Adrienne Epstein and chic Maddy—the evening couldn't have gone better. Dad was on his best behavior. He liked Amy, and knowing that she would be in St. Louis after graduation played into his long-range plans for me. Mom had Gunther's gift of gab and excelled at making the person she was talking to feel like a star. Amy's two brothers and Rand watched a Cardinals-Cubs game on television until dinner was served.

At one of our just-resumed Sunday night dinners at Claverach, I mentioned my upcoming Labor Day weekend in Chicago. I told my parents about my plans with Amy, and they were overjoyed. The three of us embraced. Of course, it was no big surprise, but with all the tumult over going public, it was a welcome respite.

Wedding plans were discussed. The idea was to marry in June, next year, at Lake Shore Country Club in Glencoe. Dad was suitably impressed, as this was the preeminent Jewish club in Chicagoland. Mom merely closed her eyes momentarily. The Feldmans would host the rehearsal dinner the Friday night before the wedding at one of Chicago's luxe hotels. Mom would take care of the details.

When the subject of an engagement ring came up, I mentioned to my parents that I might go to some of the local jewelers in St. Louis.

They were both horrified, but for different reasons. Dad wanted me to buy it wholesale on Forty-Seventh Street in New York, home to many discount jewelers. "No son of Max Feldman is going to pay retail for a diamond ring! Jewelers are thieves, marking their merchandise up two or three times what it cost them. Take it from me. Put it in a pretty box. Amy will never know the difference."

"Dad, what's wrong with you?" I exclaimed. "Amy's terrific, and she deserves the best. I'll do everything I can to make sure she gets it. I'm not bargain-hunting like you do when you buy thousands of pairs of shoes. This is a one and only, and she's going to get the best."

Mom was equally appalled, declaring that Amy was no discount bride. "And she's no dope, Max. She won't be fooled, and I will not be party to depriving her of what she deserves."

"And pay full retail?" thundered Dad.

"Yes, Max, full retail. Just as the rehearsal dinner will be at the Ritz-Carlton—and not some Holiday Inn."

"You know, Maddy, you've been rather testy since the vote. Time to put it behind you. You lost."

Mom gathered herself. "If I have been testy, Max, it's not because of the vote. It's because you've been so full of yourself and your road show tour that you're beginning to believe your own PR. Meanwhile, I'll be planning the wedding while you're touring with your sycophants. Josh and I will go to New York and make sure Amy receives a ring she can be proud of."

Dad shrugged, rolled his eyes, and sauntered off.

Mom and I visited some private jewelers in New York who were in office buildings and didn't have any retail street presence. Everybody treated Mom like a queen, and she certainly knew her stuff. But we ultimately decided on a two-carat emerald-cut ring at Harry Winston, which certainly did have a retail presence. You had to talk your way past the guard at the entrance and get through the security doors; once inside you knew to speak in hushed tones and to have a very thick wallet.

Amy later confided in me that she had hinted about her dream ring while having coffee with Mom one day. It was a forgivable conspiracy, but it cost me many times what my Porsche 911 had set me back. Ultimately, everyone was happy—except for Dad, who grudgingly loaned me the money for the ring until the proceeds from the public offering were in my bank account. "It's not the money, sonny, it's the principle. Paying retail for jewelry is not in my DNA."

Whatever minor despondency Dad suffered as a result of my retail ring was more than offset by his success on the road show. By all accounts, even Peter Kahn's, Dad crushed it. He was articulate, responsive to questioners but not so responsive as to ruffle the lawyers' feathers, and adept at explaining the numbers during the slideshow. Institutional investors loved the story. And they loved the numbers even more. Everybody wanted in. That meant there weren't enough shares to go around, which jacked up the prospective opening asking price from eighteen to twenty dollars per share.

With about a month to go before the IPO, it looked like clear sailing. I buckled myself into my car and headed north on I-55, on my way to the Tri-State Tollway and Highland Park, Illinois, and my date with Amy and the Epsteins.

The trip took almost six hours on that Friday before Labor Day, and I arrived midafternoon. The Epsteins' house was a fairly large Tudor style with Ye Olde English half-timber liberally tacked onto the exterior. Only the downstairs was air-conditioned. Amy explained to me that the breeze off Lake Michigan cooled the upstairs, and conditions were helped by a gigantic attic exhaust fan that pulled the air through the house while also pulling papers off desks and petals off flowers. But who cared? I was there to seal the deal with Amy, and that's what I did.

The Epsteins were warm and hospitable, but not hospitable enough to let Amy and me sleep together.

"It's one weekend, Josh, you'll survive," Amy declared with a wink when I arrived.

Ralph readily and happily granted his permission for the union.

On Saturday, I took Amy to a bluff overlooking Lake Michigan and asked her to marry me. She hugged me and gave me a loving kiss. I presented the ring, which, she said, was "just what I wanted!" Then she kissed me again.

Back at the house, Amy showed off her ring, and we all toasted with champagne. We called my folks, who were delighted as well. We had dinner that night at Lake Shore Country Club, which would be the wedding venue.

I then zipped back to St. Louis Sunday morning, the happiest guy on the planet.

• • •

Back at work on the Tuesday after Labor Day, it was the home stretch of our big financial transaction. The month sped by with expected highs and lows, and hiccups, as financiers call any glitch. But on October 15, 1980, Fratelli Massimo, which began with one store (the way all big chains start with one store) in 1957 in downtown St. Louis, went public on the New York Stock Exchange. Its trading symbol was "SHO." The IPO price was $24 per share, but it quickly rose to $26.25 in later trading. Lehman Brothers exercised its "greenshoe" option, which meant it could sell an extra tranche of stock and make even more money. My dad browbeat Peter into allocating an extra-large portion of the stock to Nichols & Nichols, where it just so happened that Highland Hills member Bobby Weil was a stockbroker. "Without him," argued my dad, "this might never have happened."

We began the IPO celebration party in New York, at Smith & Wollensky, at 9:00 p.m. that night. Max, Maddy, and Gunther left the festivities early. But the young I-bankers stayed late. The three analysts invited me to tag along when they departed for a so-called "discreet" gentlemen's club. The champagne flowed freely, and everyone got sloshed. Along the way, the jokes got raunchier, and the imitations more biting. One of the analysts did a perfect Harrison Balding impersonation, which sent us to the floor in laughter, momentarily taking our eyes off center stage where…

Well, I had an unforgettable night/morning. And I was relieved when they later told me that I did nothing I could be arrested for—at least in New York City.

The family's proceeds from the IPO amounted to about ninety million. We also maintained a 51 percent voting control of the company. That was good news, but if Dad went south on me, he and the public shareholders could still deny me the leadership role in the company.

I never received a check for my share. I mean, really, what was I going to do with millions of dollars? I knew nothing about investing and, aside from a new Porsche, I lacked for nothing. So Gunther arranged for my share, about twenty million, to be wire transferred to Brown Brothers Harriman, where the Berg family money was invested.

My contact at BBH introduced himself, with all the formality of an English butler, as Mr. Raymond Whitaker. He assured me that my money would be well taken care of and invested in quality stocks.

I meekly asked him if he could send me a check to cover the loan Dad had made to me when I bought Amy's ring.

After a moment's hesitation, he said, "Of course, we'll overnight it to you in St. Louis." I then told him I wanted another
twenty-five thousand dollars (for a new Irish Green Porsche
911). He assented, as if he had a choice, but offered the following:
"Just a word of advice, Joshua. Your grandfather, who opened the
account and drew up the trust, hopes that you will be prudent
with the funds and continue to preserve the bulk of your wealth
as he has in his own account for several decades."

"Sure thing, Ray." I thought I could loosen him up a bit. But,
no, he reminded me that it was Raymond.

What a year! I was going to marry a terrific girl. Each family
member benefitted financially from the IPO. And to top it off, I
learned at Christmas that I was to become an assistant shoe buyer
in 1981, so as to begin learning the secrets of my dad's success.

Chapter 16

SHORTLY AFTER NEW YEAR'S, CARLY CALLED TO TELL ME THAT DAD'S father, Sy, had died, and that Max would not be attending the funeral. Did I want to represent the family?

"Yes, of course," I said.

I loved and admired my grandfather Gunther, who had a remarkable presence, was well-connected and respected, and was always the smartest guy in the room or at the tables in Las Vegas, but Sy was my favorite. Gunther was slightly intimidating and very complex. Sy was straightforward; you never had to analyze what he said for subtle messages. His warmth, affection for me, and schmaltzy repartee made him easy to be around, and I always looked forward to our time together.

We would go out for lunch or dinner somewhere near his place, or in Miami Beach if we both had time, and kibitz about retail, baseball, politics, and America during the Great Depression and World War II. While Max's name would come up, he never returned to the family breakup episode he had recounted to me at Wolfie's on my first business trip years before.

I arrived at Miami International Airport at 11:00 a.m., rented a car, grabbed a quick lunch at McDonald's, and found my way to Mount Nebo Cemetery, where the graveside service was to be held.

I was among the first to arrive at the plot, which was adjacent to that of my grandmother Rose, who had died more than a decade earlier. I smiled when I noted that their plots were at the intersection of two asphalt walkways—a "high traffic" corner.

This was a perfect location for a retailer. There was enough adjacent space for a third plot (perhaps for their wayward son, Max?).

Fortunately, the crew had erected an open-air canvas pavilion that protected the mourners from the Miami sun—which, even in January, was brilliant.

I introduced myself to Rabbi Weiss, who looked to be around eighty years old. He spoke with a heavy Eastern European accent and offered his condolences.

"You gave him much pleasure on your visits and helped him reconcile himself to his troubled relationship with his son. 'At least Josh is a real mensch,' he would say. He loved you very much, and you gave him faith in the future."

I thanked the rabbi and declined his invitation to speak. Sy knew how I felt about him, and I didn't need to broadcast it to the dozen or so attendees—some of whom I recognized from the Ida and Milton Silverstein Home for the Aged, where Sy spent his final years.

The service was brief, and the rabbi spoke with knowledge and fondness about Sy for a few minutes before the mourner's kaddish, the Jewish prayer for the dead.

Following the rabbi's lead, I shoveled some dirt onto Sy's simple pine coffin, the traditional casket for many Jews. As the clots of dirt hit the coffin, my thoughts turned to his fraught relationship with Max, and how devastating it must be for a father to lose contact with his only son. I'm sure Sy took no pleasure in Max's successes. Nor do I think he was jealous. At one of our lunches, Sy declared that a parent or a teacher must never be jealous of his son or his pupil. "You guide them as best you can," he said, "and then hope they succeed. The credit and rewards of that success are theirs, not yours." Max, of course, would wholeheartedly agree with that last sentiment. I don't. Sy taught Max the basics, and my father built his empire on that foundation. Had Max merely acknowledged that help, it might have helped salve the wounds in their relationship. But Dad's ego would never have permitted him to utter that thought, even though Sy would have deflected it.

Several of the mourners expressed their condolences to me, which I accepted with gratitude.

As I was preparing to leave, Sy's attorney introduced himself and handed me an envelope containing a letter my grandfather had written shortly before he died.

> *My dear Josh,*
>
> *You're a bright boy, so you must know there's bupkis in my bank account, and what is there I've given to the shul where I've passed many happy hours. Attendance is shrinking. Or as we would say, Business is Lousy. They need the gelt more than you. Thank God you and your family don't lack for anything. What I can give you is some advice which I hesitated to do at our dinner at Wolfie's, or at our periodic get-togethers that followed. Why ruin good deli! I can still taste those tongue sandwiches!*
>
> *I always regretted telling you about your dad at that first dinner at Wolfie's. You were just a kid and busting your tuchus to please Max. But with my time coming soon, I felt I owed you a legacy of some kind other than the money kind. So here goes.*
>
> *Maybe Rose and I screwed up or maybe it was just fate, or maybe it's what they call genetic today, but Max is an incomplete person. God will strike me dead if I call him evil. We'll reserve that word for nogoodniks like Hitler and Stalin. But*

Max lacks what we old Jews call rachmones, and what you call empathy or compassion. He has no conscience. And dear boy, beware. You cannot trust him.

You CAN, however, always depend on Max to think only of himself and what makes him happy.

I worried at first that you would turn out like him, but thank God, you haven't. You're a mensch. Not perfect. Nobody is. In fact, I think there's a little nastiness deep in the heart of us shopkeepers. Rose might have called it a survival instinct, but she was a softy. I call it conceit, a belief that we can outsmart the customer. We smile and serve, but there's a tiny contempt for those we're smiling at and serving. "I'm going to win this round, Mrs. Sobel!"

And, I might add, every successful retailer has a bit of larceny in him, so you'll be tempted to play games with prices, stretching for that extra nickel, or maybe putting your thumb on the scale, but nothing very serious. I wish I could say that your father barely crossed the line, but he has the capacity for much greater wickedness in his pursuit of what will gratify him.

It breaks my heart as a father to speak of my son this way. But you're worth that broken heart.

I love you and wish you and your family a hundred years of happiness.

Your Zeyde,

Sy

My two grandfathers could hardly have less in common. They were night and day. But they would have agreed on at least one thing—their distrust of my dad. Each man showed this in his own way: Gunther through his endless legal maneuvers, and Sy through his loving-kindness, his very being, and his advice. They each sought to protect their loved ones from Max. For Gunther, it was Maddy. For Sy, it was me.

But for all their efforts, it would take still more time and heartbreak for Maddy and me to fully appreciate the extent of Max's malevolence, and the destruction it would cause.

Chapter 17

FOLLOWING THE IPO, DAD GOT SOME GOOD NEWS. AT ONE OF OUR Sunday deli dinners, he announced that his new best friend, Bobby Weil, had expedited his membership application at Highland Hills Country Club, and he was slated to become a member in thirty days. He was delighted and gushed about what this meant for him and the family. He credited the IPO decision, which Bobby had argued for, as well as Bobby's subsequent intervention on his behalf at the club.

"How nice for you, Max," Mom graciously congratulated him, while turning her attention to prying open the potato salad container on the kitchen counter.

Dad was determined to make HHCC a family affair and ran on about the wonders of the club. He raved about the social gatherings, the contacts we'd make with the rich and powerful of St. Louis, the golf outings, the New Year's Eve Gala, and the physical facilities. "The golf course is maintained beautifully and is one of the best in town. The clubhouse looks like an old castle in England, and the interior is very ritzy and impressive. Can't wait to join."

A grimacing Mom was still wrestling with the stubborn potato salad container. I came to the rescue and helped her find the magic tab. She then made sandwiches for the three of us. But Dad was clearly frustrated. He was like a kid with a shiny new bike that nobody noticed.

Dad told me I could take golf lessons and that Mom could play bridge at the club.

I smiled in response, and Maddy halfheartedly conceded that the club would be a convenient place for her group to play bridge. She made it clear, though, that this was Max's thing. She said she hoped that it would be everything he wanted it to be.

Dad assured her that she was underestimating what it would mean for the family. He winked at me and smiled. As if to say, just between us guys.

Dad did worry a bit about how his recently fired accountant and lawyer would vote. But not to worry: he was assured by Bobby Weil that everything was taken care of. He was, of course, voted in.

A month later, on a snowy day in late February, we three drove out west and visited the club at Dad's urging. Mom and I had been there before, but we had never experienced the grand tour.

Upon entering the grand foyer of the club, we saw blush-colored French stone walls. The floor was slate in a black-and-white checkerboard pattern. The dominant architectural feature was a fireplace that would have been at home in a French chateau. Logs were blazing against the winter cold. Window treatments and upholstery sported a gray-black-neutral palette. The only discordant decorating touch was the overstuffed, seldom-sat-on, and impossible-to-get-up-from-with-any-dignity sofa.

Hanging above that sofa were four tablets inscribed with the names of the past presidents of the club. A scan of the tablets revealed an essential truth about Highland Hills CC. Names like Belmont, Mendelsohn, Arnstein, and Baer appeared with frequency on tablets one and two. Lots of father-son combos. Tablets three and four were inscribed with names like Hirschfelder, Feingold, Taub, and Kleinfeld. To the casual observer, these

surnames are merely Jewish sounding. True enough. But the
fact is that Highland Hills was founded by Jews whose families emigrated from Germany in the last half of the nineteenth
century who were unwelcome at the exclusive gentile clubs. For
many years, those families ran the club and held events like the
annual Easter Egg Hunt and made sure that a giant Christmas
tree occupied pride of place in the club's grand foyer. It was only
after World War II that their Eastern European cousins were
admitted in any meaningful numbers. Eventually, the Easter Egg
Hunt and Christmas tree were abandoned.

We were warmly greeted by the club's all-star manager,
Andrea Marks, who gave us the tour. Andrea had been at HHCC
forever. The members quietly joked that she was abandoned,
like Moses in the bulrushes, on the doorstep of the club as an
infant and never left. After we were shown the various club
venues, all quite elegant, the four of us had lunch in the Tavern.
Hot, buttery, cheesy bagels (for which the club is rightly famous),
matzo ball soup, sandwiches, and salads were followed by chewy
macaroons.

When the check was presented, Andrea took it. "It's our treat
today. But from now on, Mr. Feldman, you'll be signing. And I
have some good news for you about your club number. Most
members have three-digit numbers, so a two-digit number is
much coveted. One of our older members, Mr. Adelstein, died
a few weeks ago, and his number, seventy-five, was available. I
saved it for you."

In one of those memorable cringeworthy moments, Dad
nearly genuflected in front of the club manager. "Thanks, Andrea,"
he said. "I can't tell you how much that means to me. And by the
way, call me Max. Mr. Feldman was my father!"

Mom's eyes were locked shut and she slowly shook her head.

"I'm sorry, but we always address our members using their last names. It's club policy."

"Sure, I get it. Thanks again, Andrea, for everything."

While Dad was reaping financial and social dividends from the company's listing on the NYSE, Mom's reward was the armistice, or at least the cease-fire, on the home front.

• • •

Fratelli Massimo held its first formal board meeting that winter. It was a seven-member board of directors, whose names were listed in the proxy statement published with the rest of our going-public documents, back in October. Even though the Feldman Family Partnership owned a majority of the stock and held four board seats, the SEC required us to appoint at least three outside directors (nonfamily members and no employees of Fratelli Massimo). Gunther suggested that the attorney Harrison Balding would be an appropriate addition. No problem there. Dad countered with Bobby Weil. Gunther nixed that, saying that the SEC frowned on stockbrokers participating on public company boards. Dad then suggested that Ralph Epstein be named. Evidently, Amy's father was already on a couple of the Crown-family-dominated boards in Chicago. Gunther thought that would present problems when I married his daughter in June. Gunther then recommended Peter Kahn and explained that a respected investment banker who knew the retailing world would be welcomed by investors. Dad, still bristling from Kahn's impertinence, argued vehemently against the recommendation, but Gunther prevailed on the merits.

For the final slot Mom nominated one of her friends who went to Smith with her, Julia Symonds, who had recently been named publisher of *Vanity Fair* magazine. When Dad asked why she should be selected, Mom told him that her position at *VF* made her conversant with business issues, particularly those in the fashion business. She was well connected with the brands, both footwear and apparel, and could offer her industry and fashion insights to the newly constituted Fratelli Massimo board.

Dad was no fool. He also knew that she was a leading figure in the Equal Rights Amendment campaign, and a leading feminist who had recently debated Phyllis Schlafly on the issue.

"We don't need her kind on the board," he told her.

"Max, she's an authority on the fashion business, and I insist."

Dad gave in, knowing full well the other prospective board members would welcome Ms. Symonds.

Six of the members attended that winter board meeting. Rand had a conflict, or so he said. We met in the Fratelli Massimo conference room, with Carly taking minutes. Harrison Balding had scripted the meeting, and he distributed a proposed agenda, which our chairman, chief executive officer, and president Max Feldman approved; he asked for comments and suggestions from the members.

Hearing none, he proceeded to the business part of the meeting and reported on recent financial results, which were impressive. Dad knew how to ring the register! A schedule of future meetings, including the annual stockholders' meeting, was circulated and approved. Board committee assignments were also accepted. Audit was chaired by Harrison, and the all-important Compensation Committee by Peter Kahn, which somewhat mollified Dad, since I-Bankers have no problems with seven-figure salaries and bonuses.

For some reason, perhaps to be gallant, Dad felt it necessary to direct some comments to Julia. He cleared his throat and began, "Julia, a lot of this stuff is new to both of us, but Maddy said you're a quick study . . . quicker than me; I know we'll both figure this out as we go along. But I do want to say, on behalf of the board, that we want you to comment whenever you think you have anything worthwhile to say. It will be valuable to get a woman's point of view—particularly from one who knows fashion—as your lovely outfit today certainly illustrates."

Julia responded, "Thank you, Max, but let's not forget Maddy. She's a female of the species, as well, and is second to no one when it comes to style. I'm sure you'll agree."

"I do, of course. Having you both on the board will certainly add a touch of class and will benefit all of us enormously."

Julia did not answer. Maddy grimaced and suggested that after our board lunch, the Feldmans meet in Dad's office.

After the meal, the three "outside directors" departed, and the Feldmans returned to Fratelli Massimo headquarters and went to Dad's office as Mom had requested.

"Well, I thought that went damn well. First time out of the box. Don't you?" Dad stated.

Mom, who was standing with her arms crossed over her chest and her eyes ablaze, stared at him. "Max Feldman, if you continue to patronize and condescend to Julia, she will cut your balls off."

I couldn't believe what I had heard Mom say.

Dad's jaw dropped.

"I won't say it again. Pretend she's a man, if you must, but treat her with the respect she deserves."

"I complimented her, Maddy, on what she was wearing. Since when is that a crime?"

"Did you compliment Peter Kahn on his Armani suit?"

"Now, why would I do that?"

"Treat her with dignity, Max, or you will regret it." Mom held her ground.

"A bit touchy since your boys banded together to make the IPO decision, eh, Maddy?"

Mom went nose to nose with Dad. "Screw you, Max. I accepted that decision and moved on. But at the meeting, you treated Julia like she was your summer intern. Telling her to speak if she had something worthwhile to say? 'Your lovely outfit today . . . you add a touch of class.' Really, Max? If Amy Epstein had witnessed that patronizing performance of yours, she'd bash your head in. Right, Josh?"

"Yeah, Mom's right, Dad. They don't want to be treated that way anymore."

Mom groaned something about the two of us and strode out of the office.

Dad, as usual, needed to have the last word. "Josh, that's a side of your mother you rarely see, but I get my fill, believe me. She can turn on that freezer of hers that she learned from Gunther. I'll be in the penalty box for a long time for that one. She probably only suggested that Julia woman have a place on the board because her boys voted against her last spring. She wants an ally."

"Dad, maybe she wanted an ally, but Julia's an icon on Seventh Avenue. She always has front row seats at the fashion shows. She's constantly quoted in the trade and business press. Julia knows her stuff, and is very well-connected. She could be helpful to you and the company."

"I doubt it. Look, I've got a business to run, let's get to work."

Work is exactly what I did, for most of that spring.

At the office I was knee-deep in paperwork, always with a pencil in one hand and the phone in the other. Monitoring sales and store inventories and harassing vendors for one sin or another was my daily routine.

By far the neatest part of the job was going to New York to visit the brands. We were treated like royalty—even me, a mere assistant buyer. As Dad would say, "He who holds the pencil, holds the power." We would be warmly greeted by salesmen, escorted into their showroom, and given what was called a "style-out," which was a presentation of what the brand thought would be important for the next season. Styles were pulled from shelves and lined up on the table. We all moved them around like chess pieces, sending some back to the shelves, asking for others, and finally settling on a fairly broad assortment of candidates.

If he wasn't there at the beginning of the meeting, Dad would appear as if by magic at just the right moment to kibitz with the bigwigs and saunter over to the table. All eyes and ears turned to him. He would walk around the table assessing the nominees and ask questions. "Why a stacked heel on this one?" or "Why a needle-toe on that one?" "Why taupe and not coffee-color?" and finally "Why's your competition showing stiletto heels and you're not?" Answers were lightning fast, debates would ensue, and modifications were made. Eventually, the line was winnowed down to the dozen or so styles that made the finals. Then quantities, price, and delivery dates were negotiated. At the end of the day, most of the participants were exhausted—and relieved.

And then it was off to one of New York's finest restaurants for drinks and dinner, all paid for by the vendor.

It's impossible to overstate Dad's importance in the process. He was held in the highest regard by both his buyers and the brand representatives. For more than twenty years, he had established himself as a superstar merchant. Everyone paid attention to him, including *Footwear News*, *Women's Wear Daily*, *Vanity Fair* (yes, that *Vanity Fair*), and industry observers and stock analysts who wanted inside information on what brands were hot and which were not. When Dad spoke, everybody listened.

On the plane ride home, he would sometimes sit next to me and give me the inside scoop on brands and representatives. He told me who the straight shooters were, who was a lying bastard, who was a thief, and who could be played, and how.

I gobbled it up. I was getting my postgraduate education from the very best, and I looked forward to more lessons and more responsibility in the years ahead.

• • •

When the Epsteins arrived in June for Amy's graduation—with honors!—from law school and our wedding, Mom and Dad took the opportunity to entertain them and introduce them to our friends. Naturally, the party took place at Highland Hills, with Andrea Marks handling all the details. Of course, Maddy was consulted, but she was happy to relinquish responsibility to Andrea, who demonstrated a phenomenal talent for party planning.

It was a giant success. Adrienne Epstein even whispered to Mom that she wished their country club, Lake Shore, had somebody like Andrea.

Rand made it to town in time for the party and was his charming self. He asked me afterwards, on the way to the car, if while he was at home this would be the right time for him to bring up the matter of his sexual orientation. I begged him not to.

"Christ, Rand, Dad will blow his top. Let's do it another time, and I promise I'll be there for you."

"Guess you're right. Wouldn't want to spoil the weekend or the upcoming wedding."

Mom had insisted that Dad, Rand, and I buy tuxes for the wedding. "You're not going to show up in ghastly rented tuxes that are pasted and paper-clipped together." Rand bought his at Wilkes Bashford in San Francisco. Dad and I went to Bergdorf Goodman and selected identical Armani models. Mom chose an Oscar de la Renta gown. It was elegant and tasteful, and she claimed she didn't want to compete with Amy or her mother. Right!

The wedding's officiant was to be the Epsteins' ultra-Reform rabbi; he was so much in demand for mixed marriages that I asked him if he were still comfortable marrying two Jews. The rabbi laughed, but Amy didn't. She shook her head with her eyes closed and asked if I had brought a filter for my big mouth.

The rehearsal dinner was held at the downtown Ritz-Carlton. I was roasted by my fraternity brothers, one of whom flashed my college transcript on the screen behind the head table and interrogated me about my many D's and F's. "You should have received a ping-pong paddle instead of a diploma!"

When one of Dad's vendor friends took the microphone, he asked me if I had shared with Amy the details of my late-night shenanigans at the Las Vegas Shopping Center convention so many years ago. "You're a legend, Josh!"

My brother stole the show. He had arranged with the Ritz to wheel in a regulation basketball hoop and backboard and challenged me to one last game of Horse. To the merriment of everybody but me, he proceeded to whup me while doing his Marv Albert play-by-play routine. Some things never change.

The wedding itself took place at Lake Shore Country Club in the ballroom overlooking Lake Michigan. It was a mid-June evening, and you could see the sailboats plying the waters and the moon's reflection on the lake. It was a spectacular view. But an even more spectacular sight was Amy. My god, she was beautiful, and she looked like a princess in the gown she had selected at Priscilla of Boston. As she walked down the aisle with her dad, Rand whispered to me, "You are definitely not worthy of her."

I asked, "What would you know about that, playing as you do for the other team?"

He raised his eyebrows. "Touché." We almost laughed.

The Jewish wedding contract—the ketubah—signed, the vows exchanged, the blessings chanted, the ceremonial glass crushed in one go . . . and it was over.

The party that followed was a rousing success even without Andrea Marks' guiding hand.

Amy and I spent our wedding night at the Ambassador East Hotel, then one of Chicago's finest. Scenes had been filmed there for the Alfred Hitchcock movie *North by Northwest* starring Eva Marie Saint and Cary Grant, who had called the valet from a room very much like ours and asked to have his suit "sponged and pressed." I didn't call the valet, as I was too busy frolicking in bed with a passionate and inventive Amy.

We spent the next month traveling in Europe, stopping off first in London, where we stayed at The Stafford London, a small, discreet, and well-located hotel that Rand recommended. Next we visited Paris, and then took a sleeper to Milan. Dad had insisted that we visit the Massimo brothers, who were both gracious and hospitable. Then we went on to Rome.

We returned to St. Louis in mid-July. Amy Epstein Feldman moved into my apartment, as it was more spacious than hers. She didn't have to report to Hotchkiss and Hamilton until after Labor Day, so she used the time to redecorate our place, discarding a lot of my junk and replacing it with admittedly more tasteful furnishings from local furniture stores. I, on the other hand, reported back to work and dug in.

Chapter 18

ON THE TUESDAY AFTER LABOR DAY, AMY AND I GOT UP EARLY, showered, dressed, and got ready for work. We both had coffee and split a bagel for breakfast. We departed for downtown, Amy in her Honda Accord ("Josh, for me a car is merely a means to get from point A to point B"), and me in my 911—a much more pleasant way to get from point A to point B.

While this was Amy's first day at work, I had been at it since early August, taking care of the last of the back-to-school deliveries and prepping for the holidays. Morale at Fratelli Massimo had never been higher. The public offering had been followed by thousands of stock options being distributed to virtually all levels of management, including store managers. Since the stock had gone up from twenty-four dollars on day one to about thirty dollars, all the stock option recipients were in the money. Everybody was bullish about the company and its prospects. The Wall Street firms that followed our stock urged clients to buy.

We weren't alone. These were heydays for many mall retailers. Regional malls had proved to be a boon not only for specialty retailers in shoes and apparel, but also for the department stores that anchored them. The early 1980s marked the beginning of a period of consolidation in the department store industry, with regional chains joining forces and changing ownership. Robert Campeau, a Canadian billionaire, entered the fray and caused great chaos. The fallout from all that corporate juggling was the emergence of two giant department store chains, May

Department Stores, whose main offices were in St. Louis, and
Federated Department Stores, headquartered in Cincinnati.

The disquieting news on the retail front was that fewer shopping centers were opening, as it was becoming increasingly
difficult and expensive to build new ones. Land prices had esca-
lated; most of the great locations had already been developed;
and local politicians who had warmly embraced malls and the
real estate and the tax revenues they generated in the 1960s and
1970s were more reluctant now because of concerns over urban
sprawl and environmental impact. But even more concerning
was that more and more women were working, had less time to
spend in shopping centers, and were beginning to find the mall
inconvenient. Off-the-mall retailers were taking advantage of
this phenomenon and were often opening in areas adjacent to
the regional malls. Discount stores, like Target and TJ Maxx, and
category killers, like Bed Bath & Beyond, were becoming increasingly popular.

Fratelli Massimo was not immediately affected by the slowdown in mall openings because we had operated fewer stores than
our competitors like Nine West and Baker's. We still had room to
grow, particularly in the Northeast and on the West Coast. We could
probably still open twenty to twenty-five stores a year for the next
five years. Wall Street liked this fact and called it our "long runway."
But the acid test for retailers was, and would always be, our performance in existing stores or comparative stores. As long as our older
stores were pumping out gains of 4 to 6 percent, our profits would
increase, and so would our stock price.

While we all felt good about our prospects, Dad was never
satisfied and continued to look for ways to improve results. His
engine idled high, and he always loved making surprise visits to

stores. He wanted to see them as our customers saw them. In his words, "Not some bullshit ambassadorial visit when everything is so perfect."

Midway through September he called me and suggested we surprise our Westroads, St. Louis store on our way home from the office.

"Back-to-school is over. Let's see how they look, and we can shop the Stix, Baer & Fuller department store while we are there."

That shopping center had opened in the fifties. It was quite obsolete, as it had only the one anchor department store and eleven smaller specialty stores. But our sales volume there was terrific, as this antiquated shopping venue was located on the fifty-yard line of St. Louis County at the intersection of two major arterial roads. Location, location, location.

Another reason for its success was Les Portnoy. Les was one of the best salesmen in the country. He had been there since the store opened and had hundreds of loyal customers who always wanted Les to serve them. They would wait for fifteen minutes or more for him, while declining help from other available salesmen. He was a phenomenon. Dad and I always loved watching him work his magic. Rotund and bald, it wasn't his looks that charmed them; it was his gift of gab and his ability to make each customer feel special as he chalked up sale after sale.

On our way to the store, I asked Dad why Les had never been promoted.

He laughed. "We tried promoting him many times, but he always flatly refused. 'Mr. Feldman,' he would say, 'I love selling. And I'm good at it ... make lots of money on commissions. And when I leave the store, I don't have to worry about nothin' like managers do. Just let me sell.' And we did!"

The store itself was in the strip of stores adjacent to the department store. We parked a couple of hundred feet in front of Fratelli Massimo and approached the entrance.

"Goddamn manager hasn't switched our window displays from back-to-school to fall. Penny loafers and lace-up shoes still on the nose, not dressier flats and heels," Dad griped.

And it got worse. He summoned the manager, Norman Hopper. "What's with the windows? And two burned-out lights?"

"I was going to get to it, Mr. Feldman, but my assistant manager called in sick."

"Don't feed me that bullshit. Why weren't you here at 6:00 a.m. switching out the window? Why does it take the CEO of the company to focus your attention on a lightbulb? I bet you have no trouble closing up on time, do you?"

"Well, no. But that's when the mall closes, sir."

"Do you wait on the stragglers or kick 'em out of the store?"

"We wait on them, Mr. Feldman."

"Bet you lock the door at 9:00 p.m., to keep more customers from entering. Norman ... "

This was brutal, and I shuddered. He loved terrorizing store personnel who screwed up. But I also knew that trying to soften Dad's tirade or divert him would make him even angrier. He would take it out on the manager. Then he would accuse me of taking Hopper's side and give it to me with both barrels later. It was a no-win situation. I swore, when I was in charge, I would never do what Dad was doing.

In any event, I slinked off and greeted Les Portnoy. He was busy wrapping up a multiple sale—two shoes and matching handbags.

"Howdy, Mr. Josh."

"Cut out the Mr. Josh crap, Les. I'm not a hairstylist."

"*Excusez-moi*, Josh. How's by you?"

"All good. What's selling? And what do you need?"

Les was encyclopedic. He gave me a rapid rundown of what was hot, what was not, and what we were missing. My pencil was flying.

"Got to run, Mr.—oh, sorry, Josh. Can't keep 'em waiting." Les proceeded to help the next customer in line in his section of the store.

Meanwhile, Dad was still (as he liked to put it) tearing the manager a new asshole. He was pointing out dress code violations. All the men in the store were expected to wear coat and tie. Several were not. There was trash on the floor. Even more serious were the store's lousy accessory sales: handbags, bows, polish, and hosiery. We made a ton of money on those items.

Anyway, Dad had worked himself into a state, so I reminded him that we were planning to visit the Stix department store. He straightened his suit, gave a parting shot to the wounded manager, then embraced Les and smilingly called him a pig for taking all the customers. "If I had one of you in each of our stores, Les, I could retire and turn this business over to Josh."

Stix, the sole anchor department store, had a well-merchandised shoe department with a longtime manager and veteran salespeople, all of whom knew Dad. He and I were greeted politely. Dad spent some time joking around with them, not forgetting, of course, to ask them what was hot and what was not. We weren't sure that they had given us the straight dope, so we'd compare what they said to what Les had said when we got back in the car.

We strolled through the department, inspecting the merchandise and making notes. Watching the customers, we took notice of what they were trying on and purchasing. We observed the fixtures to see what was prominent and eventually made our way out of the department. The manager overtook us and shared a raunchy joke, which made Dad belly laugh, and then we were gone.

On our way home, I asked Dad a question that had long puzzled me. "Stix has big assortments of merchandise, lots more styles than we stock, and many of the same brands we carry—and at the same price. How can we compete?"

"Well for one thing we have our own French Room Originals brand, which beats them on looks and price. But more importantly, we edit our assortments for our customers. Many women work and don't have time to traipse through the department store to search for what they want. And the service in most of the stores stinks." Then he added, none too modestly, "Editing and styling are my strong suits, in case you haven't figured that out, boychik.

"Oh, and Josh, don't forget that next year will be Fratelli Massimo's twenty-fifth anniversary. Hope you have it under control."

There was no way I could have forgotten this. In addition to my other duties, I was the unofficial planner for next year's big celebration. Our directors, and all the execs from the field and home office, as well as their wives, would be invited. "No girlfriends," Dad winked. We couldn't have it at Highland Hills. Andrea told him that there was a rule against business events being held there. Mom offered to help, which was a godsend. So, I lined up the Ritz-Carlton and reserved an early weekend in November 1982.

Dad was hoping that the Massimo brothers would attend. He called them and sent an invitation, but they declined. Both were in their seventies and were reluctant to make the trip from Italy. They sent Dad a lovely letter recalling their first encounter in 1950. They thanked him for jump-starting their growth and for naming the company after them, and they congratulated him on his many successes. They wished him and the company a prosperous future.

To commemorate the anniversary, they sent Mom and Dad a gorgeous Florentine sculpture crafted from Carrara marble. Mom fell in love with it and made sure it was prominently displayed in their home. I always saw it as a testament to Dad's entrepreneurship, his skill in identifying a business opportunity, and his uncanny ability to maintain warm relationships with his suppliers.

Thank God the anniversary celebration was scheduled for November and not October. I didn't know it at the time, of course, but the St. Louis Cardinals, after a fourteen-year hiatus, would be in the World Series that month, and the city, hotels, and airport were a zoo. Dad called some of Fratelli Massimo's important suppliers, the advertising manager of the *St. Louis Post-Dispatch*, and the always reliable Bobby Weil and managed to score eight box seat tickets to each of the playoff and World Series games. Mom expressed no interest in going, but after Dad virtually got on his knees and begged, she deigned to attend the seventh and deciding game of the series. Even Gunther called to congratulate Max on the Cards' victory.

While I was focused on my career and planning the party, Amy was making progress in her own career as well. She was assigned to the corporate law practice at H&H and usually worked late—and sometimes on weekends. We'd often go out to eat, and St. Louis gave us lots of options.

I had already figured out that Amy's legal skills far outpaced her culinary skills. I hadn't given it much thought. Mom depended on Nora or carryout, but I kinda figured that Amy would know how to cook. I kinda figured wrong. I didn't really mind that much.

"Amy, the warranty on the stove will expire before you ever turn it on."

"Very funny," she said, shooting me the bird. "You try working all day and cooking when you get home."

Maybe she would try to cook when we had kids. But that was in the future. We wanted to travel, have some alone time together, and party with our friends and coworkers. Kids were a nonstarter for a while, at least. And we both were anxious to succeed at the office.

Amy was determined to one day be named a partner at H&H. Corporate law paid the bills, and it was important for her to develop relationships with existing clients and perhaps bring in some new business. This would require not only expert legal work, but also social skills—both of which Amy had in abundance. She was already tagging along with senior partners when celebrating with clients over a deal's conclusion. While Amy was home most nights for a late carryout meal, she was starting to do a bit of business entertaining herself. Corporate types loved telling war stories, particularly when they won the war, and Amy was a beautiful and attentive companion. She joined the Development Board of St. Louis Children's Hospital, with some of the city's up-and-coming leaders.

All this was a reminder of her warning that she didn't intend to be another Maddy.

The early years of our marriage were blissful. Both of us were making progress in our careers. Amy was given more and more responsibility at H&H. I was learning a great deal about the shoe business.

On a weekend day, Amy suggested we take a ride in the Porsche. When I got into the car, I noticed that one of the tiny rear seats was occupied by what appeared to be a rather large doll with a T-shirt on. I looked closely at the T-shirt, which read "6 months to go, Slugger" in teeny, tiny letters. But I got the message!

It didn't come as a complete surprise. We enjoyed being with each other, and there was no slowdown in the intimacies that we shared, both protected and sometimes spontaneously unprotected.

I leaned over and passionately kissed the mother-to-be, gouging a bruise in my thigh from the goddamn parking brake. But I was feeling no pain.

Chapter 19

As happy as our personal life was with news of the baby coming, sometime in the mid-1980s I started to notice some adverse trends in the shoe business. It wasn't that business turned south, exactly. Sales and profits were still strong, but some clouds began scudding across the sunny skies we had been enjoying for so many years. Even our slowing expansion didn't hurt us, as our older stores were doing well, and we were still able to open a dozen or so stores a year. Yet there was a disquieting development.

One day I happened to get to work early, because I was now assistant buyer for our overseas-sourced footwear, and I wanted to get a look at the overnight telexes from Asia. I was wandering around my office thumbing through them when I peered out the window onto the Washington Avenue bus stop directly below. Most of our clerical staff disembarked there. I noticed that every single woman was carrying a plastic bag in addition to her handbag. And every single woman was wearing athletic shoes. The plastic bags must have contained the dressy shoes they would wear at the office.

When my secretary, Sandy, got to her desk, I watched her change her shoes from athletic to dress.

"And why are you doing that, Sandy?" I asked.

"Well, to be honest, Josh, the dress shoes we're expected to wear in the office are beasts to wear all day, so I wear Nikes whenever I can. Is that a problem?"

"No, no, no. Just curious, thanks."

That really piqued my curiosity. When I ran into Carly later that day, I asked her about it. And she confirmed what Sandy had told me.

Of course, I knew that athletic footwear was becoming increasingly popular, no doubt about it. But having grown up with Maddy and the way she dressed, and living with Amy, who drove to work wearing dressy flats or mid-heel pumps, I was surprised that some working women actually preferred Nikes and Reeboks to traditional leather footwear when they had the choice. Though I shouldn't have been.

A couple of weeks later the gloriously and prominently pregnant Amy and I were having Sunday night "kitchen supper" with my parents.

I related the observation and conversations about athletic footwear for women.

Maddy was incredulous. "How does a mature woman wear tennis shoes except when she's playing tennis or cleaning out the garage?" What my mom knew about cleaning out a garage was a mystery to me. She merely called a local handyman and went back to reading or playing bridge.

"Well, Maddy," Amy jumped in, "I've noticed the same thing at H&H. The associates and higher-ups still wear leather shoes to and from work, and certainly at the office, but most of the paralegals and others do exactly what Josh described."

I said to Dad, "That's an interesting trend, isn't it?"

"Yes, if it's a trend and not a fad," he replied, "which I happen to believe it is. These looks come and go. Women loved Candie's flats a few years ago, and they're deader than a doornail now."

"Maybe so, but Rand tells me that some of the offices in California have instituted what they call casual Fridays, and staff can wear athletic shoes and comfortable casual clothes, except for jeans and shorts."

The mere mention of my brother's name was greeted like an audit request from the IRS.

"Oh," Dad said, "your brother is an expert on fashion in the workplace now? How nice. Well, maybe anything goes in the circles he runs in. Surprised his boyfriends don't run around in jockstraps in San Francisco."

"Max, stop it this instant," Mom barked. "Rand is happy in his life. The more you mock him and denigrate him, the worse you look, and the more distant from our family he will become. So, stop it!"

I jumped in. "Dad, he's your own flesh and blood, not some store manager you can terrorize and demean. Where's your conscience?"

"That's not the question—it's where his prick is these days."

Mom piled on. "He's your son, Max. Have the decency to respect him, or at least accept him. For the sake of the family."

Rand had talked to the three of us about his sexual orientation the Sunday night of Fratelli Massimo's twenty-fifth anniversary weekend. All the guests had cleared out and the Feldmans (minus Amy, who had a late-night work session at the office) were sitting around this same kitchen table, reliving the weekend.

Rand tilted back in his chair and coolly announced, "Well, no time like the present. Josh knows, and Mom suspects it, but I want you all to know that I am gay. I am actually in a relationship with Todd Barker, who is a bartender in the

Tenderloin district. I am also quite happy in this life, and I hope you're cool with it."

Mom's eyes watered as she absorbed the news. She rose and squeezed Rand, telling him how much she loved him and didn't care a bit, that she just wanted him to be happy.

She sniffled. "I had my suspicions, as you said. You don't grow up in Manhattan without a sixth sense about these things, but I'm glad you revealed this to us, darling; it's a weight off your shoulders."

"And it will make him even lighter on his feet!" Dad shouted. "A couple more revelations and he'll be able to fly home to San Francisco without a plane."

Rand was prepared for Dad's reaction. "Look, Dad, I'm sorry I'm disappointing you, but this is a biological fact. I am wired this way, and I've known it without knowing it since high school. I've dated girls, women, but it doesn't work for me or them. It's just this way."

"It's San Francisco, isn't it? The epicenter of that lifestyle. Maybe you should move back here and get yourself straightened out. We know the top docs here at Wash U."

"Dad, it won't work, and I'm not moving back. I can't live my life here. It's not just St. Louis, but almost all of flyover country. There's an intolerance for gays. There's open acceptance of us in many coastal cities. But returning home to St. Louis is impossible."

"Well, I've just lost a son. If Sy were alive, he'd light a Yahrzeit candle."

"No, he wouldn't, Dad," I said. "He would be sad. He would know that struggles lie ahead for Rand, but he wouldn't mourn his loss. He's still very much alive, and my very own Rand the Man."

"Well, I've got one son left, thank God. Though he's a bit naïve. Tell me, Josh, how does it feel getting whipped in basketball by a faygeleh?"

"The same as it felt when we were both kids. Dad, how can you vilify and ostracize your own son? You're in the fashion business. Half the people we deal with are gay."

"No son of Max Feldman is queer. End of story. He's dead to me."

"I was never alive to you, Max. Even when you thought I was hetero. You treated me like crap from day one. I wouldn't play your game—worshiping the great merchant, Max Feldman. All you ever cared about was yourself. Your opinion means nothing to me. Nothing!"

Dad bounded up the stairs to bed.

Mom put her arms around Rand and said, "He won't come around, Rand, no matter what we say. It breaks my heart."

"Mom's right," I told him. "We love you dearly, Rand the Man, and will always be on your side."

Rand visited us rarely, coming in for important Fratelli Massimo board and stockholder meetings, and for a housewarming party. He stayed with Mom and Dad on only that occasion, and even that ended in disaster.

Mom, Amy, and I visited with him in California, and he and Todd joined us on a European trip, and again, on a trip to Asia. But I saw far too little of Rand the Man, except when I was in the Bay Area.

• • •

A couple of months after the showdown with Rand, Dad called me into his office.

"I know you're busy and trying to squeeze in as much travel as you can before the baby comes, but something's come up and I wanted to give you a heads-up."

Dad was right about the travel part. The baby was due in a couple months, and I was planning to go with the buyers to Hong Kong and Seoul, Korea, the following week to talk to our shoe resources and place some orders for spring.

"What's up?"

"Well, big news. Your mom and I have decided to move."

"Wow, that's great. I always wondered why you stayed in Claverach, particularly after we went public. You can afford virtually any house in St. Louis."

"You're right, but your mom wouldn't consider anything in Ladue." Ladue was the wealthiest suburb in St. Louis; most of the big estates were there. "'Won't be joining a garden club, sweetheart,' she said. But a house came on the market in Brentmoor Park in Clayton, just across Wydown Boulevard from where we live now. So it's even closer to Wash U, and she finally relented."

Dad gave me a copy of the listing:

73 Brentmoor Park represents a rare opportunity to own one of the impressive estates in St. Louis. This Frederick Dunn home is a neoclassical regency experience with one-of-a-kind features throughout. The Sir John Soane–inspired residence, guided by the bi-symmetrical philosophy, spans 13,000 square feet and includes 5 bedrooms, 8 bathrooms, a world-class wine cellar...

"Sounds perfect, Dad. Go for it."

"Well, we already have, despite some of your mom's reservations. 'A bit grand, don't you think, dear?'" he imitated Mom. "I reminded her that her place on Fifth Avenue was rather grand and it never seemed to bother her. Eventually, I prevailed. We close in about a month."

"Congratulations. I'll miss Claverach, but this move seems terrific to me." I made a move to leave, but Dad motioned me to stay.

"Your mom and I thought you and Amy, with a baby on the way, might want to consider buying Claverach."

"Huh. Interesting, but I've got to talk to Amy about it."

"Of course." He then named the asking price. "And a big plus is that neither of us will have to pay a commission."

"Makes sense, and I appreciate the proposal, but Amy needs to weigh in."

"Don't wait too long, but let me know when you know."

On the way down in the elevator, I thought about what my parents were about to do. It did make sense—they could afford it, and Dad was doing more entertaining now in his public role. But I also knew that things weren't good between them. The going-public drama and Rand's revelations had probably left some scars, and they likely wanted the additional space and personal privacy that Brentmoor Park would afford them. I wondered whether they would even sleep together. Or stay together. I supposed they would, or why buy a monster house?

When I got back to my office, I placed a WATS call to the pompous Mr. Raymond Whitaker at Brown Brothers, where my stake from the public offering was held—and growing nicely. I had not taken a dime from it since I repaid Dad's loan for Amy's engagement ring, except for the brand-new Irish Green Porsche 911 Targa I had bought several years ago.

I explained to Raymond what I might need if we decided to purchase Claverach, and he said it was no problem. But he strongly advised me to call Gunther before doing anything. I would need his advice, not his permission.

So I called Gunther, elbowed my way through his phalanx of secretarial protectors, and finally got my grandfather on the line.

When I explained the opportunity and Raymond's suggestion to me, he grunted and replied, "Josh, first of all, I'm very happy for you and Amy. I'm a bit alarmed at the prospect of being a great-grandfather, but I look forward to having a new member of the family and wish you both the best."

"Thanks, Gunther, I'll tell Amy. What's the deal about the money?"

"Well, back when you announced your engagement to Amy, you'll recall that I advised both of you to get prenuptial agreements, to protect the assets you both brought into the marriage. But like lots of starry-eyed couples—and you were both starry-eyed—you refused."

"That's old news."

"Indeed. But Raymond was right in suggesting that you call me. If you use some of your trust for your and Amy's mutual benefit, such as purchasing a house, it can cause a big legal battle in the unlikely event that you two divorce. The whole corpus of the trust can become marital property and in some cases be split in two. I assume you want to avoid such an eventuality?"

"Yes, but we're perfectly happy, and I am not sure why you have to cast a shadow over this whole situation," I said.

"Casting shadows, my boy, is what lawyers do for a living. Let's just say, I want you to consider an alternative method of financing Claverach if you choose to go that route, rather than taking money from your trust.

"I'm sure your mother would have no objection to loaning you, not you and Amy, but you alone, the full amount of the purchase price of the house. The loan would be set up in such a way that you'd pay principal and a nominal amount of interest monthly over the term of the loan. I might add that you would write the monthly payment checks and property taxes out of your own checking account, not that of the trust account. By structuring it that way, you would be protecting your multimillion-dollar trust. How does that sound?"

"Guntheresque, if you ask me."

"I'm flattered. Think about it."

As I hung up, I remembered something Gunther had once told me. "In the eyes of the courts and the IRS, it is not so much what you do—it's rather the form in which you do it. Take, for example, the reasons we create trusts, rather than make outright gifts."

Then I thought back to the time I watched him play blackjack in Vegas. He always made the right move, was super cautious, robot-like, and was consistently the smartest guy at the table.

After dinner that night, I broke the news about the house to Amy.

"Well," she said, "we will probably have to move from this apartment when the baby is two or so, and certainly if we have another. And I love living in Clayton. The house is great, but needs serious remodeling. Your parents have barely touched it.

Oh, and let me ask you this: Does the house have mostly happy memories for you, or do you have any negative feelings about the place?"

"Certainly, it hasn't been all peaches and cream, particularly during the past few years. But for the most part, I love the place."

"And the price?" she asked.

"Seems fair."

"And how will we go about paying for it, and also the remodeling? Using your trust?"

"Ah, well, no," I said. "I thought I could just borrow the down payment from Maddy, and we could make the mortgage payments out of my salary."

"You thought? Look, big shot, I happen to practice the law. This method of financing wouldn't have anything to do with protecting your trust, would it?"

"I guess it might have that ancillary effect."

"You guess it might have that ancillary effect? How clever of you! And from somebody who couldn't make heads or tails of the lease on our apartment! You don't fool me, mister; this has Gunther's fingerprints all over it."

"Well, Raymond at BBH suggested I call him, so we bounced around a bunch of ideas."

"You bounced around a bunch of ideas, did you? I wish I had a tape recording of your contributions to that back-and-forth. You are such a terrible liar, my dear; don't ever, ever lie to me. I don't care how brilliant your grandfather is, I'll break into that trust and you'll be lucky to get half! Are we clear?"

She went on, "And Josh, I repeat: Don't ever lie to me, by omission or commission, or in your sleep, or in your brain. I realize this is not an earthshaking deception, and if you were my client, I would have advised you do exactly what Gunther recommended.

"But I am warning you. Do not lie or deceive me. I won't tolerate it. You showed me that letter that Sy wrote you, and he said there's a bit of larceny in every retailer. I'm no virgin when it comes to 'manipulating' a legal matter to my client's advantage, but in this house, there'll be no second chances. No matter what. The truth."

"God, OK. Why are you making such a big deal out of this?" She was totally overreacting.

"I'll give you one good reason—I don't trust your father. He plays fast and loose with the truth, and I would bet a lot of money that he cheats on Maddy. I hear stuff from Jenn Weil and from some of the lawyers in the firm. And yes, I know about how he connived with Jenn's dad to confront Maddy with the IPO proposal on that Sunday. You didn't share that minor detail with me—that's lying by omission. You've been warned, mister. Are we clear?" With eyes flashing and her lips pursed, my wife shot me a very serious look.

"Crystal. Jesus, I promise. Can we please return to the issue of the house?"

"Yes, buy the house! And yes, borrow the down payment from the marvelous Maddy, and protect that trust of yours to make Prince Gunther happy."

I wasn't sure what had gotten into Amy. Maybe it was her hormones because she was pregnant, but she'd really gone over the top. *I'm not at all like my father*, I thought.

• • •

A week later, I was sitting in the business-class section of a ten-hour Cathay Pacific flight from Hong Kong to San Francisco, which, with any luck, would allow me to make my connection to St. Louis. The buyers I reported to had stayed an extra day in Hong Kong. This meant I had time to myself, and I spent it reviewing our hectic business itinerary and the rigorous negotiations we had with our Asian resources.

Doing business in Asia was unlike anything we did in New York. We had our choice of styles when we bought domestically. Overseas, we had to create our own styles, often copied from branded winners.

Negotiations were tense. Our Chinese vendors were great businessmen. Fortunately, we had an agent who spoke their language. Once we agreed on the sample, we would go back and forth over materials, workmanship, and, of course, price. They lied and I lied. They claimed the price we were getting was the "most preferred." I told them that we'd never paid that much for the shoe. We quibbled over pennies, delivery dates, and quantities. But the results were worth it. We might, for example, "create" a Capezio ballet slipper that resembled the original for twelve dollars, versus the twenty-four we would pay in New York for the genuine version. The customer could rarely tell the difference. This gave us lots of room to promote the shoe at very attractive prices. Everybody was happy. There were benefits for our supplier, our accountant, and our customer.

I got home barely in time to make my appearance at Amy's baby shower at Highland Hills. Her friend Jenn Weil Katzenberg, who was also pregnant, hosted it. I was told to stay in the foyer of the club until I was summoned. As I waited, I idly looked over the plaque listing current officers and board members of the club, and I spotted something surprising.

At that moment Dad walked in, greeted the receptionist, and noticed me standing by the plaque.

"Welcome home, Josh. How was the trip?"

"Mission accomplished: great pricing and 120 days out. I just noticed you're a board member of the club, and in charge of Finance. What gives?"

"Oh, it's really nothing. I'm helping them with the numbers."

"That's quite an honor for a new member."

"I guess. They needed someone who's used to running a large organization, and I suppose I filled the bill."

Dad was being uncharacteristically modest. I happened to know from Mom, who'd heard it at the bridge table, that the club had big plans for Dad. It seems that snagging a CEO of a public company for the club was quite a coup. Lots of successful people—lawyers, doctors, CPAs, family-business owners, and so on—were members. But there were not a lot of CEOs of New York Stock Exchange–listed companies at Highland Hills. "Big plans" could mean only one thing. One day, Omaha-born and -bred Max Feldman might very well find himself president of the club.

Mom wasn't enthusiastic about the prospect. "Your father is going to expect me to play the role of the First Lady of Highland Hills Country Club. And I will flat-out refuse. I don't want any part of this. He should do what he wants—play golf, gin rummy, schmooze with the boys, whatever. And if he wants to lead this club, that's fine. But I shall watch from the sidelines. I made that perfectly clear to him. He doesn't believe me, naturally, because it's always about Max and what he wants. But not this time. This is his baby!"

I had been stunned back when Dad implied Mom was a hypocrite by pretending to be merely a mature student while sporting thousand-dollar handbags or trying to discourage Dad from buying a grand house (which, he constantly reminded me, was no grander than the apartment she grew up in). But I was not so surprised when Mom vented about Dad. She'd been so disdainful of him, despite his professional and personal successes. So I butted in.

"You were born into that world, Mom. But he's earned it. Don't you think he deserves a little support from you? Don't begrudge him that. Look what he's achieved. I'm proud of him."

"Yes, Josh, he's a great merchant and retailer, and he's earned those honors—if that's what he thinks they are. But your dad is consumed with glorifying himself, and I won't play cheerleader for the ego of Max Feldman! Let others do it."

Dad and I were at last invited to enter the party room for the baby shower. There was a lot of girl talk, oceans of wrapping paper, yards of blue, yellow, and pink ribbon, tasteful gift boxes, oohs and ahhs exclaimed, and a careful recording of who belonged to which gift. My beloved Amy was surrounded by her friends and some colleagues from Hotchkiss and Hamilton. All were beautifully dressed and were scented like the fragrance counter at Neiman Marcus. There was a mountain of gifts on the table in front of Amy. Maddy was scurrying around, making sure the gift list was accurate and collecting cards off the packages to double-check. Adrienne Epstein, Amy's mom, was assisting her. The chatter in the room was almost deafening.

Dad and I mingled with the guests and joked about needing a semitrailer truck to haul off the loot. Then I noticed that Andrea Marks, the club manager, was standing by quietly to make sure all was in order.

All was in order, at least, in the party room.

Chapter 20

With a month to go before the baby's due date, Amy took maternity leave at H&H. She might have worked a bit longer, but she wanted to get started remodeling and redecorating Claverach, while at the same time making necessary changes in our apartment for the baby. The latter was simple: converting our small extra bedroom into something functional for the baby. The room saw a splash of yellow paint. We added an array of baby furniture and apparatuses—even blackout curtains. The furniture and paraphernalia would eventually be moved to Claverach.

Remodeling Claverach would be a much grander project. Amy and I agreed that much needed to be done, so she hired a highly recommended decorator to help. Amy had coffee with Maddy and explained the project to her, hoping that Mom would be OK with its scope and the frequent visits it would require during the next several months. Mom was cool with it, and she conceded that remodeling was long overdue.

I paid scant attention to the wallpaper samples, fabric and carpet swatches, and dozens of pages torn out of *Architectural Digest*. I had lots of work to finish before year-end and before the baby was due. I knew that once that happened, it would be chaotic around our place and I'd be lucky to have time to make it to the office.

On December 16, 1986, little seven-pound, six-ounce Allison Lauren Feldman was born at St. John's Mercy Hospital in St. Louis. We told Mom that she was named after her mother, Alice, and she was delighted, as was Gunther.

Allison was a beauty, at least to my untrained and biased eye. Each of the grandmothers seconded the motion. My mother-in-law thought she resembled Amy as a baby, and Maddy thought she looked like infant Rand. I could see no resemblance to anybody. I guess it's a skill grandmothers have, or think they have.

The granddads were great. Dad held little Allison and cooed something about being a future Fratelli Massimo customer. My father-in-law, Ralph, took his turn with her and mentioned how fortunate that her birth date allowed us to claim her as a tax exemption for 1986.

Dad passed out illegally imported Cuban cigars, a gift from Bobby Weil, and the secretaries on my floor arranged for a sheet cake celebrating the occasion. I was blessed to have a girl, they assured me, as boys were so much more trouble.

Rand was tied up with end-of-year stuff at the ad agency he was working for in San Francisco, but promised to fly in when he could. As a token gift he sent Allison a San Francisco Giants teddy bear. Dad gnashed his teeth, as Rand knew he would.

Gunther came through in typical fashion. He flew in for a few days with plans to travel to Las Vegas for the remainder of the holidays. He presented Allison, or rather Amy and me, with a sizeable check in Allison's name, or rather in Allison's just-created trust account at Brown Brothers. Ever the sentimental so-and-so, he handed me a manila envelope and asked me to read the enclosed letter, sign the trust documents, and forward the material to him.

While everybody's attention was focused on Allison, I escaped to our bedroom to read the letter and follow Gunther's instructions.

Dear Joshua,

I am overjoyed to join the ranks of great-grandfathers. I can't wait to lay my eyes on Allison and am thrilled and grateful that she was named after my Alice. By all accounts, she's precious. Her birth, of course, evokes memories of the first days following your mother's birth so many years ago. Alice and I were never happier. I was just starting my legal career and Alice was teaching third grade in one of New York's public schools. We had a tiny apartment in Chelsea.

You're probably unaware of this, but Madeline was in and out of the hospital when she was an infant. One medical problem after another, mostly with her lungs, but the little fighter pulled through, to our great relief. It redoubled our commitment to protect her to the extent parents can shield their child from life's vicissitudes. If anything, these trials created an even tighter bond—with each other, and with Madeline. You and Amy will undoubtedly feel that same protective instinct for Allison—although I certainly hope you avoid the hospital episodes.

To lay the groundwork for her financial well-being, I have established the enclosed trust for Allison's benefit. Hopefully it will grow over time and insulate her from some of life's financial challenges. A substantial trust will also enable her to choose a career path without being overly concerned with remuneration. She can be a poet, a teacher, a social worker, or anything that engages her. She will, of course, face numerous trials that can't be solved with money. The usual things— health issues, relationships, academic hurdles, social diffi- culties, dealing with you and Amy through her adolescent years, etc.

And, of great importance, there will be the issue of finding the right partner to spend her life with. Sometimes that choice can be quite problematic and a situation over which you will discover you have little control. But in the event of a dubious choice on her part, you will find that you still retain parental obligations to protect her as best you can from the pains of an unfortunate union.

Please forgive me for my little sermon. As my law partners can attest, I am increasingly given to pontificating as I draw upon my many experiences both professional and personal. It's one of the few privileges of the elderly!

With that, let me wish you, Amy, and Allison the best and happiest of lives.

Your loving grandfather,
Gunther

Listening to her squalling in the living room, it was impossible to envision Allison passing through the stages Gunther had written about. His not-too-subtle allusion to the perils of Allison's future marriage partner were not lost on me. He had done all he could to shield Mom from Dad's dark side. Yes, he'd secured her bank account, but he could do nothing to protect her from Max's narcissism or cruelty.

I filed Gunther's letter with Sy's. Both warning me about Max.

It's well-known that nothing prepares a father for a new baby. Correct, at least in my case. I was besotted with little Allison. I couldn't wait to hold her (careful with her neck!). And I couldn't get enough of that indescribable infant's skin (not against your unshaven face!). I was mesmerized by those blue eyes that she deigned to open from time to time (most babies' eyes are blue but may change over time, I was told).

Of course, there were the downsides: nighttime feedings, incessant crying, and horrible diapers—all predictable, but a shock to the system nonetheless. Amy's mom, Adrienne, stayed with us in our tiny apartment, which helped enormously. She had this talent for seemingly twirling and simultaneously wrapping the baby so snuggly in blankets that the baby almost, almost smiled. I myself never quite got the hang of it.

Mom played the whole situation like a Stradivarius. She gave Adrienne precedence, permitting herself only brief visits while Amy's mom was still there. Once she left, immediately after Christmas, Maddy became a household fixture. She was smitten with Allison. "A girl in the family, finally!" She offered Nora's services, should they be necessary, and as a Chanukah gift, promised to pay for a nighttime nanny once the holidays were over.

Althea Thompson saved the day. With night sessions taken care of, Amy's equanimity returned. I, too, could sleep through the night and remained totally unaware of Allison's screaming and crying. I simply didn't hear it.

Things began to settle down after New Year's. I spent my days at the office, which seemed serene compared to the confusion of the previous few weeks of brand-new parenthood. Amy negotiated her way around the apartment and found her footing with Allison. She was anxious to get back to work, and H&H agreed on an early January date. We asked Althea if she wanted to be our daytime nanny, once the nighttime horrors ended. She agreed, which made our life manageable.

Amy continued her work on Claverach with her decorator. She also worked on getting her figure back. She succeeded in both.

Amy's tawny brown hair had looked a bit like Farrah Fawcett's before she switched to a pageboy style. She always worried about her weight and backside, which I frankly had found fetching, ever since college days.

The evening before she went back to work, Amy and I sat down to a quiet dinner after Allison was down for the night.

"Josh, we are blessed—the baby, the house, and our little family."

"I agree," I said. "You've done most of the heavy lifting and are a star. I love you."

"Thanks. I won't argue with the heavy lifting part, and I love you too. But I want to discuss how we go forward. I met with one of the senior partners at the firm. He encouraged me to aim for partnership, and I'm determined to reach that goal."

"That's great."

"Josh, that will mean long hours, entertaining clients and potential clients, and weekends at the office. Maybe even some travel. Some off-site get togethers. I'm telling you all this because you need to prepare yourself for doing a bit more of the heavy lifting at home. Althea will be here—and you can depend on her— but I will be absent from time to time, so you're going to be filling in with daddy duty." She took a deep breath and continued.

"When you were a child, Maddy and Nora saw to it that you and then Rand were well cared for and that the house ran like a clock. Your father was off doing his thing at Fratelli Massimo. That worked in your household, but my professional aspirations make that formula unworkable. So, prepare yourself for some domestic chores when I'm not available or flattened by my work-load and Althea is not here. Are you OK with that?"

"Sure," I answered.

"And one more thing. I may not be there to cushion every reversal with your father. I will have my own reversals and my own setbacks at work. Infighting at the higher reaches of a law firm is every bit as treacherous and consuming as it is at Fratelli Massimo, so there will be times when you'll have to duke it out with Max without me in your corner. Don't get me wrong, I'll always support you, but we both know what your father is capable of—and you've signed up to do battle with him. I'll have my own battles to fight."

Amy's declaration of independence caught me off guard. But I couldn't really argue with her. She deserved her shot at partnership. And I was determined to succeed Dad. I had come to rely on her advice, which she would probably still dispense, but I would now seek it more sparingly. She had warned me again and again about my father. While I agreed with her assessment, I could see both sides of him. He was both the brilliant merchant/retailer and the glory-seeking, self-made man who would stop at nothing to satisfy his own appetites. I was betting that his love for me, his partnership with me, and my growing prowess as a retailer would carry the day.

Chapter 21

WHILE THINGS WERE RUNNING SMOOTHLY AT HOME, THEY WERE bubbling up at the office. Our chief financial officer, Walter Benning, was concerned with the 1986 financial results. Preliminary numbers indicated that while comparative stores sales were up low single digits, our profits would fail to meet Wall Street expectations. Dad asked me to join the two of them as they went over the numbers.

In-season promotional markdowns were the culprit. Tepid demand for our merchandise had led to the predictable promotional pricing. Dad, who mostly paid attention to the sales line, was fuming, as he had hinted to Wall Street analysts that the profit picture would be brighter than Walter was projecting. Dad declared Walter's estimates "dead on arrival" and ordered him to scrounge around and find some more profit dollars ASAP.

A clearly shaken Walter nodded his acquiescence and departed.

A couple of days later, Dad called me to say that Walter had dug up the four cents per share we needed to hit Wall Street estimates. To me, that seemed reasonable enough. We were a large company, and finding several hundred thousand dollars of profit didn't seem out of order.

"That's what you pay that guy to do," was Dad's reaction.

But that didn't end the matter.

While Fratelli Massimo hit Wall Street's earnings per share number to the penny, analysts were disappointed, since we usually beat the number by a nickel or so. The disappointing earnings resulted in the stock trading down a few dollars. Then the calls from analysts started.

I sat in Dad's office as he was politely grilled, but grilled he was. After all, Fratelli Massimo had never disappointed Wall Street, so the analysts were surprised, and they hated surprises—unless they were positive surprises.

Dad talked his way through the blizzard of questions and seemed credible enough to me. The analysts were careful not to actually criticize him or the company, because they often represented firms that wanted to do business with us, such as debt offerings or secondary stock deals. They were careful, but not slavishly so.

When it was all over, Dad switched off the speaker.

"Those sons of bitches—they're like spoiled brats. Nothing's ever good enough for them. Glad we're done with that, and hope it never happens again, at least on my watch."

At the time we went public, Dad had been rather dismissive of analysts and their probing. Not so fast, Dad.

It took another few weeks for the other shoe to drop. At our board meeting, when it came time for the audit committee report, Harrison Balding did the routine stuff and then mentioned that the auditors noted that the company had deferred some markdowns into the year 1987, which had the effect of increasing profits in 1986.

The very astute Julia Symonds, sensing Dad's discomfort, smiled and asked him and Walter Benning why the markdowns had been delayed. "Isn't it better to take the write-down on a timelier basis even if it means reporting weaker profits?" she declared with her eyebrows raised.

"What we did, Julia, is customary," Dad patiently answered after a brief hesitation. "As you know, our fiscal year ends on January thirty-first, but we still have markdown merchandise in February, so we moved the markdown write-off to the February sales period, which Walter indicated was an acceptable accounting practice. Walter?"

"It is, indeed," said Walter, who had been invited to attend the meeting for this very reason.

"Now, if there are no more—" Dad started.

Julia, with a lips-only smile, interrupted. "Then why have you not done that in the past? The auditors indicate that this is a change in practice—one that benefits 1986, but penalizes 1987."

Dad was doing his best to keep himself under control. Mom had warned him about Julia, and he wished to retain his testicles. I was praying he wouldn't patronize her.

After counting to ten, a prickly but cautious Dad offered this: "Julia, that's a good question. In the past, we've tried to be ultra, ultraconservative with our inventory evaluation. I gave permission to Walter to loosen up a bit this year, given the situation on the ground."

Please, please, I prayed to God again: Julia, don't ask for a description of the "situation on the ground."

"Max," Julia continued in her district attorney mode, "What exactly was this 'situation on the ground'?"

Cornered, especially with Walter Benning at the table, Dad had to fess up. "Well, Julia, a preliminary estimate of the quarter's earnings revealed a slight, very slight, profit shortfall. Wall Street doesn't take kindly to those misses. So Walter, to his credit, dug deeper and found a legitimate source of more profits that was wholly consistent with good accounting practices."

Peter Kahn piled on, "But Max, aren't you setting a dangerous precedent by borrowing from next year's profits to hit this year's target?"

Dad was embattled, so he called on his deep reservoir of bravado to save the day. "You made a great point, Peter, and I know how this looks, but I have never, in the nearly thirty years of our company's existence, failed to deliver results. Nobody at this table should doubt that 1987 will be a great year and this minor blip that Julia correctly noted will be long forgotten!"

Some grumbling ensued, along with awkward body language, chair squeaking, and eye rolls, but a crisis was averted.

After all the board members exited the meeting room, Dad turned to me and bellowed, "What a cunt! She's Maddy's revenge, I swear to God."

I couldn't help but recall Sy's admonition that there's a bit of larceny in every retailer. I'm pretty sure I would have done the same thing Dad did. The retail worth of fashion inventory is hard to evaluate. And the value of that inventory has a huge impact on profits. Will that clearance shoe sell at $22.99 or $18.99? It's a judgment call. We're not sure, and the accountants are clueless. There's always a margin for error. We retailers are famous for taking advantage of that.

As I left, Rand stopped me in the hallway, and said, "Not only is Dad a creative merchant, but he's also a creative bookkeeper!"

"Rand, honestly, these are judgment calls."

"And who's the judge? The guy who hates his own son? The guy who covets the spotlight but can't stand the heat? The old man wanted to go public—well, his wish came true. Let's see how he deals with public criticism."

"I have enough faith in Dad's merchant skills to right the ship this time. But there will be a next time, and a time after that. One of these days, he'll have to face the music."

Dad, still smarting from that February board of directors' meeting, convened a come-to-Jesus reunion of all the shoe merchandise department executives in the company's classroom.

After telling the merchants that they had screwed up, given away merchandise, and failed to find fashion winners, he cited chapter and verse of the horrors of in-season promotions. Calling it an addiction, which required deeper and deeper discounts to satisfy the customers, he focused on the Capezio knockoff situation as an example.

The full-price version of the original Capezio was $48. The starting price of our knockoff was $36, which cost us $12. We first tried a $29.99 promotional price on our version. Not much response. Then we went down to $24.99. Sales improved, but not enough. At $19.99, the shoes sold like hotcakes! But this price point scarcely covered our cost and was less than half the price of the original Capezio flat.

Everybody agreed that the customer was wising up and waiting for the inevitable price reductions. The only solution was finding merchandise that would sell at full price, whether branded or our own private label. But that was like telling baseball players that they only needed more timely hits to win games. Wow! What terrific and actionable insight.

As I saw it, we were trapped. We and our competitors had trained the customer to wait for in-season promotions. Even Macy's had succumbed to "One Day Sales." We would probably never be able to reduce our dependence on in-season promotions. Like the mouse in the basement, we went for the cheese and got hammered in the process. Unlike the hapless mouse, we could escape if we could find the right merchandise.

Which we did. Beginning with back-to-school in 1987, and continuing for a couple of years, business exploded because of one item: the Timberland boot. Every teenage girl had to have at least one pair, and many bought two or three. Timberlands were high-priced, which help boost our average ticket. We could barely keep them in stock even during the dead days of summer, when everybody was thinking sandals.

I became buyer of our private label collection as the Timberland trend was tailing off, so I knocked off that iconic boot. I underpriced the genuine version by fifteen dollars. And like many mice before me, I went for the cheese and promoted that sucker for back-to-school. I also managed to capture the latecomers and the budget-minded. How seductive and addictive that formula was!

Like clockwork, Dad's boardroom bravado and optimism had been vindicated.

Chapter 22

THE FELDMANS HAD TWO HOUSEWARMING PARTIES IN THE SPRING OF 1987. Amy and I hosted the first one as a rather low-key event, featuring cocktails, hors d'oeuvres, and a piano player. We invited our folks, friends, some neighbors, and a few colleagues. Amy even invited a client or two, and one prospective client that she was anxious to lure to H&H. Trey Baker, chairman and CEO of the biggest bank in St. Louis, was in her sights. She was dolled up for the event mostly for Trey, and she did look amazing—a fact Trey didn't fail to notice based on the amount of time he spent with her. It was all part of Amy's campaign for partnership.

Amy had done a terrific job on the house. I could barely believe it was the place I had grown up in. Out went the last of the avocado-tinted appliances, out went the basketball hoop (which was good riddance as far as I was concerned). Out went the wall-to-wall carpeting, the damask curtains and, sadly, Mom's bookshelves. In came sleek, crisp, and modern furniture along with soft window treatments and colorful area rugs. The house was a gem, and Amy and I couldn't wait to begin living a normal family life with baby Allison.

Rand flew in the morning of Mom and Dad's party at Brentwood Park. I picked him up at the airport and we headed to my house, where he greeted Allison for the first time. He apologized for the long delay in seeing her and presented her with some incredible Florence Eiseman rompers and dresses he had bought at Neiman's in San Francisco. He insisted on holding her once her diaper was changed.

"I'm your uncle, Rand the Man, little Allison, and always will be. Even if I can't prove it, since the basketball hoop has mysteriously disappeared."

We had time for brunch together before Rand departed for Brentmoor, where he would stay the night. "Mom literally begged me, claimed it would be the only time. I would have a master suite to myself. I don't think Dad had a vote," he told me.

We gathered around the kitchen table and dug into the deli.

"Looks like the folks have some big news," Rand confided. "I think they want to tell us tomorrow morning after the party, but Mom spilled the beans when we spoke last night. She seemed a bit tipsy. In any event, act surprised when you hear the news tomorrow, OK?"

"Sure. What's going on?" I was more than curious.

"Well, first, it seems that Dad is going to be named vice president of Highland Hills at their next board meeting. The next step is the presidency. Evidently, Bobby Weil engineered the whole thing. Dad couldn't be more excited. Mom is not excited. She's happy for Dad, but wants nothing to do with the club, the parties, and all that. And I guess she told him that if there's any party planning to do, he'll have to depend on Andrea Marks . . . or the 'ever-obliging Evie Weil.'"

We laughed. We could imagine her saying that. "What else?"

"Yeah, Mom's going to pursue a PhD in lit at Wash U. She's completed virtually all the classroom requirements and she's fluent in French, so the foreign language box is checked. The big task is a dissertation, which she intends to write on Henry James."

"No surprise there," Amy said, then added, "I couldn't even finish *Daisy Miller*."

"Best of all," Rand continued, "Mom is going to stop smoking the minute tonight's party is over."

"What prompted that decision? We've been after her for years."

"Not what prompted her, but who. That little twenty-pound varmint who's napping upstairs. Allison Feldman. Seems Mom wants to watch her grow up, go to college, maybe get married."

We toasted Mom with our Coke cans and ended brunch by hearing how Rand was doing in San Francisco, while I told him about my recent promotion and progress at Fratelli Massimo. Around three, I drove him to Brentmoor. We hugged, and I wished him luck avoiding Dad during his brief stay. He laughed, "I'll do my best."

Sadly, his best wasn't good enough.

The warm fall evening was perfect for the party. The temperature was in the low sixties and leaves were fluttering down from the maple and oak trees that lined the drive to their home.

After valet parkers whisked their cars away, guests were greeted by liveried members of the catering staff. Mom and Dad remained at the entrance to the magnificent foyer to greet each person. Hors d'oeuvres and drinks were passed. Tables for eight were arrayed across the backyard, where giant oak trees with brown and yellow leaves served as a canopy. Japanese lanterns lit the pathways. Heat lamps were perfectly placed, in case the temperature dipped. A quartet provided subdued musical entertainment.

Mom and Dad went from table to table to chat with the guests. They had done a careful job of arranging the tables so that the country club folks were seated together. Mom's bridge buddies and their spouses occupied a table, and her university colleagues another. Their longtime social friends filled several. Mom had urged Amy and me to invite some friends of ours. I invited some of my Pi Lam fraternity brothers and their wives. Amy, some college and work friends, as well as the Weils' daughter, Jenn, and her husband, Tommy Katzenberg. They were celebrating the birth of their son, Jonathan.

Amy, Rand, and I were seated with Mom and Dad at a table for five, although I don't recall being seated for more than a few minutes at a time, as we spent most of the evening making sure our friends were enjoying themselves.

From what I could tell, the evening was a smashing success.

Amy and I had decided to walk to the party. It was a beautiful fall evening, and I had worn a blazer and Amy, a pashmina. We held hands as we made the ten-minute stroll back to our house.

"They really know how to throw a party, Amy."

"Yes, they do. That house works beautifully for entertaining, and the caterer was outstanding. But Josh, there's trouble in River City. Did you notice that your parents barely spoke to one another?"

"They were busy with their guests. Did you expect them to be arm in arm the whole evening?"

"No, but I watched them very carefully, and your mom had her eyes glued to Evie Weil. She was openly flirting with your dad, adjusting his tie. For his part, your dad was massaging Evie's bare shoulder while she was ministering to his tie. Evie, Max, and Bobby were all laughing. Not your mom. She wheeled around and almost collided with somebody passing out drinks."

"Amy, since he joined the club, Dad's become very tight with the Weils."

"It's not the Weils I'm worried about. It's Max's 'getting tight' with Evie Weil."

"Oh, now what has your fertile imagination conjured up? Dad's having a torrid love affair with Evie Weil?"

"Josh, you're so oblivious sometimes," Amy said.

"And what is that supposed to mean?"

"It means, dearest, that I don't trust your father. Neither does your mother. And, my old lab partner, neither should you."

Amy was right. I can be clueless about relationships. And yet, while I suspected Dad was capable of having a discreet dalliance or two (Rand was convinced he was unfaithful to Mom), I was positive he would not sink to having an affair with Evie Weil. He couldn't, wouldn't, betray Mom like that, and humiliate and expose her to all that local gossip.

As Amy and I were getting ready for bed, the phone rang.

"Josh . . ." It was Rand, and he was out of breath, as if he had just run a race.

"Rand, what's wrong, are you OK?"

Stammering and stuttering, he finally got it out, "Pick me up—now—I need to sleep at your place tonight."

"But Mom made you promise to stay with them."

"Not possible—just come, now. I'll be waiting outside. Come now!"

"OK, OK. I'll have to get dressed but will be there in ten." I hung up the phone.

Amy was by my side. "What's going on?"

"I don't know, but Rand said he needs to spend the night here, and I need to pick him up, pronto."

"OK, I'll get the guest room ready. Do you want me to go with you?"

"No thanks, Amy, this is a brother-to-brother deal."

• • •

When I arrived at Brentmoor, Rand was standing on the porch next to his suitcase. He was disheveled, his tie undone, his jacket over his shoulder, and one of his shirttails hanging out. Not the fashion plate of old.

He threw his stuff in the back of the car and literally collapsed into the passenger seat.

"What happened?" I could hardly wait.

"Not now. When we get to your place." I complied and pressed my foot on the gas.

When we arrived home, Amy showed him to the guest room, but not before he silently hugged her with all his might. I got a couple of beers from the fridge and headed for the den. We settled in there, facing each other in the room that had been the scene of Maddy's little birthday rituals, but my brother was in no mood for nostalgia.

He guzzled half his bottle of beer, belched, and said, "He's a monster—no other word for it."

"Tell me what happened."

"After the party, I was having a cognac in their living room. Maddy came by, kissed me goodnight, and made her way up the stairs. Moments later, Max entered the room, spotted me, went to the bar, mixed himself a drink, sat in his Eames chair, and simply stared at me." Rand looked away.

"After a few minutes of awkwardness and, I guess, noting that my protector had gone to bed, he tore into me about my lifestyle, which he was subsidizing. Somehow, he thought I should feel guilty about that. He specifically cited my apartment in Pacific Heights as something bought and paid for by the sweat of his brow. Evidently, I had disgraced the family name with my 'escapades' and didn't deserve to be a member of the family. I had cast my lot with, well, unspeakable homophobic slurs.

"I tried reasoning with him. I live two thousand miles away. What shame could I possibly bring to the Feldman family name? I was a private person and entitled to live the way I wanted. But not on his dime, he said.

"He finally rang my bell when he went after Todd. Called him my 'screwing-the-daylights-out-of-your-asshole buddy,' and said we were breaking every law of man and nature. Josh, I couldn't take it any longer. I called him out for his creative bookkeeping at the company. Said that because the world-class merchant couldn't get it done legitimately, he went ahead and cheated.

"That really pissed him off. He jumped out of his chair and screamed that I was naïve and an ingrate. I countered by telling him that he was cheating at work and probably cheating on Mom. He stood over me, his spittle going everywhere, and screamed that I was delusional. Then he returned to his Eames chair, downed a slug, and smiled. He asked, 'If I am so deplorable, why did you vote with me to go public?'"

I stared at Rand. "How did you avoid answering?"

"I didn't. I went toe-to-toe with that bigot and shouted, 'I did not vote with you! I could never give you what you wanted. You make my blood curdle.'

"'Impossible,' he declared. 'It was 60-40. It took three of us to outvote Maddy.'

"So I said, 'And I thought you were so good with numbers, oh Mighty Merchant. Your wife voted with you! That's how you got to 60 percent.'

"Josh, you should have seen his face. I wish I had a camera."

I stood up and crossed the room. "Rand, you told him you voted against him and Mom voted with him?"

"Yup, it was time he knew the cold, hard facts."

"But you as much as told him that I voted against him too!"

Rather too proudly, Rand said, "He didn't need to figure it out for himself. I told the son of a bitch that both of us voted against him. He was dumbfounded. Incredulous. The Mighty Max looked like he had seen a ghost. And then he punched me. Not hard, but it took my breath away. He called me a shameless motherfucker and screamed, telling me to get out of his house and never come back. And that's when I called you."

I stood and faced my brother.

"Do you have any idea what this means for me? Mom swore me to secrecy about the vote. She told me Dad would never forgive me." I was starting to get a headache.

"I know, but you didn't tell him, I did."

"What the fuck difference does that make? He now knows I voted against him!"

"But Josh, don't you think that's a small price to pay for the pleasure of kicking him in the balls, once and for all?"

"You threw me and my career plans under the bus for that Kodak moment. And you threw Mom under. That was her secret too."

"You don't think he deserved it? The way he's treated not only me, but Mom…"

"Christ, yes, he deserved it, but who appointed you the messenger? Don't you think Mom and I deserved a voice in the decision?"

"You weren't there. You didn't hear his rant, his venomous, abusive name-calling. I've lived with it for years, and not just from Dad. I've gotten it from ignorant homophobes from coast to coast. I've had my fill. I won't tolerate it anymore."

"I don't blame you for being angry. But Rand, you fucked me over in the process. I have a life, too, and hopes and ambitions. Who gave you the right to put those at risk in order to vent your spleen?"

I sat down on the couch and put my head between my hands.

"Look, Josh, I know you're pissed—"

"More than pissed, Rand. I feel betrayed by my beautiful Rand the Man. You were so wound up, you saved yourself and left me fighting for my life."

"I love you Josh…you've been my biggest cheerleader since we were kids. You welcomed me out of the closet with open arms. But you must understand that I have my pride. I have to live with myself, and I couldn't go on being his piñata."

There was no point in continuing this. I didn't want to say anything I would later regret.

We cleaned up the den in silence, turned off the downstairs lights, and headed upstairs.

"Can you give me a ride to the airport tomorrow?" my brother asked. "Or should I call a cab? Plane leaves at nine in the morning."

"Call the taxi."

When I got into bed, Amy stirred and asked what happened.

"He squealed."

"Oh, sweetheart, I am so sorry."

Chapter 23

I ARRIVED AT THE OFFICE EARLY ON MONDAY, FEARING THE WORST.

Amy and I had hashed out the whole episode over a long breakfast on Sunday morning.

Of course, she was completely supportive of me but pointed out that the secret vote was a powder keg just waiting to be set off.

"And Rand was the one to light the match, dear. He's been so abused by your father that I find it hard to be too angry with him."

"Even though it means my career plans are blown up?" I was feeling very sorry for myself.

"Even though. It's time to face facts, honey. Your dad is a totally self-absorbed tyrant and cannot be trusted. Yes, he's likely to kick you out of the company, and maybe it's best to get it over with now. I don't think he ever wanted you to take his place. He's so hungry for adulation that sharing the spotlight with you or having you in it solo is anathema to him. He'll use you and abuse you, but he'll always be the Merchant Prince."

"You don't know that."

"You're right, but I know your father. He always leaves a trail of bloody bodies behind him. Think about Sy, your brother, your mom. If my instincts are right, one day it will be you. And that day may be tomorrow. You should get it over with while you're young and free to go your own way. That doesn't mean my heart isn't breaking for you, because I know you've wanted to lead the company all your life, and it's being snatched away."

"Amy, you want to be a partner at H&H. And I know you. You'll fight like hell to make it happen. Just like I'll fight like hell to reach my goal at Fratelli Massimo."

"There's one big difference, sweetie. Those who render the partnership verdict at H&H will base their decision on who will benefit them and the firm. Sure, they're human and have their biases, but their major goal is to maintain the reputation of H&H—keep the firm prospering and their paychecks growing. I need to prove to them that I can do that better than my fellow associates. In your case, Josh, your fate rests in the hands of a megalomaniac."

"I don't see him that way," I said. "Yes, he's brutal and a bully, but he, like your partners at H&H, wants the company he created to keep prospering and his paycheck to keep growing. I am the best qualified, hardest-working candidate for that position. Plus, despite all his transgressions and failings, he's never wavered in his support of me."

"Well, tomorrow may be the first, last, and only time he does waver, and you'll be history."

"No, Amy, I will ultimately survive and thrive."

"Glad you've convinced yourself, Josh, but you haven't convinced me. We shall see."

I knew Dad was royally ticked off and would act accordingly, but as I walked into the office, I was hoping he would come to his senses—if not today, maybe in the near future. Even if he was pissed, he'd never let anything bad happen to Fratelli Massimo. The company and his own reputation meant more than anything to him. He needed me there.

I spent the morning hanging out in my office doing busywork, meeting with buyers, and checking things out in the sample room. I asked my secretary, Sandy, to let me know if Dad or Carly called.

Zip, nada, nothing, all day long.

This seemingly endless workday eventually came to a close. Maybe disaster had been averted. I hadn't even gotten a tongue-lashing.

But around five, Fletcher, the security guard, popped his head around the door.

"Josh, your dad just stopped by the reception desk and told me I'm supposed to give you a message."

"And the message, Fletcher?" I could barely stand to wait.

"I don't know quite how to say this, and it hurts me to say it, but your dad, and he's the boss, wants you to pack up your office and clear out of the building ASAP. At first, I thought he might be kidding, but he assured me that he wasn't, and that you would know why you had to leave. When I hesitated, he gave me that look of his. So here I am."

So this is how it would end. Dad couldn't do it in person. Of course, there is a cowardice that lurks within all bullies. No, just our trusty security guard giving me my walking papers, which meant no chance for an appeal or stay of execution.

"Sorry you have to be the messenger, Fletcher," I mumbled. "You're just doing your job."

"I appreciate you saying that, Josh; this is the most awful thing I've had to do for the company. Um, he also told me to get some banker boxes and uh, stay with you while you packed. I hope you don't mind. I can stay out here, if you want." He stepped into the hallway.

Dad didn't even trust me enough to pack by myself, fearing I'd take some critical document with me. "Fletcher, I appreciate how you're handling this, but let's do it by the book."

So it began. I threw most of the selling report printouts in the trash, set aside the important and confidential stuff for my successor, emptied out the drawers in my desk, and tackled the personal stuff on the credenza behind my desk. My intramural ping-pong championship trophy, a sorority picture of Amy, a picture of the two of us my father-in-law took the weekend we got engaged, a composite picture of my Porsches, and, of course, a photo of Amy, me, and Allison taken only weeks ago. All of my personal stuff filled most of two banker boxes, which Fletcher offered to help me carry. I accepted his offer, gave him a hug, and was escorted, as Dad had requested, to the garage.

A teary-eyed Fletcher said goodbye and wished me luck.

I had parked my car next to Dad's parking space. There was a large sign on the wall facing his parking space:

Reserved for Max Feldman.

Chairman, CEO, President

Fratelli Massimo, Inc.

There was no sign on the wall for my space, kind of like an unmarked grave.

I stuffed the boxes on the back shelf of the Porsche and began the commute home for what I assumed was the last time.

As I drove down our street to Claverach, I saw Amy sweeping the leaves off the stairs leading to our front door. She was wearing a Cardinals hat, an untucked plaid lumberjack shirt, a pair of mom jeans, and some ancient L.L. Bean Top-siders. She smiled, waved, and shouted, "I'll meet you in the garage, slugger."

By the time she got there, I was unpacking my banker's boxes.

"I know, sweetie. I know. We'll talk all about it soon. But first, give me a hug, like those bear hugs you gave me when we were dating."

We squeezed each other hard and I buried my face in her neck. We swayed, and she consoled me, whispering those words I needed to hear. I sent a silent thank-you to God for Amy Epstein Feldman.

When we finally separated, I tried to say something, but she shushed me. "We'll talk all about it over a pizza and a couple of beers. Allison's sleeping at Maddy's tonight, so it's just us."

I changed into a pair of Levi's, an old Pi Lambda Phi sweatshirt, and a pair of sneakers and joined Amy at the kitchen table. She was slicing the pizza and opening a couple of cans of Bud.

"How'd you know?"

"I called your mom around noon today. Rand had called her last night after he got back to San Francisco. According to Maddy, he told her the whole story: his blowup with Max, the revelation of the BIG SECRET, and your reaction. He thought you would understand. 'You've always been there for him.' But you shut him down. Rand is devastated."

"He got that right, and he deserves to be devastated. He had no right to make me collateral damage in his fight with Dad. Rand won't pay the price, but I will. What about my getting the boot today?"

She looked at me. "Maddy figured that would happen. Your father went on a rampage yesterday. Rand was a 'hopeless fairy.' And Maddy a 'scheming bitch.' You, my sweetheart, were called an 'ungrateful, untalented suck-up who bit the hand that was feeding him.' And on and on. Maddy and I figured that he would get his revenge today. I guess he did."

"Yeah, he did. The gutless fuck didn't have the nerve to confront me. He sent poor old Fletcher to deliver the news, watch me pack up, and accompany me to the car. I guess that's end of story."

"Josh, dear, we'll need some time and distance to figure out next steps, and I have an idea or two. I rented a videotape of *It's a Wonderful Life*. We can curse Old Man Potter, perhaps one of Max's heroes, and cry our hearts out at the end of the movie, just like we always do."

"Sounds like the perfect ending to a horrible day." I sighed.

Chapter 24

AMY SURPRISED ME THE NEXT DAY WHEN SHE SUGGESTED THAT THE two of us escape for a week and go to England. She had already booked the flights and the reservation at the Stafford Hotel, where we had stayed on our honeymoon and on most of our subsequent trips to Europe. She had even arranged for Allison to stay with Mom while we were gone.

We needed to wait a week to depart because Amy was buried in some project at H&H—plus she had a long-standing commitment on Saturday night to dine with Trey Baker, St. Louis's preeminent banker, whose legal business she wanted to poach for the firm.

"On Saturday night. Are you crazy?" I demanded.

"In our business, the client, or the targeted client, makes the rules. Trey is what you would call a player. He's a terrific banker, but he has a wandering eye, and I'm not speaking as an ophthalmologist."

"Amy. I know you'll stop at nothing for that partnership, but..."

"Josh, you needn't worry, though I'm flattered by your jealous pique. The key with men like Trey is to attract them and then be 'reluctantly' unavailable. They always want what they cannot have, and he can't have me, love. But he'll keep trying.

"It's all part of my two-pronged—if you will excuse the expression—strategy. His bank is in a wrangle with the state of Missouri involving branch banking. And I've been digging through the relevant legislation, litigation, and court cases, and I may be on to something. It was buried in some ancient statute that his current law firm has yet to discover. I'm working with our experts in the field to see if this is the silver bullet Trey is looking for. 'Bringing home this coonskin,' as LBJ would say, could make me partner at the firm. Showing a bit of leg will be an additional incentive for the man about town."

"Well, just a bit of leg is OK, but…"

"Trust me, sweetie," she said.

"I ninety-nine percent do!"

Amy winked. "Would I have told you all of this if I was going to succumb to his charms?"

I woke up Wednesday with nothing to do. Or so I thought.

I was assigned mommy duties, with Althea assisting. At first it was fun, like a weekend day with Allison, who was a cheerful and active toddler (most of the time). We played silly games and I crawled around and played horsey with her. I let her bounce on my potbelly. But she, like Amy, had a mind of her own, and was not afraid to pout, cry, or scream if she was crossed. And to top it off, she was walking—which made me proud, but also ran me ragged trying to keep her out of danger.

Thank God, she was still on a two-nap-a-day schedule. I napped, too, collapsing on the sofa. It was exhausting, even with Althea pitching in at feeding, changing, and bathing time. Christ, how did mothers do it?

Althea seemed to take all this in stride and couldn't help smiling at my fumblings.

On Saturday evening at seven, Amy walked down the stairs in a stunning little black dress, a bright red cashmere pashmina, her hair in a French twist, and her best jewelry on display. She was perched on three-inch-high Manolo Blahnik evening shoes.

(No Fratelli Massimo knockoffs for my Amy.) I ran to the kitchen for a ruler and measured the distance between her knee and the bottom of her very short dress.

"Just a little bit of leg?" I eyed her.

"Very funny, Josh. Should be home by ten; we're dining at the Saint Louis Club, a very public place, so I'm sure Trey will be on his best behavior, after he works the room."

"I'll wait up for you, dear."

"I was counting on it, Mother."

It was my turn to give her the finger.

She didn't quite make it home by 10:00, or 10:30, but I heard her car pull into the garage at 10:45.

She was walking on air! "I'm a star, sweetheart. You may kiss me. Like you mean it."

We embraced and she then pulled her head back a bit and winked. "The two-pronged strategy worked, my love. When I return from London, the law offices of Hotchkiss and Hamilton will be engaged to solve Trey's branch-banking problem. And Trey insisted I lead the team. Partnership, here I come!"

"How sweet it is, Amy, and exactly how much leg did you have to show?"

"Well, if you must know, Trey had reserved a banquette for two, and I found my dress riding up a bit, so maybe a few inches more than you measured earlier. Trey's wandering eye noticed the gap and scooched over, which forced me to scooch over. It took all of my athletic skills to avoid falling out of the banquette on my butt. Poor Trey had to settle for a sexy, mournful 'sorry, I am not available' look on my face. You, on the other hand, can have your way with me!"

• • •

The Stafford, in St. James, just south of Piccadilly and adjacent to St. James Park, had a rather modest lobby. It was one of those small, quaint, discreet English hotels long on service and amenities, but short on grandeur. It was just perfect for our weeklong stay after the latest Feldman family crisis.

Amy had reserved a beautiful suite in the main building that featured an enormous bed and a sitting room. British TV is a disaster, so we planned to read local newspapers and books, some of which Maddy had given us before we left St. Louis.

Amy had made terrific arrangements for little Allison during our sojourn. Maddy was delighted to have some "quality time" with the little bugger, as long as Nora was willing to play part-time nurse—which she was anxious to do. "Haven't had a wee one around in a long time!" She also invited Adrienne, Amy's mom, in for a few days.

This must have driven Max nuts. He used the invasion as an excuse to travel extensively "on business," he said.

After our overnight TWA flight to Gatwick and a shuttle to Victoria Station, we flopped down on the bed and napped for a few hours. Both of us unpacked, showered, dressed, and reported to Colin, the hall porter, as concierges were then titled in the UK. Dinner and theatre reservations were made, passes for the Underground were secured, and gratuities were graciously accepted by Colin.

As was our custom, we planned to dine at Wiltons that first evening. But first, a drink at the hotel's American Bar, where the peerless Charles had long presided. The bar was placed in a narrow, rectangular area at the back of the hotel. The ceiling

was festooned with hats, pennants, memorabilia, and souve-
nirs from American and British sports teams, corporations,
military units, and universities. The walls sported photos of
the Royals and the rich and famous patrons who frequented
the establishment.

We seated ourselves at the bar. "Ah, welcome back, Mr. and
Mrs. Feldman. The usual?" This meant a gin martini for me and a
Chardonnay with ice for Amy.

We toasted each other and savored the distance from St. Louis
and the intimacy . . . just the two of us. After taking a few sips,
I felt Amy's hand on my thigh—high up on my thigh. I jerked
around and she gave me that look and suggested we retire to our
room. "C'mon, Mr. Ping-Pong Champion, time for some action,"
she said. And with that, we slid off our stools and told a winking
Charles that we would be back in a while.

"I'll refresh your drinks—how long will you be?"

Amy said in response, "A long time!" Eat your heart out,
Trey Baker!

We were all over each other in the ancient two-person
elevator as it slowly, too slowly, ascended.

Once in our room, we put the Do Not Disturb sign on the
door and stripped off most of our clothes. In the heat of the
moment, I forgot to take my socks off, but who cared? We went
at it hammer and thong, the latter item Amy had been wearing
only moments ago.

It was like our honeymoon, but better. Much better. Where
had Amy learned this stuff? How had she gotten so adept and
agile? But who cared? I lost myself in her. I thought of nothing
but her, and how she loved me and saved me. All my worries
evaporated with Amy at my side, or under me, or on top!

In the aftermath she stood naked in front of me, rested her hands on her hips, and said, "You're my life, Josh. From that first day in Field Botany, well, maybe not the first day." She laughed and confessed that she knew I had told Mrs. Eisendrath that we were a terrific team.

"I could have killed you when I found out. Behind that 'Gentle Josh' image you try to project, you are a devious little bastard, aren't you? Anyway, I fell in love with you—eventually. Your Chicago store visit and lunch at Michael's invitation was brilliant!

"But you're my partner now, not just my lab partner, but my partner for life, Josh, and I want you to be happy. And I want us to be happy. So, we're going to use this time together to figure out what makes us both happy. OK?"

Speechless, I just nodded OK.

During the first couple of days, we shopped in London and saw the sights—some familiar, some new. We ate well and drank too much. We made love frequently and varied the routine, coming up with some new tricks and playing some old favorites. The one thing we did not do was talk about Fratelli Massimo. Neither of us wanted to spoil this interlude with business talk.

Of course, we called Maddy frequently to see how Allison was doing. Maddy assured us that all was well, and that Allison was enjoying being the center of female attention.

By Thursday, we had seen enough of London, so we decided to visit Stonehenge and Oxford on Friday.

We spent some time with Colin, mapping out an itinerary. We couldn't depend on rail travel, so I reluctantly arranged for a rent-a-car. Driving on the "wrong" side of the road made me crazy. I couldn't judge the spacing with cars coming at us from the right side of the road, so I edged farther and farther to the left. That worked on wide roads, but not on narrow country ones. Naturally, I brushed against the thick hedgerows on the left—with predictable results. I managed to obliterate the passenger side mirror or, as the Brits would say, the "wing mirror." A roll of duct tape I bought in a small town near Oxford allowed me to patch it back together, but got chuckles from passersby. "Must be a Yank!" I imagined them thinking.

We arrived midmorning in Oxford, briefly toured the campus, and gazed at the gowned scholars speeding down the thorough-fares on their bikes, looking a bit like Halloween witches on broomsticks. We then rented a punt on the Cherwell and strug-gled up- and downstream for an hour, had a quick pub lunch, and headed for Stonehenge, an hour away.

After a brief tour of the visitor center and a walk over to the monoliths, we listened to the guide tell our little party all about how the stones had gotten there, where they had come from, what rela-tionship they had with the solstice, and such. After his spiel, the rest of the group returned to the car park. Not Amy and I. We found a bench with a wonderful view of Stonehenge and the setting sun. It was brisk, but we both were dressed for the chill.

"Josh, this trip has been wonderful in every way, but we return to St. Louis this weekend, and it's time to figure out where we go from here—or rather, where you go from here. So, let me ask you a question: If it were possible, would you want to return to Fratelli Massimo?"

I frowned. "I'm not so sure Dad is ready for that yet. Knowing him, he's still pretty pissed off. Maybe one day, but ..."

"Let start again, Josh. If it were possible, would you want to return after we get home from Europe?"

"Ok, we'll pretend it's possible. And the answer is an emphatic *yes*. Since I was a little kid, I dreamed of running the place when my dad stepped aside. Everything I did at that company was meant to increase my chances of that happening. So, yes, if it were possible, I would return—even with Dad's craziness.

"I once heard a female politician, I don't remember who, deride her opponent by claiming 'he was born on third base and thought he hit a triple.' That resonated with me. I landed on third base myself, thanks to Dad and his talents. That's made me even more anxious to prove to you and the rest of the world that I can make it to home plate on my own."

Amy took my hand and looked me in the eye. "You say he's crazy. That's the understatement of the year. The man is a beast. Everybody knows it. Even you know it, on some level. He's a narcissist and a megalomaniac. He's completely insensitive to the feelings of anybody but himself. Please take some time. Think again. Take another path."

I stammered, "I admit my dad is everything you think he is. I stopped trusting him years ago. It began with Sy's story. Then, how he abused my brother and how he talks about Mom. But the one thing he does respect is performance. Fratelli Massimo is his baby, more his child than either Rand or me. He treasures that company, and he will reward the person who can continue its success into the future. Underneath all that bluster and brutality is his desire to see his legacy survive. How many times have I heard him say, 'I am Fratelli Massimo'? He can't run it forever. In fact, he's already dividing his time between the club and the company. He's taking longer vacations, leaving the office for days at a time. I see him preparing to be the president of Highland

Hills, and he's probably on the prowl for a woman not named Maddy."

I took a deep breath and continued, "I believe that I'm the person best positioned to carry on the legacy that Dad created, and I think Dad knows it as well. That sounds crazy in light of what he did when he fired me. But that was just reflexive. Rand told him that I betrayed him. Dad predictably retaliated, but he will come to his senses. Not because he loves me, and I doubt he does, but because he needs me."

Amy grimaced. "I wish you would reconsider. You don't need to prove anything to me, and I don't understand why you must prove yourself to the rest of the world. That sounds a bit like Max. I wish you could find contentment in succeeding elsewhere, at some other endeavor, somewhere far away from your father. Allison's just a baby; we could move anywhere, do anything. I could practice law wherever; I so wish you would choose any path other than the one you were on. How can you make your future dependent on the whims of your father?"

"Only partially dependent on Max's whims. Results speak for themselves. I'm confident that I could build a case based on my achievements, if given the chance. So yes, if it were possible to return, I would, knowing full well that Dad can be monstrous. But we're a public company, and shareholders look at the bottom line and, as you well know, so does Dad. He's dependent on good results to keep his wealth growing, his ego inflated, and his social position secure. But frankly, Amy, I'm surprised that you keep pressing the issue knowing that my immediate return is highly unlikely—if not impossible."

Amy closed her eyes, sighed, took a deep breath, and said, "I'm pressing you, Josh, because you can, in fact, return."

I was incredulous. "Just how is that going to happen?"

"You remember that it took us a week to get ourselves organized for the London escape? Well, during that interval, I wasn't only working, making reservations, packing, and arranging for Allison. My action plan came to me as I was sweeping the leaves on the stairs, just as you were driving home on that fateful day. The next day, I got on the phone with Maddy, Gunther, and Rand and explained the situation and my strong suspicion that you would be determined to return to the company. Your family loved the plan. It even got a laugh from Gunther, who hailed me as his 'heiress apprentice.'

"Here's how it will work," she began. "Max has the power to fire you, but the board has the power to fire Max. That is wonderful leverage, my dear, but we cannot use it. You're not ready to take over the company, so he's still the key to Fratelli Massimo's short-term success. He would know we were bluffing if we threatened to fire him, and he would call our bluff. But our plan will work without having to threaten him."

Amy looked straight into my eyes. "Four of the six eligible board members—you will be excused and excluded from participating—are prepared to vote to reinstate you. This includes Maddy, Rand, Julia Symonds, and Peter Kahn. Maddy and Rand were in the bag. But Symonds and Kahn, after discussions with Gunther in New York, insisted that you be reinstated. They appreciate your achievements and future prospects at the company. In fact, Peter said that it was reassuring for stockholders that a succession plan was in place in case Max bailed or 'went off the deep end.' They were also mightily upset because Max did not consult them when he fired you. I'm not sure how Harrison Balding will vote, but that's immaterial since a majority of the seven directors are in favor of your return."

I threw my hands in the air. "But Max will go crazy. He won't stand for it!"

"He's trapped, Josh. Do you really think he would quit over this? His entire persona is tied to the company's fortunes. Oh, he'll be angry, sure. He'll shout and rant, but Maddy—and this is the delicious part—will quietly and patiently explain to him that the board has the right, in fact, the duty, according to the bylaws, to overrule him if it thinks reinstatement is in the best interest of Fratelli Massimo and its stockholders. Harrison Balding will confirm that principle. Then ever-thoughtful Maddy will offer your dad a fig leaf. There may be no need for a formal vote if Max can see his way clear to accept the informal 'recommendation' of the directors."

I was silent, and in awe. Not only was Amy clever as hell, but she had actually devised a viable strategy to keep me with the company, even though it was a path she had repeatedly asked me to reconsider.

We sat looking at each other, lost in our own thoughts. I took her hands in mine and kissed her tenderly. Words failed the both of us.

After a few minutes, Amy withdrew her hands. "Josh, you have two giant tasks awaiting you. First, you must find a way to work with Max. He may lose this battle, but he'll be looking for a way to win the war."

"I understand all too well, but I'm determined to make it work. He'll be hellish to work with for a while. And what is the second task?"

"You must find a way to reconcile with Rand."

"Now, that's a different story. He caused this mess. I'm supposed to make peace with him? If you hadn't been so clever and come to my rescue, I'd be out on my rear end because of Rand."

"He knows that, darling. And he feels terrible about it, as Maddy indicated. But he was provoked by your father. He endured a long, withering attack before he fought back in the only way he could. Imagine yourself in his shoes. He's gay and making a decent life for himself; his own father has rejected him, reviles him, and hurls slurs at him. What was he supposed to do? Simply suffer in silence? Or come out swinging? Something you, yourself, might have to consider doing one day—think about that!"

Amy went on. "You must understand, Josh. If you had been present when the fight occurred, I know you would have joined Rand. He's your best friend, and he's stood by you—always. You have to forgive him this breach. You simply must. After all, sweetie, he's going to risk your father's wrath at the board meeting when he defies him once again. And he'll do it for you, Josh. For you."

"It's not for me, Amy. Rand will enjoy 'raising his hand' to defy Max. No, what he did to me was unforgivable."

"I wish I could convince you otherwise, dear—for the sake of the family. For Maddy. For one minute, stop thinking about your own grievance, and give some thought to your mother."

Amy lowered her voice. "Maddy swung the go-public vote for Max. She never revealed the secret, and this has caused her much grief. Can you imagine how your father has treated her since he assumed Maddy voted against him? She's kept her mouth shut, taking the punishment Max has dished out. God knows how she's tolerated it. But she did it to protect you and your brother."

"I adore my mom. I'm devoted to her and will honor and respect her always. But Rand betrayed me in a way I cannot forgive."

We walked back to the car park in silence.

Chapter 25

WHEN WE RETURNED FROM LONDON, AT GUNTHER'S SUGGESTION, Julia Symonds notified Max thirty days in advance that there was a "confidential subject" she wanted to discuss with the board. Dad placed it first on the agenda. He had been wary of Julia since the very first board meeting, no doubt recalling Maddy's admonition that he not condescend to Julia, or she would make him pay. Maybe he thought he could mollify her by putting her issue as the opener, or maybe he hoped she was resigning.

The board meeting began with the usual formalities, after which Julia raised her hand and asked if she could speak. When she declared that she wanted to discuss my reinstatement, I rose and left the room—but not before I had a chance to observe my father's reaction. He was startled and angry, proclaiming, "Not on my watch. Josh is finished here. You're going to have to choose—it's me or him." And then the door closed behind me.

I found an empty office on the executive floor, closed the door, and awaited the summons to return. Despite my father's declaration, I knew the outcome was not in doubt. So I focused on the aftermath.

His reaction to the board's decision was very predictable. I could count on his bombast, profanity, and cruelty after the humiliation he would suffer at the meeting. But I'd been through similar tongue-lashings with him and witnessed countless others; I knew what to expect. As I was rehearsing for the confrontation, Carly knocked on the door and told me I could return to the boardroom.

It was like entering one of those huge meat lockers in a butcher shop. Instead of carcasses on hooks, the directors were sitting frozen in place, most with arms folded over their chests while averting their eyes from Max, who was purple with rage.

"Carly, read the minutes pertaining to the item that Ms. Symonds raised," he spat with his voice quavering.

Pushing her glasses back on the bridge of her nose, Carly read aloud that "Joshua Feldman is to resume his normal duties immediately. Further, he is to receive back pay due him during his recent leave of absence."

More silence.

I thanked the board for their confidence in me and assured them that I would work diligently to confirm their faith in me.

Max continued to glare at me. The rest of the meeting moved to a conclusion very quickly.

"I want to see you," Dad ordered, "in my office—now. That is, if the board approves," he added sarcastically. The frozen people were suddenly animated, and they scrambled for the exit.

The air was thick in his office. He sat behind his desk giving me his Darth Vader death stare. Finally, he summoned himself.

"I came within an inch of resigning."

"Bullshit, Dad, you were never going to resign. Save your breath. You could never leave Fratelli Massimo. Much as you stated so modestly at the go-public meeting: 'I am Fratelli Massimo.' Think of those poor members at Highland Hills who would be deprived of a corporate chieftain as their next president. They'd have to settle for a mere has-been."

I continued on. "Go ahead, resign! Stop taking calls from the adoring press. Stop being wined and dined by your vendors. Stop putting out puffy press releases. And just hang 'em up. I know I can count on at least four votes by the board if you depart."

Max fired back. "You think you're so clever, you and your little cohort. But I am still Boss, and, with God as my witness, I'll fire you the minute you have a lousy season, hire the wrong person, or miss a profit target. And before I do it, I will make sure the board is on my side. If they're not, I will resign and then they can hunt for a replacement for irreplaceable me. And it won't be you, Gentle Josh."

He was only getting started. "You think you're hot shit, don't you? But no, Josh, you don't have what it takes to run this business. You know that's what they call you behind your back— 'Gentle Josh.' I want to vomit. You're just like my father, the Mayor of Twenty-Fourth Street. Should have known it after your first trip to Miami. Even your fag brother has more spine than you! Imagine, pretending that you can run this empire being 'Gentle Josh.' And another thing, imagine not having the mighty Gunther, or Maddy's and Rand's shareholdings, to prop you up. You're full of brave talk, but without your protectors in the wings, you're just another hapless, dime-a-dozen numbers jockey."

"Maybe you want to stamp your feet or take a swing at me like you did at Rand. No? Well, if you're done with your rant, Dad, I have Fratelli Massimo work to do—lots of stuff to catch up on after my so-called lengthy vacation. And you'll want to get back to writing your Highland Hills acceptance speech while you're still chairman, CEO, and president of the company."

He chuckled. "You better have eyes in the back of your head, 'cause I'm going to be looking over your shoulder every minute of every day, just waiting for you to slip up. You hear me?"

"Loud and clear. I've been warned. But you'd better be on guard too, oh mighty merchant. You keep leaking info to Bobby Weil or fiddling with the books, and I'll have to reluctantly inform the board. Yeah, I know all about how you feed your patron stockbroker and puppeteer little insider tips. Amy and Jenn Katzenberg are best buds. Pre-earnings release hints to help good old Bobby and his clients make some dough. It will break my heart, but my fiduciary duty as a director..."

Dad said, "You don't have the guts to do it. I will dictate what we've just discussed to Carly. She'll bring you a copy to sign. Your next termination—and there will be a next, and final, termination—will be done by the book, with all the files ship-shape. You'll be fired for cause; the board won't be able to stop me. Understood?"

"OK. And I will add the stuff about insider info and cooking the books; leave enough space for that insertion, and then I'll sign."

"Get the fuck out of my office."

That was easier than I thought. Of course, Carly never showed up with the document. Dad and I were both bluffing, but I felt liberated saying that stuff, instead of just thinking it.

As I was leaving for the day, I riffled through my messages. Rand had called a number of times. No doubt a plea to bury the hatchet. If and when that conversation happened, it would have to be face-to-face.

• • •

Fortunately, for all our sakes, the end of the decade of the 1980s was a successful period for Fratelli Massimo. Largely because of the Timberland brand boot and our version of it, our sales and profits grew nicely and resulted in a rising stock price. This silenced nervous analysts and querulous board members. As a corollary, it increased the value of our family's holdings in Fratelli Massimo. We had retained voting control and owned more than 50 percent of the outstanding stock. As a buyer of our private label footwear, I was gaining confidence that I had what it took to lead our entire merchandising team.

During the weeks following my reinstatement, Dad and I were like an estranged married couple. We seldom spoke unless necessary, and when we did it was short—but not very sweet. He never missed an opportunity to remind me of my tenuous status. He threw obstacles in my path whenever he could: he fired Sandy, my secretary; had Walter Benning check and recheck my markdowns to make sure I wasn't cooking the books; found "budgetary reasons" to exclude me from shoe shows; and withheld my year-end bonus on a technicality.

I merely smiled and ignored the jabs and insults, assuming that he would soon tire of the campaign. Amy and I had used the same strategy when Allison would scream her head off in the middle of the night. Eventually she'd gotten the message.

But what really broke the ice was Amy's being named a partner at H&H. Mom, who must have been looking for a way to mend fences, invited us to join Max and her for a celebratory dinner honoring Amy at Tony's.

Amy was the celebrity that night, and nobody, not even Dad, wanted to rain on her parade. The champagne and vintage wines flowed. So, feeling no pain, Max and I began tentatively chatting about sports and then inevitably about the business. If not exactly renewing our vows, we established a civil relationship.

At the office it was never again a buddy-buddy connection. It developed into more of a boss and right-hand–man situation. Happily, for me, my dad was somewhat less involved in the day-to-day management of the business as he climbed the leadership ladder at Highland Hills. Dad's absences gave me an opportunity to handle more of the workload and learn more about the business. Dad, on the other hand, was scheduled to succeed Bobby Weil as president, and he needed to learn a lot in a hurry to be ready for that assignment. I gathered that the finances were not the challenge; rather, it was pleasing the members that presented him with difficulties.

On the occasional Sunday evening when, at Mom's insistence, the five of us got together, Dad would tell us tales about Highland Hills, such as the member complaints that made their way to the board. The scallops were cold, somebody's kid pooped in the pool, somebody's foursome jumped ahead of a group lunching at the 19th Hole, somebody drove their golf cart across the eleventh green, and so on.

But then he got more serious.

It seems that only men could be members of Highland Hills, and while their wives could participate in many of the club's activities, they were excluded from an important one—playing golf on Sunday mornings. The rule stemmed from the days when most men worked six days, so Sunday morning golf was reserved exclusively for them.

Times, of course, had changed. Most men worked five days, and many wives worked as well.

"No, sweetheart, I will not serve on a committee exploring the 'wives' issue,'" Mom declared. "In fact, it's shameful that it's taken Highland Hills this long to figure out it had a problem."

Dad's entreaties fell on deaf ears. Nope, she would have nothing to do with Highland Hills.

I ventured in. "Seems easy to solve. Just make women eligible for membership and all the privileges."

"Well, some of the guys don't want them on the course on Sunday mornings. They claim women will slow down play, and the old codgers complain that they won't be able to pee whenever and wherever they want—they will have to use the toilets on the course."

"Western civilization at a fork in the road!" my mom sarcastically added, a habit she'd honed when speaking of the club.

The trials and tribulations of Highland Hills were like a soap opera. Dad was consumed by them. But his petty problems at HH paled when compared to the daily challenges at FM. In addition to being chairman, CEO, and president of Fratelli Massimo, he served on the local hospital board. He was also a director of one of the large publicly held banks in town, which continued to provide us with seasonal financing. Dad's ambitions at Highland Hills were of a piece with his craving for celebrity status.

Maddy came over to our house one day while Amy was out with Jenn Katzenberg. It provided the perfect opportunity to ask about Dad's involvement with HHCC.

"But don't you see, Josh, this is an honor and a sort of crowning achievement for your dad. He's a very successful self-made man, and invariably, they're the most covetous of the trappings and titles of status. He needs constant validation of his greatness. While I understand it, I am contemptuous of that trait and am totally unable to talk him out of it.

"I suppose everybody has a folly. Mine is school. Do you think I will ever be a scholar of note? Of course not. I am pursuing a

PhD solely to satisfy my own desires. Your Porsches are your folly. God only knows what Rand's are. But your dad savors status, and nothing is more important to him than having it conferred by those he thinks are of the upper crust."

"Well, I guess that makes sense," I said. "And it helps explain why Bobby Weil has become so important to Dad. He's always had his guy friends, his golf foursome, and his industry buddies, as he calls them, but Bobby has taken him under his wing. He has guided him into the public offering and cleared a path for him at Highland Hills."

"Yes, Josh, Bobby has helped your dad, but it was hardly altruistic. Bobby himself has benefitted enormously. Going public was very lucrative for him and his firm. But there's a personal price we pay for Dad's folly and Bobby's assistance, unlike my academic pursuits and your Porsches. We are now being judged by members of the club. We are expected to behave and perform in a way that meets their expectations. To follow their rules."

After a few moments of silence, Maddy continued.

"I fell madly in love with your father for many reasons. He was handsome, sexy, and vigorous, and I think he loved me back in those days. He was also fiercely independent, roguish, and marched to the beat of his own drummer. He was a rule-breaker, taking gifts and other inducements from his vendors and cutting corners. Minor crimes, to be sure. But I found all of this to be daring, audacious, and even charming. As the Billy Joel song goes, I was an uptown girl in love with a backstreet guy.

"Don't forget I grew up with the world's most ardent establishment rule follower, Gunther Harris Berg. The law was a perfect profession for him, the straightest of straight arrows. He was always at the beck and call of the rich and powerful. But he was only as good as his last piece of advice. Yes, we belonged to the best clubs and I went to the best schools. But those institutions are peopled by the most judgmental individuals on earth. Every step you take is evaluated and weighed against their norms. Follow the rules, follow the rules, follow the rules! I hated that world.

"Your dad, in those days, was oblivious to all that. He was self-reliant and charmingly clueless about my world. He was my ticket out of there. We would be free. We wouldn't be judged by those people, and we wouldn't live with those people. St. Louis was a million miles away. I was the happiest girl in the world."

"And now?" I raised my eyebrows.

"Now, I am not so happy. Your dad's success has made him insufferable in many ways. Preening and prancing to please the powerful. And ironically, the more successful he is, the needier he has become. 'Maddy, you'll never believe what they're saying about me in *Women's Wear Daily*—have a look.' Unbelievable. He goes on and on about 'merchandising superstar Max Feldman,' blah, blah, blah."

"But you voted to go public, Mom, and you had to know where that would lead."

"Yes, I did. I've never faced a more vexing decision. Do I kill that deal and preserve what I cherished, my freedom and independence, or do I side with your father and let him achieve the public stature he craved?"

"What made you vote with Dad?"

"You boys. If you and Rand had voted—as you did!—against your dad, and I had joined you, I feared for our family's survival. An angry and resentful Max Feldman, which he certainly would have been, would have made our lives an even worse hell than it is. You'll recall how easily he betrayed his own father. Max would have become completely unhinged if we had deprived him of the adulation that sustains him.

"What good would my independence or freedom be if our family was blown up? So, in the end, it was a pretty easy, but painful, decision. Now that the big secret is out in the open, I was hoping your father would warm to me a bit, but, no. He's locked in his own world of business, and now, the club.

"You have a truce with Max, as do I. That may work in business, but a marriage should be more than merely a cease-fire! There, I said it. And one more thing, Josh. You've shut out your brother. I understand it all, but in the years to come, we three will need each other. Mend that fence!"

• • •

A couple of weeks later, when I returned from a Cardinals game midafternoon on a Saturday, there were several cars parked in front of our house. I remembered it was playdate day at the Feldmans'. Amy and some of her closest friends would be in the basement, and their preschool kids would be creating havoc. Maybe I could escape, but as I put the car in reverse, I saw Jenn Katzenberg waving to me as she and little Jonathan walked down the driveway.

"Caught you, Josh, didn't I?" she called out.

"Guilty as charged. How's the playdate going?"

"It's riotous down there. Amy served chocolate cake. Not a good idea! It will take a week to clean it up."

"How come you get to leave?" I joked.

"I promised Mom I'd help her get ready for a dinner party tonight. Your folks will be there. I can't tell you how much my mom and dad like being with them. Well, I better get going before Jonathan has a meltdown!"

As she drove off in her Jeep Wagoneer SUV, I couldn't help thinking about the complex relationship between the Weils and the Feldmans. Mom was certainly no fan of the Weils, Mr. or Mrs. I had never forgotten how Amy and Rand were convinced that the relationship between my dad and Evie Weil was not entirely platonic. Amy often wished I had a filter for my big mouth. She needn't worry today. My lips were sealed. I shook my head and pressed on into the hell in the basement.

Chapter 26

As happy as retailers are with robust sales volumes, they always, always temper that euphoria because they know they will have to go up against those robust figures the following year. What will we do for an encore?

During the early 1990s, in the aftermath of the Timberland boot bonanza, we stumbled. There was no replacement for that high-priced boot, so it was back to searching for winning styles that our nationally branded vendors showed us. But the reaction to our selections was weak, thus handicapping our private label knockoff assortments. Who wants lower-priced versions of so-so branded styles? Thus, our promotional prices resumed their steady decline that had characterized the pre-Timberland boot era. Naturally, top line sales were disappointing, as were profits.

The situation was exacerbated by the virtual halt in new regional mall openings. In fact, our store count began to decline. And for the first time in three decades, existing malls, particularly the average ones, began to experience unwanted vacancies as leases expired or tenants experienced financial difficulties. In contrast, the more vibrant malls like Roosevelt Field in New York, Woodfield Mall in Chicago, and South Coast Plaza in Southern California, were raising rents at a rapid rate because retailers still vied for those quality locations.

Dad was often AWOL at work. On many days when I passed his office, it was dark. When I asked Carly where he was, she usually said the club. Even on Mondays, when the club was closed to members? Yes. I gathered from Mom, who gave me a sly look, that during the summer Dad uncharacteristically played golf, showered at the club, and came home after dark.

On several occasions, I was asked to sign urgent, time-sensitive documents—like lease extensions—when Dad couldn't be reached. As an officer of the company I was empowered to sign them, but where was Max? He wasn't at the club, and he wasn't at home.

He was even distant when the team traveled to New York. Dad had negotiated a discount at the New York Hilton, where our people stayed in New York. But Dad started staying at the posh St. Regis Hotel. In fact, Mom didn't know he was staying there. She tracked me down once at the Hilton and asked me where he was. When I asked him why he stayed at the St. Regis, he told me he had meetings with investors, bankers, and analysts, and he thought it was important to put a good face on things, even though the numbers were lousy.

"They sniff panic or lack of confidence, and the stock price is in the toilet."

Well, the stock price may not have been in the toilet, but the bathroom door was open and the lights were on.

Dad managed to join us for some of our vendor meetings on Seventh Avenue. The routine was much the same as it had been in our heyday. There was lots of bonhomie, kibitzing, and serious negotiating. But the results weren't there. Some of the styles we (he) chose were winners, of course, but too many of our selections were mediocre at best and had to be promoted or reduced significantly during clearance.

My trips to Asia and Novo Hamburgo, the shoe capital of Brazil, to place orders for our private-label collection were geared more toward lowering the quality of our shoes than they had once been.

The reason: if we had to discount our merchandise more deeply, we needed to lower the cost of our incoming merchandise to make a decent margin. Dad instructed us to raise our opening price points so that we could slash them by 50 percent and still make money, while giving the customers what they thought was a fantastic value. This was yet another deal with the devil that I was sure would come back to haunt us. Just like our incessant promotions.

After I returned from a trip to Brazil, Carly called and asked if I could join Dad for lunch in his office. I had a laundry list of concerns I wanted to discuss, so I was quite anxious to see him. Carly took my deli order, and I typed a list of questions and issues for our meeting.

Dad joined me in the boardroom.

We discussed the trips I had made to Asia and Brazil. We were forced to concede that Jackie Fisher and Vince Camuto had brilliantly locked up production in Brazil with their Nine West brand, which forced us to scramble to find factory capacity there. I acknowledged that our quality would take a hit as a result.

"Quality means shit if we can get the styling right—which brings me to the reason for our meeting. You need to get some experience in branded footwear style selection. You've been spending most of the last several years doing knockoffs in Asia and Brazil, and the results have been OK. But it's time you took the next step. I want you to begin shadowing Herb Segal, who's been working with the domestic brands for almost a decade now. His batting average ain't so hot lately, and he needs the help."

I had been waiting for this day to come, and I was psyched. I had mastered the knockoff component in our buying formula, but the true test of a merchant was picking winners that our branded resources presented to us when we visited their show-rooms, or when they called on us here in St. Louis. Dad had been a genius at it. Though, to be honest, he had left most of the style picking to Herb in recent years.

"Sure, Dad, I'm all over it."

"Well, you need to start facing some major-league pitching. I've got my hands full with those Wall Street Airedales who need constant care and feeding. With our earnings falling short of expectations, the phone is ringing off the hook. I'm even taking the gas pipe on the bank board. They're all very polite, but the message is clear. We need to bounce back. And you need to man up."

"Great opportunity, Dad, thanks." I meant it.

"Don't blow it."

And with that, the meeting was over.

When I got home, Amy intercepted me and told me that I needed to pay special attention to Allison at dinner. She was preparing for her role as a pilgrim in the kindergarten Thanksgiving pageant at Glenridge School. Evidently, she'd been practicing her lines repeatedly since she'd gotten home from school.

So, after dinner, Allison donned her costume, which Amy had bought at Spicer's—a local variety store—and we were both treated to yet another rehearsal.

"Behold! What a bounty I see before me!" my daughter cried. "Corn from the earth and apples from the trees. We are thankful to you, our Indian friends, and to God."

And then, mercifully, she was off to bed.

Amy came downstairs and sat at the other end of the couch.

"You were on Pluto tonight, sweetie."

I told her about my conversation with Dad.

"Great news, sweetheart. You know I've always doubted that your father would honor his pledge to you. But you've earned this opportunity. And to be brutally frank, Fratelli Massimo and Max need you, given the recent results and his 'distractions.' Be very careful, though. Max has a penchant for treachery."

"You don't have to remind me."

• • •

We capped off the year by going to New York to celebrate Gunther's eightieth birthday. Maddy had made arrangements for the celebration at one of his favorite venues, the iconic Pool Room at the Four Seasons restaurant, which was the apogee of power dining in NYC. The room was festooned with holiday decorations, which beautifully complemented the seasonal décor. Eight of us were seated around a round table laden with countless items of shining glassware, china, and silver.

Naturally, Dad made a big stink about Rand's partner, Todd, being included, but Maddy shut him down quickly. "I'm giving this little soiree, dear, and I'm inviting Todd. Leave the homophobia routine in St. Louis. It doesn't play well in New York."

The family gathered in the Fifty-Second Street foyer, checked our coats, and posed for a photograph taken by a member of the restaurant's publicity department. Paul Kovi, one of its owners, embraced Gunther and introduced himself to the rest of the family. He knew Mom and kissed her on both cheeks. Kovi escorted us up the stairs to the Grill Room and pointed out the Mark Rothko painting and the curtain designed by Picasso. We then passed through a corridor to the Pool Room, where a special table had been reserved.

We toasted Gunther and enjoyed a sumptuous meal.

Gunther, who was semiretired and "of counsel," whatever that meant at his law firm, was still as sharp as a tack. After all the good wishes were spoken and the table cleared, he asked if he might be permitted to say a few words.

"I am so grateful to all of you for helping me celebrate my eightieth birthday here in New York. Having all the family members gathered around the table delights and overwhelms me. If Alice could see us now, she would be thrilled. In keeping with that thought, I wanted to ask her namesake, Allison, to repeat her lines from her school Thanksgiving program. Allison, would you please stand by me and repeat your lines so that everybody can hear?"

I feared that Allison would be too shy, but no, she stood and walked purposefully to Gunther's side. He put his arm around her little waist, and she boldly treated us to:

Behold! What a bounty I see before me!

Corn from the earth and apples from the trees.

We are thankful to you, our Indian friends, and to God.

Amid much applause a grinning Allison returned to her seat. Even the folks at the table next to us appeared enchanted. The table's captain nodded his approval and presented Allison with their traditional pink cotton candy confection, which occupied her for the remainder of Gunther's talk.

"I next want to welcome Todd to the family. You've made Rand a very happy fellow, and that's been of great comfort to me. You and Rand took on an uphill battle and are winning! And I predict that it will be easier and easier to win those battles. I hope to live long enough to see that day."

Todd nodded his thanks. He was sitting next to Rand. Todd was handsome and muscular. Fair-haired and broad-shouldered—a Levi's and plaid-flannel-shirt guy who seemed quite uncomfortable in a suit and tie and had loosened the tie a bit and unbuttoned his suit jacket. Rand must have gone suit shopping with him.

"And to Josh—congratulations on your promotion. You're also lucky in love, which is no small thing. Amy is perfect for you. She is a loving mother and wife, and an 'in-house counsel'! Listen to her well, Josh; she sees things straight and true."

"And to Max, a far lengthier tribute. First an apology. On that day, many years ago, when we met for lunch at the Harvard Club, I confess that I completely underestimated you."

Dad smiled like he was in a toothpaste commercial.

"You stunned me with the announcement of your plans to wed Maddy. I was uncharacteristically lost for words. But in thinking back on it, I should have seen it coming. You were a talented, ambitious, and determined go-getter. Nothing was going to stop you. A regular Sammy Glick.

"So, Maddy became your first prize. Your laser-like devotion to your business was the single most important reason for its success, and, of course, that trophy was your second prize. Believe me, it takes someone special to disregard the intrusions of most non-work-related distractions, to put minor family matters aside to focus on the business. Persuading your family to take it public became your treasured third prize. You are the legendary indispensable man, Max. I, along with your shareholders, hope you apply that vision, tenacity, and foresight for years to come!"

Dad was absolutely beaming. "Gunther, thanks, coming from you those were terrific compliments. If I may say something, I was never one to sit on my rear end and wait for lady fortune to arrive. And I didn't come from money. Not like some at this table. Nope, I went after the big prize from day one, and by God, I won it!"

Mom merely pursed her lips and glared at her dad.

"And now, Madeline, my dear daughter. Since you were a little girl, not much older than Allison, you have been my loving confidant and partner. You've always put me and your family first, bringing us much joy and comfort, without sacrificing your own determination to make your own way in life. No, you didn't listen to my advice at the Harvard Club. Like Frank Sinatra, you wanted to do it your way. And you did do it your way, demonstrating an admirable independence. One last thing, Maddy. When you sent me a copy of your dissertation on Henry James, I must admit I cheated a bit and skipped to your chapter on *The Portrait of a Lady*. James presents us with an independent, strong-willed, attractive Isabel Archer who ultimately finds contentment in rejecting societal expectations. Remarkably, you have many things in common with her, namely dedicating yourself to a noble and unusual pursuit. In your case, your PhD. Perhaps you will also share Isabel Archer's destiny.

"And now if Allison and the rest of you will forgive me one more indulgence . . . as we Jews like to say on such occasions, thank you, God, for allowing us to reach this day."

As we exited the restaurant, Gunther embraced each of us, hailed a cab, and returned to his apartment.

The family walked a few blocks back to the St. Regis.

Amy spoke first. "He hasn't lost his touch. Subtext and innuendo so subtle, his little speech would merely float over the heads of the unwary."

Maddy said, "You're right, Amy. You have to parse every sentence."

Dad jumped in. "Well, speaking for myself, I feel great. He publicly admitted he misjudged me, and he couldn't have been more complimentary. Who's that Sammy Glick person?"

"A character in a play—*What Makes Sammy Run*."

Dad shrugged.

Then Amy asked Mom about Isabel Archer in *Portrait of a Lady*, reminding her that she had never read it.

"We'll talk about it sometime, but his message to me was crystal clear," a stone-faced Maddy murmured.

And with that we arrived at the hotel.

When we entered the lobby, Mom turned to me and Rand and asked if she might speak with us.

"It's time you boys cleared the air. It hurts me to see you two acting like strangers with each other. Do this for me, please."

I looked at Amy, whose facial expression left no doubt she expected me to succeed at this second mission—the one she had declared on our London trip. Rand spoke to Todd, and then turned to me. "Let's get a table in the bar."

The King Cole bar at the St. Regis was sophisticated, venerable, and expensive. Dad was quite familiar with it since he stayed at the hotel, while we mere company mortals were billeted at the Hilton. His hotel bills and entertainment tabs sent our controller into a tizzy. Carly greased the skids, but the expenditures were the talk of the office.

Behind the bar was the famous Maxfield Parrish mural depicting Old King Cole sitting on his throne, with various supplicants and retainers scurrying about.

Rand had never before seen the mural, and stated that he thought it looked "like Dad sitting on his throne at the company, with his staff doing his bidding."

"You nailed it, Rand, except wasn't Old King Cole a merry old soul?"

"Yup, couldn't be Dad."

We sat down at one of the high-top tables, ordered drinks, and gazed at one another for a few moments.

"Josh, we have to end our standoff. For our sakes. For Mom. For the three of us. So let me start. I apologize from the bottom of my heart for damaging your career prospects when I had my confrontation with Dad. I have replayed that conversation dozens of times in my mind. You were right to be pissed off—or worse."

"It was bad enough that you revealed your own vote against going public. Dad would have figured out that I, too, had voted against the IPO. He's good with numbers. But why, oh why, did you have to reveal it? Throw my secret vote in his face! Why did you use me like that?"

"Because it was the weapon that would damage him the most. He had written me off years ago and must have been pleasantly surprised when he wrongly assumed that I had voted with him.

You were always his favorite. So, in that moment, after being bullied and vilified, scorned and belittled, I threw that grenade to bloody the son of a bitch. And Josh, honestly, I would do it again, though I regret making you collateral damage in the fight."

"Then what kind of apology are you making, telling me that you would do it again?"

"In a minute. Let me explain." Rand shifted in his seat, then went on. "I will always regret hurting you. You were always my champion. You never let me down. You rooted for me to succeed. I never knew what sibling rivalry was until I left home. It shocked me when I discovered that brothers were not always best friends, because you were mine. But in that moment, when Dad and I were eyeball-to-eyeball, and he was making a mockery of my life and treating me like scum, I had to use your vote to bring him down.

"You see, Dad is never content to merely win a competition with a member of the family. No, he must eviscerate, humiliate, or emasculate his adversary."

"C'mon, Rand, aren't you exaggerating?"

"No. Look what he did with his own father. Not content with going to work for his competitor, he slashed prices and drove Sy out of business. Not content to ostracize me, he needed to stick the knife in and twist it. And with that knife burrowing into my gut, I threw the grenade at that sadistic bastard. That stopped him, dead. So, while I regret using you as I did, my survival instincts took over."

He took a deep breath and continued. "And one more thing. He will find a way to not only hurt Mom, but he will also shame and humiliate her in the process. And you will be next. You will need any weapon you can find to bring him to his knees, or you will end your life like Sy, a gentle, lovely old man, defeated and impotent."

I sat back in my chair and tried to digest what Rand was saying. Was he merely trying to rationalize what he had done, or was he justified? My recent bout with Dad—dismissal, my forced reinstatement, and then his threats and tongue-lashing—revealed his ruthlessness and cruelty. I had fought back. But I held the trump card—the board's support. What if I hadn't?

I was not at all sure that Rand and I had buried the hatchet. I would call it what diplomats term a "candid and constructive exchange of views." I understood why he did what he did, but it still hurt. It would take time and sad events for us to reconnect as brothers, and as best friends.

Chapter 27

I THREW MYSELF INTO MY NEW BUYING ASSIGNMENT WITH VIGOR. Not since Dad had handed me that real estate evaluation project, years before, had I attacked a task with such energy. I was determined to succeed. Only now, the gloves were off.

I met with Herb Segal at his home in the suburbs after the holidays to come up with a game plan. Herb was a real veteran. Max had promoted him from the stores in the mid-seventies, and he had done virtually every job in the merchandising department—planner, distributor, merchandiser, and then buyer of our branded footwear. He was a font of information and was very supportive, not at all threatened or insecure about my partnering with him. In all honesty, he seemed to welcome it.

He had already filled three boxes with fashion magazines like *Vanity Fair, Elle, Cosmo,* and *Vogue* for me to take home and plow through when I had time. He suggested we schedule a trip to Milan and Paris to visit boutiques and observe what women were wearing. He even recommended I spend a day on Washington University's campus to see what the girls were wearing.

We spent a week at the office studying last year's style-by-style selling histories. What worked? What didn't? And most importantly, why? We did a style-out of expected spring deliveries. This involved devoting an entire sample room to displaying merchandise our stores would present to our customers in the February through May period. That was a sobering experience, because we could tell that we would be missing the mark if the fashion magazines and trend forecasting services we subscribed to were accurate. We might be able to cancel some of the later deliveries if we got on the horn right away, which we did. That helped, but it didn't solve the problem. For better or worse, spring was pretty much put to bed. We had to rebound in fall/holiday, which accounted for about 60 percent of our sales and 75 percent of our profits.

Herb asked me to give my dad a heads-up about spring, which I dutifully did. Dad couldn't resist lambasting Herb, calling him worthless as a pimple on a goat's ass.

Our trip to Milan and Paris would conclude with a stop in New York to visit our brands. By that time, we should have a clear idea of what was needed for fall.

Before we left, I treated myself to a mid-January afternoon on campus. Even though Amy and I lived only a few blocks away, we hadn't visited except for Mom's commencement when she received her PhD.

I don't know who was handling admissions at the school, but they must have been requiring photos attached to the applications. The girls were amazing looking.

I admit, I did a little fantasizing, but I didn't get much of a fashion read; most of the girls were wearing slim washed designer jeans, L.L. Bean hunting boots, Timberlands, or Wellingtons. And they sported puffers from Patagonia, North Face, REI, L.L. Bean, and one or two with the Moncler insignia. They were bundled up for winter. I made a mental note to return in the spring when they would be wearing shorts, skinny tees, and sandals. It would be a must on my calendar.

Not surprisingly, Milan and Paris were two of Mom's favorite cities. We often stopped there on our family vacations, but I wouldn't be staying at the Grand Hotel et de Milan or the Ritz, nor would I be viewing *The Last Supper* or the *Mona Lisa*. I would be there on business, and that meant shopping the boutiques, dropping in on a few of the luxury-brand showrooms to peruse but not buy, and observing what women were wearing. We were desperate for answers, because we needed to save fall at all costs.

On the long plane ride to Milan, Herb and I had plenty of time to shoot the bull; after a few of those bitty bottles of booze, we had what can only be described as a pity party. We gave in to the temptation to moan about the forces that were challenging our business—some of our own making, and some beyond our control.

The litany was long: too many price promotions, the colossal athletic shoe phenomenon Dad had mistakenly declared a fad, casual lifestyles that dinged our dress shoe business, and so on. Competition was fierce both inside and outside the mall. Discounters were rampant. And regional malls were fading in popularity. Oh, woe were we! But that's the world we were living in.

After landing at Milan Malpensa, we endured a $75 taxi ride into the city center. The outskirts of Milan were as drab as those of any large American city. But it was the shopping district bounded by Via della Spiga and Via Montenapoleone that was the nexus of haute couture and luxury, so we headed there after checking into our hotel and having a bite to eat. Gucci was our first stop, and from there we went to Ferragamo, Tod's, and the other luxe apparel and footwear boutiques. What an eye-opener for me. I was fascinated with classics like the little beribboned ballet slippers at Ferragamo, the little quilted flats at Chanel, the horse-bit loafers at Gucci, and the driving shoes at Tod's. The color arrays were remarkable. And their dressier fashion looks wowed us as well.

And the women . . . these were, by far, the best-dressed, most-attractive women in the world, clicking their way down the cobblestone streets in stiletto heels. Like nothing I had ever seen (or bothered to notice) before. What a pleasant education.

We spent a couple of days in Milan visiting more accessible retailers in their Galleria Vittorio Emanuele II shopping center and their upscale department store, La Rinascente, across from the Great Cathedral.

For nostalgic reasons, we stopped in at the Massimo brothers' headquarters—which were a far cry from their original workshop Dad first visited in 1950. Their sons, who now ran the company, greeted us with enthusiasm, treated us to lunch, praised Dad, and gave us a taste of Italian charm and hospitality. But it had been many years since our family's Fratelli Massimo could afford their Italian shoes. We took a quick look at the sample room, asked the sons to extend our best wishes to their fathers, and were on our way.

Our experiences in Paris were enlightening. We spent time on the great shopping streets, like the Champs-Élysées and Rue Faubourg St. Honoré, on the right bank. Rue de Sèvres on the left bank rendered us *au courant* regarding the state of fashion in Europe. Again, department stores like Galeries Lafayette, Printemps, and Le Bon Marché, with their inviting in-store boutiques, showed us many brands and looks that were popular with affluent Parisians. We even went to some of the dingier areas of Paris, near the Marais, to see what street fashion was all about.

Whenever the Feldman clan visited Paris, we saved one evening for dinner at Le Relais de Venise. Herb had never been there, but was game to try it. After waiting for about half an hour in line, we entered this glorious steak-frites joint. We enjoyed the most delectable meal, concluding with a sinfully delicious and calorie-laden profiterole, for a scant equivalent of forty US dollars per person. It was a welcome contrast after the fancy schmancy, multicourse dessert-trolley and cheese-cart restaurants we had previously labored through. These had come in around 150 dollars per person, with title, taxes, and dealer prep.

On the plane trip to New York, we plotted our battle plan with our branded suppliers. And it worked to perfection!

Visits all started with the usual schmoozing, which my partner Herb excelled at. I felt it must be a generational thing. He knew all the stories and the personalities, present and past. He could identify styles from a vendor that worked and those that were floperoos.

Then the salesmen would show us the entire line. I would be scribbling notes and Herb would be putting his hands on the merchandise and moving the samples back and forth. The sales team wanted orders, of course, and came equipped with pens and order forms awaiting our decisions. Because Herb and I had prepared so well, we had a fair idea of what would work and what wouldn't—but we wanted to go a step further. So, I broke the ice.

"What did Nordstrom buy?" I asked. Nordstrom was widely recognized as the best fashion shoe retailer in the country.

"Sorry, boys, but we can't share that information with you."

"What are you? Priests, lawyers, or doctors who can't divulge client secrets? Sign some kind of oath?"

"Well, no. But they are our biggest customer. No disrespect to Fratelli Massimo, but your purchase totals are about 25 percent of what they buy."

"What if our purchases for this coming season were zero percent of Nordstrom's?"

"C'mon, guys."

"C'mon, yourself. What did they buy? What are they betting on?"

We would frick and frack and play good cop and bad. Then we'd snap shut our attaché cases and pretend to leave. The usual.

Finally, we squeezed answers out of them. Some of the vendors would tell us outright. Others, with more scruples, merely pointed to the styles Nordstrom had purchased without uttering a sound. Whatever worked for them.

"But," we were warned, "you cannot underprice Nordstrom by a penny."

"Agreed," we nodded our heads.

When it came to their brand's performance at FM, I dragged out that brand's selling report at Fratelli Massimo for the previous year which, in addition to reporting sales and inventory levels, computed the margin that brand had generated. Suddenly, the meeting became tense.

"What financial payback does Macy's ask for when your brand's profits don't meet expectations?" I asked.

"That, my friends, is strictly confidential."

"I get it," I continued. "I've done the grunt work for you. We expect your brand to produce X percent gross margin. You fell short by Y dollars, so we would like a check in that amount."

"Outrageous. Your dad never asked for markdown money like that."

"Well, there's a new sheriff in town, and you owe us for many years of markdown money."

"Fuck you," was the response.

"Fuck you," was my answer.

Eventually we would compromise, of course, but in every case, we would receive a sizeable credit against the purchases we were writing for the upcoming season. Those credits would add significantly to Fratelli Massimo profits for the fall. And we had set the precedent for future concessions!

On the plane ride back to St. Louis, Herb gave me a skeptical look. "Those gross margin numbers you obligated the vendors for looked inflated to me, Josh. Are you sure your calculations were correct? Because if they're not that high, you screwed those guys."

"Paying for past sins, Herb. And besides, as my grandfather Sy said, 'There's a little larceny in every retailer.'"

"Your father would agree with your grandfather on that."

Results for fall, as it turned out, were excellent. Not Timberland excellent, but excellent enough to boost our annual sales and profits and dislodge the stock price from its trading doldrums, going from twenty-two to twenty-eight dollars a share.

Herb and I became a team. Our skills complemented one another. He was engaging, encyclopedic in his knowledge of the shoe business, and very wise. I was the numbers guy, and most of the time, the bad cop. Let's say that I was the not-so-gentle Josh. Hammer in hand, goddamn it. Neither of us were artistes or fashion seers, but between our preparations, number crunching, and negotiating tag-team routine, we were magic.

Dad was pleased and made a point of praising me at that February's board meeting when the previous fall and full year's results were shared with the directors. I was careful to give Herb lots of credit, though he was not there, of course, to hear it.

Then we absolutely crushed the previous spring's miserable numbers, and were on our way to another excellent year. Still, I knew that these bottom-of-the-ninth heroics could not last forever.

· · ·

Late spring was not too early to start preparing for the fall President's Ball at Highland Hills, where Dad would be installed as president, succeeding Bobby Weil. Dad brought up the subject at one of our increasingly rare Sunday family dinners.

"Maddy, I'm going to need your help to plan the ball. You attended lots of these parties in your New York life. You know the ins and outs of these things better than anybody else. Decorations, menu, table arrangements, and all that stuff. I want mine to have a 'continental' flavor, something unique—something the members will remember for a long time to come. Think of it as my inaugural ball."

"No, thank you, Max. I want nothing to do with this. I'll gladly accompany you and do the chitchat, but this is your party. Not ours. I told you that years ago, when HH reared its head. Ask Andrea Marks, or better yet, the first lady of HH, Evie Weil, to plan it."

"Please don't dig your heels in, Maddy. This is my one chance to show the club what we two can do. All the members look up to you, know your background and style, and expect something special."

"I doubt very much that they look up, down, or sideways at me, dear. You're the main man. I'm a mere accessory. Just call Andrea or Evie, who planned the last ball, which was considered a smashing success."

"Andrea does it for most everybody, and she's very talented. And Evie did plan the last ball, which was the best ever. But I know you can do better. I promise I won't ask you to do another thing, please just this year's President's Ball."

C'mon, Mom, I thought. *Just this one time . . .*

Mom sat up in her chair, cupped her chin in her hand, her elbow on the table and, Solomon-like, considered the appeal. Dad awaited the verdict with bated breath. It really meant the world to him.

"Unique and memorable. And continental and special?" Mom confirmed.

"You got it."

"I'll think about it, and we'll talk about it next Sunday."

"I knew you'd step up." He grinned.

Amy and I couldn't wait to see what Mom would come up with. Nor could Dad, who wasted no time asking Maddy what her plan was when we sat down at the table a week later.

"Well, Max, I have been giving the matter a lot of thought. You wanted a format that was unique, memorable, continental, and special. A real *wow*. Something the members will remember for a long time, right?"

"Exactly."

"Well, it will be hard to compete with Evie's boffo party two years ago. Not sure I can pull it off." She put her fork down.

"I know you can, Maddy, and so do you. Tell the kids about Bobby's installation."

"OK. Bobby and Evie came up with an absolutely smashing theme. 'A Scottish Highland's Fling,' it was called. What could be more appropriate for Highland Hills Country Club? Nothing! That's what makes the challenge so difficult." Mom took a sip of water and went on.

"All the walls were tastefully covered with tartan plaid tapestries, banners, plaques, and Scottish battle implements. There was even a diorama of the Battle of Culloden. Many of the members wore kilts. Dare we peek? Each of the tables represented a different Scottish clan, but with a twist. Instead of the 'O'Neil table' for example, it was the 'Oy' Neil table.' Unfortunately, I think O's are for the Irish, Mac's are for the Scots. But we'll call it poetic license. And, of course, the tables used the genuine clan plaids for tablecloths. A couple of bottles of single malt Scotch at each table. And the menu was an admittedly rather tough roast of beef complemented with a generous helping of haggis." She looked into the distance and shrugged.

"Dear, it was rather cruel, if you don't mind my saying so, that nobody warned the kosher people that haggis was sheep's offal, but from where I was seated, I don't think anybody cleaned his plate. Dessert was a veddy English black pudding. And to top it all off, a bagpipe ensemble entertained. They can't possibly imagine what it's like to listen a three-hour bagpipe session, can they, dear? But the coup de grace was the flourish and entry of the club president and first lady dressed as Bonnie Prince Charles and Mary Queen of Scots!"

Amy and I burst out laughing. The visual of the Weils was a showstopper.

Allison wanted to know what we were all laughing about, and I explained that it was an "adult" thing; she went back to her book.

Dad soldiered on. "Mom's described it perfectly. And that really puts a lot of pressure on me for this year's bash."

"Well, as I said, it will be tough to follow the Scottish Highland's Fling, but I thought maybe a more ethnically Jewish theme would work," Mom said.

"I'm not sure I understand," Dad said.

"I call it 'An Evening at the Kibbutz'."

"Maddy, you're joking!" roared Dad.

"Shush, darling, here are the highlights. An Evening at the Kibbutz: the ballroom walls will be festooned with Israeli flags, photos of Jerusalem, and some portraits of the political and military heroes of the country. The door to the ladies' locker room will serve as an emergency exit, in the highly unlikely event of a Palestinian mortar attack. Each of the guests will be encouraged to arrive in khaki attire with perhaps a colorful scarf for this festive occasion. Each of the wooden picnic tables (this is a kibbutz, after all) will represent one of the twelve tribes of the Jewish people— Reuben, Simeon, Judah, and so on. One table, representing the lost tribe, will be reserved for the club's few non-Jewish members. The menu calls for challah; boiled chicken—just like your mother Rose served for the High Holidays; string beans—fresh or canned, depending on availability; a dollop of fresh horseradish; a sweet potato timbale, and, of course, a tasty sponge cake for dessert. The wine, of course, will be a Mogen David selection. And entertainment will be provided by a klezmer band dreck from New Yawk, as they say."

"Maddy, that's enough!" Dad shouted.

"But you haven't heard the best part, dear. Our flourish will be performed by the klezmer band...perhaps 'Hatikvah.' And then, our grand entrance. I see you as Moshe Dayan, eye patch and all. Perfect. And I'll be Golda Meir. I'll need to strap on some Santa poundage and find a dowdy dress and matronly shoes, but no sacrifice is too great for this wonderful affair. There you have it. Your thoughts?"

Dad stormed from the room.

Amy and I couldn't hold it in any longer, and we exploded in laughter. Poor Allison didn't know what to make of the whole thing. We hustled her out of the house and into the car. There would be hell to pay for Mom.

When we were in the car, I burst out, "I didn't know Mom could be that clever and caustic."

"And cruel and reckless," Amy responded.

Sunday dinners were suspended for several months, given that evening's drama and the arctic freeze that settled over Brentmoor Park. Each parent carried on—Dad, when he managed to show up at the office, and Mom, at the bridge table—but it was chill city over there.

Midafternoon on the Sunday a week before the President's Ball, which Andrea Marks had planned, Maddy called to invite us over and asked us to pick up a pizza on the way. Evidently Dad had some last-minute work to do for the big party, and he wouldn't be at home. I was watching football upstairs, and Amy and Jenn were playing some video games with Jonathan and Allison in the basement. I called down to Amy and asked her if she was OK with Maddy's invitation.

"Sure, as long as . . . sure! Jenn's mom asked her to take Bobby to the airport around four, so she's going to leave in a few minutes. So, yeah, let's go to your mom's."

Amy, Allison, and I piled into the family SUV, stopped for a couple of pizzas, and arrived at Brentmoor Park around six.

Dad's absence was a blessing. No tension, no awkward silences, no verbal warfare. Just like old times, but without Dad. Allison showed Maddy some of the moves she had learned in gymnastics, which elicited a smile of contentment.

"I so vividly remember you boys at her age. Allison brings back those happy days to me. You and that stupid game of Horse with Rand the Man. Oh, how your father hated to see you lose!"

"Speaking of Dad, Mom, what's he up to tonight? Polishing the silver for the ball?"

"Not quite. He's at the Weils'. We just spoke on the phone. Evidently, Bobby is helping Dad with his speech. I don't get it. It's not exactly the Sermon on the Mount or Henry V's charge to the troops. But Bobby knows best!"

Amy looked at me wide-eyed and gave me a signal to shut up.

Luckily Mom's attention was diverted, as she was occupied taking the pizzas out of the oven.

Amy and I both knew that Bobby had left for New York. It didn't take clueless me long to figure out what Dad was up to.

We managed to act as if everything were normal, though we hurried things along—not sure we could maintain the charade. We made our getaway on the early side, claiming we each faced a horrible Monday at the office.

Amy and I stayed silent in the car on the way home and then sent Allison to bed. Exhausted, we flopped down on the couch.

I was lost in my own thoughts. I adored Mom. How could he risk hurting her like this? I knew Dad was no angel. I never bought his story about why he was staying at the St. Regis while the rest of the team was at the Hilton. And his unexplained absences from work? Showering before he went home from the club after playing golf on weekdays? He never used to play golf on weekdays. All very suspect. But Evie Weil, whom Mom detested?

After a few minutes, Amy spoke, mercifully skipping the "I told you so's." She shook her head. "Maddy's very likely to find out what's going on between Max and Evie."

Chapter 28

BECAUSE WE WEREN'T MEMBERS OF THE CLUB, WE WEREN'T expecting to attend the ball, but I received a phone call from Andrea Marks on the Monday preceding the affair inviting us as "special guests" of the incoming president. "Your father insisted. The board agreed. So please, come at seven thirty, a half hour before the party starts. Your dad will want a family picture."

Andrea was gracious enough to greet us at the club's entrance and escort us to Balmoral Hall, where the fete was to take place. A photographer was taking pictures of the elegantly decorated grand English half-timbered hall, the lavishly adorned tables, and the leaders of the club and their wives. My beaming dad beckoned us to join Maddy and him for a family photo. We arranged ourselves and smiled. We didn't know it at the time, of course, but it was to be the last photograph ever taken of the four of us together.

Tables for eight were adorned with china chargers flanked by ranks of sterling silver flatware and crystal goblets; dramatic floral centerpieces filled most of the room. Amy and I were to be seated at a special spotlight table along with Mom and Dad; Bobby, who was the outgoing president; and Evie Weil, Jenn Katzenberg, and her husband, Tommy. A nine hundred square-foot dance floor adjacent to a rehearsing band occupied the north side of the room. A heady air of anticipation enveloped Balmoral Hall for this biannual event.

The members and their spouses filed in, dressed in formal attire. The men were in tuxes, some in morning coats, and the women were jewel-bedecked, clothed in their fashion finery and uncomfortably perched on three-inch heels. Many were anxious to congratulate my slimmed-down, tuxedo-attired dad, and my mom, who chose to wear an Oscar de la Renta gown, along with a glittering array of jewelry. Amy had on her little black dress and the Manolo Blahniks that she wore when she dined with Trey Baker. She was on the receiving end of a lot of admiring (lustful?) looks from the men.

Out of politeness, I imagine, Amy and I were congratulated, along with my folks. Drinks and hors d'oeuvres were passed by staff in livery. Joy was in the air.

When the guests were summoned to their tables by the clang of an Asian gong, Bobby Weil stepped to the mic to introduce Dad. Bobby didn't hold back, but gushed endlessly about "my friend and our president, Max Feldman." My dad was glowing.

Dad strode confidently to the mic. After thanking "my good friend Bobby" for his kind remarks, Dad began his inaugural address. "Proud to be your president . . . from my humble beginnings on the plains of Nebraska to this crowning achievement . . . I promise to continue the club's forward momentum and maintain its stature as the best Jewish country club in the city." He saved the best for last: "And maybe the best club in St. Louis—even the gentile ones!" This last line was met with a roar of approval and a standing ovation.

Dad slow-walked back to our table, shaking hands, kissing cheeks, and soaking up the love.

He was, in Tom Wolfe's eloquent phrase, "A man in full."

Triumphant, he returned to the table where he was seated between Evie Weil and Mom.

With the band playing subdued musical numbers, allowing guests to actually talk and be heard at their tables, Mom kissed and congratulated Dad with a hint of a smile—but her eyes narrowed as she turned to Bobby and thanked him for helping Dad polish his speech. "Frankly, I was being bitchy about it; glad you were there for him Sunday night, Bobby."

"Hell," Bobby responded with a broad smile, "I didn't help him Sunday; I was in New York. Max did it on his lonesome."

"But Max, darling, you called me from the Weils' house Sunday evening. I missed the call and called you right back, and you said you were working with Bobby on your speech. You didn't get home till midnight."

There was a long moment of silence. Mom's polite smile disappeared, replaced by an expression conveying acknowledgment of a long-held suspicion. She nodded her head up and down slightly, as if to register confirmation of her discovery.

Dad was trapped, speechless, his eyes wide and his face white as a ghost.

Mom said, "Perhaps you were working on your speech with Evie? No, I think not; that doesn't make sense. 'Popular and flamboyant Evie' can't string two sentences together."

With the bit firmly between her teeth and fire in her eyes, like a racehorse nearing the finish line, Mom added, "Why, Evie, I bet you're sleeping with both the past and current presidents of the club, aren't you, dear? How proud you must be!"

"Wait a goddamn minute, Maddy!" Bobby howled. "You can't talk to my wife like that!"

"No, you wait, Bobby." Mom eyed him with total contempt. "You've engineered the whole thing, haven't you? Took us public. Pushed my all-too-eager husband through the ranks at the club. With a little bit of help from Evie, who has been so accommodating."

Evie rose from her chair. "Perhaps if you had been more accommodating in the bedroom, Maddy, Max wouldn't have been sniffing around me. Not my toughest conquest." Evie half-stumbled as she exited with a clatter of her chair, drawing attention to our table.

"Oh, Max, you've been sharing our little marital secrets with Evie, haven't you?"

In a stage whisper that could be heard from thirty feet away, my panicky dad begged, "Not here, not now. Maddy, please shut up!"

A hush had fallen over most of the surrounding tables. Even the musicians stopped playing.

"I'll shut up, Max." She hurled the contents of her champagne glass at Dad, and she didn't miss.

Dad stood, his champagne-soaked face a shade of purple, his fists clenched in a prizefighter's stance. But Mom literally beat him to the punch, slapping his face with a smack that echoed across the room.

Before he could respond, Mom spun from the table, asked Amy and me to drive her home, and left the hall. Amy and I trailed a few steps behind.

All eyes were on the drama—including the members of the band, the serving staff, and the wide-eyed club manager, Andrea Marks.

The *St. Louis Post-Dispatch*'s gossip columnist, Jerry Berger, reported the incident in Monday morning's edition:

Off script at hoity-toity Highland Hills Country Club's President's Ball Saturday night. Shoe maven and new club prexy Max Feldman's florid face fielded a glass of champagne

and a roundhouse haymaker from wife Maddy as news
of Max's extracurricular adventures with Evie Weil (wife
of outgoing president Bobby Weil) blew up the gathering.
Naughty, naughty.

● ● ●

I was summoned to Dad's office the minute I got to work Monday morning. He was pacing, a rolled-up copy of the *Post-Dispatch* in his fist. He slammed the door to his office, continued pacing, and proceeded to launch into a blistering rant about Mom. "Smug, frigid, arrogant, vengeful, and worse things I would call her, if you weren't here! How could she choose that time and place to bring me down?"

"How can you ask that question, Dad? You brought it on yourself. You lied and you cheated on her with Evie Weil, and it was revealed at that table at the President's Ball. What did you expect her to do? Suffer in silence?"

"Yes, to be blunt. To permit me my moment in the sun. I'd earned it. We could have hashed it out later, at home."

"That's ridiculous, Dad. You expected Mom to just sit there and smile? Just like you tolerated Rand's sexual orientation? No, you had to humiliate and degrade my brother. Just like you permitted Sy to stay in business? No, you had to destroy him. You weren't content to merely play Dickie the Stick, you had to be fucking Evie Weil, Mom's nemesis and a world-class gossip. You're rather good at twisting the knife. Mom's response was fair play."

"Don't go judging me, Gentle Josh. You have to be a street fighter to succeed in this business. Kill or be killed. Success wasn't handed to me on a silver platter like it was for you, your mother, and your brother. You're all spoiled. Sure, I had to get my hands dirty, while all of you were wearing white gloves. But I gave you everything you have, and I can take it—"

"Let's stop the bullshit," I interrupted. It was past time to clear the air once and for all. "You've betrayed every member of the family. You don't trust me, because I voted against going public. And I don't trust you. The only thing that matters to you is results and making Fratelli Massimo succeed. I'm the only person working at the company who you can count on to make that happen. We both know you're not about to recruit someone to fill that slot, so don't start in on that again. Who would tolerate your bullying? Now, let's wrap this up. I have work to do, unless you want to do it yourself, which I highly doubt."

He mumbled a response and then started talking again about HHCC, where directors and past presidents were meeting that very night to decide the fate of his presidency. Evidently, the outrage of the members was palpable Saturday night and was further inflamed by Jerry Berger's gossipy reporting in the *P-D*. Many were demanding that Dad step down. Ever-reliable Bobby Weil, who treasured his sketchy if not outright illegal insider relationship with Max, had advised his meal ticket to stay the course. "I'll lead your defense team and explain that a not-so-stable and inebriated Maddy touched off the melee, and you did your best to quell it," Bobby had told Dad. As for the infidelity matter, Bobby was confident that the all-male group would be sympathetic and shrug it off. Dad agreed. "None of these guys will want to throw stones in their glass houses! But even if they let me finish my term, I'll accomplish nothing. Not with a hostile board and an angry membership."

He then reported that Evie had terminated the affair. "She said, 'I can't deal with the drama of your hellcat wife, and evidently, you can't either.'"

And to conclude his list of woes, he told me, "Your mom and I are going to legally separate."

I was then dismissed, mercifully, and returned to my office where I called Mom. Nora picked up and said Mom was in bed and didn't want to be disturbed; she suggested I call back later in the day. I didn't reach her until Tuesday, when she was up and about, according to Nora. Mom and I made a date for lunch on Wednesday at the Ritz.

Dad called me early Tuesday morning. After a four-hour meeting, the board had decided that Dad's presidency should be spared. Mom was clearly the "provocateur" and had acted in an "unwifely" manner, but Dad was censured for his inability to subdue or control her. "Airing dirty laundry in public is not the Highland Hills way." The board reluctantly conceded that the "Highland Hills Incident" would continue to be fodder for Jerry Berger if Max's term were cut short—which would be unprecedented for the club. "Nobody wanted that!" Dad, for his part, promised that Maddy would not appear at the club, except to play bridge. This last arrangement was welcomed by the board, which looked favorably on Maddy's outstanding bridge playing when the prestigious and hotly contested interclub ladies' bridge matches were held.

Dad's prophecy proved to be correct; he served out his term as a lame duck with little being accomplished. His successor, a senior partner at Hotchkiss and Hamilton, Amy's firm, not-so-quietly campaigned for the presidency with the not-so-subtle promise of "restoring dignity to the office."

· · ·

The Wednesday before Thanksgiving must be a slow day in the hotel business, because we had the Ritz dining room to ourselves. I arrived a bit early and was seated at a banquette facing the entrance, so I could greet Mom when she arrived. I didn't know what state she would be in, but I needn't have worried.

At noon on the dot, she entered and strode to our banquette, and we warmly embraced. No tears, just a long and hearty hug. God, I loved her so.

Except for her low-heeled Ferragamos, she was totally Chanel, with a nubby, subtle plaid suit and contrasting shell, and an emerald brooch from Bulgari.

"Mom, you look divine, just like those women in Milan."

"Bet they weren't wearing a shaper and support hose, and didn't have crows' feet. Your father always wanted me to have 'work done,'" she laughed, "and I told him that we should go together, so that he could have his man boobs reduced and a bit of liposuction around his love handles. We declared a cease-fire. Just like we did Sunday night."

The waiter came over and took our orders, and quickly delivered her Chardonnay and my Diet Coke.

"Look, my darling Joshua, let me be frank. The end of the marriage was a long time in coming. Your father and I have been out of sync for years. It probably started before Fratelli Massimo went public, but the drama and wounded feelings that going public evoked sped the dissolution. And his inexcusable treatment of Rand left me with a raging anger with Max.

"We both wanted and needed different things. I loved privacy and your dad craved public recognition. I sought comfort in my studies, my family, and my bridge, and your dad sought comfort in his business and celebrity and, well ... in other ways, as we all have discovered."

She had a sip of her wine and continued, "The breakdown of the marriage is not completely your father's fault—maybe 80 to 90 percent. I made my own little contributions. Shutting him down in the bedroom. Refusing to help him with his little speech or serving on the 'What to do about the wives?' committee. Proposing the Night at the Kibbutz. . . ." She smiled. "Was that delicious? But costly! And I got to humiliate him and that whore of his at the club. You have no idea how much satisfaction I derived from that. I have no real regrets, other than marrying him in the first place, but then I have you two boys."

We were served lunch and Mom ordered another Chardonnay. This was becoming a worrisome habit with her.

"And why a separation, rather than a divorce?" was my question.

"Too complicated. I spoke, of course, to my father who, to his credit, didn't remind me that he had warned me repeatedly against marrying Max. Gunther's eightieth-birthday party allusion to Isabel Archer in *Portrait of a Lady* cut me to the quick that evening. Like her, I had married the wrong guy and would leave him but technically stay married to the abusive bastard.

"No, ever the pragmatist, he focused on the legal and financial quagmire the family would face in a court-ordered division of assets. Max would insist on my disposing of my Fratelli Massimo stock, for example. I can't bear the thought of relinquishing family control of that company. Nor do I relish the publicity that a divorce and its legal wrangling would entail. Instead, we will work things out in a civilized way in the privacy of an attorney's office. And we will each be free to live our lives as we wish.

"I'll buy a smaller house nearby, perhaps in University City, but more likely in Clayton. One with a downstairs bedroom. I want to be near to you, Amy, and Allison, but not too close. You will have your privacy, as will I."

"You can stay with us for a while if you like, Mom. But why a downstairs bedroom? They're hard to find in Clayton, particularly in a smaller home. You're physically fit, and climbing the stairs is supposed to be good exercise."

"Thanks for offering to put me up for a while, but thirteen thousand square feet is enough space for your father and me to coexist peaceably for a few months. And as for the downstairs bedroom, well, I am closing in on sixty-five, and on the cusp of old ladyhood. I've been a smoker for most of those years, so those steps are a bit of a strain. I'm winded every time I climb that hideous circular staircase at Brentmoor. I need to hold tight to that banister to make it to the top."

By that time, the wine was affecting her speech.

"Your father is capable of disloyalty and betrayal and has demonstrated that numerous times. I am merely the latest example. You're now the last member of the family still in a position to be victimized. And you will be. I don't know how or when, but Max will find a way." My mom looked me straight in the eyes. "Be on guard. Better yet, weaponize yourself for that day. You won't be able to throw champagne in his face and disgrace him in front of the members of the club, but you must counterpunch and retaliate."

"Rand gave me the same speech not long ago, Mom. I get it."

"And finally, dear, do everything in your power to protect your marriage to Amy. She's the right woman for you. She's no Gunther, who did his best to shield me from the worst of Max's depredations, but she's strategic and savvy, and she loves you very much. A great partner."

I begged Mom to let me drive her home. She may or may not have been on the cusp of old ladyhood, but if she drove, she'd definitely be on the cusp of a DWI.

Chapter 29

I SELDOM SAW DAD AT THE OFFICE THE FOLLOWING SPRING. I KNEW he was traveling a lot, and he often headed out to Highland Hills for a meeting, golf, or whatever. Frankly, I was grateful for his absences. I didn't have to deal with awkward personal stuff with him, and it gave me the opportunity to demonstrate my value to the business. My span of control broadened considerably in his absence.

I was able to look in on the workings of the real estate and legal departments. Now I was the one signing leases and lease extensions, and finalizing contracts and loan documents. I was getting an education. I even gained a greater understanding of the increasing role that information technology was playing, and would play, in the future.

These forays into staff functions were what I considered my extracurriculars. My business major was, of course, merchandising, so most of my time was spent with Herb Segal, either in the office or on the road. Our partnership matured and developed, and the results were excellent. He played good cop and was a rule follower, playing it straight. I played bad cop and bent the rules from time to time to benefit the bottom line. I loved that role. Maybe there was a bit of Max in me, after all.

The industry was going through a shakeout period. One-time giants like Edison Brothers Stores, which operated Chandler's, Baker's, and Wild Pair stores, in addition to a bunch of apparel concepts, went into Chapter 11. The causes of their distress were pretty much the ones Herb and I had moaned about on the plane trip to Milan.

In early May, after a fairly good Easter season, I got my first-ever email from Dad. Didn't even know he knew how to do it. He asked me to see him in his office after lunch.

When I arrived at his office, he greeted me and suggested we sit in the conference room.

In an expansive mood, he asked, "Well, Josh, how are you adjusting to the family's new lineup?"

"OK, I guess. Mom seems settled in her place in Wydown Terrace. Small house, bedroom on the first floor, with plenty of room for her card table, books, and stuff. Even an extra bedroom for an Allison sleepover or if Rand comes to town. Amy's doing great at Hotchkiss and Hamilton, she's heading up their burgeoning banking practice, and Allison's knocking them dead at school and is a little hellion at home. So, yeah, I guess we're all good. How about you?"

"Glad the drama is over. I'm doing great. I'm redoing Brentmoor. Hot new designer from New Yawk in town. You, Amy, and Allison should see it. Will invite you when it's done."

"Terrific."

"I wanted to see you about some organizational changes I want to make. Get your opinion. You've actually been doing the general merchandise manager's job, but without the title. Effective immediately, you'll be vice president, and GMM. You'll oversee shoes, both branded and private label, and all accessories. It's the most pivotal job in the company. You've come a long way since I scared the shit out of you after the Rand incident. And it's paid off. Bigger challenges lie ahead, though. Think you can handle it?"

"Yes," I replied.

"We'll see. And I know I am getting ahead of myself, but I want to get you ready to be named president in the next couple of years, the next step along the way. An important one."

"That's good news."

"As GMM, your first order of business is to fire Herb Segal. He's been a noncontributor for a long time, and a big earner. You've propped him up for a couple of years, but he's past his sell-by date."

"Dad, I appreciate the confidence that you're showing in me, but I'm not about to fire Herb. He and I ..."

"Get some balls, Josh. Take the fucking training wheels off. He's been using you, playing you, leeching off your success. He's history."

"Firing Herb will be a mistake—particularly at this point. We work great together, and the results prove it. We're buying the right shoes and we're wringing every penny we can from the vendors. Just take a look at the bottom line. Beating your old figures. With me taking on even more responsibilities, I need somebody I can trust in branded footwear."

"Maybe you're not ready to step up?"

"I'm ready, and you goddamn well know it. I've even been doing the president's job when you're AWOL. There are people in legal, real estate, and IT who don't even know who you are. But they know me. Firing Herb is counterproductive, and a nonstarter."

"Same old Josh. When you learn to stand on your own two feet, send me one of those emails."

"Herb stays, or I go. I've earned my stripes. I'm well-known in the industry. Who do you think the vendors call? And a couple have asked me if you've retired, it's been so long since they've seen you. What's selling and what's not? *Women's Wear Daily* calls me. Who attends the shoe shows? Who uses Carly more than you? Me, that's who."

"Whoa, listen to that. Josh is wearing his big boy pants. OK. He stays until the first screwup."

"Where have I heard that threat before?"

I turned and left the office.

When I discussed the Herb Segal controversy with Amy, she shook her head and congratulated me on sticking to my guns. "The only way to deal with a bully is to show strength! And Josh, sweetheart, one more thing. You enlisted in the Marines, so you can't be surprised the drill sergeant is kicking your butt. I pleaded with you to leave the company, but no, you had to re-up. It wouldn't have been my choice, but it was yours. So, deal with it."

A sobering reaction.

Later, Amy changed the topic. "I have my own news to report. Want to hear it?"

"Sure."

"I received a call from a very happy senior partner at the firm informing me that I was asked to make a presentation at a national bankers' conference. I am so psyched. It means I'll be pulling all-nighters to prepare for it, but it's the opportunity I've been itching for. To strut my stuff with the leaders of Chase, Bank of America, Citibank—all the big boys. There'll be other lawyers on the agenda, but I'm the only woman!"

"And what a woman! Amy, I'm so proud of you. How did you swing it?"

"My old friend and client Trey Baker is on the committee, and he recommended me. I'm thrilled."

"When and where?"

"In ten days, in Scottsdale. At the Phoenician. And we're flying private. Trey insisted."

Also sobering.

"What's wrong, Josh? Are you worried about something?" Amy asked, smiling, with her eyes half-closed like a lazy lion or a master of the universe.

"Not exactly, but jealous as hell, if you want to know the truth. I see the way men look at you, and I know Trey's reputation."

Amy took my hand and kissed me passionately. "Josh, you're my one and only." And then she grabbed her briefcase and told me she was heading back down to the office. "You and Allie can have a father/daughter date."

That was a rather unattractive prospect. Allie, ten with the mouth of a teenager, was cute and smart, but she was driving us both crazy. Our daughter had become sarcastic and rebellious. We were both, in her lingo, "totally lame." Her grandmother Maddy, who shamelessly indulged her, was "completely cool."

• • •

When Amy, Allie, Mom, and I got together for Sunday deli, we joked and teased, told war stories, and shared updates. Allison spoke about her adventures at school and her successes in the classroom and on the soccer field. Amy, without naming names, let us in on some of her legal legerdemain, including her coup at the Scottsdale conference, where she scored engagements from some of the banking heavyweights. I gave everybody the latest on retail and the Redbirds, both of which were going through dry spells. And Mom soaked it all up, but also let us know how her academic life was proceeding. (She was teaching a graduate seminar on guess who? Henry James.)

Sometimes the conversation turned to Dad. By an unwritten rule, we refrained from veering into the negative. Maybe it was for Allison's sake. He was one of her grandfathers, after all. No, it wasn't that. It was simply our desire, I think, to keep things positive.

It was a treat to see my mother happy again. She'd even gained some weight. Certainly understandable at age sixty-seven. Though being Maddy, she knew how to dress to disguise those extra pounds.

But I wasn't so sure Mom was her old self. For instance, she called me from her car phone after she'd parked on the street in front of the house, where the pavement is flat. "How about giving the old lady a hand up this steep driveway?" she asked. "Steeper than I remember!" Even with my help, she was out of breath when we reached the front door, but if she had parked on the steeply pitched driveway itself, she would have to get in and out of the car at an awkward angle, wrestling with the car door, which was "as heavy as a garage door."

Then there was her footwear. She used to scoff at women who wore tennis shoes instead of traditional casual footwear. But she now wore a pair of Adidas Stan Smith court shoes when she visited. If there was anyone who was more focused on what she wore than Mom, I don't know who it might have been. It was a bit out of character. Her face was sallow, and her facial features were more pronounced than ever, particularly her patrician nose, of which she used to be so proud. Her hair was still rich and beautifully coiffed, but solid gray. Maybe Mom really was joining the "old ladyhood" brigade, after all.

When I asked her how she was doing, she brushed it off with "getting old ain't easy, but it beats the alternative."

One Sunday, after Allison went up to do her homework, the three of us cleaned up the kitchen and retreated to the den. Mom, with a second (or maybe third) drink in hand, ventured a question about how Dad was treating me.

"OK, really. He's gone a lot. But we pretty much go our own way," which was true.

"And how's business?" she asked.

"As I said at dinner . . . difficult, but doable. Lots of carnage in the mall. But we're hanging in. Not much margin for error. Whole different world out there, Mom. There are scores of choices for women when it comes to footwear. Lots of discounters, like DSW and Payless, gumming up the works. We just have to be right when it comes to fashion."

"Well," said Amy as she opened up the book section of the Sunday *Times*, "it's lucky you're not in the book business. Look at this. A full-page ad from a company called Amazon claiming to be the world's largest bookstore. Millions of books that you can order from your computer. They'll ship them right to your door—and at a discounted price. They don't even operate a store."

"That's ridiculous! Who would want to buy a book on a computer?" Mom was incredulous.

"Says the woman who claimed that women wore tennis shoes only for playing tennis and cleaning out the garage! And look at you, Stan Smiths for God's sake. Not even LA Gear, or Vans."

"So sue me, I was wrong. These are the most comfortable shoes I have. And no, I wouldn't wear them to Saks. But on a cozy Sunday night *en famille*, that's what I wear. But you can take it from me, there's something tactile, almost sensual, about books that impels one to shop for them in a store, where you can touch and feel them, and open them to a page and sample what the author offers you. And if you're curious, have a question, or just want to chat, you can talk to the bookish sort behind the cash register who knows his stuff and knows what you like. Pressing a key on your computer, baloney!"

"And that business assessment from your normal ole run-of-the-mill Henry James scholar," I said.

"Laugh at me if you want. I may not know much about footwear, but I sure know books. Now, Josh, if you'll be kind enough to walk me down that awful driveway, I'll be on my way so you guys can get up to whatever you get up to."

She swayed a bit on the way to her car and held on to me a little tighter as we made our way down the driveway. I credited the two-plus glasses of Chardonnay for her shakiness.

"Sure you don't want me to drive you, Mom?"

"It's eight blocks, Josh, for Christ's sake."

She gave me a big hug before she got into her car.

"I love our little foursome, but I wish I saw more of your brother. Oh well."

As for the job, we on the merchandising team at Fratelli Massimo were grinding it out. Nothing came easily. We fought for every nickel and experimented with different promotional formulas, such as percent off, dollar values, and BOGOs. We weren't bashful about asking our vendors for concessions, markdown money, special discounts, or whatever it took. If we had a hot shoe—gladiator sandals, for example—we pleaded for quick refills and flew them in. Those brands were our partners and needed us as much as we needed them. With traditional shoe retailers failing left and right, we had some leverage, and we used it.

Even with all that, the proportion of shoes we sold at full price continued to fall, as did our average selling price on promotional units. That put tremendous pressure on our expense structure, so working with our CFO, Walter Benning, we downsized our staff, increased our dependence on automation, and closed every marginal store we could. Unfortunately, many of the weaker stores had a while to go on their leases, and the landlords wouldn't permit us to shut them down.

So far, it seemed to be working out. Sales were tepid, but profits reasonable. The stock traded in a narrow range, midway between its historic high and low, at around twenty-five dollars. The market was giving astronomical valuations, however, to the dot-com start-ups, who were the new kids in town.

I'm not sure what Dad was really up to during this period. He came in from time to time, reviewed the numbers, and sent out some emails. He continued to travel to New York, where, I assume, he had meetings with the Wall Street gang. I know he wasn't visiting vendors.

He wouldn't venture into the merchandising department when he was at HQ. The upside was that it gave me free rein over the business. And I took full advantage of it.

I knew almost nothing about his personal life, and that was fine with me.

As back-to-school was ending, he did show up and asked me to join him in the conference room.

"First, give me a rundown on business," he demanded.

I proceeded to give him some details about the challenging conditions we faced and the actions we were taking. I gave him a quick review of the numbers through September, sales, comp store sales, and projected profits.

"Not too exciting, Josh."

"I would welcome any suggestions."

"Fresh out, I'm afraid. I visited the Galleria store on my way downtown, and frankly, it looked pretty good. Went over to Dillard's department store, and I don't think you're missing much. It's just a down cycle in the business. We've been through them before—the mid-eighties come to mind, and then Timberland exploded. Something will come along."

"I hope so. Meanwhile, the grind continues." I sighed.

And then he smiled. "I think it's about time we gave you the title of president of Fratelli Massimo. You've earned it."

I wasn't completely surprised. I had been handling most of those responsibilities for months. I was ready to be president. "Thanks, Dad. You can count on me."

"But remember, there's one more rung on that ladder, and I'm standing on it. I will continue as chairman and CEO for a while, run the board meetings, handle Wall Street, and keep an eye on the business. But as for the day-to-day, it's in your hands. I'll be the outside man. You'll be the inside man."

"When we will make it public?"

"Well, I want to run it by the board, write the announcement, and take care of some formalities—like boosting your salary and stock option totals."

I knew I could do it. All the nervous Nellies in the family were wrong. It was only a matter of time before I ran the show.

Dad scrabbled around on his desk, rustling through some papers. I thought he might be looking for something regarding my new salary and stock options.

I was wrong.

"Oh, and one more thing—you'll be doing it without Herb Segal." He smiled.

"What are you talking about? We went through this last year. Herb's my man."

"*Was* your man, son. He just signed these retirement papers." Dad waved them in my face.

"Impossible," I replied. "I was with him last week in New York, and he didn't say a word."

"I guess that's because I asked him to keep the matter confidential. Ole Herb, been around a long time. He deserved a nice send-off. Made him an offer he couldn't refuse." He chuckled. "Just like the Godfather."

I was momentarily speechless—whipsawed again.

"You son of a bitch, you want me to fail, don't you? You know how valuable I think Herb is and what a great team we make. You're handicapping me from day one of my presidency. What are you trying to achieve by doing that with Herb?"

"Simple, Josh. I want you to have the chance, the same opportunity I had, to prove yourself without any hand-holding and spoon-feeding from anybody—including your old pal. He'd be gone in a couple of years anyway. Bye-bye, crutch. You like a strong supporting cast, don't you? Think what Maddy, Rand, and Gunther did for you when I fired you. Well, time to show what you, alone, can do." He cleared his throat and continued.

"You can promote someone to take his place. You can hire a successor to take your post as general merchandise manager. You'll be the boss. So, you gonna do it, or what?"

I answered immediately. "Of course, if only to prove to you that I can run this business. But you're true to form, Dad, giving with one hand, and taking with the other. If I'm president, why can't I have the man I want in merchandising? I'll tell you why, because you want me to fail. I used to admire you—even worship you. I am humiliated now, even thinking about it. I was always trying to impress you when I was a kid. Running the comp numbers. Listening attentively to your stories and triumphs. Defending you to every member of the family. I would have taken a bullet for you. I thought you were a rock star. And I believed that you were my ally." I said all of this while looking him straight in the eye.

"But at the end of the day, you're simply the irreplaceable Max Feldman that Gunther toasted, or should I say roasted, so cleverly. That's all you are, as he intimated. The ultimate self-made man of business. There's not an ounce of humanity in you. As Sy said, you're an incomplete person. Where's your fucking heart, your soul? I don't care how much civic bullshit you do. That's all for show. When it comes to the people you're supposed to love, you've crapped all over everyone. Sy, Mom, Rand, and now me."

"Are you through with your little temper tantrum, Josh? You want to hold your breath and stamp your feet like you did when you were a kid, to show me how angry you are? Or maybe take a swing at me? Oh, I forgot. You wouldn't even deck your little brother when he kicked your butt in those basketball games you used to play. You would just smile." As he spoke, I felt the air leaving the room.

He went deeper. "As for those family members you treasure so much: Sy was a real winner; he couldn't see past the big
hooknose on his face, and he was willing to see his store and the
family bank account go down the drain rather than disappoint
the neighbors. And there's the mother you adore so much, with
her pointy-headed intellectual friends counting the number of
angels on the head of a pin. Too erudite for mere mortals, like me
and my friends. And 'crapped on' is precisely what your sainted
mother did to me on my inauguration night at the club. As for
Rand, he's just a worthless fairy as far as I am concerned. I made it
on my own, and if you want to run Fratelli Massimo, you're going
to have to make it on your own, too."

Just when I thought he was finished, he offered one last
blast. "One more thing, boychik. In the world of business,
you have to be a street fighter; you need to make tough decisions. Sometimes those tough decisions seem unfair to others.
Firing people, reducing head count, cutting salaries, cutting
corners, playing fast and loose with the numbers, the whole
nine yards. So being unfair, learning to be cool with it, and,
in fact, becoming proud of it, is one of the secrets of being
an effective leader. This separates the ruler from the ruled.
Best learn that fact, or start doing volunteer work at the Little
Sisters of the Poor. Otherwise, you'll have no place at Fratelli
Massimo."

We stared at each other for what seemed an eternity. Then I
turned and left the room with as much dignity as I could muster.

I found Herb in his office.

"What were you thinking, Herb? We had a great thing
going," I said.

"I'm sorry, Josh, leaving you in the lurch, but I have to think about myself and my family. Your dad significantly sweetened my retirement package. He was unbelievably generous. Look, I know that you single-handedly saved my job over these past several years. I'm grateful. But I'm not like you Feldmans. I don't have a stash; my stock options are almost worthless. I owe on my house, and I'm still paying off college loans for my kids. I can't afford to be independent like you. You can walk out of here tomorrow and not look back. No such luck for me. Please, Josh, don't blame me—I did what I had to do."

Snookered.

Chapter 30

I COULD BARELY CONCENTRATE, SO I DECIDED TO GO HOME, HAVE A drink or two, and wait for Amy.

When I opened the garage door, I saw her little MINI Cooper parked there. This was unusual, as she usually didn't get home until six or six thirty.

She opened the door that connected the kitchen to the garage, folded her arms over her chest, and said, "Well, look who's cutting class again—just like at Wash U."

"Very funny. What are you doing home now?"

"Did you forget I had a doctor's appointment earlier this afternoon? All's OK, so I decided to come home instead of going back to the office. I saw your mom there, by the way. She's still fighting that cold she had last week. Looked a little green around the gills. And guess what? She was wearing her Stan Smiths. So it looks like we're all cheating a bit today. And to what do I owe the pleasure of your company, Mr. Feldman?"

"Nothing good, I can tell you. And I'm worried about Mom."

"It's just a cold, Josh."

"I guess . . . but the Stan Smiths?"

"Oh, I forgot. Maddy is supposed to be the icon of fashion, and here she is dressed like the handyman cleaning out the garage."

"It's a sign, dear. Her mind is elsewhere—putting comfort over fashion."

"If you say so. So how come you're home early?"

"We need to talk, and I need a drink."

I poured myself one and Amy grabbed a Diet Coke; we made our way to the den.

The front door flew open and Allison charged in.

"What are you guys doing here?"

"Hi to you, too."

"I mean, like, you're never here at four in the afternoon."

"Up to no good, Allie, when we're not home?" Amy asked.

"No, Mom. Why do you always, like, think the worst?"

"That's a mom's job, darling. Think the worst, and then be pleasantly surprised, occasionally."

"Whatever. I've got work to do, even if you two don't," said our daughter.

She scampered up the steps, and, bam! Her bedroom door slammed shut and we both saw the light flash on the phone, meaning she was calling somebody—most likely, her friend Jonathan Katzenberg. To complain about us, we supposed.

"Well, that was a nice interlude."

"Bad day at the office, Josh?"

"The worst." I proceeded to give her chapter and verse of my conversations with Dad—the presidency and the Herb story.

"Josh, this is like a broken record. And frankly, I am out of ideas—and sympathy. Despite a chorus of warnings, you insisted on going after that white whale; you're going to end up like Captain Ahab, lashed to that leviathan and dead in the water. Escape, honey. Escape. You're rich and talented, and you can succeed anywhere."

"Quit?"

"Yes, Josh, quit! Look at it this way—you've proved yourself over these past several years. Your dad's been gallivanting around while you've been running the business. You have that great satisfaction. You also have piles of money. You're respected in the industry. You're quoted more than Max. You've never touched the money at Brown Brothers, have you?"

"No. What am I going to do instead, Amy? I'm forty years old. Join Highland Hills and play golf? Go to afternoon movies? Do volunteer work, like Dad suggested?"

"You don't have to quit working, dear. You just have to quit working at Fratelli Massimo. Max is counting on your obsession to keep you there. He desperately wants you to stay. He needs you to stay. If you do, he wins, either way. If you do well, he'll take the credit and probably stick around as chairman of the board, because the man needs a big title like a baby craves mother's milk. If you don't do so well, he can fire you or—even worse—bring in a new CEO for you to report to."

"Amy, I've never worked anywhere else. I've been associated with the company for decades. Retail management jobs in St. Louis are scarce. Any potential employer would wonder why I was leaving the family business. And do you think good ole Dad would make that process easy? Hell, no, he'd bad-mouth me every chance he had. And my wealth is another strike against me. Nobody wants to hire a rich exec who can quit whenever he pleases. Employers want you to need the job. No, I'm well and truly fucked!"

"You can start your own business."

"The only business I know is the shoe business, and that's the last business I would want to start. It's like Verdun out there."

"Be fucking real, Josh, and get the hell out of there before you end up like Ahab. And that's my last word on the subject. Ever. Oh, one more thing—I don't intend to have my future happiness tied to the not-so-gentle mercies of Max Feldman. I'm a hero at

H&H, and I'm making good money. And as much as I love you, I don't intend to be shackled to that great white whale next to you. So make up your mind."

This was crazy. Or was it me. Was I crazy?

Amy's words sounded an awful lot like an ultimatum. It was only my cowardice in confronting her and a subsequent crisis that stopped me from thrashing this out with her. I couldn't bear to hear Amy confirm her threat. So, dealing with the emergency became my top priority.

It started with a call from Rand.

"Mom wants to see us, and she wants me at tomorrow's board meeting. She won't be able to attend. What's going on?" he asked.

"I don't know. I've heard nothing. I'll call, or stop over, and let you know."

I called Mom, but Nora said she was not taking calls. I offered to come over, but she haltingly said that Mom wanted to see me and Rand after the board meeting. Then she hung up.

I told Dad about Mom's request, and he agreed to rearrange the agenda to free me and Rand to get to Mom's immediately after the meeting.

As president, I sped through my report on our business: "tepid" with total sales down, but profits equal to last year. I gave an overview of the retail sector: "malls sluggish, off-price and athletic footwear surging, and online sales beginning to chip away at brick-and-mortar transactions." Luckily, the internet wasn't materially impacting shoes and apparel. At least, not yet.

No, we weren't going to buy an off-price footwear competitor, nor would we invest in a website. And yes, after a brief search, I had hired Bill Bruton from Nordstrom to succeed Herb Segal.

The board quickly approved his title, compensation, and stock option plan.

Rand and I begged the board's indulgence and skipped the traditional post-meeting lunch; we streaked to Mom's house quickly, as she had requested.

We arrived at Wydown Terrace at about a quarter past one. Nora greeted us warmly, but nothing could disguise the anxiety in her body language and facial expression. She ushered us into the living room and then departed for the kitchen, leaving the three of us together.

As if posing for a portrait or taking her place on a stage set in the opening scene of a play, Mom was seated primly in her comfortable leather wing chair. She was beautifully dressed, but that could not mask her sickly pallor, the faint odor of fear dueling with her Chanel No. 5, or the arduous effort she made in rising to embrace us both. She invited us to be seated on the sofa and asked if we would like something to drink. We declined.

"Boys, I know you're concerned about me. Rand, when you've called, I haven't been forthcoming. Josh, you've picked up on things that are unusual for me. My visage, fatigue, even my choice of comfortable footwear. I'm not much for drama, nor will I resort to euphemisms. You both deserve honesty, as brutal as it is." We remained silent, two boys sitting with our mother.

"I have been feeling weak for several months. The simplest tasks left me feeling winded. I have been feeling so tired. And then, I was plagued by a terrible cold. So, I went to see my internist."

Rand and I were on the edge of our seats, waiting for the ax to fall.

"After examining me and looking at my chest X-rays, he told me that he noticed a shadow in my left lung. Again, I'll spare you the platitudes, bromides, and comforting rationalizations doctors are trained to offer. He urged me to see a pulmonary specialist sooner rather than later."

Mom hesitated at this point, summoning the energy to continue.

"Because of your father's position on the Barnes Hospital Board, and the phone call he graciously and quickly made, I was able to see their leading pulmonary specialist, Phil Olson. He was thorough in his examination, and additional X-rays were taken, as well as an MRI. He performed an endoscopy and ordered a biopsy." She was moving along at a rapid pace.

"As you must have surmised by now, the news was not good. I'm scheduled to have my cancerous left lung removed next week, but there is no guarantee that will solve the problem. My right lung may be compromised as well. A biopsy will be performed on that lung after the surgery, and we'll know more at that time."

We were choking back tears, including Mom, but she pressed on.

"I wish to God there were an easier way to break this to you both. You're the loves of my life, along with Amy and Allison. But there it is."

Rand and I went to Mom, gently elevated her from her chair, and hugged her with all our might. We both gave in to the tears that had welled up during her recitation. Maddy couldn't hold them back either. Even Nora, who was never very good at not listening behind closed doors, joined the family and cried softly.

"Well, I'm glad that's finally over," Mom managed to say in a hoarse whisper. "Even dear old Gunther broke down last evening when I called to tell him. I've never witnessed that, ever. You can't imagine how much I've dreaded telling you boys. For me it was worse than the diagnosis, causing you both such pain. Moms are put on earth to spare their children pain, not inflict it."

"Mom, you're the best. Rand and I will do whatever we can to help you through this."

"Look, Mom," Rand said, "my freelance work in California is very flexible. I can stay here with you, through the surgery and aftermath. Todd would insist, and it's what I want to do. Josh has a business to run, but he'll be with you when he can."

"Boys, I appreciate your offers, but I think I'd rather deal with this myself. Come visit, of course—and that goes for Todd, Amy, and Allison, as well. But I need to come to terms with this myself. I'll lose myself, if I can, in *The Wings of the Dove*, and take to heart what James so brilliantly wrote about dignity as life ends."

She looked at us squarely. "And besides, you have families to take care of, just as I once took care of you."

Exhausted, physically and emotionally, she continued, her voice cracking.

"I'm told that there'll be time enough for us to gather as a family in the months that follow. Let's spend whatever time we have together, remembering only good things. Rand the Man, you can do that announcer routine you used to do when you beat your brother at Horse. And Josh, you can continue to tease me about how you were wronged by Ickle Pickle on your fourth birthday."

Silence reigned, and Rand and I simultaneously submerged ourselves in recollections of treasured memories of childhood with the marvelous Maddy.

The two of us embraced, tragedy binding us. Any lingering traces of our ongoing feud evaporated.

Chapter 31

I HAD BEEN TESTED BEFORE AT WORK, BUT I NOW CONFRONTED A two-front war, and I would need all my energy and skills to succeed at the office as well as the emotional strength to help Mom through her ordeal.

Amy offered to do anything she could for Maddy. She adored Mom almost as much as I did. Her health crisis put Amy's ultimatum, if that's what it was, on hold for a while—which turned out to be fortuitous.

When I returned to the office, Dad called to express his concern for Maddy. I thanked him for that and for facilitating the appointment with the pulmonologist. He asked if I could handle the challenges at work and at home. I assured him I could. Then we hung up.

My first stop was GMM Bill Bruton's office. I told him about the senior vice president title and the stock option that the board had approved. Both had been promised to him when I hired him. Bill was fifty years old and had spent most of his working life at Nordstrom, the best shoe merchandising company in America. The brands we bought also sold to Nordstrom. These vendors were very high on Bruton and recommended him for the post at Fratelli Massimo. His role would include responsibility for branded and private label footwear, as well as accessories—including the hot handbag category.

I traveled with him to New York for his initial trip as Fratelli Massimo GMM. He was greeted with enthusiasm, and he demonstrated a comprehensive knowledge of the branded shoe business. He even introduced me to newer brands, which Nordstrom was experimenting with. These start-ups were eager to sell to Fratelli Massimo, and I was optimistic that these newer items would spark excitement in our stores. At each of our stops, vendors brought up Amazon and the embryonic internet channel of distribution. Each laughingly assured us that they had no intention of putting their "quality branded footwear" for sale on the internet. Some called it a bazaar; others claimed it was the Wild West. All agreed that we would lose control over pricing for any item offered with that channel. Besides, we all said, "Women want to try shoes on before purchase."

We also traveled to Brazil and to Asia together. He was less knowledgeable about private label purchasing, as Nordstrom depended almost entirely on nationally branded merchandise in those days. Fortunately, we had a veteran private label buyer, Hank Jenkins, who showed him the ropes and put him through his paces.

I also hired a Washington U MBA, Roger Morton, as my assistant. My span of responsibility encompassed a lot more than merchandising, even though that function was by far the most critical to our success. But as president of the company, store operations, real estate, IT, and other important departments reported to me. I needed Roger to assist me with monitoring what was going on in these non-merchandising departments. I also asked him to work on some additional projects using Lotus 1-2-3 spreadsheets and other modern tools. Our chief financial officer, Walter Benning, continued to report to Dad, which made sense, since he and Dad handled communications with the investment community.

Despite the long laundry list of marketplace challenges enumerated at our March board meeting, we were able to eke out small comparative store increases while closing underperforming stores. We were therefore able to report to our stockholders in June that the business was on a solid footing, and that we were confident that the customary quarterly dividend of ten cents a share could be maintained barring any sudden downturns in business. The stock price traded around twenty dollars off its lows, but nowhere near its high in the mid-thirties.

On a warm spring day, Amy and I escorted Mom to Barnes Hospital the day before her scheduled surgery. Dad had worked with the hospital administration to facilitate registration and other formalities. She was quickly assigned to a private room. The surgical team promptly visited her in preparation for the next morning's procedure, which Mom told us would take place at 8:00 a.m. Once the team exited, Mom, with a stack of books on her nightstand, waved us out of her room, claiming she was happy to be finally getting it over with and didn't need us "hovering."

Amy and I had what passed for lunch in the hospital cafeteria and agreed to leave Mom alone. We would go to work and return early the next day to see her off to surgery, then await the results. Rand, Gunther, and Dad asked us to call them when we had an update.

Determined to be early, we arrived around 7:00 a.m. the next morning only to discover that her bed was alarmingly empty. *Oh my God, what happened to Mom!* I thought as I ran to the nurse's station.

That elicited what I thought was an inappropriate round of laughter. One of the nurses took pity on us and said Maddy had fibbed about the 8:00 a.m. time. Surgery was really scheduled for 6:00 a.m. "I don't need a royal send-off, like some ocean liner," she had told them. "And I don't want those kids looking at me like it might be the last time they see me alive. I'll survive the surgery, and they can fuss over me then."

Typical.

So, we waited — and waited—in one of those areas of the hospital outfitted with uncomfortable plastic chairs, a TV tuned to morning fare, and a vending machine. We each tried to catch up on office paperwork, without much success. Our thoughts turned to Mom and our prayers for her recovery.

At long last, Dr. Olson appeared and summoned us to a small private conference room.

"Your mother came through the procedure quite well. She is in 'recovery' now and will likely go to the ICU for a few days, so that we can monitor her progress and see that she is stabilized." He spoke very clearly.

"We removed her left lung and performed a biopsy on her right lung. Before surgery she actually grabbed hold of the lapels on my lab coat and insisted that I give you my frank opinion even before the path lab gives us a report. I must say, your mom is a no-nonsense person, so I gave her my word. I always wait for the pathologist's report before speculating, but your mother was insistent. I fear the news will not be good. There are troubling signs that cancer may be present in her right lung.

"I am sorry to tell you this. What I cannot know at this point is what the outlook is, what procedures, if any, will be called for—and, frankly, how much time she has. We will need to wait for the lab reports and further examinations. Do you have any questions?"

Where to start? And yet his report seemed comprehensive. His brusqueness discouraged further questioning. We could only hope that the status of Mom's remaining lung was healthier than he had concluded.

"No, no more questions, Doctor. We appreciate your candor and we'll depend on that in the days ahead. We'll pray for a different diagnosis when the lab examines the tissue. Thank you for doing what you can for Maddy." I tried to hold myself together.

With the briefest of nods, he wheeled around and left the room.

I called Rand, who listened to the report and bleak outlook with admirable calmness; he immediately offered to come to St. Louis to tend to Mom. I discouraged him from doing so until Mom was out of intensive care, and hopefully home. He reluctantly agreed.

Gunther was speechless at first, but then said, "It's what I feared. I know it sounds selfish, but I don't want to outlive my Maddy. She's the heart of the family and always has been. I feel like the Tin Man in *The Wizard of Oz*. How can I live without a heart? Please, please forgive me for focusing on myself. What can I do?" I assured him that everything was taken care of, and that we would keep him informed. A drained and depleted Gunther whispered his goodbyes.

Dad expressed his sadness about the prognosis and offered to stop by. I thanked him and told him that Mom wanted to be alone. He understood.

After visiting "recovery" and seeing Mom still unconscious from anesthetics and breathing normally, we left after asking the nurse that we be notified about when she would be moved to intensive care.

Mom was mostly out of it that first post-op evening in intensive care.

Amy and I worked out a rotation schedule that called for my visiting Mom on my way to work. Amy would visit during lunch, and we would both come after dinner.

Mom was predictably disoriented, cranky, and obstreperous during the first couple of days in the ICU. Gradually, she regained her emotional equilibrium and quietly accepted our presence, but waved away any sentimentalities and hopeful wishes.

"We'll see what the surgeon says when he gets those pathology reports."

The meeting with the surgeon was scheduled for later that week. I called Rand and suggested he fly in, which he was eager to do. I also called Gunther and told him. "It's difficult for me to travel these days, and I will be a distraction. Please call me the instant you have news, Josh."

I didn't call Dad, though I would let him know what the prognosis was. It would be awkward having him there.

On a Friday afternoon in May, the Feldmans gathered in Mom's room, which was now on a regular patient floor. Dr. Olson and a colleague came into the room and introduced themselves to everybody.

A businesslike and direct Dr. Olson spoke. "I'll get right to it. I know how much you value honesty and promptness, Mrs. Feldman. But first, I must apologize. To honor your request earlier this week, I violated a cardinal rule when I speculated with your son and daughter-in-law about the condition of your right lung before we had the reports. Please forgive me."

Mom sat up in bed and said, "What are you trying to tell us, Doctor? Out with it!"

Clearly, no patient had ever hectored the eminent Dr. Olson like this. He gathered himself and explained, "The biopsy reveals that there is no evidence of cancer in your right lung. My colleague here is the chief of pathology at the hospital, and he has studied and restudied the tissue samples we sent him. He will explain." He motioned to his colleague.

The pathology chief began, "The growth that we suspected was cancerous is actually benign and relatively harmless. I've been working with my associates to verify that conclusion. We've conducted a number of tests. That's why it's taken us so long to convene this meeting. But we are unanimous in our conclusion. In defense of Dr. Olson, I, too, thought at first it was cancerous, but our rigorous tests proved otherwise. This is wonderful news, Mrs. Feldman."

We all enjoyed a few moments of relief—a reprieve. There would be more time for Maddy. Amy, Rand, and I hugged Mom, who was still trying to digest the news.

Mom croaked, "You're sure this time? This isn't some kind of palliative to give me false hope? And what does this new diagnosis portend?"

"I don't blame you for your skepticism, Mrs. Feldman," answered Dr. Olson, "but I promise you that the news is genuine, and encouraging. It simply means that you will probably live longer and won't require another round of surgery, or chemo, at least for a while. You will need to work with medical staff to monitor for treatment in the coming months. You smoked for almost fifty years, you had lung disease when you were a child, and your remaining lung is weak and compromised. However, with care and the correct pharmaceutical regimen, you should be able to lead a somewhat normal life for the foreseeable future. But—and I stress this—your right lung is far from healthy, and it is vulnerable to a number of diseases—including cancer. At this moment, however, you are in no imminent danger."

The emotional roller coaster we had been living for the past two weeks rendered us exhausted and speechless. We were elated by the prognosis, even though we realized Mom would be living on borrowed time. Still, it was more time than we had expected. I couldn't wait to call Gunther.

He was pleased, of course, but cautious. Being the realist that he was, he did not want to give in to outright joy; he told me he would want to visit when Mom was ready to see him.

Dad was happy, too. "Dodged a bullet, didn't she?"

"Didn't we, Dad?"

. . .

Mom returned home to continue her convalescence. This required a retinue of caregivers, nurse practitioners, and aides; frequent visits by physical therapists; and Nora, of course. We installed a hospital bed in her downstairs bedroom and created a makeshift resting place in Mom's study for the overnight care-givers. We also carved out a daytime space with a large-screen TV for the aides. It was strange visiting Mom on my way to work and finding the house buzzing with activity and the TV blaring with morning fare. God, who could stand that stuff?

Mom was cool with it, though. She remained stoic and uncharacteristically accepting of her new surroundings, as well as the chattering attendants and incessant noise from the TV. She seemed reconciled to her situation and her fate. But she was still Mom. When flowers from well-wishers arrived, she immediately gave them to the staff. When books arrived from those who knew her as a bibliophile, she passed them out to her attendants as well. God only knows what they made of novels by Don DeLillo and Steven Millhauser.

Mom and I often had breakfast together in her small dinette.

"I think it's time to invite my father to town. I think I can handle it now."

"A weekend visit?" I asked.

"Whatever works for him will work for me," Mom answered.

"We'll put him in the Ritz. I think he'll be more comfortable there," I suggested. He wouldn't be able to manage the stairs at Mom's.

"I second the motion. And Josh, book him a large suite and make sure there's an adjacent room for Elvis, his man Friday."

I rose from my chair. "Can I get you anything? You must want something current to read."

"Look, kiddo, I just gave away a ton of books to my helpers; as for myself, I am rereading the classics."

"Certainly something modern would be more relevant."

"You still don't get it, Josh—the masters of literature said it all, and what they said is as relevant today as it was in centuries past. Life, death, love, betrayal, revenge, family, society—it's all the same today. Now off to work with you, and let me know when Gunther's coming."

Gunther arrived the next weekend. That was an ordeal. Approaching eighty-five, the old man was as mentally sharp as ever. But he was physically disabled and required a wheelchair to get around. Elvis, his manservant/driver, accompanied him to St. Louis. I rented a wheelchair-friendly van for Elvis to drive, met them at Lambert, and our mini motorcade made the short trip to Clayton and the Ritz Hotel.

Gunther needed a nap, so after they were checked in and had a chance to inspect and approve their suite, I left him and went downtown to the office, even though it was Saturday. Gunther had made it clear that he wanted to be alone with Maddy that afternoon and evening. Nora was busy preparing dinner for the two of them. Amy, Allison, and I would join them for Sunday lunch, after which Gunther and Elvis would return to New York.

Working on Saturdays had become a ritual for me since assuming the presidency. It was great being alone in the office except for our building's veteran access controller, Fletcher, who always greeted me warmly. He and I had grown close over the years since my brief exit from the company. Despite our closeness, he always required me to sign in and sign out.

In my office, one look at the sales numbers confirmed what I had been hearing for the past few weeks: business sucked.

Weather was certainly a factor. A cold and rainy late spring and early summer season killed sandal sales, prompting us to increase our reliance on off-price promotions. And while this tactic was effective in generating some sales, it also cut into our profits. Had weather been the sole reason for bad business, it might have been comforting, but a deep dive into the selling reports revealed that early fall business had been weak as well. The new merchandise (leather casuals, sport shoes, and dress shoes) was not working. It was way too early to get a read on fall boot sales, the traditional ATM for shoe retailers, but it was not too early to know that back-to-school was going to be problematic. A nice fall cold snap would help us, but only if we had the sport and casual shoes that teenagers wanted. They certainly didn't want them now, though.

After digging my way through the pile of paper and doing some ballpark estimates, I wrote an email to Dad with copies to GMM Bill Bruton, Walter Benning, and Roger Morton, my assistant. In it I provided an assessment of our current situation and our likely quarter-three results. My projections tended to be pessimistic, but they gave us a small chance of beating the estimates. This way Dad would be able to give Wall Street an early warning. But who knew? We might just outperform.

I finished up some routine tasks, turned off the lights, and headed home.

We gathered at noon the next day for lunch at Mom's.

Nora had set a beautiful table for the five of us and had wrested some flowers from Mom before she had a chance to give them away. She had placed them in a rather lavish centerpiece. All of this was way over the top, but I think Nora was desperate to put on a show after weeks of almost institutional living at Wydown Terrace.

My grandfather greeted me when I came in.

"How did you and Maddy get along last evening?" I asked.

"Well, your mother is looking much better than I imagined, and I'm grateful that she's as spirited as ever."

This, of course, was Gunther-speak for "she's stubborn and defiant," and as I later found out, she had refused to let Elvis help her to the dining room table, claiming she was "fully aware of its location and fully capable of getting there on my own."

"And how about you, Gunther? Fully retired?" I inquired.

"Not quite. They politely but firmly gave me my walking papers at the office," he said with a laugh. "I don't blame them. I'm more of a nuisance than a contributor. But they still call from time to time, and a few of my old clients favor me with a question or two just to assure themselves that I'm still alive and not gaga. And how's business at Fratelli Massimo?"

"Not so good lately."

"Rest assured I won't trade on this inside information."

"Speaking of trading, how is Brown Brothers doing? Are they participating in the dot-com boom?"

"Conservative and blue chips as usual, Joshua. As for the internet, it will take a lot more convincing for them to invest in those stocks. None is making any money. Lots of fancy projections. Lots of metrics that make speculators happy. But they don't pass the smell test at Brown Brothers. We will just have to content ourselves with a sideline view of the action."

It was a happy gathering at the dining room table. Mom was upbeat and caustic, Gunther sly as always, Amy was engaging, and I merely luxuriated in the love that abounded in the room. Allison and Gunther were chatting away when Allison raised her voice and politely asked her grandfather if he was at all concerned about disadvantaged people around the globe. He thought for a moment or two and said, "Of course I am. What concerns you, specifically?"

Allie told him that she and her classmates were raising funds for the enslaved Tibetans, poverty-stricken Aboriginal peoples in Australia, and the Aleut tribes in Alaska.

"And what, Allison, would you have me do for these mistreated souls?"

"Write a check, Grandpa!"

"Ah, in what amount?"

Allison, who was all of eleven years old and was thankfully ignorant about the family's resources, hesitated briefly. "Well, we have a goal of two thousand dollars for each of those tribes."

"What if I pledge half that amount for each, or one thousand?"

"Gosh, that'd be great!" she exclaimed.

"My pleasure, Allison. Please email me the necessary information. And oh, by the way," he teased, "when you start thinking about colleges, I hope you'll consider NYU or Columbia. You can come live with me and Elvis; we have plenty of room."

With a roll of her eyes, Allison said, "A college girl's dream come true." Smiles all around the table.

About half an hour before Gunther and Elvis were scheduled to leave for the airport, Amy whispered to me that we should get going. Evidently, while Gunther and I had been talking, Maddy had told Amy that we should allow Gunther and her a half hour for a private tête-à-tête. "We may never see each other again, and I have some things that I must tell him in person while we're both compos mentis."

On that somber note, Amy, Allison, and I embraced Gunther and then Maddy, and exited.

Nora was waiting for us outside.

"I must tell you what happened this morning. You know how reserved and formal your grandfather is. Always polite, mind you, but you never know what's going on in his head. Well, this morning he shows up for breakfast with, of all things, a jar of peanut butter that he had bought at the grocery store.

"I was getting things ready for breakfast while your mum was getting dressed. So I asked him what he wanted me to do with it. He asked me for a Sharpie! I rummaged through the junk drawer and found one. The next thing I know, he's scribbling on the lid. Thought he was off his head, poor soul. Then he hides it in the pouch on his wheelchair. At that point, Josh, I know he's gaga. I went about my business and your mum walked into the kitchen, bright and cheerful as usual." She inhaled, then continued on.

"She hugged and kissed her dad, and everything seemed normal. Then, before they start eating, Mr. Berg tells Maddy that he has a gift for her. He pulls the jar of peanut butter out of the pouch and places it on the table in front of your mom." Her eyes were as wide as teacup saucers.

"Your mom takes one look at it and screams, 'Oh no! I can't bear it!'"

I'd rarely seen Nora so upset.

"She was hysterical. She was bawling. She fell to her knees and gripped your grandfather's legs, laid her head on his knees and cried, 'My hero!' And by that time, he was sobbing, too, and he squeezed her head and said, 'My lovely little one, my heart and my soul.'"

Nora said she had never seen such carrying on, "especially from those two cool customers."

"Nora, what did Gunther write on the lid?"

"That's the strangest part. Just two words: Maddy's Jar."

It would be nearly two years before I learned the rest of the story.

Chapter 32

ROGER STOPPED BY MY OFFICE FIRST THING MONDAY MORNING TO say he had gotten my email and would do some supplementary analyses and "what if" scenarios. Radio silence from Bill Bruton.

Our CFO, Walter Benning, had called Carly and asked to see me. I met with him at eleven o'clock in the conference room. He said some of our lenders were getting nervous about our results and prospects. Their debt agreements with us contained covenants that called for monetary penalties if we failed to achieve certain agreed-upon financial targets; in addition, they could demand immediate repayment of the entire loan. We needed to avoid running afoul of those loan agreements. I assured him that we would move heaven and earth to do so. I also insisted he not give our lenders a heads-up. If rumors about our financial health started to circulate, our suppliers might not ship us. Dad agreed with my decision via an overseas call.

Unfortunately, these loan agreements were due to expire shortly, and we would then be forced to seek a renewal. Walter was worried that the new loans would have even tighter restrictions and would require a significantly higher interest rate to compensate the lenders for the risks they were taking. That is, if they agreed to lend us money at all!

I had always assumed we had lots of cash on hand. Dad used to boast that banks borrowed from us, not the other way around. But that was a long time ago. The usual seasonal buildup of inventory had depleted most of our cash reserves, so it was critical that we renew the loan agreements, and it was up to me to produce the numbers necessary to satisfy the lenders.

There was still no email response from Bill Bruton. I stopped by his office—only to find it dark. He was taking a personal day, according to his assistant.

Great! I had sent him the critical email on Saturday. Not only did he not respond, he was taking time off.

I spent the afternoon with Roger running different scenarios, varying sales, markup, and gross-margin assumptions. And while we could come up with some improved projections, they would require a bit of help from the weather, holding our vendors' feet to the fire, a few hot styles, and a good boot season.

When I left for the day, I put a sticky note on Bill's desk asking him to see me ASAP, the next morning.

I skipped breakfast with Mom on Tuesday and got to the office around seven thirty. No Bill Bruton. I made a battle plan for the day: a review of current styles, a look ahead to holiday arrivals, and crunching some more numbers with Roger.

There was a knock on my door around nine o'clock. "Heard you wanted to see me," Bill said.

"Fucking right, Bill. Have you had a chance to read the email I sent you Saturday?"

"Not yet. What's up?"

"Bill, I sent it to you on Saturday. It's Tuesday, for Christ's sake, and you haven't even read it?"

"We had guests, and frankly, I consider the weekend my personal time."

"Delete that thought, Bill. In this job you're never off duty. I don't care if your daughter's getting married or if the house is on fire. Read your fucking emails. I've been stewing about this for forty-eight hours, while you've been entertaining your guests. Read it now!"

It took him a minute or so.

"Wow, I see what you mean, Josh. But you don't have to be such a ballbuster. At Nordstrom, the weekends were our own. No business. I can see, though, that the outlook is pretty gloomy."

"Correct. And it's up to the two of us to figure out how to improve that outlook."

"Sure, what do you want me to do?"

"I've been working with Roger, and it looks like we can squeeze out a few cents per share in additional earnings if we get our vendors to cough up some markdown money."

"Well, Josh, that proposal makes me pretty uncomfortable. Those vendors are our partners. I mean, we bought the stuff and we negotiated a price, and a deal's a deal." He folded his arms, daring me to contradict him.

"Bill, you can delete that thought as well. Their merchandise didn't sell, and being our partners means sharing in those losses."

"That wasn't the way we did things at Nordstrom. We never went hat in hand to our vendors after the season, begging for a handout."

It took all my strength not to strangle the dickhead. Time for some Max-like medicine, I decided. I got out of my chair and stood over him.

"You've got thirty seconds to make up your mind. Do you have the balls to do this job, or would you rather spend your time entertaining your houseguests and ignoring the Code Blue here at Fratelli Massimo? What's it going to be?"

"Hey, look, Josh, nobody has ever talked to me that way. At Nordstrom—"

"If you say the word *Nordstrom* one more time in my presence, you're fired. Are you in or out?" It was more of a statement than a question.

Ignoring my threat, he responded, "Josh, I have a certain reputation to maintain. I've been doing business with most of those folks for a decade or more, long before you ever met them. I've developed wonderful relationships with them. I don't want to ruin it all over one lousy season."

"I have your answer then. Pack up and get out of my sight."

There was something completely satisfying about kicking him out of the building. I had never experienced that thrill. Maybe Dad was right. You had to embrace being a ballbuster if you wanted to succeed.

. . .

I was ready to leave Sunday evening for New York. Appointments were made. Dollar targets were established, and I had my eye on the prize. And fortunately, I would miss Dad's return to the office.

A week later, I returned and, as I had expected, Carly asked me to see Dad, ASAP.

"This is a clusterfuck, Josh. I leave on a vacation and come back to chaos. Walter's been to see me and negotiations with our lenders are iffy. Bruton's fired. You've flown the coop and I'm left with this mess. Tell me New York and Los Angeles were a success."

"New York and Los Angeles were a success," I replied.

"Don't be a wise guy. What happened in New York and LA?"

"I scrounged out two million in markdown money, cancelled forty-two thousand pairs of losers, and got concessions on some of the others. A good trip."

"OK. And as for Bruton?"

"Totally lame, as Allison would say. I booted him."

"Goddamn it, Josh, your first big personnel decision turns out to be a floperoo."

"Yes, it was. It's on me. But who necessitated that decision? Who wouldn't hear of my keeping Herb Segal around until I got my feet on the ground? Who set all of this organizational chaos in motion?"

"Pretty narrow shoulders for the guy in charge." My father smiled.

"No, it was my call, and I wish I could have a do-over, but don't you go shirking your responsibility either. You preemptively disposed of Herb and then handed me the reins. That was a shitty and irresponsibly counterproductive thing to do. And you'll never convince me you didn't know how it was going to turn out."

"Well, Josh, you could have walked away. Another mistake on your part. They're mounting up."

"Tell me something, Dad. In that Bible story about Abraham being commanded by God to slay his firstborn, were you rooting for the deed to get done?"

"Now you sound just like the Queen of Literature, Dr. Madeline Berg Feldman."

"I have nothing more to say to you. I have work to do."

"See you at the board meeting."

That board meeting was short, but not very sweet.

Mom was welcomed back after having missed two meetings because of her health.

I brought the directors up-to-date regarding Bill Bruton and the grim outlook for the second half. The only bright spot was our boot business, which was encouraging. If that trend continued, we might be able to pull out a decent holiday season.

Most of the meeting was devoted to a summary of our new borrowing agreement. As Walter had predicted, the term was short: one year, expiring on January 1 next year. The interest rate increased by two percentage points, and restrictions were stringent. We were in no position to get relief.

The issue of the dividend was discussed, and while our lenders preferred that we suspend it because of our weak third-quarter performance, we prevailed and declared it once again. Any signal to Wall Street that we were in trouble would freak out our vendors, who would tie up our merchandise and demand payment on receipt, rather than the regular terms. That would signal the beginning of the end for Fratelli Massimo.

Chapter 33

FOURTH-QUARTER 1997 BUSINESS REBOUNDED. A LATE-NOVEMBER snowstorm reminded customers that winter would arrive soon, which stimulated higher-priced boot sales, and trips to the mall resulted in excellent traffic through the holidays. Our lenders were pleased, as were our stockholders, as better-than-expected earnings prospects boosted the stock price by a buck or two, ensured another quarterly dividend, and fattened our bank account.

This was all good, but my attention turned to spring.

At our early February 1998 board meeting, after reviewing 1997's results, I cautioned the directors that we were likely to experience negative comp store performance during February, March, and April. Boot sales had been so strong in the holidays that we were short of clearance merchandise, which accounted for most of our revenue in January and February. And with additional store closings in the offing, total sales would likely dip by 5 to 10 percent in the first quarter—which would probably produce the first loss ever for the company.

That news set off a flurry of questions I had been prepared for. I answered them as intelligently as I could. Dad was mostly silent and sat Buddha-like at the chairman's end of the table.

Walter Benning announced that he would be working with Roger, my assistant, to see what impact those projections would have on the various restrictions in our loan agreement. He promised to keep the directors apprised.

Having just about emptied my bag of tricks with our vendors, I was left with the clear mission of finding merchandise that would sell well at full price.

After our board meeting lunch, I headed to the Galleria shopping center to visit our Fratelli Massimo store. I wanted to have a conversation with Les Portnoy, who was still the company's leading salesman. His insights through the years had proved invaluable. He was now close to retirement, but still had a section full of customers waiting for his attention. He had physically slowed down, and so had his customers, but he still possessed that selling magic my dad and I had enjoyed watching years ago. He knew our customers, and I was eager for his help.

He waved me over, gave me a hug, and agreed to take his break in fifteen minutes so we could grab some coffee.

"It's as dead as a doornail out here. February 3, thirty degrees, and dirty snow on the ground." He shook his head. "What brings the newly installed president of Fratelli Massimo to our humble store? Oh, and belated congratulations, Mr. President."

I gave a shallow smile. "Thanks, but I'm not so sure congratulations are in order, given our crappy business. Condolences might be more appropriate. Any reactions to the spring merchandise?"

"Tepid at best. Who wants open-toe dress shoes in this weather? And stripling sandals? Forget it until it warms up. A few Valentine purchases of stiletto heel 'fuck me' styles to the Guidettes. But basically, we're selling the 70 percent–off clearance stuff, and there ain't much of that."

"Look, Les, when I was working in the stores, we used to look at all the incoming merchandise and try to predict winners and losers."

"Yeah, we still do that. In fact, I'm the official scorekeeper. I'd say it's about fifty/fifty on the stuff we've seen."

"When we get back to the store, show me what you guys think will work, and what you think won't."

"Sure, free advice and worth every penny."

"Any other free advice?" I asked him.

"Yeah. Sell your Fratelli Massimo shares and invest the money in Amazon, like I am."

"Very helpful."

We spent some time in the stock room looking at how the salespeople evaluated the new merchandise. Frankly, they seemed as confused as I was. No common denominators among winners and losers. Colors, materials, heel heights—whatever. Zero help.

I thanked Les and the crew and went to visit the competition: Marmi, Nine West, Precis, Aldo, Dillard's, and Famous-Barr. Unfortunately, there was nothing exciting. Everybody was still on sale. Customers were scarce, and the new stuff on display looked a lot like ours.

All in all, it was a frustrating, wasted trip.

I was about to get in the car when my cellphone rang.

"Where are you?" Dad asked.

"Visiting Galleria."

"OK. Look, I need to talk to you. How about meeting me at Highland Hills; you're only a few minutes away and you won't have to fight rush hour traffic. In half an hour?"

"I'll be there," I said.

I got there in fifteen minutes.

Andrea Marks gave me a nice smile in the foyer and told me that Dad was on the phone in one of the private card rooms upstairs. She invited me to have a table in the Tavern, where I could order something to eat and drink and sign Dad's name on the tab.

The club had been redecorated since my last visit, whenever that was. It was tasteful, as always, with updated colors, carpeting, and wall décor. I could see why the members loved the place. It just wasn't for me.

I walked down the hall to the Tavern. It was a large and cozy room with a dozen or so tables and was intended for casual dining. In Highland Hills lingo, this meant that gentlemen needn't wear ties.

The walls were covered in distressed pine paneling, giving it a very clubby feel. The carpet was chocolate brown, with a cream-colored geometric pattern. The very comfortable chairs were covered in nicely distressed leather.

I scanned the room and noticed that three or four tables were occupied by older women, Mom's age. This obligated me to work the room, Highland Hills style, with what might be described as country club stop-and-chats. A ninety-second time limit punctuated with a short list of acceptable topics: health and status of family members, life events, problems with the golf course, and (in hushed tones) complaints about the food. That was it.

I made my way around the room. I was greeted warmly as I struggled to remember their names, their kids' names, and most importantly, their grandchildren's names. They, of course, remembered mine! These folks were family-tree savants.

I spotted Jenn Katzenberg holding forth at a table for four and sauntered over.

"Josh, how is Maddy doing?" she wanted to know.

I updated the table and asked about her son Jonathan, Allie's best friend. I departed to the sound of well wishes for my mom.

The friendship between Jenn and Amy had ebbed a bit since the schism that developed between the senior Weils and Maddy after the scandal at the club. They spoke frequently, but Amy felt a hint of a chill in the relationship. Amy sensed that Jenn was not altogether pleased with her success at H&H, her happy marriage to me, and her barely polite interest in what was going on at Highland Hills Country Club, which was Jenn's Mecca.

Jenn was an accomplished bridge player, and she participated in some community endeavors, but basically, she was a creature of the club. She and her clique were a powerful force at Highland Hills. "Lesser" members catered to Jenn, seeking her approval and a coveted Saturday night date with the Katzenbergs or an invitation to one of their parties. Amy's independence of and indifference to the social dynamics of the club, along with her professional triumphs, insulated her from Jenn's power and influence. The fact that Jenn's husband, Tommy, was openly seeing other women, while Amy's marriage was solid, only exacerbated Jenn's frustration.

At least that's how Amy saw it. Amy also knew that while Jenn traded in gossip, she would never betray Amy. Years ago, Jenn had confided a deep, dark family secret to Amy. Amy had never revealed it to a soul, including me. Jenn treasured Amy's discretion and returned the favor by honoring Amy's confidences, no matter how gossip-worthy they were.

As I left the tables in the front of the room, I was summoned to the rear of the Tavern, where four familiar faces turned to greet me.

"Josh, it's so nice to see you," said Susan Fox, one of my mom's bridge buddies. In fact, they were all members of Mom's bridge group. No wonder—it was Friday, bridge day at the club. Mom had a doctor's appointment, so she was absent.

They all started talking at once, asking about Amy and Allison, and mostly, about Mom. I told the foursome that Maddy loved them all. They were her best friends, and had been for more than forty years. They had befriended her back when she was a strange New Yorker in a strange land.

I embraced each in turn. All were teary-eyed, including me.

And then the ladies began smiling and chattering about Maddy.

"Statuesque . . . dressed to kill . . . warm, but what a mouth she has . . . master bridge player . . . never criticizes a partner's error in bidding or play, merely closes her eyes and slightly shudders . . . revels in her three B's: her boys, her books, and bridge."

An image flashed in my mind. Suddenly, I saw the *Post-Dispatch* photo of Mom posing with Max in front of their first store, with her Mona Lisa–like quizzical smile.

Oh Mom, oh Mom.

Half an hour later Andrea tapped me on the shoulder and escorted me to one of Highland Hills' private card rooms, where Dad was seated. I sat across from him. Atop the card table was a house phone, a dog-eared tablet with heavy scribbles, and Dad's Montblanc pen.

"Josh, sorry about the wait. I've spent the afternoon after the board meeting talking to analysts, institutional investors, and a reporter or two. All of them want to know why the stock has fallen in recent days. Naturally, I had to be careful, since our fourth-quarter numbers won't be public for a few weeks, and I don't want the Securities and Exchange Commission lawyers up my ass for disclosing the undisclosable."

"What did you tell them?" I asked.

"Well, we publish corporate and comp sales monthly, so I was able to repeat those numbers, the strong November and December, thanks to boots. I blamed the slow January on a lack of clearance. I tried to emphasize that those boot sales would likely yield higher margins in the fourth quarter, 1997. The lack of clearance merchandise was a good thing, but it meant lousy sales in January, etcetera, etcetera."

"But that stuff was all in the press releases."

"That's what you try to do with those jerkheimers, just repeat stuff that's already public. But it didn't work; they all sense a lack of enthusiasm for spring, so they're dumping the stock. What could I say and stay out of jail?"

"I guess you were in a tough spot."

"Joshua, no, I guess *we* are in a tough spot—you, me, and Fratelli Massimo. We need some answers, but most of all, we need results. Any clues at Galleria?"

I gave him my downbeat report.

"This is serious. If we blow through those loan restrictions this spring, there will be hell to pay. The stock will drop like a rock and the banks will be all over us, asking for those umbrellas they loaned us on a sunny day. Our vendors will get nervous and may refuse to ship on the usual terms. You have no idea, kid."

"Dad, any advice or thoughts would be welcome. Meanwhile I am dedicating all my energy and focus to improving business for spring."

"Not distracted by your mom's health issues, are you?"

"No. Mom is quite independent. She has Nora and periodic visits from a medical person to check her status. I care deeply about her, but the doctors feel she's stabilized and can engage in normal activities. Mom's not distracting me; it's the business that has my full attention."

"Better be enough."

And with that, our meeting ended.

When I checked my cell, which I had turned off when I entered the club, I discovered that Amy had called several times, asking why I was late. The last message indicated that she and Allison would have a girls' night out. I could "fend for myself."

• • •

Roger and Walter were waiting to see me when I got to the office the next day. They had come armed with a sheaf of spreadsheets, which we pored over for about an hour. The bottom line was that if my board projections were realized, we would not meet the necessary financial requirements in the loan agreement. Walter asked again, as he had the year before, whether we should prepare our lenders for that event. Even though it was often better to warn stakeholders of potential problems, I urged him not to, in this case.

"We can't trust those lenders to keep their mouths shut, and if word leaks that we have debt problems, not only will the stock crater, but the business will be on life support." I paused for a second. "No!" I told him. "Let's hope that results are better than I projected, and we'll be able to comply with those loan covenant provisions."

It just was not smart to start a panic over the possibility that business might be soft. I then asked Roger to destroy the sheaf of spreadsheets and prepare another scenario: the sales level we would need to achieve to comply with the loan restrictions.

Walter grumbled; he understood the dilemma, but he wanted to check with Dad—which I encouraged him to do. Dad, of course, agreed to keep things quiet, as long as we could.

In this case, patience paid off. Bit by bit, business improved during the spring. The weather cooperated by producing record-high temperatures in March and April. TV weathermen were warning of drought conditions because of a lack of rainfall. The farmers may have been worried, but I was elated.

The calendar was also favorable with an early Easter, which meant dress shoes got off to a fast start and we found ourselves reordering and—more importantly—receiving refills of dozens of the hot styles. Open-toe casual and dress shoes did very well, and our sandals (especially sport sandals) started selling much earlier than usual. Hot brands included Nine West, Steve Madden, and Birkenstock. Some high-priced dress shoes from Stuart Weitzman and Via Spiga contributed as well. With an increased proportion of our merchandise selling at full price, we reduced the number of promotions and the size of the discounts. The handbag business, especially the Coach brand, was also on fire.

Instead of the 5 to 10 percent decline in total sales that I had originally projected, we managed to squeeze out a 1 percent total sales increase because our older comp stores were up 5 percent for the first quarter. And without the profit drain from stores we had closed, earnings perked up. The stock rose to about seventeen dollars a share. I was looking forward to our upcoming board meeting, when I would share the good news with the directors.

Dad was thrilled. There was certainly a bounce to his step. When we ran into one another, he'd give me a high five or a thumbs-up and an "atta boy." I, like Sisyphus, had pushed that giant rock to the mountaintop's peak and wasn't about to let it roll back down!

Dad may have had the chairman and CEO title, but I was running the business.

Chapter 34

Two seismic events rocked my world in 1998.

St. Louis Cardinal Mark McGwire and the Cubs' Sammy Sosa spent the summer bashing home runs at a phenomenal pace. The nation was transfixed by the battle. As the season wore on, even Maddy tuned in to watch Redbird games. McGwire won the duel by hitting a record seventy homers. Or seemingly hitting seventy homers. Seemingly, because he had a trick up his sleeve, literally—steroids.

McGwire wasn't the only one with a trick up his sleeve. Mr. Max Feldman shook up our family's world with his own sleight of hand.

When the board assembled for the April meeting, Carly notified us that Dad would be a little late. I was to begin with the president's report.

I first provided the members with an unaudited preview of our first-quarter sales and profits and summarized the major factors that had contributed to our performance. Not many questions! Rather, lots of praise and sighs of relief. Walter Benning, usually the epitome of impassivity, actually applauded and stated that we would easily avoid loan covenant trouble—and would likely do so again in the second quarter.

He moved that we declare the usual ten-cent per share dividend. Unanimous approval.

"I vote yes!" declared Dad, as he jauntily entered the room. "I apologize for being late, but I had to take a very important call—which I must share with you." He settled himself into his seat, and went on.

"First some background. Last January, I was in New York for a National Retail Federation meeting. I happened to run into Ed Gottlieb, an old friend, who is CEO of Missouri Atlantic Group, or MAG. As many of you know, it is a huge private equity concern that specializes in retail companies. He casually mentioned that MAG might be interested in taking a stake in Fratelli Massimo. He likes our concept, real estate, and buying power. I will explain why later. I told him that a formal expression of interest from MAG would require me to inform the board of that overture.

Mom, Rand, and I exchanged worried looks. He was prepping us for bad news!

"For those of you unfamiliar with how private equity firms work, let me outline it for you briefly. When those firms are interested in acquiring a company, they typically aggregate a pool of equity from partners and borrow substantial sums to purchase the targeted company. MAG then operates the company, usually making significant changes in management and operations, which presumably yields a stronger, more profitable business. After several years, they put the company up for sale, at a significantly higher price than they paid. This creates a windfall of profit for the investors after paying off the loans they made at the time of acquisition.

"I informed Ed that the board meeting was scheduled for today, and he called this morning to inform me that he had secured expressions of interest from lenders, banks, and financial institutions like insurance companies. He also has aggregated a group of investors, including me, who have committed capital for an investment in Fratelli Massimo.

"With all these arrangements in place he, speaking for MAG, formally expressed an interest in buying all of the outstanding shares of Fratelli Massimo. Their board has approved an all-cash offer of $20.50 a share, about a 20 percent premium over yesterday afternoon's closing price. He will confirm all this in a letter, which I expect to receive shortly via facsimile. I closed my eyes and shook my head. The much forecasted day of reckoning with Max was here.

"I thanked Ed for his interest but cautioned him that the board had an obligation to get up to speed on the offer, and that we would not have an immediate response."

A flurry of hands went up, but he continued. "Another element of the transaction is important to mention. We are required to publicly disclose the offer even before we have a chance to evaluate it. As a result, other bidders will have a period of time to match or exceed MAG's offer.

"Before answering your questions, let me explain why MAG is so interested in purchasing Fratelli Massimo, as well as some of the conditions he mentioned." Dad then looked up and over in my direction.

"But before I start, hats off to Josh, who manned up and made spring a success, with a little help from the weather and calendar. That performance impressed the hell out of Ed and his partners."

This brought another board ovation. He had surely given me a compliment, but—"manned up"? But this was the least of my concerns. There would be worse to follow.

Dad went on with his presentation.

"MAG is very impressed with Fratelli Massimo's positioning and recent results. They're optimistic about our future and think we can convert some of our underperforming stores to their discount shoe division. And, importantly, we can begin sourcing some of our shoes from MAG's factories.

"You mentioned some conditions?" came a question from the table.

"Well, they have to examine our books and get the blessings of their accountants and lawyers. They also require unanimous approval by *all* members of the Feldman family. They don't want any drama." Dad paused and gave Mom a long look. "They want to close the deal before the holidays." Board members were captivated by Max's presentation.

"And they insisted that I become a financial partner in the deal, which means I have to personally plunk down seventy-five million dollars, which represents my proceeds from the proposed sale of Massimo Fratelli. It will also cost most of what I have socked away through the years. They want me fully invested in this.

"And, of course, they want me to continue to run the company. They need a world-class merchant in charge. Ed Gottlieb said, 'You created the company, grew it, know it inside and out. Without you, there's no deal.'"

Smiling broadly, Max added, "I will recommend, with the board's approval, a generous severance arrangement for Josh— not because he is my son, but because of his many years of commendable service to Fratelli Massimo."

I was shocked. I was speechless. My face was totally frozen. I was out on the street. Me, the guy whose efforts had saved the day for Fratelli Massimo. I had made this deal possible. Dad grinned at me, kind of a "sucks to be you" smile.

Hands again shot up, but this time it was our board lawyer, Harrison Balding, who quickly took the floor.

"Thank you, Max. But before we get into the details and begin discussing this proposal, it is my responsibility to inform the board of the duties and obligations that this proposal requires of us.

"Because of the nature of this bid, and Max's involvement, we need to set up a special committee to review MAG's offer, and any others that might surface once the announcement of MAG's bid becomes public. We must do what's best for all stockholders. Max, the board, and the special committee must each engage counsel and investment bankers to advise them."

Then the discussion started.

I could barely pay attention; it was quite clear what this transaction would mean for me. My lifelong dream of being CEO of Fratelli Massimo was out the window. Dad, like Mark McGwire, did indeed have a trick up his sleeve. If Dad took charge, with his old buddy Ed Gottlieb at the helm of MAG, I would be odd man out. I had to hand it to my father. He figured out a way to have his cake and eat it too—and get a second helping by getting rid of his son.

The three Feldmans had their eyes on me; Dad was still smiling triumphantly, while Mom and Rand wore mournful looks. I remained poker-faced while my stomach churned.

The next item of official business was the establishment of the special committee to consider the offer. The board agreed that Peter Kahn, Harrison Balding, and I should take on the task.

The promised letter from MAG arrived and was circulated, and it contained much of what Dad had said.

As we adjourned and were about to depart for the Noonday Club lunch, Dad asked if he could see us Feldmans in his office for a few minutes after the meal.

"We won't be there, Dad," I replied. "We need to call Gunther first."

"And why do you need to do that?"

"He'll be very helpful to us, and we will want to hear what he has to say." I turned to Mom and Rand, who signaled their concurrence.

"Gunther's past his prime and is at death's door. Surely there are other experts you can call if you think it's necessary," he said.

"Max, I, too, am past my prime and at death's door, "Mom said. "But both Gunther and I are in full possession of our faculties, and I know of no one whose opinion I value more than his in matters like this."

Dad regrouped and uncharacteristically tried the conciliatory approach. "Look, Maddy, you don't want to spend whatever time you have left in court fighting this thing."

She raised her eyebrows. "How unusually thoughtful of you, Max. We'll let you know when we're ready to proceed."

"Have it your way," he said and shrugged.

I asked Carly to work through lunch to prepare a rough draft of the board meeting minutes. I planned to email those, along with the letter we had received from MAG, to Gunther. I also called him and asked if he was available later that afternoon to talk to Maddy, Rand, and me about a proposal the board had received, which I would be sending him in an hour or so. He was glad to help.

Mom called a friend from Washington U and reserved a conference room in Brookings Hall, which was equipped with a modern telephonic hookup. We didn't want to call from Fratelli Massimo offices. We needed neutral ground.

Mom and Rand drove to the university together, and I followed. Once there, we situated ourselves in the meeting room and made sure all the conference call equipment was in working order. We had to call a tech guy to instruct us and help set things up.

Before we called Gunther, the three of us had an opportunity to discuss what had transpired at the meeting. I expressed my skepticism about the "chance meeting" with Ed, the scenario that Dad had presented. Mom and Rand agreed with my conclusion, but we realized that it was moot. The proposal had been made, and the ball was in our court.

"Seems to me that we don't really have much of a choice," Rand said. "We have to publicize MAG's offer, and it's sure to have an effect on the market—and may even elicit other bids. I don't think we can stop it. Sorry, Josh, but Dad strikes again."

Mom turned to me. "Josh, sweetheart, I know you must be feeling awful, and it's important to get Gunther's take. But I'm afraid I agree with Rand. I don't think we can head this thing off."

"It's partially my fault, my blind spot," I told them. "I ignored countless warnings about Dad. He is loathsome. 'You have a chance to prove yourself, son.' All of those phony thumbs-up and high fives. What the fuck! And all the while scheming with his pal Ed to sell the company and cut me loose. He's a real shit."

"Josh, you're preaching to the choir," Mom said. "But your father is who he is. We need to figure out how to proceed. Gunther will help."

After some mechanical and electronic gyrations, we managed to get him on the line.

"Hello to all of you. I've had a chance to read the minutes and MAG's letter. I must admit I enjoy getting back in the fray, if only in an advisory capacity. I warn you that my billing rate per hour is four figures, but you are in luck. Today and today only, a special friends and family discount is on offer. That's a retailing gimmick, isn't it, Josh?"

"Yeah, Grandpa, I'm familiar with that gimmick and welcome the bargain. It's nice to be on the receiving end, rather than the giving end."

"Well, good. Before we discuss the proposal, congratulations to you, Josh. Nice going. I don't know anything about those styles or brands, but I know a lot about sales, earnings, and dividends. Bravo! Now on to the MAG proposal.

"Assuming MAG is as financially solid as their statements seem to indicate, their professionally worded and vetted offer is legitimate and requires the response that Harrison suggested. Max's version of the contact with MAG, and subsequent offer and MAG's reasoning and conditions per the board minutes, are textbook—which suggests Ed and Max's interaction was not a 'chance meeting.'" Gunther was picking up speed.

"Harrison's instructions are textbook as well. The special committee. The need for independent advisors, and the prompt disclosure of the bid. I will, at the end of this conversation, present a short list of lawyers and investment bankers I consider to be unmatched, in terms of expertise and discretion."

He paused, then asked, "But first, how do the three of you analyze the offer?"

Rand spoke first. "It seems to be a good deal for the stockholders, but unfair to Josh."

"And you, Maddy?"

"I echo Rand's sentiments. It's hard to imagine a better deal for the shareholders, which I might add, include all of us. But Josh pays a heavy price."

"Josh?"

"Rand, Mom, I appreciate your sensitivity, love, and support, but this is business. And what Harrison said doesn't leave much room for sensitivity, love, and support. We must do what's best for the stockholders, but who knows? We may be able to better reward the stockholders by rejecting the bid and staying the course with our current team. In fact, I have a strategic alternative that might just require a reassessment of the MAG offer."

"I am anxious to hear about that strategic alternative, Josh," Gunther said. "We need to have all the available data before the board decides. Josh, how do you think the company will do in the months ahead?"

"Candidly, I have no idea. I thought spring would be a disaster. It turned out great. Last fall, boots bailed us out. But tomorrow's retail business is anybody's guess. We are wholly dependent on finding hot new merchandise. And some luck with the weather. A warm November and December will kill our boot business, for example. And frankly, our business model is dated and leaking oil—but still functional."

"Sounds like me, Josh, dated and leaking oil—but still functional. But I wouldn't want you guys to invest in me at this time. Why do you describe it in those terms?" Gunther asked.

"Let me clarify without getting overly detailed. Most of our stores are in good regional malls, but many of those shopping centers are declining in appeal. We are heavily reliant on 'friends and family' promotions, and the customers are wise to the gimmick and demand bigger and bigger discounts. But the elephant in the room is the internet. It's growing in popularity every day—use is up 50 percent, last year alone. The numbers are still small, but the internet is sure to become a powerful force in the years ahead."

"Is that channel of distribution, the internet, your strategic initiative?" Gunther asked.

"It is. In a nutshell, I believe that shoes can be sold on the internet. This defies the conventional wisdom in the shoe industry. It is the same conventional wisdom that dismissed the threat of athletic footwear. The same conventional wisdom that urged us to use constant promotions as a cure-all for sales woes. But Zappos, a privately held West Coast start-up that relies almost exclusively on the internet, is showing early signs of success. Overnight deliveries and free returns are attractive features for the customer. Except that, unlike most web operators, Zappos does not discount. Customers are willing to pay full price."

Gunther quickly said, "Are you suggesting that Zappos would be willing to consider a merger with or acquisition by a traditional brick-and-mortar retailer, like Fratelli Massimo?"

"I believe they might be. I'm friendly with Tony Hsieh, Zappos's founder. We can bring some critical things to the party: shoe merchandising expertise, a valuable company name in Fratelli Massimo, decades-old relationships with the shoe brands that thus far are reluctant to sell on the web, and our own private label merchandise, which Zappos currently can't offer."

"It's a bit pie-in-the-sky," Gunther said. "But the combination of the two companies could be a real winner." He thought for a moment, then concluded.

"As intriguing as that alternative appears, Josh, any transaction like that is bound to take time—several months, at least. The MAG offer requires an immediate response. Will the board be willing to reject MAG's offer and risk seeing it disappear while you test the waters with Zappos? And will your father support the initiative? Without the agreement of the company's CEO, the board will almost certainly accept the MAG proposal."

"I agree, but it's worth a shot. I will meet with Dad," I told him.

We all knew how things would end. Mom and Rand shook their heads in unison. Gunther finally broke the silence. "A bit of advice for you, Josh. As a Delaware corporation, the board has much discretion, but unless you are thoroughly convinced that Fratelli Massimo will perform better as an independent company—with or without a partner like Zappos—you are well advised to accept the best bid if the acquirer is financially qualified.

"And one last personal aside, if you will permit me. You realize that Max is 'betting the ranch' on this. I would imagine that if things work out according to MAG's internal spreadsheets, he could be worth half a billion dollars or more with a successful exit strategy. If things don't work out, it will be a different matter entirely." I understood that much.

"And now, Josh. Knowing Max as I do, I believe the probability of your convincing him to approach Zappos is close to nil. He hungers for the bigger stage that MAG offers him and his potential nine-figure exit. That being said, your mere mention of the Zappos alternative will almost certainly be relayed by Max to Ed Gottlieb. The silver lining may well be a sweetened offer."

After he presented the list of lawyers and bankers he recommended, we thanked Gunther profusely, and he signed off.

I thought back to that pivotal meeting when we voted to go public. I selfishly wanted to stay private because I knew that path would materially improve my chances of running Fratelli Massimo one day. Once we went public, we would and did have a responsibility to outside shareholders. Max held that trump card when he conspired with Ed Gottlieb. Mom, Rand, and I could not hold back the tide of public shareholders, institutions, outside directors, and, ultimately, the wishes of the CEO.

How glorious he must feel. This was his dream come true: a big payday for the stockholders, some puffed-up title at MAG, the opportunity to be as rich as Midas, and to crush me in the process. Max had won this round, but I would stop at nothing to win the next one. And there would be a next one. My mission was to figure out exactly what it would take to claim victory. No matter how ruthless I had to be, no matter how much blood was shed, I was ready. "Gentle Josh," as they said in *The Godfather*, slept with the fishes.

. . .

Rand went home with Mom. I went home to Amy, who was sympathetic but made it plain that she was glad it would be over. "No chance the board would reject MAG's offer, or a better one, if it were presented," she said.

"Josh, you didn't slay Moby Dick, but you didn't drown, either. Give yourself a chance to mourn your loss, but remember you're loaded with money and talent and were single-handedly running the company for the last couple years. You must put your talent, experience, and expertise to use. You agree, don't you?"

"Yes, Amy. It will take me some time to wrap my head around this. I've spent my life preparing to run Fratelli Massimo. Even as a kid, I dreamed of it. Those were dreams that Dad encouraged. So yes, I need to sort things out. But you can rely on one thing, Amy. I will retaliate. I have learned from the master—Max Feldman. I don't know how, or when, but he will go down at my hands!"

Chapter 35

DAD RECEIVED ME IMMEDIATELY THE NEXT MORNING.

I confirmed that Gunther said we were required to make an immediate public disclosure of the offer, and that it would be up to the special committee to evaluate the MAG bid, as well as any other bids that might come in. The committee would then make our recommendation to the board, and it would either accept or reject it—or negotiate with the bidders.

I then outlined my Zappos proposal.

Dad closed his eyes, shrugged his shoulders, and smiled. "Out of left field, sonny. It's a nonstarter, the very definition of a Hail Mary pass. Too little too late, podnah." He then rattled off the usual litany of reasons why selling shoes on the web would never work, and then he proceeded to give me some advice. "Look, Josh, a great merchant you will never be. You're a good businessman, a smart retailer, and a magician with numbers, but you strike out as a visionary. You'll land on your feet. Wherever you end up, stick to what you know how to do."

"I'll keep that in mind, but I do intend to talk to the special committee and apprise the members of the Zappos alternative," I said.

"Then you'll want to tell them that I am absolutely opposed to your nonsensical proposal, which risks MAG pulling their offer. Even if the family wants to support you, which I doubt, I will have the votes to win. Those independent directors are scared shitless about stockholder lawsuits. In fact, Josh, please see that

I am scheduled to address the special committee when you're finished."

Dad was taking no chances. Gunther was on the money once again.

With nothing to lose at that point, I asked Dad if he had any regrets.

"Hell, no. I've dreamed of this day since I went through the wringer back when we met to decide whether to go public or not. Imagine me, the creator of Fratelli Massimo, the company's brains and talent, stuck with a measly 20 percent of the company. And I was supposed to be grateful that you and Rand saved the day from your mother's stubbornness? It turned out you and your fag brother betrayed me, voted against me, and promptly hid behind her skirt until the truth came out. The great lady voted with me. Wanted to keep peace in the house, did she? A hell of a lot of good that did her. I have to laugh." And he did. Then he went on.

"Regrets? You kidding? I'll never, ever forgive your mother for humiliating me at the club. I look forward to becoming one of the richest and most respected men at HHCC. And it won't be because I inherited it. It's because Max Feldman had the vision to create Fratelli Massimo, build it, reinvest in it with MAG, and reap the harvest."

Max Feldman, ace merchant, could only focus on what this transaction meant for him—vindication and redemption. As Sy had written in his letter, Dad would do only what was in his best interest.

The special committee gave my proposal short shrift. I couldn't blame them. They had a sure thing with the MAG offer and would incur business risk and stockholder wrath if they voted with me. But in my head and in my heart, I knew a combination with Zappos could be a long-term winner for the company.

I stopped at Mom's on my way home and filled her in on the details of my conversation with Dad.

"As always, Dad focused solely on himself and his greatness, and had nothing to say about the collateral damage the MAG deal caused."

"Josh, honey, what did you expect? All of us Feldmans have experienced his treachery. No surprise."

"Then you're reconciled to selling Fratelli Massimo? Doing precisely what Dad wants?"

"Yes, I am. And not for all the fancy legal reasons. My father taught me many lessons. First and foremost, play the long game. Keep focused on your most important objective, even if you lose some skirmishes along the way. And boy, did we lose some skirmishes—including the MAG takeover.

"But think of it this way. Rand, you, and I are wealthier than we ever dreamed. Your father is betting his entire fortune on turning his hundred million into half a billion—or more—in a few years. He wants to be the richest man at Highland Hills, assuming that will redeem his tarnished reputation. And he wants to play on the national stage; MAG offers him that opportunity in New York. Maybe it will work for him. Maybe it won't. In the meantime, Josh, he has set you free."

"Indeed, Mom. Free to bring him to his knees," I said.

"I hope I live long enough to see that," Maddy responded.

• • •

Once the announcement of MAG's offer was made public, several other bidders expressed interest and made respectable offers. And like clockwork, just as Gunther had predicted, MAG sweetened the bid to twenty-six dollars per share. I could just imagine my dad urging them on and throwing more of his own money into the pot. After all, we were talking vindication and redemption—can't put a price tag on that.

And so, MAG and Max won the day.

The day the final MAG deal was announced, I stopped in at Simon Hall to talk to the dean of the Olin School of Business at Washington U. Fratelli Massimo had done some recruiting there, and we chatted about how valuable WU grad Roger Morton had been. He had ultimately landed a job with MAG, and I was bullish about his future. I then switched gears and spoke to him about my desire to teach a retailing course at the school, after the deal was closed in August.

"I noticed that the current bulletin includes no retail courses, and I'd like to give teaching one a try," I told him.

"Josh, not a bad idea. I've often fielded this kind of request from CEOs who are retiring from their posts. I warn them that there are twenty-six class sessions in the semester and that they might run out of war stories. You must be willing to create a rigorous syllabus, commit to being here in St. Louis, and promise to not rely too heavily on guest speakers. Most of those CEOs take a pass when they hear that."

"I think I understand," I said. "I believe I can commit to the last two requirements. I intend to stay in St. Louis, and I'm confident I can do most of the teaching. As for war stories, mine might be too bloody for student consumption. Oh, and one other thing

I should mention. If you look at my undergraduate transcript, you will find it rather lackluster. Just wanted you to know."

"As the politicians say," he said, smiling, "'just a youthful indiscretion.' Not a problem, Josh. If you can come up with a decent curriculum, I'm sure we can fit you into this fall's class offerings."

The fact that the Feldman Family Partnership had donated twenty-five million dollars to help fund the Department of American Studies at Washington U did not hurt my chances in the least. The dean was quite familiar with the gift and size of the partnership, and his Cheshire cat grin signaled his optimism about our future relationship and potential dividends therefrom.

I met with the head of the Marketing Department, who helped me create a syllabus using Harvard Business School case studies on companies like L.L. Bean, Staples, Walmart, Best Buy, Macy's, and others. I was in business. And opening day was approaching on September 1, 1998.

I soon discovered that I loved teaching. My students were bright and articulate, and they didn't hesitate to grill me if they disagreed. Retail is such an accessible subject. Everybody shops. And, like advertising, everybody has opinions. I taught—and continued to teach—a fun course, usually oversubscribed, and immensely rewarding—though not monetarily, of course. In the years to come, I would walk away with several teaching awards, and maintain immensely satisfying relationships with many of my former students through email or when they returned to St. Louis for a reunion.

My work as an educator also allowed me to stay up-to-date with what was happening at retail. I invited guest speakers from different segments of the industry, and I attended trade shows, kept up with the trade papers, made courtesy calls on vendors, and managed to stay in touch with shopping center developers at their annual convention.

In addition to keeping me in the game and available for a major retail leadership post, staying current and relevant allowed me to focus laser-like attention on how Fratelli Massimo fared. All the fanfare and confetti showered on Max's "brilliant transaction" would evaporate if Fratelli Massimo failed to perform. If the company went under, my father would be virtually penniless, having invested almost every dollar he had in the MAG transaction.

The clock was always ticking, and I was constantly watching. I had long understood how fragile the company's formula had become and how distracted my father had been, reinventing himself. For a while, I was content to bide my time.

• • •

About a year after the sale of Fratelli Massimo, my grandfather Gunther passed away. By that time, Maddy was too sick to travel to New York for the funeral. Rand and I went, of course. Allison wanted to go, but had finals. Mom met with us at Wydown Terrace before Rand and I took off for LaGuardia.

"It's a blessing, boys, that his body gave out before his mind shredded up. And I'm thankful that he died before me. No parent…well, you know."

We knew.

We reminisced about Gunther, all of us in awe of his brilliance. Even though we had become closer to him through the years, he remained an enigma. He was pragmatic, insightful, jocular, and a terrific storyteller, but still a mystery. Many of his utterances needed careful parsing to understand. I think Amy put it best when she had said to me years ago, "When your grandfather speaks, there's always the apparent meaning, then the subtext, and then the sub-subtext that require interpretation."

When we were about to leave for the airport, Mom asked Rand to stay behind for a few minutes. I got the car started and waited for him. About ten minutes later, he slid into his seat, fighting off tears.

"I'll never see her again, or if I do, she won't be Maddy."

That truth sank my spirits as well. When I pulled myself together, I asked Rand what they had talked about.

"Tell you later, Josh."

As Rand feared, our conversation at Maddy's house did turn out to be the last conversation the three of us would ever have. It was as if she were determined to survive Gunther, saving him from the grief of burying his "little girl."

Riverside Memorial Chapel in Manhattan was crowded for Gunther's funeral. Generations of his former associates and law partners were in attendance; leading figures from the business community, judges, and other dignitaries were there, including former Mayor David Dinkins. Representatives from the development offices of MIT and Harvard were prominent and made their presence known. His bridge comrades expressed their condolences. Even two of his gambling buddies from Vegas showed up (the car dealer from New Jersey and the guy who owned frontage on the Strip). Elvis stood to the side and was greeted by many, as he had greeted them when they had called on Gunther.

There were even a couple of reporters there from the *Times* and *Wall Street Journal*.

Rand and I took the dais, welcomed everybody, and explained that his daughter Maddy was unable to be at the funeral because of illness.

Rand said, "The rabbi who spoke posed the eternal question, 'Who among us can understand the ways of the Lord?' We ask you, 'Who among us can understand the ways of Gunther Harris Berg?'"

We each shared some memories of our grandfather—his love for us, and our love for him.

We were mobbed by well-wishers after concluding our remarks. They shared stories about our grandfather touching on his brilliance, his incisiveness, and his clairvoyance. "He had an amazing ability to foresee the future and the skill to prepare for the inevitable," one of his former clients put it.

His personal estate attorney asked if we could meet with him briefly after the service. We joined him in one of the empty chapels after the crowd filed out.

"I know you both are heading home, but I wanted a few minutes to tell you that I will be in touch with you about estate matters over the next few months. I know your mother is indisposed now, but I would appreciate your relaying that message to her when you return to St. Louis, Joshua."

I assured him that I would.

"Oh, and one other thing. The will is a simple, straightforward, six-page document, but he established more than twenty trusts, which are anything but simple and straightforward. No surprise there. It will take a while for me and our associates to figure out how to deal with them.

"A quick question: I have known your grandfather for decades, but I must admit I was puzzled by three of his bequests, which seemed completely out of character. Perhaps you can shed some light on them. He specifically requested that upon his death, ten-thousand dollar checks be sent to the Free Tibet organization, the Friends of the Australian Aborigines League, and the Tribal Chapter of the Aleutians. All in honor of his great-granddaughter, Allison Feldman."

I just shook my head. Who, indeed, could understand the ways of Gunther Berg?

I was leaving from LaGuardia and Rand from JFK, so we shared a cab partway. I asked him what Maddy had said to him.

He laughed and said, "Mom always worries about you. About me, the gay son, not a care in the world. But you, my straight brother, worry her. When you were young, she worried you would become a clone of Dad. A horrible fate! Then as time went on, she worried that he would crush you."

"And now?" I asked.

"She's not worried any longer. You did battle with Dad, proved yourself, and survived—and will find your happiness in other pursuits. She chuckled about your determination to even the score with Dad and wished you luck. And you have Amy, another of Mom's triumphs. She told me this because she always used to implore me to be strong for you. Then she smiled and said, 'I'm at peace now.'"

The taxi dropped me off; Rand and I hugged, thinking that it was only a matter of time until we met again at another funeral.

But with Mom, there was to be "no funeral, no memorial service, no fuss, no flowers, no eulogies, no rabbi, no nothing. Just cremation and it's dust-to-dust." Those were her orders.

In the weeks before her death, I visited with her often at home, where she wanted to spend her last days. I would find her in her bedroom, in the hospital bed we had rented. On the nightstand were vials of pills, a drinking glass, a pitcher of water, and a stack of books. And for some reason, the gift that Gunther had given her on his final visit. Mom's jar of peanut butter, emblazoned with *Maddy's Jar* on the lid.

I asked her what made it so special. "Josh, when I was a kid, I would dash home from school, make for the butler's pantry, and treat myself to a spoonful or two or three of peanut butter. My mother was disgusted by this, since the entire household shared the same jar of peanut butter. We fought and ultimately compromised. I could have my own jar of peanut butter. The rest of the household, its own." She smiled, hesitated, perhaps reminiscing.

"When your grandfather presented me with this jar with my name on it, I lost it! All those memories came flooding back, including the breakfast I had with my dad before my wedding, when I dipped into the New York jar for the last time."

That explained, Mom asked me to help her live a little by tasting some peanut butter. I was to dip the spoon in the peanut butter jar and hand it to Mom. She savored it. But as the end grew near, she lacked the strength to feed herself, so she asked me to get a teaspoon, skim the peanut butter, and put it on her tongue so she could savor the flavor. Afterwards, she would look at me with teary eyes, touch my hand, and smile lovingly. I teared up as well. There'll never, ever be a mom like my mom.

She also wanted me to read to her from some of the classics that had given her so much comfort. But as her attention span rapidly weakened and her pain relievers blurred her thoughts, she asked only that I recite the passage that concludes *Middlemarch*.

It refers to the fictional Dorothea Brooke, who was one of Mom's heroes. And I could do it by rote.

> "But the effect of her being on those around her was incalculably diffusive: for the growing good of the world is partly dependent on unhistoric acts; and that things are not so ill with you and me as they might have been is half owing to the number who lived faithfully a hidden life, and rest in unvisited tombs."

Chapter 36

SHORTLY AFTER MOM DIED, I NOTICED THAT A PRIME STOREFRONT location in downtown Clayton had become available. I was itching to get back into retailing. Teaching was fun and it kept me up-to-date about the industry, but ringing a cash register was in my DNA.

I called the landlord, signed a lease, and opened a bookstore.

This was certainly no substitute for the bigger stage I was determined to perform on. But it got me back to the basics. I would be the merchant, selecting titles, determining product placement and pricing. I wanted to talk to customers. It had been so long since I was on a sales floor, and I was genuinely curious about what my customers had to say. And I welcomed the opportunity to motivate a staff, create displays, craft a buying plan, and worry about beating last year's figures. It would help me strip the rust off.

Clayton was a pretty busy place during the day. It had many high-rise office buildings and law offices, as the county courthouse was just down the block, so lunchtime was always a prime time for us to do business. We were never open at night or on the weekends.

The store offered a nice assortment of fiction and nonfiction, bestsellers and literature as well as trade paperbacks at full price. I swore off promotions. I had been down that path and I knew how it inevitably ended. We did offer clearance, damaged, and remaindered books on a mobile bookcase by the front door.

Sure, some got stolen, but at least the thieves were readers. Mom would have approved.

We were happy to special order books and would notify customers when they arrived. But if they were in a hurry, we would suggest they log onto Amazon.com and order it on their own. We were also pleased to give them our well-considered personal recommendations, not computer-generated algorithms, if they wanted advice. There was a coffee shop next door, so we mutually benefitted. Lots of coffee drinkers are readers, and vice versa.

After the store opened, I was there much of the time when I wasn't teaching or doing my prep work for my inevitable future bout with Dad. My ultimate goal was to play a major role for a prominent national retailer. In the meantime, I hired a terrific manager, Lisa Stark, a WU graduate, to run the daily operations of the store. She had majored in American Lit and once took a course my mom taught. Lisa was a book person, not a retailer, but she was always gregarious and engaging. Most of all, she loved books, and she loved the store hours! To this day, we do business from ten in the morning until six in the evening, five days a week.

I found this work to be very satisfying. When I wasn't on the sales floor, I took care of the back-office operations, ordered books, met with publishing reps, said yes to the horde of locals asking for modest advertising bucks, and did the bookkeeping, all while perusing sales and inventory reports. Pretty basic stuff.

I also planned special events, such as author appearances and book signings. Ever since Amazon had become a force, publishing houses and authors were much friendlier to us independent booksellers.

And I spent time keeping track of Dad, reading *Footwear News* and *Women's Wear Daily*, and having lunch with Roger Morton, who'd been assigned to Fratelli Massimo as head of planning. I never tipped my hand to Roger or any of the other contacts I had in the shoe and shopping center business. I just expressed friendly curiosity about my old stomping grounds.

While the bookstore was four thousand square feet in size, the lease included a huge vacant space on the second floor. Part of it was the simple office where I did my work. One wall was devoted to storing Mom's classics—I guess you might call it a shrine to her. But that's rather an overstatement. It's just some built-in bookshelves filled with the books she loved that we moved from Wydown Terrace after her death.

Mom's "shrine" was adjacent to bookshelves filled with family photos. While this area was technically my office, where I attended to bookstore tasks, tracked what was going on at Fratelli Massimo, and plotted my future moves against Max, it also served as a bit of a sanctuary for me.

I sometimes swiveled my chair around and looked at the family photos on the bookshelves. Maddy in her twenties aboard the Fire Islander. Mom cutting the ribbon at Fratelli Massimo's first store opening. A picture of Sy and Rose. Childhood pictures of Rand and me. Amy and me mugging in front of my first Porsche. A professional portrait of Amy, Allison, and me taken when Allie was five years old. The family photo taken at the Four Seasons restaurant when we celebrated Gunther's eightieth birthday. I would invariably lose myself in a sort of trance recalling what once was.

During one such trance, at about six fifteen, Lisa Stark knocked on the door and asked whether she should lock up the store. I told her that I would take care of it, and asked her to simply lock the front door. I would turn off the lights and make sure the store was properly closed. Amy and Allison were having a girls' night out, so I would be on my own.

I indulged myself in a ritual I'd done from time to time since Maddy's death: I would take her favorite Henry James novels off the shelf and flip through them, reading the notes she scribbled in the margins. One of my favorites was in *The Portrait of a Lady* when Isabel Archer leaves her abusive husband. Mom's note: "Serves the bastard right. Should have done it sooner." Gunther sure nailed that one at his birthday dinner. Another was in *The Golden Bowl*, when a woman receives confirmation that her husband has been screwing her best friend: "I'd claw her eyes out." And then there's—oh well, never mind, it was all rather silly, but it helped me to deal with the only real loss I'd ever suffered.

I returned the books to their rightful places and turned off the upstairs lights. I went downstairs and turned those lights off, opened the locked entrance door, went out, and locked it from the outside. I was halfway down the block when I noticed that I had forgotten to turn off the lighted sign above our door.

MADDY'S
BOOK SHOP

Chapter 37

ON A MONDAY A FEW YEARS AFTER MOM DIED, I RECEIVED AN EMAIL from Dad asking whether we could meet at his office in the Fratelli Massimo office building downtown on Wednesday. He didn't state a reason for the request, but I knew why he'd invited me; it was only a matter of time. My intel on the company was solid.

Amy had figured it out as well. As she and I were relaxing after dinner, she mentioned that Max was in town and had had lunch with Amy's longtime client, Trey Baker. "This is not confidential, Josh, but the word on the street is that Fratelli Massimo is in trouble. He's been talking to all the local banks about loan extensions or modifications and has been shot down. Everybody is nervous."

"Perfect, Amy, perfect."

We both concluded that Fratelli Massimo needed a cash infusion, and who better to get it from than the Feldman Family Partnership, which was worth several hundred million dollars? Brown Brothers Harriman had managed the money effectively. Added to that were our proceeds from the sale of Fratelli Massimo in 1998. Gunther and Mom had also left much of their personal fortunes to the partnership. Rand, Amy, and I were its partners.

As we sat at the table, we both smiled at the delicious irony of Max coming to me to bail him out. My first reaction was to reject his request out of hand. But no—that would be what "Gentle Josh" would have done. It would merely be justifying the refusal as a "business decision." But this was personal, and I wanted to crush him.

I began to figure out how to do just that. I started scribbling numbers on my paper napkin. I shared my ideas with Amy, who loved the idea and shouted, "Hallelujah! Go get him, cowboy!"

She grabbed her legal pad and started making notes. Page after page was filled as we fine-tuned and choreographed our strategy. Close to midnight, we finished. "Josh, it's not too late on the West Coast to call Rand, bring him up-to-date, and get his approval."

The call lasted fifteen minutes.

"Amy, Rand is more excited than we are. Yes, yes, yes! His only request is that he be there to witness it."

"Wonderful, Josh. First thing tomorrow, I want you to buy one hundred thousand shares of MAG stock, the company that owns Fratelli Massimo. Place the buy order with Bobby Weil himself, the bastard who kick-started the public offer years ago.

"Then call Brown Brothers and have them short one hundred thousand shares of MAG to minimize any risk of insider trading. That way, you cannot profit from the transaction. Your owner-ship position is neutralized." She had worked out every detail.

"And be coy with Bobby; he'll be curious about the transac-tion and may well suspect that you know something. With any luck, he'll pile into the stock himself. Wouldn't that be delicious?"

We both laughed and turned in, but not before Amy and I went at it like college kids. Only once, though. It was one in the morning, and we were in our forties, after all. Then she whis-pered sleepily, "What a wonderful lab partner you turned out to be! Love that microscope of yours!"

I'm usually zonked after sex. In fact, Amy often chided me for my quick return to my side of the bed and immediate slumber. "A little post-fuck cuddle wouldn't kill you." I'm usually asleep halfway through her little rebuke. But tonight was an exception. I was wide awake. Maybe I was still on a high in the aftermath of the plan we had hatched.

I tossed and turned for ten or fifteen minutes, and then quietly extricated myself from bed without waking Amy. I went downstairs to the kitchen table where we had left all our work papers. As I reviewed them one more time, I marveled at the plan. Clever—fiendishly clever. And that thought suddenly jolted me. The plan was wicked, almost sadistic. Amy and I had gotten so carried away that we had concocted a scheme which would not only punish Max, but would also eviscerate and humiliate him.

Was I actually capable of carrying this out? After all, Fratelli Massimo was likely headed for the junk heap if we did not agree to the loan. Couldn't we simply tell him the family declined to lend FM the money and let nature take its course? He'd be angry and hurt, but knowing Max, he would find a way of rationalizing the rejection, manage by hook or more likely by crook to prolong FM's existence for another six months or so, and perhaps live to fight another day, or at least cling to a life raft.

But didn't he deserve the death penalty for the way he had treated Sy, Mom, Rand, and me?

Maybe, but he was my father, after all, the man I had once idolized, the man who had taught me the business, the man who had made me rich. Didn't he at least deserve "life in prison without a chance for parole"?

And could I deliver the coup de grace inherent in our plan? Wasn't I doing precisely what Max had done to his father, Sy? Not content to let Sy's grocery store struggle for a few years, Max had virtually put him out of business by cutting prices to the bone in his own competing grocery store. Sy ended up getting very little for what remained of his store.

But wait a minute! If I merely turned down the loan request, wasn't I reverting to "Gentle Josh"? After Max's constant treacheries and betrayals, I had made up my mind to shed that moniker forever and grow some balls.

Max had brought this catastrophe on himself. He brought forth the very dictionary definition of hubris. There he was, seeking glory and riches, regardless of the consequences for others, only to see his empire crumble. Hadn't he forfeited any consideration of mercy from the court?

And here he was, hat in hand, seeking money from the family—money that would soon be squandered trying to breathe life into a dying company. Show him mercy? No!

At that moment, I managed to convince myself that I could—and would—get the job done. But judging from the sleepless night that followed, I still had my doubts.

• • •

Putting aside any qualms, I called Bobby Weil just as the market opened Tuesday morning and placed the order. "Let me get this straight, Josh, you want to purchase one hundred thousand shares of MAG? That's more than a million dollars. Their stock is trading around ten dollars or so on light volume."

"Yes, Bobby, please proceed," I said.

"My antenna is up, Josh. Anything I should know about?"

"Bobby, my lips are sealed. Please just execute the order, and let me know when it's complete."

"OK, Tiger, happy to have the business. Not even a hint?"

"Neither of us wants to go to jail, Bobby."

Bobby chuckled. "I get it." He promised to call me when the order was affected.

I then called my guy at Brown Brothers. The Feldman Family Partnership was worth five hundred million dollars, so he answered his cellphone promptly. I asked him to short one hundred thousand shares of MAG. "Are you sure? The stock just jumped a couple dollars on huge volume."

"Positive." Maybe good old greedy Bobby Weil took a plunge as well? Probably placed his personal order right before our one hundred thousand share order in order to take advantage of the certain run-up ours would produce. It was known as "front-running," another Wall Street gimmick. A gimmick that would cost Bobby millions if our plan worked. I was beginning to like the sweetness of revenge.

I spent the rest of the day calling contacts, and I set up a war room in the empty space on the second floor above the bookstore. I contacted an IT consultant who promised to provide us with hardware and software by Friday. I then phoned the bookstore's accounting firm and asked if they could lend us a hand with some analytical work next week. Of course they could. My last call was to Herb Segal, my old partner in merchandising.

"Happy to talk to you, Josh. When we parted, you weren't so happy with me."

"Water under the bridge, or over the dam, or something, Herb. You available next week for some heavy analysis? A small project with a big payoff?"

"Details?"

"Trust me, Herb, I won't disappoint." I gave him the bookstore's address. "I will call you Saturday with more info."

Amy had spent Tuesday making sure that our plan was on firm legal ground. It was, so she and I prepared for my Wednesday meeting with Max.

Dad and I had rarely spoken since the sale to MAG. We had run into each other from time to time and exchanged greetings—but that was it. I knew from the press and local gossip that he had sold the house in Brentmoor and moved to a luxury condo in downtown Clayton. He had also purchased a lavish condo on Fifty-Seventh Street in Manhattan, after being turned down by some of the co-op boards on Central Park West. I can only guess that reports of that humiliating evening at HHCC had been circulated among members of those boards that had the power to reject prospective purchasers for any reason. Dad had also purchased a small bungalow in Miami Beach.

He was splitting his time between St. Louis, New York, and Miami, taking advantage of MAG's private jet fleet, and spending just enough time in St. Louis and Miami to avoid paying New York state income taxes.

Still, it was as if Dad had an opportunity to redeem himself in New York—or maybe reinvent himself. He'd lost no time joining some of the more prestigious boards of charitable organizations while also gaining membership in some of the less exclusive city clubs. Max Feldman 2.0, with fresh new business and social connections. New affiliations with noble philanthropic institutions. His rebirth earned him the description of a "man about town."

Women's Wear Daily reported on his exploits. There was also the occasional story or photo on gossipy Page Six of the *New York Post*. Dad was often accompanied by younger, very attractive women. "Making up for lost time," he said, winking at the *Post* journalist. The *Times* and the *WSJ* offered more sober accounts of business at MAG. Fratelli Massimo was now a private company, wholly owned by MAG investors, and this meant that there was no independent reporting of FM's results—which was likely a great relief for Dad. From my sources I knew the line score, if not the box score.

The current buzz was that the shoe business was tough. Not just at Fratelli Massimo, but for virtually every mid-price, mall-dependent shoe and apparel retail operator. Trends that had begun years ago continued to take their toll. We saw the rise and growing popularity of athletic footwear and increasing reliance on off-price promotions. Lesser malls continued to lose popularity. But the latest culprit was Zappos, offering a virtually limitless assortment of branded footwear, in all sizes and colors. A customer could see the inventory and know that Zappos stocked her size. Shoes were delivered to consumer homes overnight and could be returned the next day at no cost to the buyer. The small pleasure I derived by being right about Zappos was subsumed by my regret that my last-minute attempt to convince the special committee was too little, too late.

• • •

I arrived at Fratelli Massimo headquarters on Wednesday, about fifteen minutes before our scheduled meeting. It was the first time I had set foot in the building since that dark day in 1998, several years before, when MAG took over. Happily, my friend Fletcher was still behind the reception desk.

"Mr. Josh! Welcome. I notice a few gray hairs, my friend."

"And I notice more than a few on your head, my friend."

We chatted for a moment about the Cardinals and family, and then he waved me through without having me sign the register. We smiled at each other at this security breach, and then I caught the elevator to the fifth floor, where Dad's office was located.

And there sat his loyal retainer for many years, Carly, gray-haired and dressed in business attire, guarding the door to his office.

She slowly made her way around her desk and we embraced warmly. She clung to me for a moment or two and gazed lovingly at me. "Oh, for those grand days when you worked for your dad."

"They weren't always so grand, Carly."

She smiled sadly in acknowledgment.

We traded stories of old times and cherished memories. After a few minutes, she indicated that Dad was on a call and it was likely to be a while. I could wait on a nearby sofa. But I told her I preferred to wander about and gave her my cell number; I asked her to call me when Dad was free.

I took the elevator to the lower level where I had worked back in high school days. No longer was there the clatter of comptometers and typewriters. Instead, the room was virtually silent, with giant computers diligently going about their business. I gracefully declined a tour. There was nothing of interest to see.

I next took the elevator to three, the merchandise floor. The pleasant smell of leather was in the air. The layout was the same—corner offices for the merchandise managers, rows of offices along the windows for the buyers, and locked sample rooms and cubicles for the distributors. I recognized no one, and no one recognized me. Several people asked if I needed help. I declined, and they were content to let me wander.

If I was hoping for a wave of melancholy or a frisson of nostalgia, I was not rewarded. Instead, the tour of the third floor evoked mostly unpleasant memories that I'd just as soon forget. Crisis meetings about our cash position, saying farewell to Herb Segal, firing Bill Bruton—those sorts of things. My cellphone buzzed, breaking the spell. Dad was ready to see me.

Dad's hand-tailored, blue pinstriped suit, enhanced with a foulard tie and brilliant pocket square, was a far cry from the zoot suit he had worn to that fateful meeting with Gunther and Maddy at the Harvard Club, almost fifty years ago. Dad came out from behind his desk and shook my hand. He had gained weight but wore the extra pounds well. Word had it that he had recently suffered a mild heart attack and was following doctor's orders.

He was robust, tanned, recently barbered, and manicured. Still, even the overpowering cologne he was wearing could not hide the stench of fear that trailed after him like a shadow when he came to greet me. He invited me to sit in a club chair that faced the sofa where he planted himself.

He asked about Amy and Allison, and I filled him in. I mentioned that I was teaching retailing and he laughed, "Easier to teach it than do it, son!" I heartily agreed. And then we got down to business.

"I assume that the Feldman Family Partnership is doing well."

"Yes, Dad. Brown Brothers has managed it very well through the years." Of course, I was not about to reveal how well.

"Well, cutting to the chase, I have an offer—or I should say, MAG has an offer you would do well to consider. Josh, I poked and prodded them to come up with a great package. It's particularly lush in this era of low interest rates."

I was silent and waited for him to get on with it.

"What would you say to a 20 percent interest rate? On a short-term, two hundred million dollar, one-year loan to Fratelli Massimo?"

I remained silent and listened.

"A cool forty million in interest. And with a dynamite holiday season, we could pay it off even quicker than one year. You'd still get the forty million. Pretty enticing, eh, Josh?"

I spoke. "Why are we, the Feldman Family Partnership, the recipient of such a generous proposal? If I'm correct, banks are lending at 6 or 7 percent. High-yield bonds are priced at 9 or 10 percent."

"Josh, you better than anyone know how difficult those banks and institutions are to deal with: mountains of paperwork, hordes of lawyers, and accountants up the wazoo. The family partnership can make a quick decision, while those other guys are fiddle-farting around."

I was ready with questions. "What sort of collateral is MAG offering us? Their office tower in New York? Their fleet of Gulfstream private jets? What exactly should I tell the family—Rand and Amy—about collateral?" I already knew the answer, having done a deep dive into MAG's financials.

"Well, Josh. Those assets are not in the cards. Those are MAG assets, not Fratelli Massimo's. Besides, some are already leveraged with debt. But, as for collateral, the family would be pledged all the assets of Fratelli Massimo. And that's if things go south, which they won't."

More silence.

"And if things do go south, you will own the company and realize your dream of running it yourself. It's a win-win. If Fratelli

Massimo pulls it off this holiday, the family walks away with a cool forty million. If the worst happens, you own the company lock, stock, and barrel. You can't lose!"

I calmly looked at him for a few seconds and quietly nodded my head. He was following the script precisely as Amy and I had predicted. I even hammed it up a bit, pursing my lips, rubbing my chin, squinting, and then nodding. And with a skeptical tone, I repeated, "So the Feldman Family Partnership could earn a quick forty million in interest. And if the shit hits the fan, the family would once again own Fratelli Massimo..."

"See what I mean, Josh? You can't lose!"

I smiled as if I had won the lottery. "Dad, I would have to get Amy and Rand's OK, and we would need to review all of Fratelli Massimo's financials, selling reports, leases, financing agreements, the works. Because Fratelli Massimo would be our only collateral. I mean, I have a fiduciary responsibility to my partners. You understand, don't you?"

Dad sat back, grinning. "Yes, yes. I get it. Must be cautious, Josh, as always. I will get all that material to you by Friday. All three of you will have to sign confidentiality agreements promising not to disclose that information to others. When do you think we can consummate the deal?"

I spent a few moments scribbling on the tablet I had brought with me. "Well, this proposal comes as a surprise, and we will have a lot of due diligence to do. We need to dig through all those financials, selling reports, leases, and other obligations. I'll have to get some help, so please send a few more confidentiality agreements. I don't want to stray over the line."

Max laughed heartily. "Always with the belt and suspenders—you never change. But time is of the essence, son."

"I get it. I guess, if we get the material by Friday, we will need at least a week to digest it. Then Rand, Amy, and I will have to sit down and thrash it out and, ultimately, decide. It's a big decision."

"You always were slow on the draw, Josh. You need the Max Feldman sense of urgency here. How about a week from today, next Wednesday?"

"I'll have to get back to you on that. I think it will take a week or more after we get the material before we would have an answer. We could meet with you and Ed Gottlieb in New York, if that would make things easier."

"Great. I'll check his calendar."

"Oh, and you'll want your finance and legal guy there."

"Done. Call me when you can commit to a time."

"Will do, Dad."

"Let me just say something, son. Ed Gottlieb discouraged me from talking to you, but I said, 'I know my boy. Any proposal that includes the possibility of running Fratelli Massimo will ring his chime!' And I was right. Your dream job is just around the corner if things go south. Knew you couldn't resist."

Uncharacteristically, he hugged me. It took all my willpower to refrain from kneeing him in the balls.

My equivocations about the plan Amy and I had come up with, and my doubts about my ability to see it through, completely disappeared. It wasn't enough that he had screwed each of us mercilessly in the past—now he wanted to do it again. Max wanted Amy, Rand, and me to lend him two hundred million. It would be enough to prolong Fratelli Massimo's fragile existence for a year or so. This would give Max enough time to find a safe haven, before the whole enterprise collapsed. And it would be an event he would blame me for.

Hasta la vista, Gentle Josh.

Chapter 38

Ten bankers' boxes of documents and the confidentiality agreements arrived early on Friday at the bookstore. Amy, Herb Segal, and I spent the weekend upstairs in the war room going through the records and sorting them. We distributed store leases and abstracts on one of the banquet tables I had set up, financial statements on another. On another one, we organized the style selling reports and on-order files. My IT guy set up the computers, gave us a tutorial, and stuck around to see whether we had any questions. On Monday morning, two staffers from the bookstore's accounting firm showed up, and I gave them their marching orders.

We all dug in. The key question was: What was Fratelli Massimo's true financial status? I needed to know the details. What was the company's cash position and flow? That's where the accountants could help. How valuable was its inventory? That was Herb's bailiwick. And then there were the leases, which were my assignment. How valuable were they? What percentage of their hundreds of stores had A-plus locations and lease terms, how many were A situations, B, C, and so forth? Amy analyzed the legal, financial, and terms leases and summarized Fratelli Massimo's remaining obligations to the landlords.

By Saturday, after working nonstop for eight days, we began finalizing our findings, checking and rechecking our numbers, doing worst-case scenarios, and determining a range of outcomes.

I called Rand with the final analysis and asked if he was still in. I made sure he was aware that there was financial risk involved. He did not hesitate. "I'd pay one million dollars just to see the expression on his face." I checked his availability for the New York meeting.

We spent Sunday formalizing our presentation. The staffers and IT guy helped professionalize it, and we shut down the war room at seven in the evening, sending everybody but Amy home. I then called Max on his cell and told him that Amy, Rand, and I could meet with the MAG team on Tuesday in New York.

"Hoping it would be earlier, but OK. I'll let you know time and place tomorrow. Oh, and bring your checkbook with you!"

"I guarantee you I will."

"Atta boy."

The meeting was set for 2:00 p.m. on Tuesday at the Harvard Club. Ed Gottlieb was a member, having earned his MBA at Harvard Business School. He had reserved a small conference room for the meeting. This location ensured that the matter and our discussion would be confidential.

We Feldmans arrived in New York on Monday evening and stayed overnight at the Sofitel, which was next door to the Harvard Club on Forty-Fourth Street. We breakfasted at the Red Flame, a diner down the street, then returned to our suite to rehearse. Amy and I were psyched about the meeting and its likely outcome. Rand was beyond elated. Turning to Amy and me, he spoke loudly. "You two came up with a brilliant plan. This achieves the three 'R's. We have Revenge, Retaliation, and Redemption! How sweet it is."

Amy responded in a businesslike tone. "Rand, appreciate the compliment, but it's premature. I've done enough deals to be cautious. You never really know, until the signature is on the contract. And just another word of caution. Even if the deal is done, it could cost us a small fortune."

"Amy, dear," Rand said, grinning. "I know all that. And know you must do your lawyerly bit, but I am confident the deal will get done. If the family partnership loses ten or twenty million, it's a small price to pay for Revenge, Retaliation, and Redemption! I've lived with this hurt since I was a kid, and I want it healed."

"Ditto," I added.

When we left the hotel for lunch, I suggested the Harvard Club.

"But none of us is a member," Amy reminded me.

"I'll talk to the manager," I told her.

When we arrived at the front desk of the club, I asked to speak to the general manager. The receptionist made a call, and within a few minutes, a tall and distinguished-looking man with silver hair arrived and introduced himself. "How may I help you?" he said.

I told him that we were not members of the club, but that our grandfather, the late Gunther Harrison Berg, had belonged for sixty years.

"Oh my, Mr. Gunther Berg. A legend. I was at his funeral. I believe both of you gentlemen spoke. Yes, an unforgettable man."

"We were hoping that you could show us where he liked to sit in the main dining room."

"With pleasure. He liked the table in the southwest corner, with his back to the wall, so he could observe the entire room and see who was entering. I will show you." He motioned for us to follow.

The table was unoccupied. "Would you three be my guests today for lunch? In honor of your grandfather."

I smiled. "You're very kind. Thank you so much."

He seated us, leaving the Gunther chair unoccupied, and went to speak to the maître d'.

A waiter soon arrived and took our orders.

We gazed at the Gunther chair, each lost in our own thoughts. Mine focused on what a giant he had been, and how protective he had been of his daughter, Maddy.

Amy spoke. "To think, almost half a century ago, Max, Maddy, and Gunther sat at this very table and discussed the marriage and the business. Both would be seminal in our lives."

"I wonder what they would say if they saw us sitting here, poised to bring Max down?" I said. Would Gunther have approved of our plan? I think he would have endorsed it—and probably improved on it.

My thoughts then turned to Sy. Would he have approved of our plan? Out of some paternal instinct, would he have wanted to protect his son? Or would he, too, have wished to see Max humbled? Gramps was a softy, so I felt he would have wanted to be more merciful. But today there would be no stay of execution for my father.

• • •

The three of us arrived at the conference room at 2:00 p.m.

Max and Ed Gottlieb were already there; they introduced us to their in-house attorney, Fred Miller, and the chief financial officer, Chuck Fairbanks.

We took our seats facing the four of them and unpacked our briefcases.

Ed opened the meeting. "Well, I am delighted to welcome you. Josh, I remember you when you were following your dad around the convention floor at a shoe show—must have been twenty years ago, and, of course, on the day we closed the deal with Fratelli Massimo. Amy and Rand, it's a pleasure to meet you." He smiled and continued.

"Max tells me that you have expressed interest in the proposal he made to you almost two weeks ago. We assume you've had time to do your due diligence and are prepared to proceed."

"Ed, we have had that opportunity," I replied, "and we have come with a proposal."

My father, so anxious to get the deal done that he failed to hear the word *proposal*, interceded. "Josh was excited about making the loan to Fratelli Massimo: lucrative interest income and complete downside protection with the assets of the company as collateral." He sat back in his chair with a self-satisfied grin on his face.

Fred Miller removed some documents from his attaché case. "These papers prepared by our outside counsel contain the provisions Max spoke of. Amy, I understand you are a partner at Hotchkiss and Hamilton, so perhaps you would like to review…"

"Thanks Fred, that won't be necessary," Amy said.

"Well, a handshake won't suffice. Even though Fratelli Massimo is owned by MAG investors, MAG, itself, is a public company and is subject to SEC scrutiny. This agreement must be airtight—for both parties."

I then spoke. "We desire an airtight agreement as well. But as I mentioned, we have come with our own proposal, which varies from my dad's."

Ed countered. "All due respect, Josh, but we're not here to hear a new proposal. If you have some minor changes to what

Max presented, we are authorized by MAG's board to amend Fred's documents, as necessary. Let's get going."

"Well, if you do not wish to hear our proposal, then we will be on our way."

Max jumped out of his chair. "We didn't come here to play games, Josh. I spoke to you in good faith, and I expect you to act accordingly. Ed's a busy man, and so am I. And if you were just running out the clock, we'll sue you for every penny you have!"

An exasperated Ed added, "I am not getting involved in a family spat. Are you or are you not ready to come to terms on the deal?"

I answered, "We are prepared to present you with a proposal we think is superior to the one my dad offered me. If you do not wish to hear it, then so be it." With that, we started refilling our briefcases.

Our strategy had anticipated this eventuality. Amy stood up. "As an attorney, it is my opinion and maybe my duty to tell you that MAG would be well served to hear what the Feldman Family Partnership, a multimillion-dollar entity, proposes. If you decline to hear it, the consequences may be significant. You can always reject the proposal, but refusing to listen to it will invite legal peril."

Fred Miller nodded in agreement. "What Amy's saying, Ed, is that if Fratelli Massimo, uh, stumbles, and has refused to listen to a proposal from a financially qualified entity, some of our stockholders, to say nothing of our creditors, might take us to court."

Max stood, put his hands on the table, and shouted, "This is bullshit! You lawyers can play all the games you want, but the deal I offered Josh is the deal we're sticking with!"

"Ed," I asked, "are you ready to hear our proposal?"

Ed walked over to where Fred was seated and had a whispered conversation.

"As advised by counsel, yes, proceed. Max, sit down. I know you're upset, but please listen and keep quiet. I have no intention to go to court over this."

As we had rehearsed, I started. "Before I pass out our formal proposal along with an executive summary, I would like to acquaint you with several of the items we discovered doing our due diligence. Items that need not appear in writing, anywhere. Are we clear?"

"Yes," Ed responded. "What kind of findings?"

"Well, here's a brief summary. First, a cash flow analysis revealed that, unless Fratelli Massimo receives a cash infusion of at least one hundred million dollars in the next few weeks, you will be unable to pay your bills or honor your loan agreements in sixty days. Should that occur, word of your financial distress will make the rounds, and vendors may get nervous and decide not to ship you."

Ed turned to Chuck Fairbanks, the company's chief financial officer. "True?" he asked.

"Well, we may have to stall some payments to some of our suppliers and withhold payments to contractors and other service providers." He scratched some numbers on a tablet. "I think ninety days is a better estimate."

"So," said Ed, "somewhere between sixty and ninety days, we're on the balls of our ass. Because Seventh Avenue is like a sieve. They'll close us down, won't they?"

Chuck answered, "Well, some may not ship; others may require cash on delivery, which would put a crushing strain on Fratelli Massimo, and ultimately on MAG itself—effectively ruining fall and holiday selling."

Ed jerked his head back as if he'd been smacked in the face.

"Second," I went on, "gross profit at Fratelli Massimo for the last two years has been overstated significantly by deferring necessary markdowns, which were then taken in subsequent periods, calling into question, shall I say, the accuracy of MAG's income statements dating back at least two years. And this has significantly overvalued Fratelli Massimo's current inventory. Should your CPA firm discover this problem, you will be forced to restate your earnings for the prior two years—at a minimum."

Ed rose from his chair and faced Max, who refused to make eye contact with him. Chuck blurted, "I depended on Max for those evaluations—as did our internal accounting staff and outside auditors. Valuing fashion merchandise is an art, not a science."

"Max, is Josh correct about this practice?" Ed asked.

Max shrugged his shoulders. "We're all big boys here. We all know how fashion retailers do their books. This is standard practice in the retail business. Shit, I taught Josh all about it."

"Yes, you did, Dad. But Price Waterhouse and MAG's stockholders may not be as forgiving as your board was."

Ed returned to his chair. "I have fifteen divisions reporting to me. I can't possibly know every detail of their accounting practices. How did Price Waterhouse allow this to happen?"

Chuck said, "Well, first of all, they, like me, depended on the operating head of the business to faithfully and honestly evaluate their assets. And they required that person to certify that in writing. In the case of Fratelli Massimo, they felt their numbers were de minimis in the context of MAG's billions of dollars of sales and assets."

Ed shook his head. "What a clusterfuck."

"And finally," I continued, "there's the questionable situation of MAG corporate officers' use of the four corporate jets for personal use. The IRS has some rather strict guidelines..."

Chuck instantly responded with righteous indignation, "Ed, I warned you we were on shaky ground!"

"Stop! Stop! Stop!" bellowed Ed, barely holding it together. He asked us to excuse ourselves and return in fifteen minutes to present our proposal. The MAG team wanted to go into executive session. We packed our folders in our briefcases, left them and our coats behind, and exited the conference room.

We waited in the corridor and heard voices raised, fists slammed on the table, and at least one chair overturned. Rand could barely contain his glee, raising his fist in triumph. Amy was still cautious. I was nervous.

When we were invited to return, we filed in and took our seats.

Ed turned to me. "Present!" he said.

There was no turning back now, and it took me almost a minute to summon the courage to continue. I forced myself to avoid looking at Dad and focused on Ed instead.

"Well, as you yourself so aptly put it, Ed, within sixty to ninety days Fratelli Massimo will be on the balls of its ass. Or, said in a more formal way, Fratelli Massimo will be facing the specter of bankruptcy proceedings. Our proposal is designed to avoid a Chapter 11 filing, which would envelope MAG, cost its stockholders tens of millions of dollars in legal fees, and tie you up for several years.

"The Feldman proposal will see to it that your obligations to creditors and lenders are fully satisfied, because you must maintain friendly ongoing relationships with them. You have many other subsidiaries and divisions that need financing and credit. Poisoning those relationships with Chapter 11 proceedings will be detrimental to MAG. And we will conclude this process within ninety to one hundred and twenty days."

"And how will this 'miracle' solution work?" Ed asked.

"We would accomplish this by immediately liquidating the assets of Fratelli Massimo," I told him matter-of-factly.

"Over my dead body!" Max thundered, and I closed my eyes. "You used me, you motherfucker. You conned me into sending you all that confidential information. Well, there's no way we're liquidating."

Ed interrupted, "Max, if you cannot keep quiet, then please leave. Josh, how would this liquidation process work, and what guarantees does MAG get that it will be effective?"

"We have formed an LLC, FMLCo., known formally as Fratelli Massimo Liquidation Company. As your executive summary indicates"—Amy passed out the booklets—"FMLCo. will take full responsibility for liquidating Fratelli Massimo's assets via several steps: a going-out-of-business sale with graduated markdowns designed to maximize the yield on current merchandise, the sale of Fratelli Massimo's on-order merchandise to competitors at mutually agreeable price points or cancellation by vendors, and the cancellation of all orders that have yet to go into production. We will contact landlords. In some cases, those operating healthy malls will pay significant amounts to take back real estate in underperforming Fratelli Massimo locations. By avoiding Chapter 11 proceedings, they will exercise much more control over the disposition of their properties. We would sell off fixed assets, including the St. Louis headquarters building, distribution centers, and any other saleable assets, like computers, office furniture, etc." I exhaled.

"We have worked hard to estimate what those measures will yield. That number is very close to what your debts and loans currently amount to: four hundred million dollars."

Ed asked his CFO if that number was correct. The answer was, "Yes, give or take."

Ed then asked, "Why don't we just do it ourselves?"

"First of all, we doubt you want to get into that swamp. Second, we will *not* charge you a fee for our services, and we have the benefit of knowing your stores, locations, landlords, and the value of your merchandise. Do you really want to take on that project?"

Ed grimaced and wagged his head. "What if your estimates are wrong, and you are able to collect, say, three hundred and fifty million instead of the four hundred million we owe?"

It was Rand's turn to speak. "That is a risk that the Feldmans are willing to take. If we fall short of the four hundred million figure, the Feldman Family Partnership will write you a check for the difference. MAG won't be out a nickel."

Ed's face brightened a bit. Then he asked what the assets of the partnership were. Rand requested that Ed sign a confidentiality agreement. After he signed it, he was handed the partnership's last monthly statement from Brown Brothers Harriman. He reviewed it. "That's fucking awesome."

Max slowly raised his hand.

"Yes, Max?"

"Look, Ed," Max said. "We've been through the wars together. For decades. You know how this business works. We are one hot shoe, one great boot inning, one blockbuster holiday season from getting out of this hole. This liquidation proposal is insulting and premature. I and my team will get us out of this jam. We always have and always will. There's nobody in this room or in this city who knows more about finding hot merchandise than I do!

"Josh suckered me into sending him all those financial records. He had no intention of lending us the money. What these schmucks have done is aggregate the money I generated for them in the family partnership and used it to screw me. I won't stand for it."

"Max, we *have* been through the wars together, but given Fratelli Massimo's dire situation, which had you scrambling for cash, the rather bleak outlook for its future, and the exposure MAG may or may not experience, I would say that their proposal is worthy of consideration. As to your own future, Max, we shall discuss that in private," Ed said.

My dad slumped in his chair, no doubt feeling his future, his reputation, and his fortune vanishing.

I ended my presentation. "You have forty-eight hours to decide. But remember, every passing hour decreases the value of your inventory, takes time off your valuable leases, and allows more merchandise to enter production. The four-hundred-million-dollar guarantee is based on FMLCo. getting the go-ahead by Thursday at, say, 4:00 p.m. Eastern time. Our proposal is final, nonnegotiable, and will expire at that time."

"That's not reasonable," Ed countered. "I need to consult with my board."

Amy rose. "Perhaps this will help facilitate those discussions. A strong legal principle holds that if a company knows it is close to insolvency, its primary fiduciary responsibilities transition from its stockholders to its creditors. I believe Fred will back me up."

Fred nodded his silent assent.

"Well," said Ed. "You've done your homework. But what about MAG's stockholders?"

"Ed," I said, "I am a substantial stockholder in MAG. I cannot speak for other shareholders, as their interests might differ from mine. But if you go down an alternative path that disadvantages MAG either monetarily or in its relationships with lenders, vendors, or developers, I, and perhaps other stockholders, might have to consider legal remedies."

A long silence ensued, in which Ed cupped his chin in his left hand and shook his head.

Max broke the silence. In a measured but quaking plea, he said, "What about me? I created and built Fratelli Massimo, single-handedly. Without me, there would be no Fratelli Massimo, no Feldman Family Partnership, hell, no Josh, and no Rand. I cannot and will not stand by and allow this travesty."

Ed responded. "I'm sorry, Max, but it's out of your hands now."

"But Ed, no fashion business can exist without a merchant."

"Agreed, Dad," I said. "But Fratelli Massimo will cease to exist. It will be gone. It will have no need for a merchant of your world-class stature. Disposing of its assets will depend instead on a solid businessman who understands retailing and is good with numbers. These are qualities with which you graciously and frequently used to describe me, your son."

Amy ended the meeting with a reminder that there was a 4:00 p.m. deadline, Thursday.

Ed, Chuck, and Fred gathered their papers and their copies of the Feldman family proposal and filed out of the conference room. No pleasantries were expected, or exchanged. As they reached the door, I silently handed Ed my business card with my cellphone number. Ed nodded.

A haggard Max haltingly followed several paces behind his colleagues, looking very much like a punctured balloon in the Macy's Thanksgiving Day Parade on a windy day—disfigured, deflated, and lifeless.

Watching Dad, that bolt struck me again as it had during the sleepless night when we'd first come up with the plan.

Amy and Rand were about to high-five, but I didn't join them. "I can't celebrate. I will meet you back at the hotel."

The corridor was narrow and the elevators close by; I distinctly heard my brother ask Amy, "Who stuck a pole up his rear end?"

She reproached him, "Shhh, Rand. He's just feeling guilty."

I had written the script and followed it, and now I needed to accept the consequences. Maybe Rand could revel in Dad's destruction. After all, Max had savagely abused him. By this time, he and Max were strangers, separated by a continent and diametrically opposed lifestyles. As for Amy, she wasn't blood. Max had been an irritant and a scoundrel, but Amy had thrived even with Max's depravations.

But what had I done? What had I become?

Chapter 39

ED CALLED AT NOON ON THURSDAY TO ACCEPT OUR PROPOSAL. HE mentioned several minor changes and the need to finalize the agreement with the lawyers. I agreed to the changes he suggested and said that Amy would fax him her draft of the agreement. She would fly to New York Friday to meet with MAG's attorneys. My wife was empowered by the Feldman Family Partnership to sign the final contract on behalf of FMLCo. Before hanging up, I asked him if we could borrow Roger Morton for the liquidation period.

"He'll be on your payroll?" he asked.

"Of course, and as we agreed, MAG will issue the public announcement as required by the SEC after we have approved it. Let me remind you that our proposal stated quite clearly that the announcement must express that there is a remote possibility of a Chapter 11 bankruptcy filing, depending on the success of the liquidation process. I fully realize that it is extremely unlikely, even impossible, under the terms we discussed. But I need that leverage with lenders, vendors, and real estate developers."

"I wish you wouldn't insist on that Chapter 11 sentence. That will send tremors down Wall Street," he pleaded once again.

"It will in the short term, Ed. But the liquidation process will be successful—as we have guaranteed. We need the Chapter 11 sentence for leverage. Without it, the deal is off. We will never generate the dollars we need."

"I get it."

With business matters concluded, Ed asked if I had a few minutes to discuss some personal issues.

"You are one smart dude, Josh. Your preparation, presentation, and proposal were masterful. As your father stated, you are a shrewd retailer, a savvy businessman, and you are great with numbers. I would add that you also possess your father's ruthlessness—for better or worse. You were absolutely cold as ice when you delivered his death sentence."

That was true, but hearing it from Ed seared my soul.

"I say all that because there may come a time when MAG could use you and those very qualities. We face many challenges . . . reductions in price credibility, the decline of the mall, the rise of the internet. We will need a warrior here. Someone not bashful about wielding a machete. I'll keep you in mind.

"And finally, and sadly, your father is understandably depressed. Not suicidal, but really down in the dumps. I've known him for thirty years, and I've never seen him so low. I have visited with him to try to buck him up. I explained that MAG was left with no choice. If we had turned the proposal down, we would face a host of challenges including lawsuits and damaged relationships with our suppliers and bankers. That much, he understands. But he feels utterly betrayed by you."

"I know where's he's coming from. Thanks, Ed. Let's stay in touch."

I couldn't wait to hang up.

• • •

The announcement was approved and issued late that Sunday night.

Naturally, the press started calling first thing Monday morning. Ed and I had agreed on our response, which basically reiterated what was in the announcement. But speculation about MAG's prospects was rampant and set the stock price tumbling— as Ed had predicted. I tracked it on my computer. It fell to six dollars a share at one point. Bobby Weil called several times, but I didn't take his calls. I inferred, with some satisfaction, that he had piled into the stock when I placed my one hundred thousand share order at ten dollars a share, a couple of weeks before.

The Feldman family was protected because I had shorted a hundred thousand shares simultaneously. Raymond at Brown Brothers must have thought I was a stock-picking whiz. Bobby Weil must have thought me a prick. The feeling was mutual.

The MAG story faded away, but the St. Louis Post-Dispatch gossip columnist, Jerry Berger, quipped in his Wednesday column: "MAG's press release stated that FMLCo. stands for Fratelli Massimo Liquidation Company, but a member of Highland Hills Country Club confided that their members are calling it the Max Feldman Liquidation Company!"

• • •

On the Monday morning following the announcement, the ten-person liquidation team met in the war room above the bookstore. I welcomed Roger Morton, who expressed his pleasure at being reunited and getting "out of the morgue at Fratelli Massimo."

"Not so fast, Roger, you will need to work out the details of Fratelli Massimo's 'going out of business' sale, and execute that strategy. We have some preliminary simulations, so you can refine, as necessary. Maximize yield on the in-store inventory, that's the objective. And when you are not implementing the liquidation strategy over there, you will be in place to check the progress of our other initiatives and keep me posted. Understood?"

"Gladly," he said.

Herb Segal was taking on his own major assignment, selling off Fratelli Massimo's excess inventory to competitors, rerouting incoming goods to those same companies, halting production of merchandise ordered by Fratelli Massimo, and negotiating settlements with manufacturers. "Remember, Herb, scrounge as many dollars as you can from those competitors for new stuff and stop vendors from beginning production on Fratelli Massimo orders. Make small settlements with those stuck with raw materials. Remind those producers that MAG is still alive and well and will want to do business with them. Squeeze them as much as possible. Remind them that Fratelli Massimo faces the possibility of a Chapter 11 filing if you're not successful. That's your trump card."

I smiled. "And by the way, Roger and Herb, there's a half-million dollar bonus awaiting each of you, if you achieve targets."

That set them scrambling.

I had the task of maximizing the value of Fratelli Massimo's store leases and disposing of the company's headquarters and distribution centers, along with other assets. Our due diligence revealed that FM had a large number of very valuable store leases at well below current market rents. Those developers would be eager to take those locations back and re-rent them. They would also be anxious to avoid the bankruptcy route with skyrocketing legal expenses, time wasted, and the vagaries of decisions made by bankruptcy judges. I had tons of leverage because of that "remote possibility of Chapter 11 filing" in the press release.

Our luck ran hot and cold. A local brokerage firm with national aspirations bought Fratelli Massimo's headquarters at a price that netted us twenty million dollars after paying off the mortgage. Amazon wanted our distribution centers. As expected, they drove a hard bargain, but we netted ten million from those sales. That was the good luck.

We overestimated the yield from the going-out-of-business sale at FM and took a hit. But we recouped most of it from Herb's masterly disposition of incoming merchandise to other shoe retailers. That man knew how to schmooze!

As we closed down the liquidation effort, we toted up the take: $387 million. So, I, in the name of the Feldman Family Partnership, hand delivered Ed a cashier's check for the remaining $13 million in New York. Ed was very gracious and conceded that the liquidation process was a success and left MAG in a stronger position, as the soaring stock price attested to.

I asked him how Dad was doing. "Better. Getting his mojo back. He's looking forward to moving to Florida. We're still friends, despite it all."

"Glad to hear that. Ed, I have a question, if you don't mind. What type of severance arrangement or parachute did my dad have?"

"Unfortunately, not much of one. He put everything he had and more into Fratelli Massimo. He was dead sure he could multiply his investment several times over. A great merchant can be like a great athlete who doesn't know when to quit. Willie Mays is an example. We bet on Max, too—to our regret. But that is the risk you take in our business." I was instantly reminded of Gunther's assertion that Max was "betting the ranch." Indeed, Dad did and had lost it all.

After a brief pause, Ed asked, "Why did you ask about severance?"

"I was struck by what you said when we last spoke—you know, the part about my 'betrayal' and the icy way I delivered the message. There's a long family backstory I won't bore you with, but betrayal seems to be in our DNA." I thought for a moment, and then continued.

"I lack the courage and chutzpah to console the guy. It's like the old joke about the kid who murders his parents and then begs the court for mercy because he's an orphan. I will have to learn to live with my conscience, and with what I did."

He looked at me, and I at him.

"In the meantime," I said, "I'll do what rich guys do when stricken with guilt. I'll write a personal check to MAG. Contribute it to his severance, if you will. The amount is meaningless to me, but it will be meaningful to him. It won't salve my conscience, but I want to make the gesture. And I want it to be anonymous."

"I'll make up some story and keep your name out of it. He will appreciate the extra dough. What goes on in some families defies understanding. You know, I once envied the way you idolized your dad. You hung on his every word at those shoe shows. I wished my own kids were like that. But it sure didn't end well with you and Max."

Epilogue

I HEARD FROM JENN KATZENBERG, WHO HEARD FROM HER MOTHER, Evie, that Dad retired from MAG and sold his heavily mortgaged St. Louis and New York condos. He also declared personal bankruptcy. Florida law protects private residences against creditors and bankruptcy judgments, so he now lives in Miami Beach.

His bungalow is exactly five miles east of the Ida and Milton Silverstein Home for the Aged, where his father, Sy, spent his final days.

When I now retreat to my sanctuary above Maddy's Book Shop, I do not permit myself the indulgence of rereading the notes Mom made in her books. I don't deserve that pleasure.

Maybe that's because I have come to believe that she would have rejected the plan to destroy my father. Had she sat in the Gunther chair with Amy, Rand, and me at the Harvard Club, she would have urged a more merciful denouement. I can almost hear her speaking.

"I know how monstrous Max can be. Believe me, I do. But does he really deserve what you plan to do to him? Josh, you could just turn down the loan request. That alone would be the death knell for Fratelli Massimo. It would be a fitting and humbling punishment. But by personally liquidating the company, you will be publicly emasculating your own father. It's so reminiscent of what Max did to his very own father. That you are capable of such Max-like cruelty breaks my heart."

That message from my mom literally brings tears to my eyes.

Not satisfied with merely rejecting the loan request and allowing Fratelli Massimo to slowly fade away, I had chosen to crush my own father. It was just as Max had done with Sy. Exactly as Max had done with Rand. The same as Max had done with Maddy.

Gentle Josh is dead. My dark side, the Max in me, won out.

I am disgusted with myself. What's done is done. But who am I?

I am my father's son.